I0737682

IN SEARCH OF
INA BYERS

IN SEARCH OF INA BYERS

A Novel

LARRY SPENCER

Copyright © 2021 by Larry Spencer

All Rights Reserved. This book or parts thereof may not be reproduced in any form, stored in any retrieval system, or transmitted in any form by any means—spoken, written, photocopy, printed, electronic, mechanical, recording or other wise through any means not yet known or yet to use—without prior written permission of the publisher, except provided by the United States of America copyright law.

This book is a work of fiction. Names, characters, businesses, organizations, places, events and incidents either are the product of the author's imagination or are used fictitiously. Any resemblance to actual persons, living or dead, events, or locales are entirely coincidental.

Library of Congress Control Number: 2021905688

ISBN Paperback: 978-0-578-25288-9
ebook ISBN: 978-0-578-95885-9

Book Cover and Interior Design: Creative Publishing Book Design

Cover photo: Michelaubry

Author photo Laurie Spencer @ Lolo Spencer Photography

To Lolo: my constant support system.

The most painful thing is losing yourself in the process of loving someone too much, and forgetting that you are special too.
—Ernest Hemingway

CHAPTER ONE

The fading shrill of a train whistle blasted through the midnight chill like bad opera bouncing off the ceiling of a pitch-black sky. But there was comfortable warmth inside the empty club car I occupied near the window. I stared out, watching the barren, terrain whipped by. It reminded me of this foreign film I once saw that started off with this panoramic view of a combat zone—then the camera moved in and we discovered this courageous, naive unseasoned Russian soldier charging across a battlefield, and suddenly he's caught in a vicious crossfire—instantaneously hit in the chest. Whap! And everything turned to slow motion, as the young soldier fell to the ground and his whole life flashed before him. And that's the movie. This young guy's life in flashback. His triumphs, his defeats, his loves, his heartbreak. His obsessions. And as the guy finally hit the ground—the movie ended. And his life was over. Fade out. The end.

But the point is, I think, that even though his life was brief, he'd been deliriously happy. Key word: *deliriously*.

Okay, I'm not dead and I'm not a Russian soldier but I have walked through a minefield and recently flashed on a good portion of my life, and I think finally figured out how I let things spin so insanely and deliriously out of control.

On the seat next to me is a messenger bag filled with my most cherished belongings—an unopened bottle of Silver Oak Napa Cabernet Sauvignon, a dog-eared copy of Kerouac's classic *On the Road*, a photo of my mother and me (at six months) on a California beach, a felt-covered ring box, and a crumpled check for $65,000. My life savings. When this is spent, I'll be penniless unless I considered working a menial job or selling my mother's diamond wedding ring. For now, both options were out of the question.

My mouth was dry from a lack of conversation, while riding the rails for the last two days, running from my past. I'd consider uncorking the Cab, but the sentiment behind it prohibited me. A gift from my mother to my father was to be opened on their twenty-fifth wedding anniversary. Her untimely death at the eight-year mark scratched that celebration. I kept the bottle as a reminder that life can be cruel and that breaking a promise can be forgiving.

I closed my eyes and rested my forehead against the cool window pane. After no more than a minute I am suddenly interrupted by the distinct smell of sulfur. I opened my eyes to see a seventeen-year-old girl inexplicably standing in the aisle, provocatively leaning against the seat in front of me, lighting a cigarette—a *Nat Sherman Natural*. Her preferred brand because it represented her unconventional style. She blew a picture-perfect smoke ring. This was Ina Byers. Dark eyes, dark hair, pale skin, rough around the edges. She's dressed in black jeans and a tight black T-shirt. Dark colors suit her. Mysterious fits her. Her eyes met mine; she smiled vaguely. I turned away, facing the window, and now spoke to the passing rugged topography.

"Ina Byers. My own personal anguish. She was perfect. Not your conventional hot body that gets you crazy-excited perfect. But provocative, cunning, and flat-chested perfect."

"I'm not that flat, Sharp Guy," she said as she ground out her cigarette with her heel.

"Also hostile and defensive," I said flatly, still peering out the window.

I then turned back to Ina, but she was gone. Vanished. Only the smoke ring remained, floating gently in the air. "Despite her imperfections, she was *my kind of perfect.*" The window fogged up just saying that out loud.

BAKERSFIELD, CALIFORNIA—AUTUMN 2004

Our family diner, widely known as *Ben's Diner*, is located directly on the main stretch of highway about five miles from the center of town. It has every ingredient a small roadside restaurant would have—except for what was needed the most, a frequent invasion of customers. Relegated to the suburbs, it coexisted with a hardware store and the local animal feed supply. The diner was showing signs of extensive wear and tear, as did its patriarch and founder—my father, Ben Reilly.

As usual he hovered over the grill, frying a cheeseburger, which will eventually be smothered with his homemade chili. A broken-down, broken-hearted Vietnam vet in his mid-sixties, he gripped the spatula like it was a grenade. You can be sure he got panicky when he was backed up with orders. A touch of PTSD is the root of his anxiety.

After a generous beat, I rushed in the back screen door. It bounced a couple of times before it slammed shut with a solid bang. My dad flinched and ducked for cover, reacting startled as if mortar shells were bombarding him. He then glanced at the wall clock and showed me his frustrated, pissed-off face. I go into my customary apology and a defensive alibi.

"I know. Late. Sorry. This teacher cornered me in the library and tried to get me to join the French Club. I asked her, where in Bakersfield would I ever need to speak French? She said, in her French class. Miss Sutton. Two hundred pounds of sarcasm. A real motormouth. I think she's on uppers. Has no understanding that every once in a while you need to put a comma in a sentence."

Suddenly, I realized me being late and using French Club and an overweight teacher as an excuse made no difference. My father, who was focused exclusively on the hamburger patty, heard nothing. Mesmerized by the sizzling that sounded like burning flesh, he never took his eyes off that slab of meat.

I dropped my school books on the counter, grabbed an apron off a nearby hook, and then noticed he's wearing a frayed green Army issue T-shirt and flannel pajama bottoms, that sagged in the back where an ass should have been.

"Dad, it's almost three and you're still in your pajamas. What's the deal?" I asked.

He remained obsessed with the now smoking hamburger patty and answered, "It's a matter of comfort, Jakey. Gives my balls room to breathe. I always hated confinement of any form."

"Freedom's just another word for nothing left to lose," I replied and got nothing but a blank stare from him. I clear up the confusion.

"Janis Joplin. 'Me and Bobby McGee,' 1971. Otherwise, you're okay, though, right?"

My father cocked his head to one side. There was always frustration brewing just beneath the surface.

"We need to end apartheid and slow down the arms race," he barked, "provide shelter for the homeless, change the abortion laws to protect the right-to-lifers, while at the same time maintaining a woman's right to choose. You should be writing this down for Congress to give serious thought to."

I just stared uncomfortably. He continued to rant. "We also have to control the influx of the goddamn illegals." He slammed his hand down on the counter.

"Pop, you know what you just said was kind of riddled with contradiction . . ." I stopped myself from offering a logical explanation, which usually did no good, but made me feel like I was trying to have a meaningful conversation with my father. Instead I comforted him with a pat on the shoulder and some encouragement. "You're doing good, Pop," I said, even though the signs of a brewing mental disorder were evident.

"You think I'm doing good?" he asked, full of hope.

I pried the spatula from his grip. "I got it from here, soldier," I said. "Beat a retreat."

"Yes, sir," he responded with a modest amount of energy, then dismissed himself, doing a swift about-face and almost falling over. He headed upstairs, probably to take some sort of medication. After he was out of sight, I flipped the now inedible burnt burger into a trash can and dropped a fresh patty on the grill. I sighed despairingly, knowing my father had major issues that he was powerless to remedy.

The man had a really tough life after my mother died. Running the family diner—flipping burgers with one hand and balancing a crying, damp kid with the other. I was raised on top-quality greasy food and learned about life from waitresses and truck drivers. I was able to change my own underwear and a flat tire on a sixteen-wheeler by the time I reached the terrible twos.

As it became necessary, the waitresses gave me the inside scoop on sex and using protection, unless I wanted to be a parent at a very early age. They emphasized treating a woman with respect and not just as a piece of ass. I had my first taste of beer when I was ten and experienced my first marijuana high at age twelve.

A side note worth mentioning: my mom, Michele Reilly, died of cancer when I was just five. She always looked like she was going to a party. Glowing skin, with long blonde hair and bright blue eyes, she was a vision of beauty and kindness. She held on for days. I thought I heard her say my name before she gasped her last breath. Maybe not. Maybe it was just me hoping the last thing she uttered was—*Jake*. I was five. My hearing was not that acute. *Jake* could have been *cake*. Perhaps she wanted a piece of cake. Either remark, I cried myself to sleep that night, while my father sobbed into his pillow.

My father's infallible remedy for dealing with his pain and suffering was his daily dose of Jack Daniel's. He argued that while the English took tea breaks, his preferred indulgence was Tennessee whiskey. He started drinking at dusk, and stopped when he either puked or passed out, whichever came first. It was a pathetic existence but this palliative treatment seemed to work for him.

Since my mother had passed away, the lack of a female perspective had never become an issue. My dad made sure of that by bringing home a new woman from the local bar just about every Saturday night. In the morning, he'd introduce me to Betty. Her name was always *Betty*. Why? Who the fuck knows? He'd then make us breakfast. After that, he'd send her on her way, drive her home, or call a cab. Always made sure I understood that Betty would never take the place of my real mother. That Betty was just a body for him to have sex with or he'd have a nervous breakdown. Exposing his (sexual) dalliances to a seven-year-old was not as much of a shock as you might suspect. We communicated. We had an honest father-son relationship. Bullshit was not tolerated. His extracurricular activities went on for several years, until his anxiety got the best of him and he forgot where the bar was located or couldn't remember the name Betty.

⁂

On this particular cloudy Monday afternoon, business was at a steady flow. Maybe eight to ten customers. For us, this was the busy lunch crowd. The usual sights and sounds of truckers, a couple regular soup and saltines seniors, and a FedEx delivery guy treating the manicurist from Pampered Hands nail salon to an iced tea and a Cobb salad.

Waitress Helen Mayfield, forty-five, was working the shift on her own today, because the second girl called in with a migraine. And the third girl ran off with the second girl's boyfriend over a month ago. Which worked out fine because business was weak and we really never needed a third girl.

A lot of the regulars said that Helen was a real stunner in her day. Could've been a model if she hadn't gotten pregnant at seventeen. Jumped by two boys one summer in the local park, she never reported it to the cops and lived with the consequences—having the baby. Instead of facing the ridicule of her schoolmates, she dropped out. When her parents disowned her for being a tramp, she was forced to get a job and started working for my father to cover the cost of motherhood. She had been a single parent ever since and a surrogate mother to me, filling in the emotional gaps when a hug was needed and a chest cold cried out for aspirin and Vicks VapoRub.

Two older men, early eighties, if not older, weathered from too much sun and too much bourbon, wait impatiently for their split pea soup to arrive. They always made an issue about those thrilling days of yesteryear. The topic never seemed to change—it was always centered on how country legends Merle Haggard and Buck Owens gave birth to what was known as the Bakersfield Sound in the late 1950s. It was their legacy to the world of country music. Other than that, Bakersfield was nothing but a bathroom break/gas fill-up stopover on the way to Fresno, Sequoia National Park, and San Francisco.

Suddenly there's a loud crash with a *goddammit* following the distinctive sound of dishes splintering. All heads turned to witness what was now a river of split pea soup free-flowing on the cracked checkerboard tile. I crossed the room and gave Helen a hand, wiping up the mess.

"Sorry, Jakey," she said, "I'm a bundle of nerves lately. Involuntary slippage. Sweaty palms. Stomach in knots. All stems from worrying about your dad. How's he doing today?"

"Today he's burning burgers in his pajamas. What's it going to be tomorrow, pissing in the lemonade dispenser?"

"His days are definitely getting darker," she said.

I nodded in agreement. The scary reality reminded me of the Army ammo box hidden under the counter. Wasting no time, I rushed over and pulled it out. It's labeled: Lt. Ben Reilly—US Army. I opened it, revealing a .45-caliber pistol and a box of ammunition. Helen gave me a wary look. Our minds echo the same degree of alarm that this was a potential danger zone. I suddenly became noticeably silent, cataloging various gun accidents that took place in the home. Accidental deaths were not uncommon during the holidays. Fourth of July, New Year's Eve, a reveler fires his gun into the air and a stray bullet would find itself lodged in some innocent victim's skull. A little boy, playing cops and robbers, accidentally shoots a neighborhood kid with his dad's loaded gun. A pointless playtime tragedy. Then there was the poor guy, suffering from a life of depression that eats his gun for breakfast. That's the one I worried about. The one tragedy I needed to avoid happening during the breakfast rush. I moved the arsenal to a much safer place. Out of reach, as if I were dealing with a five-year-old. First chance I got, I planned to hide the ammo box in the safest possible place. The attic, inside a suitcase. It's pretty much a given, he wouldn't be taking any trips in the near future. That gave me some sense of security, so I went back to the kitchen to resume my chef duties. Not a task I relished.

I openly admitted—to myself anyway—the hard fact that I never really loved growing up in this environment. Only when the sign turned from Open to Closed did I ever feel a sense of home. The working day was over. I could finally have my parents back again. There was an innate feeling of family that I missed from sunrise to sunset. That was then. Nowadays I just can't handle the restaurant business. It's a grind. The meager flow of customers is not enough to make a decent living. My parents had a good thing going when they were younger and first opened up. People came in droves to sample a home-cooked meal. Today, we can't keep up with the fast-food restaurants, which offer a full meal at 1975 prices.

I finished grilling a fresh burger to replace the one that my dad destroyed, and walked it over to Dave Hardwick, a regular, who always sat at the counter on his favorite stool, well-used from his 195-pound physique. If the stool were occupied he would hover until it was vacant, then swiftly move in and climb aboard. At seventy, he prided himself on being a confirmed bachelor who has told me several times how he had a serious crush on my mother. Wanted to take her out to a first-class restaurant and order a bottle of fine wine, but never got around to asking for fear that she'd say no, and that the rejection would be too much for him to handle. He had always regretted it and kicked himself for not having the courage to go after what he so desperately wanted—the woman of his dreams.

"'Here you go, Dave. Medium-well, stark naked, nothing but beef on a dry bun. Bon appétit."

I had started to walk away when Dave threw me a curve that prompted me to swing back and take notice.

"Today I'm adding ketchup. I'm altering my lifestyle. Making a change."

"Good for you, Dave. Change is good."

"Bigger news. I'm thinking of getting married."

"What? That is huge. Ketchup and marriage. Very exciting." I slid the ketchup bottle closer to him. He looked at it for a beat before carefully unscrewing the cap, as if he were a defusing a bomb.

"So, who's the lucky girl? A local or out-of-towner?"

Dave recapped the bottle. His attempt at altering his life seemed to be put on hold.

"The girl? She still remains a mystery. I'm just visualizing matrimony out loud. Wanted to hear how it sounded, if in fact I decided to walk down the aisle. Curious to see how people would react, hearing that old Dave Hardwick was getting hitched. You're the first to hear that it's even been on my mind."

"So, there's no fiancée? No wedding? Nothing? Just a random thought, huh—you were testing me?"

He shrugged, and then shrugged again for emphasis. I played the game to indulge him, and to see where it was headed. It's always a head shaker when having a conversation with Dave Hardwick.

"So, how did it sound to you, Dave? Saying you're getting married, when you're not.

This time I uncapped the ketchup.

"My stomach did flip-flops. My biggest fear, Jake is that my wife, whoever she may turn out to be, will die on me. That I'd be left a widower, unable to eat, sleep, or think straight, because the loss would be too devastating for me to function. Coming here on a regular basis would probably end, because I'd lock myself in my room and become a recluse."

"I understand where you're coming from, Dave."

"How your father ever survived and managed to keep his wits after the death of your mother, I'll never know."

"Make no mistake, Dave, it was damn hard on him. Still is. He couldn't eat or sleep for the longest time. Dave, there's a simple solution to all this."

"You seem to have the answers to difficult situations that for the life of me I can't shake loose in my head."

"It's a little mean-spirited, but it should work in your favor."

"Lay it on me, Jake."

"Don't ever get married and you'll avoid having a wife die on you."

"That occurred to me. I just needed to hear it from someone else other than myself. Thanks."

"I think that's the best way to go. Stay away from the altar. You still considering the ketchup?"

"No. It was strictly a diversion, maneuvering around the real issue—coping with an imaginary dead wife."

And then the floodgates opened up and he started to cry openly. What could I do or say that would assure him that he wouldn't be left to die alone? This was the central point of this whole discussion. He could give a crap about getting married. He just wanted to make sure that when his time came, whenever that might be, someone would be by his bedside to hold his hand. I made him that promise. Unless by some fluke I went before he did. Then I guess he'd have to find someone else to sit and watch while he passed away. But I didn't tell him that.

Although Dave seemed to be off his meds, he's normally a perfectly stable guy. It's the heat and the constant emissions of truck exhaust that have clouded our sound judgment in this town. Most of us feel like we're trapped in a sand dune snow globe and can't find a way out. I hoped I'd get out before I cracked like Dave and developed a fear of ketchup.

As I headed back to the kitchen, I saw in my peripheral a very attractive girl coming through the door. She's wearing dark clothing, sunglasses, and displaying a frown. The fragrance of her perfume is pungent. Patchouli Sandalwood. Not that I have a nose for heady scents, but I know, from being up-close, what this girl splashes on herself. I adjusted my position to get a full head-on glimpse. I know her. It was the first time I'd seen her away from the school grounds. I swallowed hard. Her presence manifested that roller coaster feeling in the pit of my stomach. This was Ina Byers. This was, in my judgment, a paramount sighting. What could possibly bring her in here? Directions to a more favorable eatery, perhaps? Didn't matter; now was my chance to initiate a formal introduction that had been long overdue. Up till now, it's mostly been nothing but a polite nod. A broad smile. Asked if she had the time. Obscure hidden mysteries like that wouldn't exactly strike up an in-depth conversation and let her know you wanted more than just the time of day. You wanted all the hours of the day and night and the in-betweens.

I checked myself out in a stainless steel napkin holder. I looked tired and unkempt. My sandy blond hair, disheveled. My bright blue eyes, dull. I asked myself—what are the chances she remembered me from the ninth grade? A ridiculous notion. In the ninth grade I had this epiphany. This was a key period when my taste in girls went from virginal shyness to rugged individualism. Warm, with a sunny disposition, suddenly became a turnoff. Vanilla was no longer a flavor that whetted my appetite. What turned me around, I had no clue, but I preferred girls who, for the lack of a better interpretation, were rough around the edges, with a more caustic timbre. The popular, more sought after girls—like the prom queens and the cheerleaders with their ample breasts, shapely legs, and miniskirts that barely covered their thighs—didn't interest me. Don't get me wrong; I'm a big fan of breasts, legs, and thighs. But I preferred them to be attached to a girl with a freewheeling mind. This fixation of mine spread through the entire student body at Bakersfield High like wildfire. Why? Who knows? But I was suddenly the central figure of gossip. This gave birth to the insults, the cruel name-calling. When I tried to explain how I was drawn towards a more radical, hard-nosed, bad girl persona, I was condemned by the guys as a Nazi sympathizer and probably had a pinup of Eva Braun taped inside my locker. I knew what type I was keen on but didn't have the balls to go after her. Like Dave, rejection wasn't something I wanted to face. It would've shattered my ego. Today, however, was different. I suddenly got the courage to act on my fantasy. I primped as best I could, tested my breath in cupped palms, and then took off the apron to lose the slovenly waiter look.

I was riveted as I watched her slump into a booth. She flipped open a pack of Sherman cigarettes, knocked one out, lit it, inhaling and blowing the perfect smoke ring. I found myself reacting out loud—just loud enough for Helen, who's on the second pea soup run, to overhear my ridiculous aspiration:

"I'd give anything to be that smoke ring."

"So, why aren't you?" she said, as if that were a fait accompli. She then asked me a critical question: "Am I waiting on the girl with the exciting full lips, or are you?"

I just exhaled, which Helen knew was code for *I'll handle the lips and the rest of her anatomy, thank you very much.*

I first filled a glass with water, ice, added a slice of lemon to be trendy, grabbed a setup, lingered a few seconds before making the journey to the center of table number four, where I set down the water glass. It spilled. So much for making a good first impression. I made myself pull my focus from the floor and looked at her directly. Apologized under my breath, swiping the spill off the table with my hand, as if spilling water on customers was a practice that happened here all the time.

"Nice move. I gather you're not the regular waiter."

"You'd be correct. Your waitress is cleaning up the pea soup that spilled before you came in."

"So, what's the deal—everyone that works here is clumsy?

"It's been a hectic day." I wanted to follow up with the question about the ninth grade, but something told me this wasn't a good spot to do that. Instead, I went with conventional protocol.

"So, have you decided?"

She fired back with absolute certainty. "Yeah. I've decided that most guys are a complete waste of flesh."

Whoa. This kick in the teeth seemed really unjustified. But I indulged her. "Would you like a side of fries with that vicious insult?"

"Okay, I deserved that slam, but like you, I've also had a hectic day." She took a beat, probably to decide whether or not to go on or just get up and leave. Finally: "My so-called boyfriend and I . . . we had this fight—doesn't matter what it was about—he was wrong. He was always wrong. Relationships. Know what I'm saying?"

"*There is always some madness in love. But there is also some reason in madness.*"

"You said a mouthful."

"Friedrich Nietzsche."

"That's your name?"

"That's who said the mouthful. It's his quote, I just borrowed it," I explained.

This little jolt of wisdom jogged her memory. She then asked me if I was the *sharp guy* in her English class who nailed all the answers and fucked up the class curve. To avoid any conflict, I just nodded. But I had to admit, I loved the fact she identified me as the *sharp guy*. Having an endearing name always made the connection distinctive.

She took another deep drag off the Sherman. My focus went straight to her lips pulling on the cigarette. I'm intoxicated and she knew it. Her carefully painted violet fingernails offered me the cigarette.

"Wanna hit, Sharp Guy? Sherman Naturals. Very avant-garde. A mellow experience," she said, tilting her head for emphasis.

I responded without taking a breath: "You make a bad habit seem very enticing." Being a devout non-smoker, I have to admit I was torn.

I mean, the thought of my lips touching her lips, even via a cigarette, would be a major move for someone who had been infatuated with her since she was fifteen. Even then she dressed in black, favored dark eyeliner and purple lipstick, and smoked at every opportunity. The girls' lavatory was a breeding ground for smokers, druggies, and make out artists.

For me, that was my sexual revolution. The turning point of my formative years. Serious masturbation came into play and I dreamt about Ina Byers incessantly. She was different. I ate up different. I liked that she wasn't afraid to be independent and think outside the box. I liked that she didn't conform to approved standards of behavior. Her bad girl image won me over. But I was always too much of a coward to pursue even a harmless invitation: Can I buy you a drink after class? *After class* seemed a bit juvenile, so I would've couched this in more mature language. As if I was talking about going downtown to a softly lit cocktail bar. All the while being hopeful that sort of atmosphere would intrigue her offbeat tastes, and she'd jump at the chance of grabbing a shot of tequila or a dry martini. I was seventeen. I was grabbing at straws. I was delusional.

Taking a hit off her cigarette still would have fired up my imagination. As I reached for it, she withdrew and turned her attention out the window where a nice-looking older guy, I'm guessing twenty-one, headed towards the door. She reacted and quickly submerged the cigarette in the glass of water; it sank and hid below the lemon slice.

"Look, my uncivilized boyfriend is about to make a grand entrance and probably cause trouble. Why I'm drawn towards social misfits is a mystery." Next came a warning that this guy had a mean streak and carried a switchblade hidden in his boot, ready if and when that streak ever reared its ugly head. A weapon that was popular with young delinquents back in the '50s seemed to have made a resurgence.

I could talk my way out of any hostile situation with clever dialogue. As far as defending myself with a knife in my face, not sure how I'd react. Probably wave my dad's .45 in the air and see if that gave me the upper hand against a switchblade. I would say yes.

With that safety net cemented in my head, the boyfriend, a lanky dude with a tanned complexion, loped inside, slumped in the same booth directly across from Ina. He's combative and wasted no time defending himself. He nervously finger-combed his hair before his verbal assault.

"All I said was you need to sometimes let the other person jump in with a fucking suggestion once in a while. You make it seem like it's a crime to have an opinion. You're really very controlling and it's becoming stale."

"Stale? Then leave," she said. "Call it quits and end this over-worked boy/girl thing we share that seems to get in the way of you expressing your point of view."

He looked at me as if I was going to save him from hanging himself.

"Perfect example of what I'm talking about. Wouldn't you agree she's controlling?"

"I don't know her well enough to form an opinion."

"I mean, chicks in general. They dominate the air around us. They rule the roost. Always need to be in the damn driver's seat."

"And what would you like me to do about it? Change the way she thinks, just so you can win this argument?"

I might have stepped over the line because he hesitated longer than I would have liked. There's no nod. No eye contact. Not even a blink.

Nothing. He stared mutely into space like a zombie. I shifted back on my heels just in case a switchblade was about to settle under my chin.

Then finally . . .

"If you have the power to change how any woman thinks, I want the fucking recipe," he said.

Ina jumped in, looking straight at me with a challenging stare.

"Go for it, Sharp Guy. Alter my point of view. Change my mind on how I think. How I dream. How I look at the world through my eyes. How my boyfriend, and I use the term loosely, thinks he's the superior sex in this relationship."

Although I felt, with enough time, I could change her point of view, I threw my hands in the air and surrendered.

"I learned a long time ago, you don't screw with the female psyche. The constant badgering, tormenting, and persecution could drive a man insane." I laughed to mock my own idiotic interpretation. Ina laughed too. The boyfriend shifted in his seat, wiped his dry mouth with the back of his hand, started to drink the water with the soggy floating Sherman, but caught himself before downing the blended brew. Ina, seemingly now disinterested in this entire conversation, began to pick the polish off her thumbnail, like she's chipping paint. Meanwhile, the boyfriend, realizing he had no chance of being victorious, took the smarter course and gave up. He placed his hands so that his palms faced up on the tabletop. I suppose to show he's got nothing up his sleeve or that he's about to recite some sort of incantation to raise the dead. I don't know. It's all a guessing game until he finally speaks.

"Okay. I get it. You're looking for an apology." Then begrudgingly: "I apologize. Satisfied? Don't make me grovel in front of the fucking waiter, who I'm sure thinks I'm some sort of loser who can't handle his girlfriend." He then turned to me and opened up. "I've been with lots of women. Not all of them pleasant. Some rough around the edges. Others temperamental and high-strung. A few emotionally troubled babes who needed to be smacked around, but I never laid a hand on them. Anyways, this is the first time I've had to apologize for me being me. Condemned for letting down my defenses and allowing people to see my weak side."

I gave the guy points for being honest and offered an opinion. "Look, your sudden weakness is not going to hurt your image, if that's what you're worried about. You can apologize and still be the nasty prick you seem to demonstrate." I hoped this idiot saw this as a compliment and not a total insult.

Ina, having had enough of this pointless conversation, slid out of the booth, and turned to me. Her cigarette breath in my face was awful but I endured it, since this was the closest I'd ever been to her.

"Do I owe you anything for the lemon water and the idle time I used up in your booth?"

"You're in luck, there's no charge for water and idle time today."

She gave me a kiss on the cheek. I wanted to reciprocate but didn't for fear I'd be pushing the affection envelope a bit too far. Plus, I think the kiss was only planted to make the boyfriend squirm. Which I'm sure worked and would be discussed and argued on the way home.

"Thanks for the use of the hall, Friedrich Nietzsche." She headed for the door.

Before she left, I called out, "Just curious. Any chance you remember me from the ninth grade? I was much younger back then, not as tall, and wore a different shirt than the one I'm wearing today. . . . Plaid, I think," I added, trying to be cute and clever.

She stood leaning against the doorjamb, her arms folded in front of her, seemingly lost in thought—either searching for a much more clever retort or deciding if she should ignore it and just get the fuck away from the heavy apathy of the diner. Then came . . .

"No. Yes. Maybe I remember you. But probably not. Ninth grade was the first time I experimented with weed. Middle school was all a blur."

And then, in a whisper, she was gone. And although I never got around to introducing myself properly, I loved her indecisiveness and the slim chance she might have remembered me.

If nothing else, this was a breakthrough moment for me. A one-on-one with Ina Byers. As I returned to my chef duties, quiet eyes followed me to the edge of the kitchen. I pivoted and turned to the cast of onlookers. "What?" I barked defensively. I got a round of applause.

Old Dave Hardwick was the first to speak up. "You did good, Jake. Handled yourself appropriately. You didn't back down from the boyfriend, who was a total prick. You have a knack for conversation and an innate way of influencing the opposition."

Was he being facetious? Or did he mean what he said? Who the fuck knows? I didn't care. I had a significant exchange with Ina Byers and that's all that mattered.

Helen crossed from delivering breakfast at table four and placed a supportive arm on my shoulder. "Jake, sweetie, considering you had an audience of critics, you managed to be witty and charming. You lived out your dream. Casual contact. This was progress. You want more, you got to put yourself out there again, Friedrich Nietzsche."

CHAPTER TWO

After a long, arduous day, I went upstairs to the apartment that's located above the diner. Nothing fancy. Two bedrooms, living room, bath and a half, and a postage stamp-sized kitchen which was hardly used for obvious reasons. As a family we ate most of our meals downstairs in the diner. Thanksgiving, Christmas, birthdays, anniversaries—whatever the occasion, the diner was our gathering place. I was raised an only child in what would appear to be an unexciting living space crammed with pots, pans and a never-ending supply of condiments. Even so, I was still able to appreciate that this was home. My room, my escape from reality, had a smallish desk with just enough top space to accommodate a swing arm metal desk lamp that resembled a long-necked crane, a secondhand Smith Corona typewriter, and a Folgers coffee can that housed pens, pencils, paperclips, and Liquid Paper. This is where I studied and put my brain to work. This is where I wrote an outstanding book report on

Bridge to Terabithia by Katherine Paterson. Not exactly my chosen reading but it was required in my English class. Judging by the class grades, I guessed I was the only one who took the time to read it. Moreover, this inadequate workspace was where I also began writing my novel, under the lamp that kept flickering and threatening to burn out while I crafted intrigue and multiple red herrings onto paper. I perceived the flickering lamp was sending out a continuous SOS code of distress—and that this annoying flutter was a sign that what I was painstakingly typing was pure crap. To this day I've struggled, never making it past page three. The wastebasket overflowed with balled up attempts at a brilliant story. I became disillusioned and locked away the Great American Novel inside a bottom drawer, used the typewriter as a doorstop, and resumed my unimaginative career as a fry cook.

It was nearly midnight when I served my dad his late-night snack. This ritual usually consisted of a bowl of his homemade chili, a Heineken beer and a Cigarillo Swisher Sweets cigarillo. He was getting more absentminded by the day, so him falling asleep with a lit cigar could prove to be risky. This was how my life flowed these days—furthering my education at Bakersfield High, helping out at the diner after school, and caring for a broken man who'd wake up screaming in a pool of sweat, caused by recurring nightmares of him trudging through the Mekong Delta with shrapnel lodged in his leg. Which accounted for his distinctive limp.

I stood at the open doorway waiting for him to swallow the last morsel of chili. The routine then went like this—I took the dirty dishes downstairs, and made sure the alarm was set and whatever was supposed to be off was off. Lastly, I headed for my room and hit the books for a good hour. Usually asleep by two, up at six thirty when

Helen opened up and made the first pot of coffee, allowing me to hightail it to school and embark on my last semester until graduation and the freedom that awaited me.

However, tonight's routine was interrupted by a loud, almost angry/panic-stricken knock at the diner door. The tendency was to ignore it. Probably a drunk thinking this was a cocktail lounge or a druggie having the munchies. This was not an uncommon occurrence. But this was different. Not your normal door knock. So different that it freaked out my dad who heard the banging from his bed upstairs. He bolted upright and went into battle mode. The knocking may have triggered the sound of strafing bullets or incoming mortar shells. A reminder of being under fire. He became alarmed, disjointed. Illogical. He took cover under the bed like it was a foxhole, then yelled down to me in the kitchen. I had just made sure the back door was locked and secured.

"We're under attack, soldier!" he yelled, his voice cracking as he spouted orders. "Grab your weapon. It's in a box under your bunk. On the double!"

I yelled back upstairs, trying to reason with him. Reminding him where we were and safe from the enemy. But the knocking came again at a rapid pace, which freaked him out even more. "Lock and load. They're coming over the top!" he screamed.

A little concerned myself. I haul ass back up the stairs, taking two at a time. His meds. *I need to get his meds*, I repeated aloud to myself. When I found him hidden under the bed, I tried to persuade him that it was safe. That it was all-clear. But he had gone completely off the rails.

"You need to kill the gook. He has come to cut off my balls and hang them in his trophy cabinet."

I doubt that any Vietcong soldier has a trophy cabinet. I take it a step further. Improvise. Drop a 60 mg Valium into a glass of wine, along with a cigar. Slid it under the bed and convinced him it was from his buddies celebrating the end of the war. He bought it. Drank the wine. Lit the cigar. Within a few minutes the pill started to take effect; he settled down and crawled back into bed, under the safety of the patchwork quilt my mother had made. My dad regarded the bedding as protective camouflage.

The knocking continued. I rushed to the open window, looked down and saw a puff of smoke rising towards me.

Frustrated, I hollered, "We're fucking closed! If you're desperate for coffee, hit up the 7-Eleven." And then a familiar face looked up at me. A cigarette dangling from her lips. A piercing voice seeped through the thin layer of smoke . . .

"I need to use the phone, Sharp Guy."

Identifying the voice as Ina Byers, I once again got that anxious roller coaster dip in the pit of my stomach. Why so nervous? Who knows? She had that effect on me. After making sure the Valium had taken full effect and my dad was now semi-comatose, I headed downstairs and opened the door. She was dragging on her habitual Sherman, looking both enchanting and pissed off, if that's possible.

"It's after midnight. I hope this is an emergency," I foolishly said.

"I'm not trying to be difficult," she said. She moved past me and entered without invitation. "My life has somehow turned to complete and utter crap right in front of your diner," she added.

"Sorry to hear that."

"My uncivilized boyfriend, the loser who you met, dumped me, both literally and figuratively. Which I wouldn't mind if it was for a good reason, but not because he can't keep up with me emotionally and/or intellectually."

"I understand. He's intimidated."

"Exactly. I mean, is that not a moronic excuse to call it quits?"

I didn't want to take sides but she did force his hand and give him an out if he wanted it. He called the relationship stale and her controlling. She told him to walk away if he was so unhappy. Seemed he did just that. Now she's at my doorstep, complaining. Thing is, this wasn't a conversation I wanted to have at this time of night, or ever. Even so, I offered a flimsy opinion.

"Actually, most guys are usually pretending to be something they're not, and their big fear is that a smart woman like yourself is going to see right through them." I made a quick correction so as not to appear insincere. "Us. See right through us."

"You got me all figured out, don't you, Sharp Guy?" she said, almost exhibiting delight.

"Well, not everything, but most everything. The important stuff, like how this conversation irritates you, so you put up this shield of toughness so nobody's ever allowed in." She nodded slightly with a smirk.

"*Every form of refuge has its price,*" I said.

"Another German quote?"

"Noted American rock group. The Eagles."

Her smirk coolly shifted into a broad smile. I seemed to have struck a favorable chord. She moved past me further into the diner, sitting on Dave's exclusive perch at the end of the counter. I wasn't sure if I liked her forward assault or not, but what I witnessed of her controlling nature didn't surprise me. "A phone, you wanted to use the phone, if I remember right," I said.

"Yeah. To call for a cab. Unless I walk home, which is not a safe idea at this time of night. Or you could be a really nice guy and drive me. It's just fifteen minutes. On Elm. Near the Safeway. My grandmother's place. An older ranch style house that was meant to be part of a development that never happened. You can just drop me off."

I explained how I couldn't leave my father. I started to call her a cab when she stopped me.

"What's the hurry? You got anything to drink—beer? I could use a beer. Or wine would be better. Any flavor. Any color."

"I think there's some wine we sometimes use for cooking."

"Perfect," she said. I crossed to the fridge.

"Do you have a girlfriend? I bet you have two. A blonde and a brunette. One for each mood."

"Wrong on both counts. No girlfriend, and my last one was a redhead. But not a natural redhead, so yeah, she may have been a brunette."

As quickly as I got the wine, she changed her mind. Finally picked up on her really bad timing.

"Jeezus, where's my fucking manners? I'm way out of line. It's late. Your dad is asleep. It's a school night. And here I am crying on your shoulder about my tragic excuse for a relationship. I'll call that cab." She reached for the phone. Lifted the receiver. Started to dial, then stopped and made a rash statement that threw me off balance.

"As of tonight, I may swear off guys completely. By sunrise, I switch sides and go stark naked lesbian. It's the only solution to my men problems." She arched an eyebrow at me. "Whaddaya think?"

"One can only hope the sun never rises," I said, hoping she got my subtle meaning, that since she was recently unattached, I'd like to apply for the position. She got the hint, putting the phone receiver back on its cradle, then turned to me with what I perceived to be a sexual stare. She then pulled me closer to her, kissed me on my earlobe, and then stuck her tongue in my ear. It was truly amazing that I was able to think clearly and maintain my balance with a tongue shoved inside my ear canal. Once she removed her tongue I was able to speak again.

"So, Ina Byers, how bad a girl were you, exactly? Tell me about the first time you did it." She didn't hesitate or tell me it was none of my business, which I expected. She jumped right in with a matter-of-fact account of her first sexual encounter.

"I lied and said I was sixteen when actually I had just turned fourteen. Older seemed more impressive, since he was a nineteen-year-old, delivering pizza. It all took place while standing at the front door because my grandmother was in the living room watching TV, and he didn't want to soil the other pizzas in the back seat of his car. I lifted my skirt, he pulled down his pants. No underwear. Made it easy. I muffled my moans by cradling my forearm over my mouth."

"Your first time was with a complete stranger?"

"I was ready to kick my virginity to the curb and he was readily accessible. Yes. A stranger."

"Was it good?" I asked.

"The pizza or the sex?"

"What do you think?"

"They were both adequate. Both satisfied a hunger."

By now I was pinching her nipple through her shirt.

"Did you come?"

"Why? Is that important?"

"Did you?"

"Can't remember," she said. "I might have faked it to appear experienced, as well as to make him feel he was a superb fuck."

"You plan on faking it with me?"

"I didn't plan on you stroking my nipple, so the answer is, let's give it a shot and find out."

This was staggering. My wet dream was about to come to true. Admittedly I was a little nervous that I wouldn't live up to the standards of the uncivilized loser boyfriend. I got the feeling he was the porn star type in bed. A lot of noise, acrobatics, and hand strumming like he was playing an air guitar. Would I have to compete with this sort of conduct? Only way to find out was to dip my toe in and test the waters.

After no more than ten minutes of foreplay, I was lying naked on the cold, hard, tile floor, while Ina Byers straddled me, pumping and flailing her body like she was riding a mechanical bull. Christ, in the heat of it all, I had forgotten about the advice the waitresses gave me about using protection. Too late. Sex was in full swing until she suddenly stopped mid-pump for a splash of honesty, which could have waited until we were done, but for her this was an important confession. She admitted that I was the kind of guy she usually strayed from. Was never attracted to my type. Good looks with no rough edges. Smart, ambitious, well mannered. The kind of person who avoided trouble. No emotional or physical scars. I suppose I felt special that I gave Ina Byers a bit of a challenge. And a different perspective on a guy much more astute than a pizza boy.

We fucked one more time. Groaning and panting loud enough to wake the dead. In the end, she lay half beside me, half on top of me. Pretty sure she didn't fake anything. I didn't dare ask. But if she did, so what? I was trembling from my own crescendo and it might sound selfish, but I got what I dreamt of—a night with Ina Byers.

While we were getting dressed, I noticed my father standing over us fully dressed in his Army fatigues, holding a toilet plunger over his shoulder like an M16 rifle and chewing on the remains of the unlit cigar. He was truly a sad, worrisome sight.

"Guess it wasn't the damn Vietcong after all," he said.

I got her a cab, walked her to the door, then properly introduced myself. Shaking hands seemed like a foolish gesture after what we had just done. Nevertheless, we sealed this unexpected liaison with a manly handshake. She claimed she knew my name all along.

"Nice meeting you, Sharp Guy," she said, using her preferred handle for me.

I then turned to my dad, who had been watching this farewell gesture from the bottom step.

"I hope to God her name isn't fucking Betty," he barked, knowing that *Betty* was code for a *one-night stand—do not repeat under any circumstances.*

I assured him that Ina was not a Betty, even though I was skeptical about believing it myself.

I stayed home from school that day and kept a watchful eye on him. This was a definite mental relapse. But I was confident he'd pull through. He had to. There was no way I was about to put him in a VA psychiatric ward. They'd just overload him with pills. Keep him in a vegetative state until he couldn't remember his name, rank, and serial number, then he'd finally succumb, dying with his dick in his hand. I couldn't and wouldn't let that happen. I was committed to keeping him alive and well balanced for as long as I could.

CHAPTER THREE

A full moon was perched directly above us like a dazzling silver dollar. Neon lights flickered through the darkness. A chorus of crickets almost drowned out the sound of a mediocre rock band (made up of amateur musicians) coming from the amusement park in the distance. This was Collins Fun Zone, a teen hangout on the outskirts of town. It's draped in blue and gray crepe paper—Bakersfield High School colors—solely for the purpose of celebrating the graduating class of 2004. The place is overrun with drunk and drugged-out, students commemorating their recent triumph of navigating four years of maintaining the status quo. During the regular school year Collins was the place everyone met on the weekends to drink, smoke weed, or—if you came with the right partner—get a hand job. This was the place where, at age thirteen, I first fondled a girl's breast. Through her sweater, so it felt more like getting a handful of cashmere than breast. In any event, the Fun Zone had a sentimental attachment for a lot of us.

I leaned beneath a support beam of the roller coaster with my friend Parker Rowe. Parker was still unsure about his future. College? The workforce? Backpack it through Europe and travel until the money ran out? As for me, my destiny was decided in advance. Hanging my diploma above the serving window in the kitchen diner as a reminder that I had the opportunity to do more, but traded that in for family responsibility. Hopefully, one day I'd get the chance to fulfill my aspiration of becoming a serious author. But for now, the only thing I'd ever see of Europe would be in history books and on the Travel Channel.

Tonight the roller coaster was stuffed with graduates leaving behind their formative years and taking on a life with greater responsibility. This scared the piss out of most of them. As for me, my only fear was growing old attached to an apron and a spatula.

The coaster cars whipped by us overhead like a boa constrictor coiling around its prey. The structure shook violently like it was about to weaken, fall apart, and hurl the travelers to their deaths on the hard ground below, their bloodcurdling screams ending with a wet sickening splat. A bit of a gruesome image, I agree. But this was the weed and the wine sharing space in my head and thinking out loud without my consent.

I took a drag from a spliff that was given to us by a fellow student, and then passed it on to Parker, who took a healthy toke of his own. As he dragged on the joint, he spotted an avant-garde babe, and spoke to me while still inhaling.

"Ina Byers sighting at six o'clock," he said, nodding in her direction as he exhaled.

"Sighting at six o'clock? What am I, a sniper?" I snapped back.

"Don't fault me for being accurate."

Stoned but fully aware she's only fifty yards away, I followed the scent of her perfume to where she stood quietly next to a water tower. Dressed in her trademark skinny black jeans and a black scoop neck T-shirt, she looked insanely hot. She had just polished off a hotdog, then headed down an embankment, stepping over a stack of old railroad ties, while maneuvering her way through some heavy undergrowth, and finally coming out on the other side to join her friends—the usual suspects—rogue, cocky, anti-establishment types. Black and leather defined their temperament. Parker and I moved closer to get a better look at what was going on. Those guys were always up to some sort of sketchy mischief. Delinquency was their sport. I would hazard a guess none of them would graduate with honors, or attain a college degree, or even want to go to college. Most graduated by cheating the system in some underhanded fashion. But they got a diploma, which I'm sure made their parole officers proud. Sure, I realize branding everyone in black pants and leather jackets as criminals and stupid was an unfair evaluation. I had no evidence to prove otherwise. Besides, I was only thinking it; saying it out loud probably would've been disastrous. A punch in the face, a swift kick in the balls, followed up with another punch to the midsection and me left gasping for oxygen. This group had a penchant for violence, as demonstrated by their favorite pastime, which I was just in time to witness.

Partially hidden behind a patch of overgrown weeds and a grove of eucalyptus trees, Ina was handed a loaded .22 pistol. Her target was a row of empty beer cans that sat lifelessly on the window ledge of an abandoned train depot once used by the Santa Fe Railway when Bakersfield was just a sleepy little town off the beaten track. The signs of decay were apparent. Shattered and boarded-up windows, termite damage that weakened the structure to almost total collapse, and even a weathered Bakersfield junction sign, dangling and ready to give way come the next heavy windstorm.

The depot was a reminder of the past, but in the present, these kids had adopted this place as their private shooting gallery, tailoring their own game called *Kill the Can,* a variation on the classic kids game, *Kick the Can.* Ina took aim and waited for her cue to shoot. However, she sensed my presence peering through the deep vegetation and blurted an arrogant assumption without taking her eyes off the beer cans.

"Keep your eye on the tin cans, Sharp Guy. You're about to be blown away by my dexterity and self-control."

On cue, the group anxiously awaiting her display of marksmanship hollered a resounding KILL. Ina fired off several rounds at the targets, nailing each one with a bullet hole and sending them flying into the night air. Impressed, her friends coolly congratulated her. Once the adulation faded, Ina became bored, handed the pistol to the next shooter, and walked off to entrench herself in a book. A book? Who reads a book at a graduation celebration after murdering tin cans?

Whatever it took to disconnect her from reality would be the reasoning, I guessed. She was not easy to decipher. Parker noticed my blank stare and satisfied my curiosity.

"I heard she got accepted to an art school in Chicago. Talented chick who knows her way around a gun and a charcoal pencil."

"Wonder why she's totally avoided me since that night we had sex?" I mused. "No eye contact whatsoever. I saw her in the cafeteria—shunned me. In class, she dodged me like I had the plague. Embarrassed, maybe?"

"Possibly you were a lousy piece of ass and you didn't rate a casual nod."

"I made her come three times."

"Maybe she faked it."

"Why don't I ask?"

"You're gonna ask Ina Byers if she faked a climax?"

I just nodded to avoid further discussion.

"And what if she says yes, she faked it?"

"Then I ask for a do-over or my money back," I quipped.

As I walked over to her, Ina reached up to light the Sherman that's pressed between her lips, accidentally dropping her book, Kerouac's *On the Road*. We both reach down for the book at the same time. As she bent over, I couldn't help but see directly down the front of her T-shirt. She was not wearing a bra. Nothing I haven't seen before. But it's still a turn-on. Ina looked up and met my gaze.

"Lemme know if you can't see my nipples and I'll lift my shirt high enough to catch sight of the areola in the moonlight." She found her comment cute and smiled.

I didn't even try to defend my glazed stare, so I just handed her the book and opted to go with a literary review. "*On the Road*. The Bible of the Beat Generation. Most memorable passage: the fourth trip. Sal and Dean take off for one last ride down to Mexico, where they spend a wild night with prostitutes and hang out with this Mexican grandma who's a ganja dealer." Her cute demeanor suddenly changed to one of annoyance.

"Way to go, Sharp Guy, I just got the book and now you've ruined it for me."

I try to cover my fuckup. "Therein lies the beauty of *On the Road*. It can't be ruined. It's perfection. You can't ruin perfection." I take a breath. "In any form." She looked at me and as usual, she was impossible to read. I'm not sure where to take it from this point. Is this the opportune opening to ask why she's been ignoring me, or should I just leave it alone? What the hell, if I don't ask it would haunt me. I paused, so I could do this in one sentence without interruption. She knew something was coming. It was like she was fucking psychic.

"What do you want to ask me?" she said. "Wait. Stop. Let me take a stab—why have I totally snubbed you since that morning when the sun came up, right?"

This time I remained silent, presuming she'd rather have stayed home and read a book than had sex with me. But then, come to think about it, she kind of initiated it, just by knocking on my door and removing my underwear with her teeth. No one does that just to get a ride home, after being dumped by a boyfriend. Well, maybe she does.

"Look," she went on, "let me save you from wasting your time forming a theory that is totally incorrect. You saw that night as something special. For me it was simply a revenge fuck, to piss off my boyfriend. Bottom line, you and I aren't happening. Consider yourself fortunate on several levels. You are, in my opinion, a spectacular guy. That's not hard to see. But I wouldn't wish me on anybody. I'm trouble. Besides, I'm leaving for Chicago at the end of the week. Putting this town in my rearview. If I've hurt your feelings in any way or shattered your self-esteem, I expect you'll get over it because you're a strong-minded person. Look, we shared a moment that I guess belongs in the scrapbooks of our minds. It was nothing else but a great moment to look back on now and then when you're recalling your high school days with your friends." She kissed me on the cheek. "Try and make the most of your life, Sharp Guy."

She walked away, trudging back through the underbrush and climbed over the scattered railroad ties, leaving me a bit thrown that she didn't take me seriously. I discovered later, through town gossip, that her move to Chicago was only a clever ruse to divert and distract unwelcome followers. Predominantly stalkers. Also, scandalmongers who bad-mouthed her because she didn't fit the standard profile of a high school coed. Stalking is not my MO. I saw myself as strictly an intense admirer, hoping to form a closer relationship. If it didn't work out in my favor, I'd walk away. But I truly believed that she wouldn't have had sex with me if there wasn't something brewing between us.

I actually followed her, purely out of intrigue and nothing else. Where did Ina Byers go after a night of commemorating the end of her adolescence? I found out as she reached the edge of the Fun Zone, where a Chevy Camaro barreled up, and came to a screeching halt. I noticed it had no plates. Possibly stolen. What am I, suddenly a detective? She slid in. She instantly stuck out her tongue and the driver set a pill on it like she had just received a communion wafer. I'm guessing it's OxyContin. The driver's older. Good-looking with a rough veneer. In truth, I couldn't compete with this guy, even if I wanted too. His steely eyes caught me skulking behind the bushes. I felt like a degenerate voyeur. He turned the corners of his mouth up at me, and then drove off.

Although sneaking around like some jealous boyfriend gave me a low opinion of myself, I still did some digging, mostly out of curiosity, and found out that the security guard at the front entrance knew him from an overnight stay in the Orange County lockup. Arrested for assault in a bar fight and grand theft auto. I had him pegged. Ray Astemendi. He had a temper to go with his steely eyes. Was I surprised that Ina was attracted to (the) bad boys? Not at all.

Parker suddenly crept up behind me and whispered in my ear. I flinched.

"That's all she wrote, buddy boy, the chase is over. C'est la vie."

"Fine. I can accept defeat. I have more pressing issues, anyway. Caring for my ailing dad. Running the diner. Who's got time for a social life? Not me. Dating and trying to maintain a steady relationship are no longer a priority."

"That's the spirit, Jake, deprive yourself of living a life," Parker said.

"I have no choice and you know it."

"I don't know it. Tell me why you can't get a college education over the internet? Or write a page a day of your unfinished novel—in between babysitting your dad and flipping burgers. People multitask all the time, and you're good at juggling balls in the air."

I realized Parker was in my corner, trying to get me to forget about Ina Byers and move on. Easier said than done. You just don't cast intense feelings aside, like nothing happened. Like you never fucked a girl you were obsessed with on the floor of your diner until the sun came up. Maybe the reality was, this was nothing but one of my dad's one-night Bettys. *Love 'em, then call 'em a cab.*

⌇

After graduation I fell into a deep depression for several weeks. Moped around the diner. Didn't eat much. Had a horrible bout of insomnia. Lost a good ten pounds. My clothes hung loose. Shaving was a chore. Avoided phone calls unless it pertained to my dad's health. And the kicker, I started smoking—Sherman Naturals, no less. All of these symptoms were not hard to comprehend—I couldn't get Ina Byers off my mind. It wasn't tough to evaluate my own disorder. I was experiencing a form of separation anxiety. Pathetic.

Opening up to a real shrink would seem to be the smart approach, but I didn't have the time or the cash for such a luxury. So I learned to live with my weaknesses and talked it out with friends and a few customers who were patient enough to listen to me spill my guts. The big question that was always on most people's minds: why the fuck was I so attracted to a girl that was immersed in the dark side? And if I liked dangerous, eccentric girls so much, there were hundreds out there, lurking in the shadows—the kind who shaved their heads in lieu of shaving under their arms, just aching for attention. For now I decided to put aside my proclivity for budding femme fatales until my depression passed, and I was psychologically fit again to chase after abnormal women with pierced navels and had no need of a hairdryer.

CHAPTER FOUR

Five years crawled by at a snail's pace. The days and nights seemed to take forever to wade through. Naturally, lots of things had transpired. I was emotionally cramped by two relationships, both with volatile, high-strung personalities that caused tense living conditions for both my father and me. Claudia and Karen. Two very attractive women. Guess I went for looks more than compatibility. Neither had any ambition. Karen and I lived together for six months. Six months too long. A nightmare. So I was relieved when she hooked up with an equine saddle and tack dealer who was headed for the Texas panhandle. Besides, according to my father, she was a user. A star manipulator. A thief, stealing us blind from the cash register on a regular basis. Roughly $1,500 in cash and a 10-quart commercial mixer worth at least $700.

Then, six months later, Claudia D'Angelo came into my life. Italian with a terrible temper. Liked to yell and throw objects when she didn't get her way or was disagreed with. The last straw was when she threw a meat tenderizer mallet in my direction, during an argument about getting a pet cat. I was chronically allergic to cats. She didn't care. My breathing became hampered. Don't breath around the cat—that was her fix. To be honest, I hated cats. I'm not a cat person. I liked the kind of pets that chased cats. This argument did not end well. At the appropriate time, I threw Claudia's clothes out the front door. Told her to go fetch. When she did, I changed the locks.

There's no one to blame for any of this. But how many more wrong choices could I possibly have made in one life if I'd been trying?

Another month of fighting my personal war on nerves and anxieties had passed when this guy from my graduating class came in and ordered a tuna melt. A fucking tuna melt. I hadn't made a tuna melt in almost a year. I wasn't about to start the process again. I told him I was out of tuna. He ordered a BLT on rye. Not white like a normal person, but rye. Okay, I was obviously still harboring a lot of pent-up anger to be this upset about fucking bread choices.

First thing I noticed about this guy, he was wearing a jacket and tie. That alone should have tipped me off—he was not who he claimed to be. This was Bakersfield. People don't wear a jacket and tie inside a diner, where condiment stains are sure to find their way onto suit pants or a clean white shirt—unless they're trying to hide their identity.

He introduced himself as Jack Lucas. Claimed he recognized me. I couldn't place the face or the name, but we exchanged niceties anyway. Then he dropped the good guy persona and got to the point. Wanted to know if I kept in contact with Ina Byers? Of course I was blown away that he brought up her name, and that he assumed she and I kept in touch. I told him I hadn't seen her in over five years.

Since graduation. *Why?* He ignored the why and shifted into asking me a series of intricate questions. Had she contacted me in those five years? If so, from where? I answered that question with another *why?* He goes on: was she looking for a place to stay? This time a *none of your damn business* rolled off my tongue. Did she try and borrow money? Okay, enough. This was not a look back high school moment by any means. It became more of an interrogation. I insisted he tell me what this was all about before I said another word. He finally opened up with the truth. Seemed he was fishing for clues to so-and-so's whereabouts, because Jack was working with a Midwest collection agency, trying to track down Ina, who had maxed out five credit cards without a single minimum due payment on any of them in over six months. He was in search of Ina Byers for fraud.

"And you came to me because . . .?"

"Because on all of her credit card apps, she listed you and a Friedrich Nietzsche as references.

"Really? Me and Nietzsche?"

Jack just shifted in place, then loosened his tie. A tie that already displayed mustard stains from a previous eatery, which I'm guessing also refused to make him a fucking tuna melt. I got back on track.

"Clever girl, Ina. You can forget about Nietzsche—he's dead. Died in Germany in 1900." But I was flattered my name was listed, actually. And here I thought she shoved me aside. Abolished me from her life. This was an unexpected treat.

"So," I said, "you were lying when you said you went to Bakersfield High?"

Jack, obviously trapped in his blatant lie, turned bright red from embarrassment, while a bead of flop sweat rolled down the side of his cheek.

"You just said that to establish a friendly rapport," I persisted, "and gain my confidence hoping I'd give up Ina Byers, right?"

"Just doing my job," he said, smirking.

"Thought you collection guys did your business over the phone, in the safety of your cubicle, afraid to show yourself in case someone takes umbrage and wants to break your face for being a pushy sonofabitch."

"I'm not the bad guy here. I'm just tracking down the offenders."

"Maybe she had good reason to default. A sickness in the family. Medical bills. College tuition. Bought blankets and food for the homeless."

"She was shopping all over the Midwest."

"Shopping for what? Expensive designer clothing and a diamond tennis bracelet?"

"I'm not at liberty to say."

"Am I in any way responsible for her debt?"

"No."

"No. So, I guess this interrogation is over, sir. You've reached the end of the line. Now, swivel your butt towards the door and get the fuck out of my diner, before I call a cop and have you arrested for being a nuisance and a cocksucker."

He headed for the door but not before setting his business card on the counter. He didn't lie; his name was in fact Jack Lucas. A special investigator for Mid-Century Collection Agency located in Michigan. I may have gone too far calling him a *cocksucker*, but it suddenly occurred me, it took balls for Ina Byers to use my name as a reference and it triggered a great deal of anger. Especially after claiming I was nothing but a "revenge fuck." I clenched my jaw before hurling a pot of chili against the wall. People jumped. Some ducked for cover. No one ordered the chili for the rest of the afternoon.

On May 30, 2010, at 9:08 a.m. to be exact, my dad died from congestive heart failure. This sad episode also fell on my twenty-third birthday. I woke up expecting to find a cake on the diner counter. This was always the routine ever since I was a kid. Cake for breakfast, along with fifty dollars in cash to spend as I pleased. Usually, I socked it away for my college tuition. These days college was a moot point. He'd bake me the cake the night before. White cake. Two layers with strawberry jam spread between the layers and topped with chocolate frosting. Instead, I found him slumped over the mixing bowl, gripping a wooden spoon. Not the happiest of birthdays. I've never eaten white cake with chocolate icing since.

Being a Vietnam vet, he was given a military funeral and buried at the Veterans National Cemetery here in Bakersfield. I took the initiative and buried him in his full dress Army uniform rather than his pajama bottoms. It was a meticulous, by the book ceremony. I was handed an American Flag folded in a triangle, in accordance with tradition, as a reminder that the USA appreciated his service—and so did all the loyal customers who came to the diner and celebrated his life on that gut-wrenching day.

I've done my best to drag the diner kicking and screaming into the twenty-first century. A few coats of paint, reupholstered booths, vintage jukebox; raised the prices to meet the cost of economic growth.

Three o'clock. A slow period until the dinner rush. There was only one customer in the diner, sitting by herself at the far end of the counter: an older woman named Virginia who came in every Friday with her husband, until he died four months back. Now she came in by herself every Friday, never much for chatting, just sat eating a piece of apple pie that she and her husband always shared. Every so often she turned her attention towards the door as if she was expecting him to show up for a bite.

I left Virginia with her pie and her memories and went out back for some much-needed fresh air. Leaned against the trash dumpster and lit a cigarette. A Sherman. The first one I'd had today. Tried to blow the perfect smoke ring. Nothing doing. Choked and coughed and stomped out the cigarette, as fast as I inhaled. There was no doubt that burying my dad, and now taking on the full responsibility of trying to keep this business afloat, would mentally and physically take a lot out of me. I felt numb. Like my insides were blocks of ice. I thought about hanging it up, before the dinner rush. Going inside and flipping the Open sign to Closed and turning off all the lights. Going dark. I cried instead. Entertaining that kind of absurd fantasy proved I wasn't thinking straight and was just reacting on pure sentiment and not paying attention to the harsh reality. I was stuck here for the long haul. And closing the doors would devastate Virginia, who was trying to maintain her apple pie ritual.

Suddenly I was jolted out of my reverie by a cloud of black smoke seeping through the screen door and engulfing me like a dense fog. I rushed back inside.

Helen was standing in the middle of the kitchen, fanning with an apron a small oil fire that started in the deep fryer.

"This baby finally took a big hit," she said. "Electrical wiring problem. Jury-rigged. This would be Ben's handiwork during one of his more muddled episodes."

"Just add this to the list of casualties," I replied. "Neon sign, two letters flickered out a week ago; toaster oven dead; any day now the freezer is about to take its last breath. Roof leaks, plus I think a family of raccoons are living under the foundation. Things are crumbling all around us, Helen."

"Maybe it's a sign. Time to kick this old girl to the curb, sweetie, and call it a day. I think even Ben would approve."

I looked up at a photo of my dad in younger, happier times that hung over the pickup window. It's one of the few moments when you'd see him smiling; I think he was high on some mood-altering drug when it was taken.

"A real shame. Prime of his life," Helen opined somberly.

"Aloneness. That's what killed him," Virginia chimed in. "Going the rest of the way on empty. It's what takes us all down." She got up, taking her slice of pie—along with the plate and fork—home with her.

"Truth is, he lost his compass," I said as I turned to Helen.

"It happens to all of us sooner or later."

"Does it? I wonder. Does it really?"

"Maybe not. Maybe I'm way off. Maybe I'm just searching for a reason as to why he did what he did, which was to die on your birthday. Is there some crazy omen behind it? A sign?"

"There's no sign. You die when you die. Death comes when it happens. When you take your last breath. There's no sudden warning." I paused, then posed a paramount question. "So, where's the line between guilt and responsibility? You have any idea? I could never figure that one out."

"You have nothing to feel guilty about, Jakey. You of all people deserve a life. Deserve a top-tier education. Write that book that percolates inside you. Fuck your brains out. Escape from this ham 'n' egg prison, before it's too late and it's *you* fryin' burgers in your pajamas."

I must've been listening and taken her suggestion to heart, because two weeks later, I put the diner up for sale. I was finally making a break for it. *It* being liberated from all the responsibility. Don't even ask me where I was going or if I had a plan, because I had crap. But knowing I was going over the wall made it all worth it. Made it seem okay without feeling pangs of conscience.

Two weeks never came because I closed three hours earlier than usual on that following Monday. The sun hadn't even set yet. The idea of selling and calling it quits agreed with me. I started to wander aimlessly around the restaurant wondering what should I save, if anything, as a keepsake. Nothing grabbed my attention. Why would I want a reminder of a business that destroyed my mother's reason to live, believing that inhaling the scent of bacon grease and tainted meat caused her cancer? Not a well-founded reason but she was a chronic overreactor when it came to her health. She had a sweet disposition. Only wanted the best for her family and other families who didn't have much. Fed the homeless and gave money to the church, even though her prayers to God for one more year of life were not answered. I would've loved to sit with her and talk about, well, anything relevant. Hell the selfless woman was my hero. Bottom line, I wouldn't save crap since the rigors of the diner also took my father down. I made the executive decision to sell everything under the roof, under the foundation, under the dirt beneath the foundation.

I crossed to the window to lower the blinds and shut out the sunlight from ever peeking in for the last time, when something caught my eye. Interrupted my final step of posting a handwritten sign to the door that announced we were closing forever, while thanking the loyal customers who stood by us for so many years.

A classic 1978 Mustang coupe that had seen better days limped into to the parking lot, steam spewing from under its oxidized red hood. I was in no mood to deal with someone else's catastrophe, so I quickly moved behind the counter, trying to look inconspicuous. Obviously not inconspicuous enough. There came a rap on the door, then a voice criticizing my lousy attempt at making myself hidden from view.

"I know you're (in there) hiding. I can see your shadow. Look, I read your sign. Sorry you're closing forever. Liquidation is a pisser. I get it. But I just need water for my ailing car. Plain water—no ice, no lemon."

Caught, I crossed to the door with a deep sigh, peeked through the blind slats, and made contact with this persistent woman in aviator sunglasses, who needed a drink of water for her sickly car. It was situations like these that convinced me I was making the right decision in getting away from this dust rag of a town.

I guessed she was in her late twenties. I took a closer look and she looked familiar. Recognizable enough that my breathing became irregular and ramped up. I wanted to sit down but my body wouldn't respond. I was frozen. Unsettled. All those things that cause a person's gut to stir up plenty of bile.

"It's Ina Byers," I said aloud just to make sure I was conscious. She looked good. After all these years, she was still wildly attractive. Black was still her color of choice. She lifted her aviator sunglasses and peered through the window, her hands cupped alongside her deep blue eyes to shade the glare.

"Hey, I could really use some help," she said, almost desperate. I made a solitary decision and opened the door. Slowly, so as not to traumatize myself when I came face to face with her.

"Sorry to bother you, but my car is a piece of shit, and I never know when it plans to show me what a piece of shit it actually is."

She kicked the fender. It had been over six years and Ina Byers pretty much remained the same. Angry, temperamental, yet still hard to define. I could feel my thoughts scramble in my head. Did she remember me? Did it matter if she did or didn't? I could remind her. Just as an opener. Idiotic. She and I fucking and me pinching her nipples would not be the wisest conversation opener. Although I was feeling uneasy, I managed to take control. I first loosened the hot, rusty radiator cap on the Mustang. Propelled by a geyser of lime-green coolant, the cap shot into the air. After it cooled, I grabbed a hose and refilled the radiator. No ice, no lemon as she requested. While I was giving her *piece of shit* car a healthy drink, she grabbed a pack of Shermans from the visor and fired one up. A familiar scene as she took a deep drag and blew the perfect smoke ring. I couldn't help but stare at this proficient skill. She sensed my stare.

"Want a hit?" She offered me the cigarette. Saliva and lipstick glistening on its filtered end. I'd be lying if I said this wasn't inviting.

"You make a bad habit seem very enticing. But I'll pass, since I stopped smoking. Never really started, actually. Had three cigarettes, coughed incessantly. Been on the nicotine wagon ever since."

"Interesting story," she said, trying to be polite but coming across purely sarcastic. We shared a laugh, knowing how mundane this conversation was going.

"But it's never too late to try a bad habit again," she added with a grin.

The muffled ring coming from her cell phone, located in her car, interrupted this indefinable moment. She struggled to open the passenger door. It was stuck, as if someone had welded it shut. She had to yank on the handle several times before it finally sprang open. Frustrated, she looked at the door, then kicked it, putting yet another dent in the already mutilated panel. She raised the question: why didn't she just drop this hunk of metal into an industrial compactor and take a damn bus? I didn't offer an opinion; I smiled, just to keep myself on the neutral side of her car troubles.

She walked away for privacy, leaning against my metal mailbox with a horse shit-green patina that rested on a weathered piece of two-by-four. As she spoke, she fiddled with a matchbook. Never checked the caller ID; she just clicked on and began to talk as if the conversation had been ongoing and she just took a break from it.

"Not to seem overly critical on the subject, Ray. . . "

Ray—that name seemed to ring a bell. She continued:

". . . but I told you your stepbrother was a real tool. No, I did. I absolutely did. Forget him, we'll find someone else to fill in." There was a pause. "What? Jack who? Never heard of a Jack Lucas from a collection agency. Yeah, yeah, I understand. If he tries to contact you again, just tell him to fuck off. Don't challenge him. No interaction. No engaging. I'm dead to him. Moved to Canada. Find a reason to get him off my back."

She ended the call. Pissed, she stomped out her cigarette, and then flung the matchbook into the open end of the mailbox. Of course it was obvious that part of this conversation was about her credit card dilemma. For now, I chose not to mention that Jack Lucas had shown up asking a lot of questions. Instead, I went with courteous social etiquette.

"Everything okay?" I asked. "I mean, except for your car troubles." She ignored the question and switched gears, following up with her own totally off the subject question:

"Was this place once a laundromat?"

I took several beats before answering because it kind of shattered my ego, that she didn't remember me or the diner or the sex. But she certainly remembered my name to use as a reference. I chose to overlook what I desperately wanted to ask: *don't you remember us having sex on the floor of this laundromat?* Again, I didn't force the issue.

"Not a laundromat," I replied. "A diner for twenty-two years."

"Hey, my teen years are a complete blur. I wouldn't have eaten here. Well, maybe I would have. I did weird, unconventional things back then. I took chances. Sure. I could've eaten here—I'm Ina Byers, by the way."

She extended her hand. I, of course, had to stop the action and didn't offer my hand just yet. It was very disappointing that I was not a part of her blurred past. As I recall, she once said the ninth grade was also a blur. God, am I some kind of tool like the stepbrother, because I recalled conversations I had with her over six years ago? Or did I just have an exceptional memory for insignificant facts?

I finally extended my hand, about to introduce myself, when her cell phone rang again. I quickly retrieved my hand while she took the call. It was the local cemetery reminding her that it was almost time for her grandmother's funeral. I never knew her grandmother, but I was pretty sure it was the grandmother who raised her when her biological mother died at childbirth. This could've justified why she rebelled against society—blaming the establishment for not saving her mother's life. I discovered this was the solitary reason she returned—to lay the old lady (her term) to rest. When I showed some remorse for her loss, she invited me to tag along.

"Think I'll pass," I said. "Really not in the mood for a funeral."

For some reason, she pushed it.

"C'mon, it'll make the death of your diner seem meager compared to putting a body into the ground." She pointed to the Closing

Forever sign. She may have hit a like-minded nerve, but I still wasn't interested.

"Appreciate the invite, but I shouldn't be attending a funeral for a stranger. It almost seems sacrilegious. Disrespectful to the family."

"Here's the thing—Grandma had no friends or relatives or close acquaintances, except for me and her Japanese gardener who didn't speak a word of English. She was basically a recluse. Like Howard Hughes but flat broke and more of a hypochondriac than he ever was. Anyway, it's been my experience that it's always better to have at least two people at a burial: A family member to do the crying, and someone else to comfort her. Which, in this case, would be me." She made this last remark with extreme seriousness.

I agreed to tag along for one reason and one reason only—I needed her to admit she remembered me.

We got into her car, that ran like the clunker she advertised it to be. A radio that got one station—country music/news. And a left turn signal that occasionally worked on its own. We weren't a half-mile down the road when she noticed me shifting uncomfortably.

"Do I make you nervous?" she asked.

"Nervous? Not at all," I lied.

"Sometimes I have that effect on people. Look, there's a joint and a bottle of Valium in the glove box if that'll settle any nerves you don't have. Take your pick."

"I'm good."

"So you don't smoke cigarettes and you don't smoke weed. What do you do that might be considered an addiction?"

"I read and write."

"Like letters?"

"A book. I'm writing a book. A novel, actually. In the same style as Kerouac's *On the Road*. An adventure into another time and place. You ever heard of the book?" I added to test her.

"Started it once. Beat Generation shit, right? But I lost the book somewhere along the trail. Never picked it up again."

"If you ever get the impulse again, I recommend it."

"The only thing I have time to read these days is highway signs. Where I'm going and where I've been."

Out of nowhere, it started to rain. Heavy. A relentless downpour. Streets were flooding fast. It was tough to see through the windshield. She didn't bother to turn on the wipers as the visibility has reached zero. But the turn signal decided to function.

"Uh . . .Did this car come with wipers?"

"It did," she said flatly. I waited for her to turn them on, but—nothing.

"Wouldn't it be a smart idea to use them?" I suggested.

"Yes, it would. Smart. But they don't work. Meant to get them fixed, but why spend the money on a car that's nearly reached the end of its life span? It, too, will one day drop dead like my grandmother and your diner."

"Sure. But until then why not fix things for safety reasons?"

"Now I get the sense you're nervous."

"Yes. Afraid that we might get in a head-on collision with an oncoming car that we can't see coming due to faulty wipers. Then we'd be dead like your grandmother, my diner. The radio that only gets one station would be the only thing to survive."

"I'd say you're more paranoid than nervous. Is that a fair evaluation?" she asked.

"Fair? Maybe. Maybe not. Why not compromise and pull over until this downpour stops?"

"Damn, you need to learn to relax, Sharp Guy," she said. Her *sharp guy* reference caused me to quiver inside. In a good way. Either this was an endearing name she lobbed at every guy, or she knew exactly who I was from the time she drove up to the diner, and the laundromat comment was nothing but her trying to rattle my cage and throw me a curve.

She took my advice and we made a pit stop at a local bar called Guthrie's Alley Cat. Dark ambience. A real dive. The barkeep was a chubby guy who I'm pretty sure I went to school with. Harry, Barry, or Jerry. Ina ordered a shot of tequila. As for me, it was too early for tequila, but I could use a drink to settle the nerves that I had finally developed in the last few minutes. A bourbon and seven did the trick.

The barkeeper recognized Ina. "Ina Byers, right?"

"My God, have I not changed at all?"

"Archie Harrison. I went by Arch. We attended the same school together."

I never even came close putting his face to the right name. Ina didn't hold back asking him if they fucked, or if he ever bought drugs from her. He wasn't as shocked to hear this as I was. His answer came as a disappointment, but also in the form of a compliment.

"Nope. We never did it. Not that I didn't want to. You were a hot fucking babe," he said, trying to be cool and distant.

"I wasn't carrying so much weight back then," he went on, "Still, I figured I wasn't your type, so I never even tried to make a move. I did brush up against you once. My only physical contact."

"And you preserved this memorable moment of rubbing up against Ina Byers as if she were a rock star?" I asked.

"Hey, I'm not embarrassed to say my life was dull as crap back then—until I started working here."

"And what, rubbing up against girls has become a regular routine?"

"That happens to be one of the many perks that comes with the job." He laughed. Ina and I kept a straight face.

This dude weighed at least three hundred pounds. In high school, I couldn't imagine he was svelte. Not that svelte was the prerequisite for persuading chicks to fuck. But having a three hundred pound guy on top of you, I'm guessing would have been a deal-breaker for most girls.

Then came a surprising revelation. Ina gently patted my hand while she spoke softly, so as not to draw the attention of others.

"Jake here wasn't my type and I fucked him," she said with no second thought about damaging her schoolgirl reputation. I reacted big. Maybe too big. While chewing on a piece of ice, I chomped down on my tongue. It hurt like a motherfucker. Let out a scream that sounded like I was being tortured. Blood oozed like someone had turned on a faucet. Archie the bartender quickly handed me a towel to stop the flow. I needed a transfusion, not a fucking towel.

"You okay, Jake?" Ina asked with an easygoing tone.

So that I wouldn't appear like a pussy, I went for minor mishap rather than catastrophe. "Fine. Nothing to be alarmed about. Bit my tongue eating a piece of ice." Blood was now dripping into my glass. It was an embarrassing sight.

A drunk in the back spoke up with a clever suggestion: "Put ice on it to stop the swelling." This produced a few random chuckles.

The blood oozing on the counter didn't seem to faze Archie the bartender. He continued to interrogate, and asked if we were a couple. His inquisitiveness I perceived to be more of a sarcastic comment than just an impromptu remark. Ina interjected, making sure our relationship was not misunderstood by this bulky man, who wiped his nose with the same towel he used to dry shot glasses.

"A couple? No way. He's cute, but he's still not my type. He's just helping me bury my grandmother."

"Sorry for your loss. *People die. It happens,*" he said, as if this was an excerpt directly from the New Testament.

I had this overwhelming desire to grab a swizzle stick off the bar and jam it in his ear. But I controlled my urge.

Anyway, this was how I found out Ina Byers recognized me. But she wasn't done expounding. There were more intimate facts she had an impulse to share with the room, such as describing our sexual encounter in detail.

"Six years ago. We—you and I—fucked on the cold hard floor of your diner. Your father was upstairs knocked out by a Valium. At first we dry-humped. Very sexy. This got you off big time. Then we undressed each other. You removed my dark purple panties with your teeth. My hairless vadge turned you on so much you came a second time without any stimulus from me."

By now I'm drowning in embarrassment. Ina looked at me, unfazed by the fact she made me feel small and insignificant in front of strangers. I was noticeably bummed by her revealing our rendezvous to an audience of drunks, who saw this as sordid rather than romantic. I slugged down the last of the bourbon, Seven, and blood combination. Swiveled around on the bar stool and, without saying a word or even nodding, headed for the door. I could feel the sympathetic stares from the head-shakers. I reached the door. The handle was cold in my hand. Beads of sweat bubbled on the back of my neck, my tongue was now throbbing. And then her voice resonated throughout the bar.

"Jake, come back here! I was just fucking around. A really cruel joke. I'm a dick. You were actually magnifico. I loved our time together. I swear it was memorable. I remember us quitting when the sun came up. You made me climax three times. Unheard of, considering my insatiable sexual appetite."

The few patrons in the back of the room gave me a round of applause, like the curtain had just come down on some low-budget off-Broadway play.

Reluctantly, I turned back. Was I a weakling for accepting her apology? Was I still that hung up on Ina Byers that being insulted in front of a bunch of drunks had no effect on my self-esteem? Damn, I wished she hadn't come back into town. Archie, our hefty bartender, poured us at least another four more shots of tequila and a bourbon on the rocks before we staggered outside into the rain. As we stood there being pelted by the downpour, I had to the ask the obvious question:

"Curious—why not mention all this when you first drove up?"

"Why? Why do I do anything? Why is the sky blue, then sometimes it's dark and cloudy? Why are fat girls ignored for their beauty?"

"What? You're making no sense."

"I know, but that's all I can give you when I'm drunk and have a hard time being coherent and giving straight answers."

Few minutes later, we were weaving along the slick highway to go bury her grandmother, Pauline. I made a promise to myself that after I helped bury the old woman, I'd put an end to this insane obsession I'd had for Ina Byers since I was fifteen. She was not the only offbeat attractive woman on the planet who wore black, drank significant amounts of tequila, and had a dead grandmother.

"Do you think I'm a rude, insensitive person?" she asked.

"Yes. Without question. No argument. Rude and impudent."

"So then, why didn't you say something the instant you saw me peeking through your window? I would have expected you to whip open the door and, with all the energy you could muster, shriek, *Holy fuck, she's back.* But no, you let me wade through all the bullshit and the laundromat inquiry. We both know why you didn't speak up."

"We do? Enlighten me."

"Ego. You wanted me to flatter you first. Put my arms around you and say that I missed our time together. That I missed the incredible sex and the clever German quotes you flung at me. I would think by now you would get me. I am not that kind of person who dangles sincerity in front of a guy. It's not my style. I came to bury my grandmother, not to resurrect old, meaningless times. Know what I'm saying?"

"I understand—meaningless. But some form of recognition would've been nice. Instead, we played your game. Which accomplished nothing but having this pointless conversation about who remembered whom and who didn't want to be the first to admit we had a past. Christ, it's like junior high all over again but without the pimples."

"I'm getting a fucking headache," she said in a quiet voice.

Then out of nowhere, she took her eyes off the road, leaned over, and kissed me. Don't know why. Didn't care why. Didn't question it. Just enjoyed it and was relieved we didn't swerve across the lane and crash into an oncoming car.

"Can we just go bury the old lady and be done with all this craziness?" It bothered me a little that she called her grandmother *the old lady*, but I wasn't surprised by her lack of respect. Let's not forget this was Ina Byers we're talking about. Loveable and caring inside, but with a tough, sometimes unkind exterior.

So there we were at the historic Union Cemetery. I was not unfamiliar with this place; my mother was buried in this same cemetery, near a spreading oak tree that provided her with plenty of shade. I suppose the appropriate thing to do would be to swing by her grave and say hello. But I chose not to because I just wanted this dark day to end, and head back to the safe harbor of the diner—which I still planned to abandon and sell to the first sincere buyer with a decent offer.

At the gravesite, a lone man awaited Ina's arrival. He wasn't Japanese, so I assumed he was just a cemetery worker. My age. Young. A depressing sight, actually. Besides us, not a single person in attendance. No friends, relatives, coworkers, or neighbors, as she predicted. The pouring rain didn't help the somber mood. I rued the fact that neither Sharp Guy nor his Dark Crush had thought to bring an umbrella. Ina took her place next to the open grave, where a closed casket rested on one of those devices that lowered it into the earth—not unlike a car that's on a lube rack. I stood behind her inconspicuously. I expected the worker to be sympathetic and say something comforting. I was wrong. The guy got personal, staring at Ina. He cleared the phlegm from his throat and said, "Sorry to interrupt in your time of grief, but I think we went to school together. Bakersfield High. Class of 2004."

"Small world. Now, can we get on with this?" she said.

"I asked you out but you ignored me. Even after I shaved my head and pierced my nose, hoping to get your attention."

There you have it—in a matter of one hour, I encountered two obsessed guys who were hung up on Ina Byers. I was not the only victim who couldn't resist her striking allure. Her reputation as a hot, easy chick preceded her. She never apologized to this guy for causing him to change his appearance and alter his nose.

"We all tried out new ideas," Ina remarked with an impatient edge. "It was a time of experimentation. You took it to another level. Out of my hands. Now, can you please push the damn button? I'm in a rush, and if I stand here any longer I could drown."

At dusk, her grandmother Pauline was finally lowered in the ground. No comforting words by a clergyman. No tears, no whimpering or sobbing by heartbroken mourners. Nothing but the groaning of the lowering device motor sending this dead old woman to her final resting place. Another five minutes and this ordeal was finally over. The sky seemed to open up even more as we headed back to her Mustang. I was noticeably upset, but tagging along was my choice. Feeling a sense of manipulation could've been avoided if I had just said, *Fuck no, I won't help bury the grandmother.*

"Look," she said, "I know you're still pissed off with me for insulting you in the bar, in front of strangers. Drunken creatures who could give a crap about who I had sex with and will never remember your name or what you looked like."

I said nothing. Just let out a frustrated sigh. She tried making me feel better.

"I apologize. Tell me how I can make it to you?" It wasn't a difficult request on my part. We couldn't pull our pants off fast enough and fucked right there, shielded by a decent-sized headstone whose thoughtful epitaph read: *Here Lies My Beloved Eleanor. Devoted Partner And A Crackerjack Bridge Player. 1921-2011.*

I lost control of my earlier ill feelings. Everything I said about backing off from Ina Byers disappeared as I entered deep inside her. "I think you're the most beautiful girl I have ever known," I said with fluency. There was this long pause while my frankness took her by surprise. Finally, she spoke, saying she was headed out of town and didn't plan to ever return. Any kind of long-term thing between us would be a horrible mistake. Sure. I got the message—a horrible mistake. Didn't need repeating, but I said it to myself anyway. *Horrible.*

We got in the car and headed directly back to the diner. She fired up a Sherman, exhaled out the window, then tossed the cigarette out after one drag. After that came an exasperated *dammit.*

"What are you angry about now?"

"That my grandmother, Pauline died and left me the house."

"And that's not a good thing, because . . .?"

"I have no pets to worry about. No plants to water. No repairs to perform. No responsibility except to myself. What do I need with a fucking mortgage hanging over my head?"

"So why not just sell it?"

"I'd get more from the insurance, if I paid someone a couple bucks to just torch it."

"You'd do that?"

"In a heartbeat."

Why would I try and convince her this was unethical? I wouldn't. A waste of reasoning. So I changed the conversation to a less volatile subject, suggesting I make us dinner. The final meal ever prepared at Ben's Diner. Then we could lie down on the cold hard floor and end the night with a repeat performance. There was a long pause while I waited for the word *horrible* to pop up again.

"Dinner and sex," she said. "God, that sounds really tempting, but I'll have to pass. I have this job, in Texas. If I leave now I'll only be thirty-two hours late."

Naturally I was disappointed. She dropped me off like a delivery package and gave me a warm farewell kiss on the cheek.

"At least give me a phone number," I begged. "In the event I accidentally find myself crossing into Texas, alone in a bar, craving a drinking partner, or a powerful desire to have sex in the local cemetery." Instead of a number she gave me this life-affirming speech.

"Move on with your life, Sharp Guy. Sell your diner to some fanatical joe who thinks he can make your twenty-year-old failing restaurant a huge success again. Find yourself a nice blonde girl who drinks daiquiris, will never have sex in daylight, and blushes when you regard her vagina as her pussy. Forget me. I'm not worth the trouble or the price of a home-cooked meal. Besides, you don't really know me. I'm a wanderer. A rolling stone. I have a locker in every bus station across America."

She hit the gas and the car skidded forward about fifty feet, then she suddenly braked, stuck her head out the window. "Hey, thanks for helping me bury the old lady."

"Sure, anytime," I said, like there'd be other old ladies she planned to bury in the near future. Her tires squealed on the slippery road and she was gone in an instant. I watched the Mustang's taillights disappear in the downpour. Seeing her again was almost therapeutic. Beneficial, healing my state of mind. I'd like to say I'd miss our thought-provoking discussions but I knew we never really exchanged stimulating dialogue.

I was soaked to the bone. My mind, a scrambled mess. I needed a shower and a hearty bowl of hot soup to take the chill off. I grabbed the mail and slipped inside, tossing what appeared to be mostly a pile of past due bills onto the counter. A book of matches flew out from between two envelopes onto the floor. I picked it up and studied it for a second. Staring back at me was this caricature of a potato wearing shades and playing the piano. The caption read in bold italics: *The Baked Potato—food—drink—R&B—Lubbock, Texas.* It wasn't hard to figure out this was the matchbook Ina had tossed into the mailbox during her heated cell phone conversation with Ray Astemendi. My first guess, this was where she works. As a waitress or a hostess. Unless she was a jazz singer, which I doubted. But you never know about someone's hidden talent. So, the question I asked myself—what do I do with this knowledge? Use it and hit the road to Texas? *Or forget her and find myself a nice blonde girl who drinks daiquiris and won't have sex in daylight hours?* I phoned Parker to meet me at the diner in the morning. I didn't mention the matchbook, only that I needed some ill-thought-out advice.

CHAPTER FIVE

The next morning. Bright and early. Clear skies. It promised to be a good day. I had just finished serving Parker probably the last steak and eggs breakfast ever to be served at Ben's Diner. No charge, by the way, and I used the good white china with the blue ring around the rim.

I ran the entire Ina sighting by him. Left nothing out. The burial, sex in the cemetery, nearly biting my tongue off in a public place. How she vividly remembered us fucking on the diner floor over six years ago.

Parker and I stared at the matchbook cover that rested quietly on the counter as proof of my encounter with Ina Byers. It was as if we were waiting for it to come alive and talk to us. Parker voiced his opinion before the matchbook spoke.

"This is not open for debate. You wouldn't catch me going to Texas on the advice of a one-dimensional cartoon potato."

He didn't have to say how he thought chasing after a girl based on happenstance was silly, if not just plain insane. I tried to influence his position. Sway his vote. That this chance meeting was not an accident. It was meant to be. Someone or something was encouraging me to follow through with the fantasy I've had for over ten years.

"Maybe it's my mom sending signals from the great beyond," I said, searching for anything to convince even me this was the right move.

"That's ridiculous, but let's go with your *great beyond theory*," Parker said. "Question: when and if you finally catch up to her—this is assuming the matchbook is an accurate clue—what are your intentions? You have a plan?"

"I haven't thought that out yet. Probably play it by ear."

"I'm going to open up a can of worms and talk reality for a moment."

Reality wasn't something I wanted to hear. Reality would only confuse my fantasy.

"Ina Byers, in high school, was a very loose chick. To be blunt— would just about sleep with anyone with a big back seat in his or her car. She was and maybe still is profoundly immoral. Unsympathetic to the needs of others. Gave teachers a hard time. Was once suspended for selling reefers during a fire drill. The bigger question being—is she truly your soul mate? What do you have in common with this chick? Besides having sex in a cemetery, which is not that unusual, people do this all the time."

"I intend to find out. I'm sure there are plenty of common areas."

"I hate to play devil's advocate here, Jakey, but I doubt it. You're West Side Story, while she's Rocky Horror Show. In other words, you're cultured and she's schlock."

"What does that even mean?"

"It means you need to face facts—you share no interests, no common ground. You appreciate balloon animals; she's the kid who comes along and squeezes the life out of them while fragile children look on in horror."

"Even with all your negative assertions, I still really like her."

"There's a difference between really liking someone and just liking the idea of her."

He wasn't totally wrong. Still, I rationalized.

"Maybe you're right, but the important thing is, I feel good being around her and she makes me feel good about myself. It's like she exudes this intensity. A passion that I've never felt before."

"It's your life, buddy boy. Stick around or take your feelings on the road. But don't come back crying the blues when those feelings get bruised and you realize you've wasted a good portion of your life in search of a meaningless, inconsequential romance."

I felt a shot of alarm, then annoyance. I knew Parker was right but I still pursued a line of questioning.

"So answer me this. Why do I want to subject myself to such a self-destructive situation?"

"How the fuck should I know? You like a challenge? You're a glutton for punishment? Your life works better under pressure? You have this growing desperation to find a mate? Pick one. They're all just lame excuses. Thanks for the breakfast. Steak was chewy. It's a good thing you're closing your doors."

With that, Parker gave me a gentle pat on the back, then left me alone to ponder my uncertain fate.

⌇

Three hours of ragged sleep was like lying in a bathtub with your ears half submerged. Bolting up in bed every twenty minutes.

65

Tossed, turned, sweated right through the sheets. Thought about taking one of my dad's old Valiums. Wondered if an expiration date really meant it had gone flat. Took half a 30 mg. Did nothing. Three in the morning, swallowed the other half. Did nothing. I was still wide-awake at the break of day. Got dressed. Made a strong cup of coffee flooded with cream and three teaspoons of sugar, then went outside and yanked the For Sale sign from its roots in front of the diner. My insomnia gave me a chance to think about my next move. Ina's impulse to burn down her grandmother's house was not as out of reach as it seemed. I vacillated between going through with burning down the diner or leaving it for the city to board up and declare it in an unconscious state with no hope for resuscitation.

My verdict was conclusive. As I was dousing gasoline along the edge of the building, a thousand things ran through my mind. The highlighted ones were: guilt; committing arson; taking the coward's way out and not sticking around and trying to make it work. Not to mention destroying years of some good and also forgettable memories.

I walked the perimeter gripping a road flare. My Jeep Wrangler positioned a hundred yards away, ready for a speedy getaway. Bags packed with needed wardrobe: mostly jeans, T-shirts, a couple long-sleeved white shirts, one sport coat, a lambskin biker jacket, and a pair of Wolverine work boots. My most cherished souvenirs also were stored in their own box. A photo of my mother when she was pregnant with me, my dad's army picture at Fort Ord, his .45 caliber pistol, and my high school diploma that had wine stains on it from an overzealous celebratory grad night. I brought nothing that would remind me of the diner. Not a saltshaker or a spatula. My throat was dry. I could barely swallow. Six a.m. It's *showtime*! My hand was shaking but that was to be expected. As I was about to ignite the road flare, a deep baritone voice from behind me halted the action. I nearly pissed my boxers.

"Don't do it, my brother."

I swung around expecting to see a godlike figure wrapped in a shroud, about to strike me down for committing this immorally wrongful act. Instead, staring back at me was a filthy indigent standing beside a shopping cart filled with what I assumed were his worldly possessions. His hair matted. His face covered by a full beard. His fingernails long, yellowed, I guessed from scrounging for cigarette butts and loose change in the gutter. The stench of his body odor lingered in the air. Genuinely nervous, I backed up for safety reasons before I spoke.

"What is it you want? Money? I'm tapped out my friend. Food? The cupboard is bare. The diner is terminally ill. Incurable. I'm closing permanently. So, it appears you wheeled your basket of odds and ends up to the wrong customer. You might want to give yourself some space, because I'm about to commit arson and put the place out of its misery."

"That would be a shame," he said. "A perfectly good structure destroyed, while there are hundreds of homeless people in need of a roof over their head. You should be ashamed of yourself, Jake Reilly."

I flinched at the mention of my name.

Him knowing who I was caused me to question what I was actually doing here. I mean, this guy could ID me. I could go to prison, if they believed his story.

"Do I know you?"

"Perhaps from AA, the free clinic, the Union Rescue Mission on Thanksgiving, the day they crowned me Mr. Congeniality 2001," he said in a singsong rhythm.

"None of the above, I'm afraid." He then threw me a curve.

"Then try Bakersfield high, class of 2004. I was its class president. Anything jog your memory?"

This took me a few seconds to process. And then it hit me—"Fuck, you're Ricky Salvetti, right?"

"Not anymore. It's *Richard* now. *Ricky* didn't really convey the right ring of respect, considering my status. I've since grown as a man, become a person of outstanding reputation. A self-confessed street urchin, if you will." He said all this as if he were reciting Shakespeare.

Unless you're clairvoyant, you could never foresee anyone's future. The attractive prom queen who gained weight, became unrecognizable and despondent. The popular captain of the football team, who seemed to have everything going for him, before he knocked up the prom queen and was forced to sell used cars and pass up an athletic scholarship. And now the sad transformation of a class president, who I recalled had political ambition but who now stood in front of me a homeless, destitute figure of failure.

"What happened to you, man?" I asked. "You had such potential."

Richard sniffed, then wiped his runny nose with his sleeve. Judging by the white residue under it, I surmised his sniffles were the result of an acute cocaine habit.

"A simple case of mathematics. My alcoholic, drug dependent parents spent my tuition money on amphetamines and other drug-related paraphernalia. Seemed I followed in their footsteps." He sniffed again.

"Sorry to hear that. Look, I have a few dollars. It isn't much but it might get you through the night." I started to reach for my wallet.

"I appreciate the handout, but what I really need is a place to stay. A place to shelter me and my fellow vagrants from the elements. A place to take a leisurely dump, other than in an unsanitary gas station commode without a toilet seat."

"I wish I could help."

"Don't be so fucking disingenuous. The answer to this riddle is standing right in front of us. This lovely structure you're about to torch is the perfect solution."

"Thing is, you're absolutely right, Richard. Sure, I'm planning to burn it down. But for selfish reasons you'll find hard to understand."

"Try me," he challenged.

"I mean, you have any idea what it's like trying to follow your old man's dream and realizing no matter how many coats of paint you slapped on, some dreams are meant to fall by the wayside? And why am I explaining my personal anguish to a guy wearing a trash bag for a coat?"

"Right, I wouldn't know about failure and adversity," he said.

"You're missing the point. It's not about failure. It's about false hopes and unrealistic expectations." I took a moment and looked back at the diner with a pained expression. "Poor, tired old dreamer. Loneliness didn't kill my dad. He died of the *Bakersfield Syndrome.* The front door hardly ever opened. Loyal customers stopped being his friend and ordered their bacon and eggs from the new Denny's in town, because the waitresses were younger and had sizeable cleavage. I can't compete with tits and ass and all the Grand Slam bullshit."

That was when I ignited the road flare, and where Richard backed off. He suddenly got heartfelt and sentimental.

"This isn't the answer, Jake. What's it going to accomplish? You can't just burn away lousy memories. They'll always be there to haunt you, no matter how much gasoline you pour on them."

All right, maybe this guy was smarter than I gave him credit for. Not that I thought he was an idiot. You just assume being on the street diminishes a good chunk of someone's perceptiveness. Not the case with Richard. I couldn't just burn my family's dreams. Especially in front of this transient, whose family had really fucked him over. I dropped the flare and stomped out the flame. I paused before handing Richard the keys to the front door.

"Here, you live with my memories," I said.

"You're doing the right thing. I guarantee we'll both sleep better at night." With that came an appreciative hug, his plastic trash bag coat scrunching between us. The smell of his breath causing me to gag.

As I began to slide into my Jeep and start the arduous journey to Texas, Richard, not thinking, struck a match to fire up a fully tamped cigarette, that he had probably stashed in his shirt pocket for a special occasion. This being one of them—a permanent residence at last. I thought nothing of it, until Richard unconsciously tossed the still-lit match onto the ground. It unfortunately landed atop a thin trail of gasoline that led to the front porch, that continued inside the diner, swirling around the Naugahyde booths and coming to an end at the kitchen's gas intake valve. While the fiery red river began to make its way along the path of inevitable destruction, I had a sudden rush of panic and remembered I left behind a close friend, who'd been with me since childhood—my Smith Corona typewriter. It's remarkable what goes through a person's mind when trapped in a devastating situation. For me, it was either save the typewriter or write my manuscript on a legal pad, using a No. 2 Ticonderoga pencil.

I started to head back inside, but I was too late. I didn't get as far as the mailbox when I felt the world around me explode. The blast was tremendous. Debris was lifted into the air like the building had just been hit by an EF five tornado. The force literally tossed me from the Jeep onto the dirt driveway like I was fluff. I landed on my back with a *fuck* and a groan. My breathing became rapid. My hands began to sweat and the back of my neck went cold. My skin tingled. I managed to yell out for Richard, but there was no response. I couldn't see anything through the billows of black smoke. Was he badly hurt? Engulfed in the flames, maybe? It felt like the kind of war zone that my dad often recounted, while using explosive sounds to highlight the realism and the horror of it all. When I was five it scared me; when I reached ten, his incendiary noises sounded less dangerous and more farcical. But he meant well, reenacting the same stories over and over.

A good fifty feet away, I managed to crawl back to my Jeep, grabbed my cell and called 9-1-1. In my cloudy state of mind, I noticed Richard furiously removing his trash bag coat that had caught fire, while running from the scene. I was relieved he had survived, but pissed the poor guy was homeless again before he ever got to move in.

While I sat on the ground leaning against the Jeep, watching the structure burn to the ground, waiting anxiously for the fire department to show up, a strange thought crossed my mind in the wake of this tragedy: I never knew how my parents met. A realistic portrayal would be when my dad was in the Army, stationed in Norfolk, Virginia. Met my mother, working as a waitress, either at a bar or restaurant. Fell in love after the fourth cup of joe. Wasted no time and got married before deploying to Vietnam. Marriage at such a young age was not unusual for a serviceman who wanted someone to come home to. This was all speculation on my part—but wonderfully romantic. Unfortunately, the definitive answer now laid badly charred somewhere in the belly of the diner. Letters, postcards, marriage license. I fucked up and would have to live with the void of never knowing the answer.

Sadly, my typewriter and the first three pages of my manuscript also perished in the fire.

⋙

Five minutes later—maybe fifteen if I was really paying attention to the time, which I wasn't—I decided not to wait for the first responders and left the scene. I couldn't face the police or the fire department. The truth would get me arrested. A lie would only delay the inevitable—handcuffed, arrested, get the third degree until I confessed to setting the fire and finally branded as an arsonist.

I headed down Main Street doing at least sixty. Maybe close to seventy. My blood pressure was sky-high and my breathing was rapid and jerky. I ran a red light. Not smart. Up ahead there were several fire trucks and police cars headed directly at me with their lights flashing and sirens blaring. I pulled over and ducked down on the seat as a safety precaution. I never understood that stealthy move, because while the first responders were flying past me at such a high rate of speed, was there really going to be someone on the fire truck who would notify the driver to stop, because he saw a suspicious character lying down on a car seat? I think not.

Even so, I stayed out of sight and made a whispered call to Parker, as if someone on that fire truck could actually hear me. Parker worked as a reporter on the *Bakersfield Californian* daily newspaper. Of course, he's totally on top of the situation and was about to call me for an exclusive. I gave him nothing over the phone purely out of fear. We planned to meet in twenty minutes at the outdoor amphitheater at The Park at River Walk. Twenty minutes later, I'm there. The venue was empty. I was seated near the stage when Parker arrived. He inched his way across the aisle and slumped down in the seat next to me.

I took a breath before I started to explain myself. "I saw the Doobie Brothers perform here a year ago. Paid through the nose for tickets. Took Becca Stillwell. A mediocre date at best. She was a Mormon. Made the mistake of challenging her belief that God came from another planet, like Mr. Spock. She left before the opening song—'Jesus is Just Alright.' Musically, an unforgettable, momentous occasion. As date nights go—a washout."

"Jake, you're procrastinating," said Parker. "Why the covert operation?"

I really didn't have to explain to him the anxiety I was feeling. He saw it in my eyes and heard the quiver in my voice. He wanted answers to what caused the explosion that rocked two city blocks. Electrical? Gas? Grease? Before making any kind of formal account of the event, he had to agree not to record the conversation. I didn't want my confession to come back and haunt me. He agreed. Nervous, I stood up and started to pace in the aisle.

"It was an accident. Sort of," I said.

Parker had his own theory. He presumed I deliberately torched the place to avoid the responsibility of trying to nurse an ailing restaurant back to health. Took the easy way out. Burned it to the ground, to look like the handiwork of an arsonist. Intended to collect the insurance money and live with the guilt, he speculated.

I stopped pacing and sat back down. I admitted that torching it was my first objective, until Richard Salvetti unexpectedly showed up on my doorstep and talked me out of it. The Salvetti connection threw him. He had no idea the guy was homeless and destitute. Parker knew about his parents being drug addicts because he wrote an exposé on the Bakersfield drug scene, which included his parents' story—desperate for drug money, they were caught robbing the grave of a wealthy woman who was buried with her jewelry. The irony was the dead woman's son, also a junkie, buried her in costume jewelry and kept the real stuff to score high-grade drugs.

I gave all the arson credit to Richard Salvetti who started the blaze by tossing a lit match onto the gasoline-soaked pyre. It was not intentional on his part. Strictly an unprovoked act. A stupid mistake made by a dismal man adrift from reality.

"Okay. Fine. Understood," Parker said. "Nevertheless, you fled the scene of a crime. They'll suspect foul play and when they find evidence, like the gas can and remnants of the road flare, you'll be their prime suspect. They'll come looking for you, thinking it's some sort of an insurance scam."

"Unless I do what, turn myself in?"

"Either way, you'll probably serve jail time."

"Great, then I'll be tagged with a criminal record. Mug shots taken. Fingerprinted. Labeled a firebug. Having to endure the humiliation that every time there's a kitchen fire or a towering inferno, I'll be pulled over and frisked for hidden matches and a can of gasoline."

I knew right away that turning myself in was not an option. I had a plan and I intended to stick with it.

"Look, jail for me is out of question. I'm headed to Texas in search of Ina Byers. Tell the authorities whatever you need to tell them. Make it heartfelt and emotional. Attest that my father left instructions in his will that if the diner should fail, burn it to the ground, collect the insurance money, and give it to a deserving charity. Like the Police Benevolent Association, or the Veterans Benefits Administration."

"I'll do my best. Whatever goes down, just remember, I've got your back, Jake. On a positive note—you're one of the lucky few to get the fuck out of Dodge."

Hugs were exchanged. But a definite uncertainty lingered.

Parker finally left, and it was time to make the long journey to Texas. I had to admit, I was so *not* prepared. I had a change of clothes. A bottle of water, my dad's gun, my high school diploma (proving to myself and others my awe-inspiring academic achievement), four hundred in cash, and hidden in my sock, an extra two grand that I had saved for college tuition, but which was now more of an emergency food and travel fund.

I climbed in the Wrangler and sat there for a quiet moment, staring into space—bewildered. The awful truth was beginning to dawn on me. I was now nothing but a pathetic outlaw about to run away from his responsibility. I gazed up and, stuck between the visor and the headliner, was my motivation—the matchbook cover. The cartoon potato illustration peeked out just enough, giving me a contemptible look. If it were real, it would most likely be scratching its potato head, thinking what a fool this dude was, chasing after a dream that could wind up being a really pathetic escapade. I let out a sigh before putting the car in gear. Nerves were rattling inside me, and it didn't help my confidence that I puked out the window while I sped up the freeway on-ramp.

CHAPTER SIX

Four hours and 257 miles later, I pulled into Needles, California. Not exactly a paradise. It was a real uncomfortable heat. The kind that sucks all your energy and sizzles the palm of your hand when you grab the car door handle. Easily 103—felt like 123. My shirt was sticking to my body. I was tired. My car was even exhausted. We both needed a breather. I rolled into a gas station. One of those combo mini-marts with two-day-old sandwiches that came with a dollop of fresh mold. I filled up on gas, then went inside to grab some free air-conditioning and use the restroom. I peed, then took my sweaty T-shirt off and dried it under the hand dryer. On my way out, I stopped and bought a couple bottles of cold water and two chocolate-chip Clif energy bars. The clerk behind the counter tried to sell me on the tuna sandwiches that were on sale for half price. Tuna and half price. Those two words in tandem are code for food poisoning ahead.

Five thousand people lived in Needles, and when I headed back to my car, three of them were leaning against it. They did not look like they were from the Welcoming Committee. Three boys. Nineteen-year-olds, if not younger. Tough, angry, and scruffy. I could sense they came with attitudes. These weren't your standard local gang members, but punk kids looking to terrorize unsuspecting travelers out of a few dollars to feed their drug habit. Strictly speculation without evidence, but my instincts were usually right.

As I approached, one of the kids, who had a buzz cut, spit in my direction; the loogie landed just short of my shoe. I stopped in my tracks, holding up a Clif bar as a symbol of peace.

"What's happening, fellas? Care for a Clif bar? A natural source of complete protein."

They instantly got defensive.

"Fuck you, fuck your protein," a kid wearing a torn Black Sabbath T-shirt fired back at me. The other two kids forced a derisive *yeah* just to be in the mix.

"So, I'll take that as a *you'll pass*," I said. "Okay, so with the niceties out of the way, I suggest you guys move the fuck away from my car, or I'll call the law."

"Cops don't scare us," the third kid, a pimply-faced scarecrow, chimed in. "We could cut your balls off by the time they show," he threatened, producing one of those stainless steel five bladed tactical knives.

"So, what is it you want? Cash? Blood? Maybe some *big boy respect*, since I'm guessing the girls in this town see you guys as a joke."

"Enough talking, wise-ass," said Buzz Cut. "We want fifty bucks, or we slash your fucking tires and cut you open, spilling your guts on the sidewalk."

The smart thing for me to do at this point would have been to retreat. Don't mess with these kids. Go back into the safety of the mini-mart, call the cops, and let them handle these young rebels. Doing that, however, I ran the risk they'd slash my tires and just take off like the worthless, contemptible punks that they were.

So, I stayed and stood up to them. By now, the boys had me surrounded. Made me slightly nervous. I moved and tried to shoulder my way through their barrier, but backed off when Black Sabbath Boy waggled a box cutter in my face. I raised my hands, conceding defeat.

"Okay, you win. You have convinced me you mean business, and that you have no misgivings about slicing my tires and gutting me like a mackerel. The money is in my glove box. I'll give you seventy-five if you just let me be on my way." The idea I was offering intrigued them. They huddled to talk strategy. Buzz Cut did most of the talking, while the other two just stood there glassy-eyed, nodding stupidly. When they turned back, I found myself having to negotiate a new course of action.

"Listen," said Buzz Cut, "if you got seventy-five, you got a hundred and seventy-five. You get a pass for one seventy-five."

"Sure. So, the one seventy-five saves my tires and gives me safe passage to the freeway on-ramp. Right?"

They simultaneously nodded in agreement, and then I opened the car door on the passenger side. Slowly reached into my glove box, first revealing my wallet that I waved in the air for their examination. They looked pleased, flashing wide grins and licking their lips, like they had scored big time.

"We're taking the credit cards too," demanded Black Sabbath Boy, who had suddenly grown a set of balls and brandished his box cutter.

I agreed on the credit cards, and then I shocked these losers with something they hadn't counted on—my own form of protection. I swiftly produced my dad's .45 pistol and strategically rested the barrel directly on Buzz Cut's forehead, while at the same time cocking the hammer back like I knew what I was doing. The click resonated against this kid's temple like a small tremor. He shuddered. The other two instantly dropped their weapons in fear. The boys then attempted to weasel their way out of this new dilemma, insisting how they were just joking around out of boredom.

"I fail to see the humor in threatening to slice me open with a box cutter," I said.

Pimply Face flipped out and sounded off mindlessly: "Did we say that? I don't remember saying that exactly. If we did, I apologize a thousand times over. We're stupid. We're punks. Living here has fried our brains. Our parents are weak and have no control over us."

Suddenly Buzz Cut began to cry. Black Sabbath Boy and Pimply Face joined him. It was pathetic. I softened, and gave these kids a second chance to redeem themselves.

"Using your T-shirts, wipe the road bugs off my windshield and grill and I'll give you a reprieve. A stay of execution."

They quickly ripped off their T-shirts and scrubbed everywhere they saw any sign of a bug, bug splatter, and lingering bird shit. After I inspected the job, I set them free and watched as they sprinted away back to the security of the rock they had slid out from under.

Fifteen minutes later, I'm back on the road to Lubbock. I hated myself for scaring those kids. What was I thinking? I was thinking that if I didn't have the gun I might be driving to Lubbock on four new tires and a deep abdominal incision. Perhaps I was becoming a true outlaw on the run. First arson, and now assault with a deadly weapon. Couldn't complain. This was what I wanted—leaving the doldrums of Bakersfield for a much more exhilarating life. By the way, the gun was not loaded, nor was there a bullet in the chamber. This was purely a bluff that obviously worked in my favor.

Just before I left the Needles city limits (in my rearview), I zoomed past a sign inviting me to Come Again. Not a chance. If there was a way to avoid ever setting foot in this town again, you can bet I'd take the long way around.

A few miles out, for no good reason, I blew on the matchbook cover. In the same way gamblers blow on dice to evoke Lady Luck. A symbolic gesture, hoping it would make my journey trouble-free. A ridiculous notion, but I'd take it if there was even the slightest bit of truth to this myth.

Interstate 40. Twelve hours and forty-five minutes from Needles to Lubbock. The Jeep rolled through Kingman, Arizona, as day turned to dusk. I was bushed, so I decided to stop at a Red Roof Inn and stay the night for forty-nine dollars. A bargain. The air conditioning vent rattled and kept me awake most of the night. I couldn't turn it off or I'd melt by morning. The TV was the size of a microwave. Or maybe it was a microwave and the room didn't come with a TV. Either way, I didn't bother to use it.

In the morning I inhaled a stale glazed doughnut and a weak cup of coffee and headed west. The temperature dropped to a cool 98 degrees. The scenery was flat. Hardly a tree in sight. Saguaro cactus was plentiful, as were the damn kamakazie tumbleweeds I kept dodging. On the side of the two-lane highway, a family watched as their father dangerously changed a flat tire on their minivan while cars whizzed close by, nearly sideswiping his ass. A toddler peed on a rock—I guessed for safety measures, because peeing next to a prickly cactus could be risky. That was the scenic route I viewed out my windshield. It never got any better.

It was nearly nine o'clock in the evening when I passed a sign that read:

WELCOME TO LUBBOCK
Slow Down—Armadillo Crossing

I asked myself the elusive question: How does an Armadillo know to cross the highway at that particular point? A sixth sense? It was common knowledge among the Armadillo community? I ignored the ridiculousness of that query, and focused on the fact I was inching closer to Ina Byers. This once again produced that nervous roller coaster feeling in the pit of my stomach. As I rolled onto Main Street I saw the NTS Tower. Designated the tallest building in Lubbock. Twenty floors. Just a bit of Lubbock folklore—it was a known fact that this building was where the despondent locals took the elevator to the rooftop and called it quits.

I passed the Buddy Holly Center (another Lubbock highlight) then pulled over to get my bearings. According to the map inside the matchbook, the Baked Potato Bar and Grill was a few blocks away, settled between Ink-fluence Tattoo & Piercing and The Daybreak Coffee Shop.

It was now 11 p.m. when I caught sight of the shades-wearing neon potato glowing in the night like a beacon for R&B music lovers. I'd arrived at my destination and parked in front of the coffee shop. The parking lot for club patrons was empty and its entrance chained off. Unusual I'd say for a high-profile joint like this. You'd think it'd be crawling with big drinkers and jazz freaks snapping their fingers and tapping their toes to a tribute band version of the Miles Davis Quintet. I got out, stretched my legs, took a much-needed deep breath and approached the entrance.

The door resembled a large piano keyboard. Just as I was about to grab the handle and head inside, the neon potato sign went dark and soon after a full-bearded guy wearing tinted shades exited with a handful of keys and was about to lock up. I assumed I was late. They must close at eleven, which explained the lack of cars in the lot.

"Hi. Sorry to bother you, but is Ina still around?"

He ignored me and continued to lock up, sliding a metal security gate across the piano door, and then slamming it shut in a pissed off manner. He then locked it with a heavy-duty padlock. He finally acknowledged that I was standing three feet from him.

"We're closed. We close at eleven on Mondays. Reopen tomorrow at noon," he said in an unfriendly-pissed-off manner.

I guessed the fact it was a Wednesday had no relevance. Bottom line, they were not open for business.

"I'm looking for Ina Byers. Dark hair, dark blue eyes, dark persona. Kind of attractive cynical."

"Fired her two days ago." His unfriendly demeanor suddenly changed to red-faced anger with a touch of hatred. "She's got a major self-control problem, that girl." Conversation over. He started to walk away. I pushed it just a little.

"Medical self-control or something in the area of multiple personality disorder?"

He stopped and turned back. He didn't appreciate my remark and told me to go back to wherever I came from. I felt the need to tell him I'd driven all the way from Bakersfield just to contact Ina. He could give a crap. I know this because he said, "I could give a crap." He kept walking towards the parking lot. I pushed again. Maybe too much pushing and not enough decorum.

"Maybe you got a home address. A phone number. Any clue would be helpful." I added in a desperate moment of sarcasm: "A piece of clothing I can sniff to track her scent."

"I got crap," he said. He seemed to like using the word *crap* to emphasize that he was tough to get answers out of. Failing to get anything useful, I went with a lie, figuring I'd have a better chance of finding her—said I was a relative and that our grandmother died. And that she was in the will and her signature was needed to release money into Ina's bank account. "She came into a lot of money. Family jewels. A treasure chest of memorabilia. A house. I'm sure she'd like to know . . ."

He's heard enough. Stopped in his tracks and stuck his face close to mine. I could smell the liquor that emanated from his beard. Also, he was fooling nobody. He was wearing a rug that was not centered and tilted to one side, like a mother bird that had constructed a haphazard nest while she was drunk.

"Bullshit. Your story is sheer bullshit. Her grandmother, I happen to know, died over a week ago. Look, let me set things straight. I'm not a big fan of Ina Byers. She's an unscrupulous piece of shit. She stole from me. Over the past year I'd say in the neighborhood of four grand. Should've had her arrested but I couldn't prove it. My bad luck. Smart move is for you to stay clear of that cunt."

"Sure, I can understand your contempt. Like you said, you're not a big fan. I don't agree with your assessment of her, but that's me. I tend to give people the benefit of the doubt before condemning them as a cunt. But that's me. I'm a liberal. Open-minded."

"So, what exactly is your connection with her? I know you're not an ex-boyfriend. Not even close to being her type. You're too . . . oh, what's the fucking word, I'm looking for?" He snapped his fingers, as if that gesture would help him come up with the answer. I gave him some suggestions:

"Wholesome? Squeaky clean? Old guard traditionalist? White middle class?"

"Sure, all those work."

"I knew her in high school. Nothing real tempestuous," I said. I could tell by the way he blinked, he had no idea what *tempestuous* meant, so he just groaned and rubbed his scruffy bearded chin.

"You might want to try the coffee shop next door," he said. "She eats there on a regular basis. A free piece of advice: watch your back with this chick. She's not to be trusted. Pretty sure, as a sideline she's a grifter. A scam artist. Always on the lookout for the short con." His demeanor suggested he might be a racketeer himself.

It was not what I wanted to hear after driving all this way, but I didn't expect anything newsworthy. This time it was my turn to give a courteous nod, and then I headed directly for the coffee shop, hoping by some chance she'd be there.

❦

Inside, it looked nothing like my diner. This place was sterile. Had no charm and no stubborn Vietnam vet cooking in the kitchen. I glanced around the room to see if I could spot her. Nothing. Only about a half-dozen weary nighthawks eating, talking, and staring at me because a stranger just gained access into their personal space. Once they decided I wasn't a threat, they went back to their over-cooked sunny side up eggs and rubbery breakfast steak.

A bleached blonde waitress, with dark roots, balancing a carafe of coffee in one hand and what looked like a bowl of hash in the other, motioned me in the direction of an open booth. I slid in, and while I perused the menu, I was immediately given a cup of coffee even though I never asked for one. She must have been clairvoyant, as she began to write on her order pad while asking, "How do you want your steak and eggs, sweetie?"

"What?"

"They're on special tonight. Truth is, day or night, they're always on special. You look like a medium rare, sunny side up kind of guy."

I didn't agree or disagree. I just let her continue scratching on her order slip.

"Refills come free with the special."

She took a breath so I jumped in.

"Ina Byers, has she had the special here recently?"

"You a cop?"

"Me? Jesus, no. Do I look like a cop?"

"These days nothing surprises me. Cops come in all shapes, sizes, and styles. You want your sourdough toast buttered?"

"I didn't ask for . . . I'll leave it up to you. Anyway, I'm a friend from out of town. She said if I was ever in Lubbock to look her up. I tried the bar but it seemed she got the axe. I was told she ate here on a regular basis. So, I'm just asking, trying to track her down. Sorry if this feels like some sort of interrogation."

"You have a lot to say for not being a cop."

"I'm an aspiring novelist. The words I don't use on paper, I incorporate into real life."

I think I confused her, so she just gave me a little curl of a smile. According to the clock on the wall, it was now ten to twelve. The waitress told me Ina might show up at any time. Said she was a midnight eater. Cheeseburger, fries, a Diet Coke. End of yet another meaningless conversation. She walked away with her carafe to top off a table of three men, and report why I was there and if I carried tin (a badge).

An hour ticked by with no results. I started to have doubts about anything anybody had told me in the past few hours since I'd landed in Lubbock. I had a decision to make. Should I drink another carafe of coffee or sit in my car and stake out the place, hoping she'd show? And if she didn't show, what then? Come back tomorrow night, occupy another booth, and wait for the clock to strike midnight? Thing was, Ina could have gotten a job near another coffee shop. In that case, should I patronize every fucking diner in Texas? I hadn't come all this way to go home without at least a sighting. Decision made. I paid the check for the Special she ordered for me, which I never touched because the meal looked like it had already been eaten by somebody else who sent it back. Left a decent tip and headed for the door. Halfway there the waitress got my attention.

"Hey, novelist."

I turned back. I liked the sound of someone calling me a novelist. It smacked of a touch of respectability.

"You wanna leave her a note if she happens to come in? Let her know you're in town, where you're staying? Use some of those leftover words you were mentioning."

Seemed like a smart idea. As I wrote the note on a napkin it occurred to me that this was a very bad idea. This could scare the crap out of Ina. This entire set of circumstances could make me look like some sort of serial stalker. Come to think of it, if I were looking at this under a psychological microscope, I was, in an alarming way, trailing her like an animal narrowing the gap before it pounced. This was not a pleasant way to look at the situation. I pondered the growing desperation in my loins. After serious thought, I considered throwing in the towel and giving up the search. As I reached for the door handle, a familiar voice echoed from the back of the room.

"Hey, Sharp Guy, rumor has it you're lookin' for me."

I swung around to see Ina nonchalantly sitting in a booth against the wall in the back of the room. She smiled with her usual arrogance, showing her perfect teeth. I scanned the room trying to figure out how she got past me. Magic? A hidden panel?

"There's a back door. Come and sit. We'll talk and you'll enlighten me on the purpose of your visit."

As I crossed to the booth I gave the waitress an incredulous stare.

"I made a phone call. I heard the desperation in your voice and it bothered me," she said with a shrug.

Ina, as always, looked like she just stepped off the cover of a gangland magazine. Dark, dangerous, with a hint of cigarette smoke wafting in the air. She wasted no time asking the paramount question.

"Okay, spill it. Why're you fucking here?"

"I followed the directions on this matchbook cover." I set the matchbook on the table, and slid it towards her.

"You're serious?"

"I am, yes. Idiotic and illogical, I won't deny that."

"From where I sit, Jakey, this qualifies as an act of fucking insanity and warrants a trip to a mental institution."

I didn't need that unkind analysis to help me realize how bad this looked for me.

Anyway, after she said she was only putting me on, and was flattered by my enthusiasm, she told me how she got fired for stealing. She claimed the other barmaids set her up. They were jealous because she got more attention from the usual drunken cocksuckers than they did. Now it was my turn to bring her up to date. I went into detail about the fire. Left nothing out, putting the newsworthy event into perspective:

"What's left of my diner could now sit in an ashtray."

"Very colorful description. Always going for clever, right, Sharp Guy?"

"If it helps to illustrate the facts and hold people's attention, why not?"

We made small talk about unimportant matters that neither of us gave a shit about, not really listening to each other, until one of the customers shouted from across the room.

"Hey, Ina, you interviewing for a new boyfriend?"

All heads turned waiting for her to answer. I waited along with them.

"Why, you want to apply, Charlie?"

"My wife would kill me in my sleep."

"Wife? And all this time I thought you were, you know, strictly a man's man." She then turned back to me.

"I can see it in your eyes, and the way you're fidgeting in your seat, that the boyfriend remark is doing cartwheels across your stomach." She took a beat. "Yeah, it's true. I'm in this relationship," she said like she was tossing the thought away. Like it was an empty admission.

I'd be lying if I didn't admit that it upset me. Once it really slammed home, it was obvious this trip was a mistake. There was no doubt in my mind that I needed to get the fuck out of Lubbock and scream at the damn potato for giving me the wrong advice. But what seemed like an obvious reason to leave at once changed when she leaned into me and shared her disappointment.

"I thought it would be different. That we'd share the same interests. That he would get me. Not happening. I've had it with clueless fucks who have no insight when it comes to knowing who I am and what I expect."

A sigh of relief. This was a positive sign. She was unhappy in her current relationship with someone who didn't understand women. At least couldn't fulfill her emotional needs.

I took a breath and tried to make her feel better about herself. Went with a quote that I've used before. *"There is always some madness in love. But there is also always some reason in madness."*

"Friedrich, the German guy. You mentioned him once before, Sharp Guy. You need to turn the page and adopt a new phrase."

The waitress brought Ina her cheeseburger, fries, and Diet Coke. "Thanks, Ruthie," said Ina, shoving a fry in her mouth.

"Anything I can get you?" Ruthie asked me. The look that passed between us was interrupted by a man's voice. He spoke with a quiet intensity . . .

"Ruthie, I'll have the special and an ice pack to bring the swelling down from this guy's jaw."

"Always the charmer, aren't you, Ray?" Ruthie blurted.

This was Ray Astemendi, thirty-something. The boyfriend. He was exactly how I imagined he would be—rock star good looks, sinewy, rugged demeanor. Dressed in worn everything—jeans, boots, leather jacket. Despite the fact it was midnight he wore vintage Ray-Bans. I made an attempt to introduce myself and assure him I was not a threat, but he ignored me, laying a wet kiss on Ina. He then slid in, crowding her. She shifted, giving herself space. Her attitude was guarded. "So, what was that kiss for, Ray—your subtle way of saying you're sorry for acting like such a shit-heel most of the time?"

Ray flipped his shades on the top of his head. They stared at each other with kind of mock seriousness. She wanted him to promise that every once in a while he'd at least pretend he cared about their relationship. There was an uncomfortable pause while the world waited for his answer. I filled the void.

"How many times can a man turn his head and pretend that he just doesn't see?" Ray gave me an incredulous look. I explained: "Dylan. Bob Dylan. It seemed appropriate during this tense moment you guys were having."

"Don't rile him, Jake," said Ina. "He's batshit crazy."

"So, who is this guy?" Ray demanded. "And don't leave anything out."

"I'm Jake."

"I asked her."

"I'm still Jake."

"This is Jake. A distant friend."

"Very distant."

"Stop fucking interrupting," he said to me in a threatening manner.

"We went to high school together. He's aspiring to be a writer and also quotes dead German philosophers. Where'd you get the sunglasses?" she asked, to change the mood from hostile to more conversational. Ray hesitated, taking a drink of Ina's Diet Coke before answering.

"From a guy."

"What guy?"

"From a guy who now needs to buy new sunglasses. So, what is this Jake doing here?" Another digression, back to anger.

"Ask him. He can speak with the best of them," Ina said.

I shifted as the focus was about to be directed at me. Even before a word was said I got the feeling it wasn't going to go well. It was a vibe I had regarding Ray. A premonition he was a rough character who used fear as a method of persuasion.

"What do you do, Jake, when you're not using other people's words because your own vocabulary fails you?" Took him a long time to get that out, but he did it without pissing off Ina.

"I once ran a diner in Bakersfield, until it burned to the ground. We catered mostly to truckers and seniors on a budget. Once in a while someone under the age of twenty would come in by mistake. Never stayed because they thought it reminded them of eating Thanksgiving dinner with their grandparents and their perverted Uncle Joe. And I don't have to tell you that every family has a perverted Uncle Joe."

"Stop and answer the damn question. What do you do *now*? In this time zone."

"I'm seeking answers. Looking for a reason to move on with my life," I said with a drizzle of truth.

This took Ray by surprise.

"Still doesn't tell me what you're doing in Lubbock."

"Like so many tourists, I'm a big fan of Buddy Holly. Once a fan, always a fan, right? You don't stop being a fan once someone is dead. Came to maybe buy a T-shirt or a mug." "Ray's in the Jesus business, by the way," Ina said, getting back on track. For a second I thought she was going to claim he was a man of the cloth. Not so. It seemed Ray worked security for Emily Easterday. A big-time, new wave, fake miracle worker evangelist.

"Who gives hope to the poor wretched fucks of the world," Ray said defensively.

"While at the same time taking advantage of pathetic religious fanatics," Ina added.

"Why do you always feel a need to explain my life to strangers out loud?"

"Because it eventually comes up in conversation and it's embarrassing. Your job is humiliating."

"Fuck you, Ina."

"No, fuck you. Face it, you're nothing but a rent-a-cop for a quack blonde evangelist with big tits."

"Oh, and being a barmaid is a much more respected position in life?"

"At least I have a high school diploma."

Ina turned to me and said, "You're a smart guy. Point out who's right and who's wrong."

"Look, it's not my place to interfere. Besides, there is no right and wrong." I turned to Ray. "Ina thinks your job is lowly. You argue her being a barmaid is inferior. End of exchange of views. You're making this a dick-measuring contest. It's not. This is part of what goes into a relationship. Each has an opinion. Each takes a stance. You're doing what most couples don't do—communicate." I suddenly felt like a marriage counselor. Didn't come all this way to balance their rocky relationship. If anything I came here with the sole intention of generating my own relationship. I wanted to be the guy arguing with Ina Byers about religious fakes stealing from the wallets of naive worshippers.

They continued to look at me. Staring uncomfortably. I took a stand and refused to support either one. Ray, angry that the outcome didn't work in his favor, slammed his fist on the table. I flinched. He then tried to intimidate me, this time pounding his fist into Ina's cheeseburger. The plate broke, splintering in several directions. His fist was left with residual condiments mixed with his own blood dripping from his knuckles. Still not taking his eyes off me, he wiped his hand off on a napkin. This was my introduction to Ray Astemendi.

Ray's tantrum triggered a response from the cook, who was also the owner—a sinewy Black man with a commanding voice. He stuck his head out the kitchen pickup window.

"Ray, calm down, or I call the cops and have you arrested for being an asshole."

It was interesting to see Ray back down.

"I'm cool, Marcus."

"No, you're not cool, you have serious temper issues," Marcus fired back. Ray played it smart with a silent nod and a smirk. Although under the table he was giving Marcus the finger. Very courageous of him.

The sound of screeching brakes directly outside the coffee shop, followed by the agonizing crunch of metal hitting metal, was a welcome interruption. Sitting in the back booth hampered our view. Ruthie rushed to the door, stuck her head outside, and confirmed the inevitable, announcing to the room that a Jeep Wrangler had just been rear-ended and crunched by a pickup truck in the parking lot. I tried to remain calm, as if it wasn't my car that was involved. As if I didn't care. As if the Jeep was not my only mode of transportation out of Lubbock and now I was stuck. But I couldn't contain my frustration. The *fuck* I screamed at the top of my lungs could've shattered crystal, if there were any crystal in the diner, which I doubted.

The entire coffee shop crushed for the door to survey the crash. As advertised, a pickup truck was humping the back end of my Wrangler. Its front end was pleated like a concertina. From the crowd I heard a curious voice asking if anybody had been killed. Accidents drew people who wanted to see blood. Broken bones. A body that had to be extricated by the Jaws of Life.

Leaning against the crushed pickup was a discombobulated old man, pushing at least eighty years old. He wore a faded plaid flannel shirt. His fly was open and the front of his baggy pants was stained from urine. There was a small cut above his left eyebrow. He had his head in his hands and was mumbling to himself. Mumbling was not a good sign for someone his age. I crossed the parking lot to make sure the old guy wasn't too badly hurt. I asked about his condition. If he wanted to sit down? Needed a doctor? Did he have chest pains? He didn't respond, just kept mumbling incoherent, unintelligible words. I asked him his name. He looked up at me with confusion in his eyes. He finally answered me.

"I don't remember my name. Maybe you can help me choose a name," he said. I figured he was hit in the head during the collision. Rattled his senses. I guided him to the curb and had him sit down. This was when Ray decided to intervene, looking sinister with his shades now down over his eyes. He whispered to me from the side of his mouth.

"Get his personal shit off his driver's license. Name, address, age. Find out if he's donating a well-used body part to science."

Since that wasn't a half bad idea, I asked the old guy for his license. He muttered that he had no license.

"The DMV bastards took it away. Said I was a danger on the road." It was apparent the DMV bastards got it right.

The shrill of sirens in the distance rocked the night. This translated to the timely arrival of the local police and an ambulance. I got nervous. Question was, did I want to file a police report? My name would get fed into the system and the Bakersfield cops would know where to find me. I repeated my arson troubles to Ina, who said to let her handle everything. She turned to Ray and gave him a nod, while gesturing to the old man. Seemed they had a way of communicating through gestures. Ray then sat down on the curb next to the old guy like he was going to have a heart-to-heart with his granddad.

"You got a name, old man?"

The man thought hard but nothing came out but a frustrated sigh. "Like I said to the other young man, it slipped my mind at this particular moment. Pretty sure it's not ethnic in origin."

"Mind if I call you Bob?"

"Actually, Bob could be my name for all I know. It rings a bell. About three months ago everything started to become fuzzy. Names, dates; even the color of salt and pepper were a mystery to me."

It was apparent this poor guy had a touch of Alzheimer's. Nevertheless, Ray did not let up and gave this old man the third degree. "Pay attention to what I'm about to tell you, okay, Bob?" Ray got a small nod. "There's no doubt, you screwed up here. For one thing, you're driving without a fucking license, which is against the law. But that's between you and the court. So, you have a couple choices. Upfront cash for the damages on the Jeep Wrangler. I'm guessing at least two grand. You can take it out of your Social Security benefits, your pension plan. Or, let your insurance company pay and your rates go through the roof. Then the bottom falls out—they repossess your pickup. Life for you becomes unbearable, and you have to go live in a rest home that smells like feces and stale urine. Understand?"

"Sure. I'm old, but I'm not a fucking idiot. But the thing is, sir, it's not my truck."

I overheard the old man confess *it's not my truck* and my stomach once again changed direction on its own.

"I borrowed it from my grandson who was passed out on the kitchen floor from swallowing too many Oxys. I just wanted to get some scrambled eggs and a slice of sourdough toast with butter and jelly. Where's this rest home located? Does it have a view of a body of water? A fountain maybe. I like to hear running water. It helps me piss."

Ray then crossed over to Ina and started to tell her what she was already aware of.

"I know. I get it. This poor fuck's mind is tapioca. He can't summon up what happened an hour ago, let alone his past."

A very unfortunate but accurate diagnosis. I could relate to this man's sickness. Although my dad died of congestive heart failure, he also suffered from a failing memory. How do you respond when your father claimed his only son drowned in a terrible swimming accident in Lake Tahoe? You nod, tell him you're sorry for his loss, and then give him a hug, in hopes that comforted him enough to fill the void he'd felt.

The paramedics took the old guy to the emergency room; they were hoping to locate the grandson, if in fact he really had a grandson, or maybe he just plain stole the truck and was faking his dementia. Here's a crazy theory, but not implausible—maybe this dude was all part of an auto theft ring, made up of grizzled car thieves out to supplement their pathetic Social Security payments. Think about this: I noticed there were no keys in the ignition, which could mean he hot-wired the truck. In the cab, in plain sight, was a screwdriver. The one tool that's used in the ignition to illegally start up an engine. And something else did not escape my notice: the old fart was wearing gloves. Who wears black latex gloves while driving? A person who was making sure he didn't leave fingerprints.

I was convinced this old man was a scam artist. Even if my theory played out to be fact, I was still screwed. Damages were gonna run me a pretty penny. The cost for replacements parts would deplete my savings. Worst-case scenario—I'd be homeless and destitute, wearing a plastic garbage bag for an overcoat as they hauled me away for my day in court. All because I was out of control, chasing a woman who obviously knew that I was on her trail, seeking her affection. What had become of my common sense? How much more of a sign did I need to leave Lubbock and give up this pathetic chase? A diagnosis by a shrink that it was a pointless endeavor?

CHAPTER SEVEN

While my car was being towed to a garage to undergo serious rehab, Ray and Ina slipped me a bottle of Jim Beam to settle any nerves I might be experiencing, then dropped me off at the Journey's End Motel, a modest, artless accommodation for a nightly rate of thirty-four dollars. I could handle the fare and checked in under the alias of Robert Zimmerman. Anybody who was a hard-core Dylan follower would know this was his birth name. I paid cash so as not to leave a paper trail. It was weird being on the run. Your lifestyle choices became your prime concern. You walked with your head down half the time. You didn't look people directly in the eye. Being friendly was risky. You limited conversations to mostly one or two words and an occasional nod. You always wore your sunglasses indoors. And once in a while you walked with a limp and used a foreign accent. I know, this was the behavior of a paranoid person. I read about this entire stratagem in some crime novel. I followed none of the aforementioned traits and except for the name change, kept my true identity intact. Maybe I limped a little when I registered at the front desk.

The room smelled from cheap perfume and nicotine. I hazarded a guess: it was last occupied by a chain-smoker who was entertaining a prostitute. Or his wife, who had no taste in cologne or men. That was just my vivid imagination running amok. Bargain basement prints of the Lubbock countryside hung on the fake knotty pine walls. The bedspread was a canary yellow—one of those chenille covers that looked like a large bathrobe without the matching waist belt. After a long shower rinsing away the road grime, I positioned myself on top of the chenille bedspread and fixated on the cracked ceiling, while I left an anxious message for Parker on his mobile.

"Hey, it's me. Need a big favor. Will you, or anybody with common sense, please tell me what was I thinking? Was I that naive that I thought she'd greet me, a pump and run from her distant past, with open arms? Pathetic. As soon as my car is able to travel again—I was rear-ended by an old man with no memory of the world he lives in—I'm headed back. Unless the Metro cops have a warrant out for me, then I'll change the scenery to somewhere south of the border. I would love a response as soon as possible, or sooner." My voice trailed off; as I was about to hang up, I added a postscript: "I don't exactly love my life at this point and time. In truth, I hate the choices I've made. If you've got a smart way for me to climb out of this funk, written proposals are welcome. I mean, other than the obvious—suicide. Calm down, I'm not serious about the latter."

I sighed, only because I hadn't sighed for some time and felt it was a necessary audible once in a while. You lived, you learned. You stared at the ceiling, and tried to seek answers from the cracks in the same manner a palmist would read your lifeline. An abstract concept that didn't deserve to be repeated in public, unless you didn't care that most people would think you have emotional problems. Especially if you happened to slip up and admitted you sought the advice of a cartoon potato. I realized being hung up on this whole matchbook potato thing was on the brink of being psychotic.

I remained motionless on the bed, and tried to fall asleep. I was exhausted. I turned off the ugly bedside lamp. It was pitch-black. I couldn't see the damn fly buzzing around my head. I swiped at it and actually got lucky and killed the annoying little threat to my slumber. There was a welcome silence. A million things danced around in my head. Burying the old lady in the rain, fucking Ina in the rain, the diner burning to a crisp, my dad's funeral, threatening those punks at the gas station with my dad's gun. Once I repeated *my dad's gun* at least ten more times, I realized the gun was still in the Jeep. I quickly switched on the ugly lamp and bolted for my clothes. I teetered, hopping on one leg as I attempted to shove the other leg inside my pants. I was a little panicky, knowing that if the body shop found it, I'd be investigated. It was almost two o'clock in the morning. Not thinking straight, I phoned the body shop. I got a recording that said they opened at nine a.m., leave a message at the beep. I didn't mean to scream *fuck me* at the top of my lungs, but I did.

With another seven hours to go, I thought I could arrive early, wait for them to open, and retrieve the gun without being noticed. Or at least go unsuspected of any slick undertaking. It wasn't exactly a sure-fire plan of attack. For one, how would I get there? Walk? Cab? Besides transportation being a problem, I was running on paranoia. I needed the peace of mind of having the gun in my possession—tucked under my pillow. I sat quietly for a second. Felt the pulse in my neck. I began to pace and realized I needed the help of a burglar. A person who knew the ins and outs of breaking and entering. Who better than Ray Astemendi? There was none better that I knew of. I made the call to Ina, in hopes she could convince Ray to help. But why would he? He thought I was a douche bag. So I had a strike against me from the get-go.

Surprisingly Ina was wide awake, and I was not surprised she was high on weed and drunk on tequila. Ray, I was told, wasn't around. "He sometimes pulls an all-nighter. A likely fucking story," she slurred. "He thinks I'm some kind of naive moron who walks around blindfolded, and doesn't see that he's balling that evangelist whore after hours. One more drink and I'll be right over."

It baffled me why she stayed with this guy. Couldn't be love. Couldn't even be the thrill of infatuation. Maybe he had something on her. Maybe an audiotape of her conspiring to overthrow the government. Planned to blackmail her. I looked at myself in the mirror just as I said that. My lip curled up, my brow furrowed, my face flushed a glowing crimson, and all because I knew what I just proposed was a ridiculous, insane notion.

Twenty-five minutes later, Ina showed up. She was sucking on a spliff. She offered me a hit. I passed. I was not about to get high before breaking into a body shop. I needed to be *compos mentis*. Five minutes into the ride, I told her about the gun being a treasured family memento from when my father served in Vietnam.

"Your dad must've been a brave man."

Until she said it, I hadn't thought of my father as being brave. But I guess he was courageous for fighting in an unwinnable war that lasted twenty years.

The residual marijuana smoke started to have an effect on me. I was getting a classic contact high. I rolled down the window. In my hazy condition, I began to have some doubts about keeping the gun. In my mind, I wanted to be sure that the pistol was only a symbol of his efforts. Nothing else. That it didn't make me a hypocrite for cherishing a piece of memorabilia that killed Vietcong guerrillas.

Ina took a hit off the joint. The car swerved into the next lane.

"Should I be driving? I asked.

"No." She then squeaked out a question while exhaling: "Do you consider yourself a chronically obsessed person?"

"Chronically obsessed?"

She clarified: "Excessively preoccupied—with me," she blurted. "Like you've fallen hard and lost all common sense in the swirl and storm of emotion that left nothing but a confusion of desire without words. That you'd been so swept up in the momentum of a person, you can't eat, sleep, or think straight. Anything?"

Jesus, where did that statement come from? I loved how she just pulled all that together from out of nowhere. It was impressive. I wasn't sure how to answer that without making it seem like I was some sinister stalker. This was the moment of truth—the time to unload my intense infatuation.

"Okay, time for me to be honest. Honest with you. Honest with myself." I took a beat. She waited patiently for my answer. It came out fast: "You consumed me. Your look, your personality, your point of view, your tastes. How you handle yourself in mixed company. How you chew your food. Sorry if this is making you feel uncomfortable. It's making me uneasy revealing all this. I'm just this guy who got caught up in the perfect dream. Haven't you ever wanted something so much that you dwelled on it until you either got it, or gave up because it finally seemed pointless?"

"No. There was nothing in my life, that meant that much to me, that I wanted it badly enough to make myself nuts over and follow the really thin lead of a matchbook potato."

"Right. I get it now. You think I'm eccentric. Quirky. Maybe even a little off-center. Freakish."

"Yes. All those traits apply."

I certainly couldn't disagree.

"But that's what I really love about you, Sharp Guy. You have a great sense of the bizarre. You understand why a person wants to join the circus and be a clown. While most of us have no fucking idea."

If you gave me a week to analyze her last clown remark, I still couldn't tell you what she was trying to say. But the fact she admitted that's what she loved about me made it an exceptional statement, and I was even more attracted to her.

Before we hit the body shop, we took a circuitous route to a twenty-four-hour McDonald's. She ordered a dozen double cheeseburgers. I assumed she had the munchies from all the weed. I was wrong. They were meant to be used as a diversionary tactic that Ray put to use when he was jacking high-end cars in Florida. That's all the explanation I got. Ray, Florida, cheeseburgers. Not exactly a master plan of attack. But who was I to judge the crafty mind of a seasoned criminal?

Breaking into the body shop lot seemed like it was gonna be a snap. There didn't seem to be any motion sensor lights, security alarms, or cameras in sight. Unusual, I thought. Ina thought different. She knew what to expect—*guard dogs*. With guard dogs roaming the yard, they'd be constantly setting off alarms and motion lights. A never-ending security nuisance, for sure.

A twelve-foot padlocked chain link fence surrounded all the wrecks waiting to be hammered back to their original shape. I spotted my Jeep, looking forlorn, sandwiched between two cars. One being the old man's truck. The other a Pontiac Gran Torino with its front end pushed in, like it had gone twelve rounds with one of those monster trucks.

As we approached the fence, I was prepared to climb. Ina stopped me. She made breaking in a snap, picking the lock like a professional. Another handy skill that Ray schooled her on.

We cleared the gate like combat soldiers—quietly. We crept along the edge of the fence so as not to disturb, maybe, a night watchman and his dogs, anxious to take down trespassers. The annoying ring of my cell phone broke the silence. We both flinched. I couldn't shut it off fast enough. The caller ID indicated that it was Parker calling me back. I took the call, frantically whispering that it was a bad time to give me advice about my life. I punched off. Unfortunately, the ringing had awakened the welcoming committee—two enraged Dobermans—barking, snarling, and barreling towards us with their teeth glistening and tongues dripping saliva. That was the frightening picture of mad dogs anxious to bite into us like squeaky chew toys.

I started to retreat but was advised by Ina to freeze. Do not show any sign of fear. I did as she said, stood perfectly still. This was where the burgers came into play. She tossed four in their path. Honestly, I had no faith that a $1.69 burger was going to stop these guys from attacking. And I was right. They kept charging. We were their preferred Happy Meal.

The next move was a lot riskier and, it goes without saying, laughable. While Ina tried to distract the dogs with a tape recording of a cat in heat, I was supposed to grab the gun from the glove box, and then run like hell to the exit. There was no time to disagree that her plan seemed flawed and utterly ridiculous. Even so, she switched on the recording on her iPhone, then ran in the opposite direction. Amazingly, the dogs were stupid enough to take the bait, and chased after the sound of the shrieking cat. This actually gave me enough time to seize the gun, and then scramble for the front gate. But halfway, guilt seemed to overpower me. I couldn't just leave her alone to tangle with the dogs. I turned back, but my heroic deed came too late. In the distance, I saw Ina darting out from behind a battered green Mercedes, running full speed towards me with a Doberman close on her heels.

"Run! This fucker wasn't fooled by the meows!" she screamed. She almost made it to the gate but tripped over an exhaust pipe and fell flat, skidding on her stomach, like she was sliding headfirst into home plate. Thinking fast, she leapt to her feet, removed her shirt and distracted the dog, waving it around her waist matador style. This action, she told me later, was called a *veronica* in bullfighting parlance. It was an amazing sight to watch, as the Doberman charged like a raging bull. After several passes she was able to maneuver and corral the dog into the back of an open van, and slammed the door shut.

Since the second dog was nowhere to be seen, this seemed like a good time to escape. But our hasty getaway was stalled. As we approached the front gate, a greasy hulk of a man—who, according to the nametag on his shirt was Smitty—was waiting for us. He was gripping a shotgun and began shouting orders.

"Freeze, goddammit" We obeyed. "Drop to your knees, hands behind your head, don't move a muscle or you're dead meat. A simple enough request that I won't repeat twice."

"You'd kill us in cold blood, just because we infiltrated your body shop?" I asked.

"I wouldn't hesitate."

With that threat still on the table, we did as he ordered and dropped to our knees. The second dog, by the way, was now sitting patiently by his side, waiting for its instructions to probably attack and kill.

"Can we explain?" I asked, hoping he'd be a reasonable man.

"Sure," he said, "but first let me explain the term trespassing. It means I have every right to protect my property by any way I deem fit. In this case, assault with a deadly weapon seems fit."

"Look, settle down. This is not what it appears to be," Ina said.

"It's exactly what it appears to be, miss. Breaking and entering. Grand theft auto. I've been dealing with your kind all my life. Think you can just waltz in here, grab a car, strip it for parts, and sell it on the black market right under my nose? Not happening."

Ina made a request.

"You mind lowering the gun so it's at least not pointing at my vagina?"

"How's that, girlie girl?"

He moved the barrel so it was now pointed at my crotch. I shifted nervously.

"Girlie girl. Only drunks with wandering hands at the Baked Potato Bar and Grill call me girlie girl. You, I suspect, are a vodka on the rocks drinker, with nimble fingers. Right?"

Smitty took a closer look and recognized Ina.

"Right. You're the barmaid with the sweet ass and the wise guy disposition," he said.

"Okay. So, now that we're the best of friends, can we get off our knees?"

"Just don't make any sudden moves, or the dog just might sink its teeth into the fleshy part of you thigh."

"Look," I said, "we had a specific purpose for breaking in that involved retrieving an important artifact from my glove box."

"Artifact? Like what? A Chinese urn?"

"Not as valuable but still worth a great deal on a more heart-warming/personal level," Ina said. "A handgun from the Vietnam War. His father's gun, that eliminated the enemy and saved your life while you were sleeping comfortably between your dogs. A gun that he brought back from the bloody trenches of the Mekong Delta as a memento of his courage fighting for the freedom of American lives. The kid was afraid that one of your light-fingered shop flunkies might want it as a souvenir, so here we were getting it back before you opened."

Ina said all this with as much theatrical timbre as she could muster. Smitty paused as he tried to soak in her claim as true or bullshit, then said, "Hey, I resent the fact you accused my guys of being thieves."

"Loose change from cup holders, sunglasses from the visor, forgotten cell phones in the glove box. Tell me the kid had nothing to worry about."

"I swear everything she just said is true," I chimed in. "I'm a worrier. A restless sort of guy." I showed him the pistol and the handle where my dad had his name, rank, and serial number etched on it. "Proof. Lt. Ben Reilly. 544-33-12."

I could tell that this grease monkey doubted that we were on the up and up. Probably thought we were smuggling drugs hidden in the door panels. Nevertheless, we were spared and left unharmed with the .45 and three cold cheeseburgers that were never used for bait. As for my car being fixed in a timely manner, it was doubtful, since Ina had called his auto body techs light-fingered flunkies. What a night.

❦

Minutes later we're in the car, saying nothing. Total silence except for the rough sound of the Mustang rattling. She was driving unbelievably slow. Her mind was elsewhere. Me, I had my head stuck out the window like a dog trying to suck in oxygen. Suddenly Ina made an urgent request: "Hunt down a liquor store. I need to get this dreadful night's taste out of my mouth and alcohol is the only remedy."

Twenty minutes later she was guzzling from a bottle of tequila. I was now behind the wheel. My idea. Purely for safety reasons. The tequila seemed to quiet her nerves and brought up a sensitive issue.

"Hypothetically speaking—in the event, let's say, I were mauled to death by those Dobermans, or that lunatic accidentally pulled the trigger and shot my head clean off—but you got lucky and survived the ordeal, I have a request."

I had no idea where this was going but I guessed it wasn't headed for a more civilized discussion. "Okay, go for it."

"Cremate me and spread my ashes in a place called *Mascota*—the bullfighting capital of lower Mexico. You got that, Sharp Guy? *Mascota*. The further away from Lubbock and Bakersfield, the happier and more peaceful I'll be in the next world. If there is a next world. Which I doubt."

"Shouldn't Ray be the one to, you know, handle this delicate chore? Considering he's almost family."

"Ray couldn't flick an ash from a cigarette into a sandbox without fucking it up. I want you to take control if, in fact, I should die before you. Mascota. Lower Mexico. Do I need to write it on the palm of your hand?"

"No. I got it. You die first, I set you ablaze and scatter your ashes in Mexico."

"Specifically *Mascota*. No other place," she barked, nearly drowning as she takes another healthy swig of tequila. I backed off because, well, I wasn't really sure if she was being serious or just putting me on. I let it play out the way it ended, with her raising her voice as if she was convinced she would die before me. The more I was with Ina Byers, the more I learned what a messed up chick she really was. But I stuck around, hoping I could find the off switch that controlled her unconventional social habits and snapped her into a more, I don't know, normal person. Okay, maybe *normal* was stretching it.

It was three in the morning when we pulled up to my motel. The idea of her staying was hers. She was too drunk to drive any further. Ina passed out on the bed fully clothed and finally woke at daybreak. She kissed me goodbye. Her morning breath was tainted with booze and cigarettes. I was sober and just plain tired and fell back to sleep with my dad's gun safely tucked away under my pillow. Ina had slipped out around 6 a.m. and headed back to her apartment to shower, get sober and change clothes.

⌣

Since my car wasn't even close to being repaired, Ina picked me up the following evening to go and witness the work of Emily Easterday and her magic fingers, which turned cripples into pole-vaulters. A large, pristine white canvas tent that looked like the *virgin circus* was in town was set up on a vacant lot on Lubbock's outskirts.

Ray was nowhere to be seen. Not that I missed his dazzling personality, I was just curious to see him in his element as a security guard. I could only imagine his rough demeanor being an asset in a job like this. Pushing people around who tried to either mock God or manhandle Emily Easterday inappropriately.

Inside was an experience in itself—a worshipping asylum. Packed with young Christian sinners, waving their arms, clapping, swaying, rocking as Miranda Grace and the Heaven Seekers, the ecclesiastical house band, ended their up-tempo rock spiritual.

A pin spot tracked Emily Easterday, a twenty-two-year-old natural beauty, striding across the stage with incredible confidence, charisma, and swagger. Everyone, including me, listened with rapt attention.

"I'm Emily Easterday and welcome to the rebellion," she said, in her best stentorian voice reaching all the way back to the parking lot. She pumped her fist in the air as cheers and a chorus of *amens* and *hallelujahs* filled the canvas arena, as if a rock legend had just taken the stage. Her sermon continued with a punch to the midsection:

"For you Rebel Newbies, we are the truest expression of the fully committed believer in Jesus. We are a counterculture, with a commitment to the radical doctrine of Christ. We're all about Skateboard Bible Groups, Christian Punk, Goth, Evangelical Tattoo Parlors." This generated louder cheers. She sat at the edge of the stage and looked out into the audience with a beguiling grin. She was hot and she knew it. She definitely appealed to a brand of followers who idolized her as a disciple, or something close to it anyway. I found this to be distressing, that a woman was taking advantage of naive parishioners using her sex appeal as bait.

A half hour later, *the show*, I'll called it, was still going full force while Ina and I lingered in the back of the tent. We finally met up with Ray, who was in a dark suit and wore a Secret Service-type earpiece. I wondered who gave him orders, Emily or God? We were told to stay clear of him as he collected the evening's take from staffers, who funneled hundreds of dollars from their collection tills into the large black leather bag Ray held with a tight grip. We finally approached. I gave him a friendly nod, which was ignored. Expected. Ina peeked over his shoulder into the money bag.

"How's God doing tonight?" she asked lightheartedly.

"Low-end crowd. Maybe five thousand and some chump change."

"Seems even God is a casualty of the economic slump," I said. Ray was offended by my remark. He turned to Ina. His brow furrowed.

"Does this friend of yours need to comment on everything under the sun?" It wasn't difficult to sense the strain between Ray and me. Ina grabbed me by the arm before things got out of hand.

"We're moving," she said, as she led me away from Ray's wrath and back into the main tent area, where Emily Easterday continued to preach her moral guidance—walking along the edge of the stage like the rock goddess she was, touching the outstretched hands of devotees. I listened and watched with an intensity that actually gave me chills. Not that I agreed with what she was selling but, rather how she sold it. Her sermon, if that's what you call it, was suddenly directed towards the unenlightened, which viewed sex, drugs, and rock 'n' roll as a rebellious curse of the youth. But according to her, they were dead wrong. These people had no clue because they had not experienced misdeed firsthand, she bellowed. They saw themselves as perfect. She took a deep breath, exhaled, then confessed even she might sin herself once in a while, but that didn't make her a sinner, she proclaimed—that made her a freaking human being. The crowd erupted in applause. Not everyone in attendance was buying her sales pitch. A worked up voice boomed from the heavens.

"Sorry to dispute your homily there, miss, but the Lord sort of passed me over when he was thinking about human beings engaging in sinful acts of pleasure."

The tent fell silent. Emily gestured to a stagehand, and a red spotlight was swung upwards revealing an obese, desperate-looking salesman type sitting precariously on a (support beam) in the darkened rafters, hugging a leather briefcase like it was filled with diet pills and flowerless cake recipes that had no effect on him. An uncomfortable murmur was heard throughout the crowd, as the congregation wasn't really sure whether this was on the level or part of the worship service.

"What seems to be your quarrel with the Lord, sir?" Emily responded.

"Quarrel? I have no quarrel. I have contempt. When *He* was sitting around creating yours truly, He didn't know when to stop." The man pulled himself up, stood shakily on a guy-wire. "No worries, I'm very agile for a large man," he said convincingly. But his enormous weight—he had to tip the scales at 340 or so—was causing the taut wire to weaken. Whatever the noise was a wire made before it snapped, was what everyone now heard. Screams were heard. I noticed anxious people turning away, anticipating this was not a performance. The big man teetered, just enough to cause his briefcase to slip from his hand. It snapped open as it plummeted to the stage, propelling an array of naked photos revealing every inch of his beefy frame.

"For those wondering," he explained unashamedly, "those are pictures of me in the raw. For you to see how your God shaped me, not in his likeness but in the form of a large glob of mozzarella cheese."

I turned to Ina, also expecting the worst possible outcome—which would be a swan dive into the crowd below.

"This dude's gonna take a header," I said. Somebody needs to call someone with a very tall ladder. Get Ray up there to talk down this fat guy, before he kills himself and kills someone else falling on top of them."

Ina claimed this was all part of the show. *A leave 'em shaking their heads on the way home miracle.* There was uncertainty in her voice as she said this.

Emily called up to the man, saying he was making everyone a bit nervous.

"Nervous? Think how nervous I must feel standing up here with nothing but a thin wire holding up my 350-pound frame that your God created."

"Your large frame is not God's doing, sir. This is your misconception of the Lord. He has not stuffed your face with fatty foods, greasy burgers, and tacos. You are an example of someone who has not taken care of his health and is trying to blame Jesus Christ for your gross physical shape. My followers, be they large or lightweight, I'm sure have a problem of you taking the Lord's name in vain." She then turned to the audience and addressed her flock. "Can I hear an amen?"

An *amen* rolled through the audience.

"So what you're saying is that God has no use for fat people."

"No, sir. What I'm saying is God is not walking amongst us to help trim your waistline. The power has to be within you."

"Power? I have no power. That's why I'm here. To seek a higher power to guide me from thick to thin and slenderize my wretched soul."

"I think it's time you accepted your fate and came down off your perch before you fall from grace."

"*Fall.* That is the operative word, isn't it, madam?"

Ina and I exchanged knowing looks right before the fat man stepped into mid-air and plummeted like the ill-fated Hindenburg.

I know. I know. That's a terribly mean description. But an accurate depiction of this terrible spectacle.

For some reason, at that moment the world went silent on me, as I mentally obliterated the horrible screams coming from the stunned crowd. Their faces distorted in unbelievable horror. When my hearing returned, all I could hear was the sound of screaming sirens and the remaining assemblage—the ones who didn't run for the exits—praying out loud.

Suddenly, a man wearing a peacoat and watch cap, rushed the stage and knelt down next to the motionless body. A ship's doctor, perhaps? Possibly trained in CPR? The fat man was still breathing. Barely. His coming out of this alive was highly unlikely. The Samaritan made no attempt to save him. Instead he whispered what seemed to be the last rites in his ear. A moment after, the *fat man* gasped his last breath and expired. Gone. That was that. His life was over. Gaining more weight and being mocked by mean, narrow-minded people had just become inconsequential. At this point, an imposing Ray approached, then dragged this seafaring gent by the collar and escorted him off the premises. You had to at least be curious about who this guy was. Can an unordained person administer last rites? Don't think so. And would an undercover priest attend an evangelical assemblage just to witness a hoax firsthand? Maybe. But I doubted it. So I put my overactive imagination to work and surmised that he was some lunatic who, because he designated himself a maritime captain, thought that entitled him to play God and administer last rites to any stranger who leapt to their death. He was placed in a police cruiser and questioned at the scene. The man had no credentials or identification to speak of. His peacoat and watch cap came from the local army-navy surplus store. He was released on the basis of a unanimous consensus of opinion—he was nothing but a drifter with a deluded sense of himself as a formidable healer, while Emily Easterday was nothing but a fraud draped in sheep's clothing. His words. The nutcases were out in full force tonight.

Ina drove me back to the Journey's End Motel, while Ray stayed behind to help scrape up the mess, to talk to the press, and, of course, to console Emily Easterday in her time of bad publicity.

CHAPTER EIGHT

A crescent moon was cradled in a starry sky as Ina and I sat by the motel swimming pool, each slugging down a Dos Equis. Me lying back on one of those cheap webbed lounge chairs, badly frayed. Ina by the edge of the pool, her feet dangling in the water, the ever-present Sherman in her hand. The fat man's suicide had thrown us for a loop. We said nothing for a good twenty minutes, until I broke the silence with an unsportsmanlike question.

"You believe in God?"

This threw her.

"What? Really? Ask me a less divine question."

"No. This is the one I'm sticking with. Do you? Yes, no, maybe?"

"I don't know. I haven't spent a lot of time thinking about if I believe there's a God these days. Why do you ask?" She leaned down, and nervously skimmed her hand along the surface of the water, for no other reason than to maybe test the temperature.

"Just trying to get a better perspective on the man who came up with the concept of suicide," I said. "I assume it was *Him.* Or not. Maybe it was first adapted by an ancient culture and had nothing to do with a higher power. What's your take on it?"

Ina popped a perfect smoke ring, then: "I have no take. It was disturbing. As much as I fucking detest Emily Easterday, it wasn't her fault the man took his own life. This was his choice. No one pushed him. He performed that half gainer strictly by choice."

"I disagree. Society pushed him. A collection of people who regard fat people as unsightly beer-bellied social outcasts."

"I think you're overreacting. Looking for any excuse to justify this dude taking his own life. Now cut the sidetracking and tell me what's really on your mind, without bringing God, religion, or bulimia into the conversation."

I told her how I was contemplating my next big move. How my car should be ready in the morning and whether I should get away from Lubbock or not. Yes? No? What was keeping me here? All that ambivalence rattling around.

"Everything's an indecision with you," she said.

"I'm a Libra. I have doubt. I vacillate. Yes. No. Maybe. Do you have any idea what that's like?" I asked as I took a sip of beer.

"You have doubt. Join the club. It's not exactly a rarity."

I got off this merry-go-round and changed the subject.

"So, you and Ray—how long have you guys been together? Just curious. Nothing more than curiosity, so don't read anything else into this."

"Is this important to you? Is my answer going to determine whether you stay or not?"

"Probably not. But it might. Look, if you feel awkward answering, don't. Or do. It was nothing but a throwaway question to get off the subject of indecision and obesity."

Ina shifted, finger-combed her hair to stall, I'm sure asking herself whether she wanted to delve into her private life about Ray, who was obviously a very complicated man with anger issues. Then . . .

"I've invested a lot of time and energy. You can't force people to show affection. Am I right? Of course I am."

"I agree, *romantic* should come natural," I said with conviction. "So you were saying? Or were you done?"

She splashed the water in anger with her fist.

"Okay. So the newest gripe is holding hands in public. He claimed he has this problem with public displays of affection. Although, he's got no problem shoving his tongue down my throat in front of Ruthie, the waitress. I'm not avoiding the question, it's just you reopened a wound. We've been together on and off since, Christ, I was in high school. Our first date was when he picked me up on grad night at the Fun Zone. He was three years older than me. Experienced. I liked that. I didn't have to play fucking mind games. We fucked in his car. Did that satisfy your curiosity, or do you want a blow-by-blow account of the sexual foreplay?"

She was now noticeably pissed, and I'm pretty sure regretted she'd opened up and revealed her inner feelings. I felt embarrassed, pushing for answers like some malicious gossiper. I didn't mean to pry and go that deep. Her personal life with Ray was none of my business. But no doubt I made it seem it was my business. I decided not to mention how I saw her jump into Ray's car on grad night. Or that I had it on good authority that Ray spent time in the Orange

County lockup for assault. Instead I went silent, realizing I didn't belong here. That I was nothing but a guy who had crashed a party without an invitation.

Ina doused her Sherman in the pool. Knocked another from the pack. She turned to me looking for a light. I happened to have the Baked Potato matchbook on me. One match left. I decided to use it and pocket the matchbook cover as a reminder of my odyssey. The glow of the flame illuminated our faces. Ina, never taking her smoky eyes off me, registered a slight smile.

"I'm not usually attracted to nice guys," she said. I nearly burned my fingers on the match as it flamed out. She pulled on the Sherman and softly blew a smoke ring. It hung in the air between us—this thin layer of white fluff—the only thing keeping us apart.

"And I'm obviously not attracted to nice girls," I came back with. Another beat and I kissed her, softly. She didn't pull away. It seemed to last forever. When we broke, I got dangerously carried away.

"You're so beautiful," I said softly and as meaningfully as I could. Her response was not what I had hoped. You tell a woman you think she's beautiful and you kind of expect at least a thank-you or a blush from the unexpected compliment. Not from her. From Ina Byers I got a declaration . . .

"Know what's great about you and me, Sharp Guy? We came from the same tragic past. The identical urge to break free from the bonds of small-town mediocrity."

I would have loved to think that her intuitions were right. But they weren't even close. My past was not tragic. Heartbreaking was the better word, and I'd coped with what was handed me as best I can. But it was somewhat nice that she put me in the same category as her. I was still waiting for her to respond to the beautiful remark. At least a thank-you or a modest smile. Nothing. Just dead silence before she put a lid on that topic completely.

"It's late. My night is over. Going to bed."

As she stood, I noticed for the first time a small tattoo on her ankle, a heart with the name *Dean* inscribed across it. I ran my finger around the heart.

"Old boyfriend before Ray?"

"You're pressing me again, Sharp Guy."

"I know. I can't help myself. It's a trait I can't seem to shake. You run a diner, you get to know your customers' private lives by prying. They return when you ask how their wife, kids, and dog are doing. Familiarity breeds people who eat breakfast, lunch, and dinner."

"My son."

"What?"

"Dean is the name of my son," she said under a blanket of sadness. Of course I reacted. But not with a look of shock but more of a half nod, appreciating that she felt comfortable enough to share that with me and not keep it hidden from view. I said nothing. Ran my finger around the heart a second time. She started to open up. I stopped her, saying it wasn't necessary for me to know. She continued anyway.

"I had these plans—you know, like everyone else. Art school in Chicago. Go on a healthy diet. Quit smoking. But life can change in an instant, as you found out when your father died and you lost the diner. I had this boyfriend at the time. I always had a boyfriend at the time. But he never knew. I wanted to make the best of it, you know? I read all the right books on how to raise a kid. I wasn't given a baby shower for the simple reason I didn't have those kinds of friends. So,

I maxed out a heap of credit cards buying infant gear. Crib, stroller, clothes, disposable diapers by the truckload. Whatever it took to give him a good life. I was prepared to be a mom." She swallowed hard. "But Dean had lousy luck. He didn't make it. Died at birth. Game over. I bought a carton of cigarettes and gave all the kid paraphernalia to the first pregnant woman I saw having trouble crossing the street."

I didn't mention that Jack Lucas, the collection agency asshole, paid me a visit. It would accomplish nothing but create more emotional grief, and putting her in the awkward position of explaining why she used my name as a reference. Now it became painfully obvious why she was a bad risk with the credit card companies. A valiant attempt at motherhood. I couldn't judge her for that.

I thought this was something she rarely did—let down her defenses. She actually started to tear up so I held her in my arms. Her head rested on my shoulder. She was cold and shivering. What should I do to comfort her? What should I say to make things better? Nothing. This happened a long time ago and unfortunately it was a heartbreak she'd always have to live with. Except for the onslaught of crickets, the moment remained silent until I walked her back to her room, and she asked that I not say anything about her son's death to anybody. Especially Ray.

"Nobody needs to see my dark roots. Ray thinks Dean is the name of a childhood pet. I realized it's awfully gullible of him to believe I'm telling the truth, but it's the story I chose to tell. So if you could just keep this between us, I'd be grateful."

I gave her my word that I'd keep her secret to myself. But I couldn't hide the fact that knowing Ina Byers lost a baby was upsetting. I went to bed that night feeling down. Stared at the ceiling hoping that reading the cracks would help me sleep. Not this time.

This time I was kept awake while I lingered on the name Dean. Over and over in my mind. That name meant something but I couldn't for the life of me figure out why. I finally fell asleep at 4:30 a.m.

I woke the following morning to my annoying motel room phone shouting in my ear. It was Ina telling me she and Ray were coming to pick me up within the hour. No, I don't want to be picked up, I said loud and clear. She wasn't listening. Said they were taking me to a local rodeo. I tried to get out of it using what I thought was a reasonable excuse: "I hate rodeos and horses scare me pissless. As a kid, a pony once ran away with me while I held onto the saddle horn for dear life. It tripped in a ditch and sent me flying into a clump of thorny bushes. I've had this phobia of horses and thorny plants ever since." I hung up. Tried to fall back to sleep. It rang again. She didn't buy my story. Knew it was all just a lie. She continued to push, push, push. A force that I was familiar with.

"No one is asking you get near a damn horse or a thorny bush. Professional riders will be taking all the risks."

I tried another path of least resistance: "I'm leaving town in less than thirty minutes."

I ended the call and slammed the receiver down. Twenty-nine minutes later, I found myself in the back seat of Ina's Mustang, having been dragged out of bed against my will. I attempted to get dressed while the car was moving down the highway, jostling me back and forth. Trying to get my pants on was an acrobatic feat to behold.

Ina was behind the wheel. Ray was behind his Ray-Bans. I was suspicious about this sudden day trip to the rodeo. They wanted to hook me up with some hot rodeo girl. Why? I got no straight answer. Only some ridiculous justification.

"Because you're in desperate need of female companionship," Ina said. "It's not healthy to deprive yourself of sex or you'll have a nervous breakdown."

"Sex? You're already convinced I'll be sleeping with this cowgirl?"

I never got a direct answer, just a sly grin from Ray. My guess was, they were up to something. Something questionable. I can't stress enough how bad this timing was. I repeated my need to leave Lubbock as soon as possible. According to Ray, my car wouldn't be ready for another few days. How did he know that? He confessed, "I made sure of it."

"So what's going on, I'm being kidnapped?"

"Yes. But in a truly productive way," Ina said.

Ray suddenly turned benevolent.

"I misjudged you, Jake," said Ray, "and since Ina mentioned that you're on the run and basically homeless, why not help you hide out for a brief time until the coast is clear? I've been there man. There's nothing worse than being hunted down by the law."

I was not for a minute fooled by Ray's kindness. I hadn't known him long, but it was pretty evident he was not a team player. If anything, he was a user. Manipulated others for personal gain. I pressed their reason for keeping me around. They were vague and said when the time was right they'd reveal a plan they'd devised that would make us all a lot of money. Now I was even more suspicious and wary, but for the moment I let it slide and didn't insist on more details. Whatever the real reason, why did I need a blind date to make their moneymaking plan work? Only thing I could think of—she was a stimulant to keep me close by. A dangling carrot in leather chaps. Get me laid and I'd agree to anything.

⌘

At the rodeo, the three of us watched from the half-empty grand-stands as Buckley Griffin, a seasoned rider, lassoed a calf from atop her charging horse, leapt down, flipped the calf on its side and tied three of its legs together with a short rope she held between her teeth. She accomplished this feat in ten seconds. On the male rodeo circuit the world record, I was told, is six. She was young, highly skilled and attractive. I understood, from Ray, that she was a hometown girl who came from old money. Ina could sense my interest. She turned to me.

"You like her, I can tell by the glint in your eyes. Come on, I want you to meet her."

Glint? What glint? There was no glint. It was crusty crud in the corners from lack of sleep.

Five minutes later, Buckley was tossing her saddle onto the bed of her Dodge Ram. While Ray and I watched from a short distance away, unseen behind a horse trailer but within earshot, Ina tried to sell Buckley on me. Judging from her body language, Buckley wasn't jumping at the chance of hooking up. Her words spoke even louder.

"Forget it, Ina. I'm wiped out. I smell like a horse, and I just want to go soak these aching loins in a hot tub."

Ina fired up a Sherman before she continued her sales pitch.

"Look, the guy's from Bakersfield. He's alone. He's cute. He's in Lubbock. He's looking for a little fun before he dies."

"He's dying?" Buckley responded incredulously.

"Eventually we all die, Buckley. I'm not asking you to fuck him, or introduce him to your friends and family. Just show him a good time—the same good time you've shown thousands of other young cowpokes in your extensive social life, when you're not straddling a horse. I'll throw in a pair of handmade ostrich boots."

Ina's lure failed to arouse Buckley's interest.

"I can buy my own boots, thank you very much."

"Sure. But how many pairs of boots come with two front row tickets to see Miranda Lambert in concert at Texas Stadium? It's been sold out for a year."

"You may have struck the right chord, Ms. Byers," Buckley said.

"Look, maybe this guy is worth being with for a few hours. He's unlike anyone you've ever met or been with. Smart, clever—he quotes German philosophers and has aspirations of being a novelist. Take a break from the horsey crowd and cultivate a little culture in your life. What's the harm?"

"Jesus, you sound just like my mother, always trying to get me out of the saddle and into a more polished lifestyle."

"At least you have a mother. His mother died when he was five. He craves female companionship."

"So what is this, a mercy date?" Buckley asked.

From my ringside seat, I witnessed the discussion becoming a bit more heated. Profanities were hurled. Arms flailed. Heads shook. Eyes narrowed to slits. Buckley began to pace. Christ, it was obvious that this girl did not want to meet me. So why force the issue? I decided to intervene and put a stop to what seemed like a futile attempt at an introduction. Besides, I never really wanted to meet this girl in the first place. When I started to come out from behind the horse trailer, Ray blocked my path.

"Relax," he whispered. "Give it two more minutes. Let Ina do her stuff. She's a natural born liar and can talk an Eskimo into buying a fucking sno-cone franchise."

"That's an ignorant, racist remark, Ray. It's a strained, artificial situation we got going here. I'm leaving. Walking out of Lubbock if I have to. Wish you guys all the best."

I had started to walk away when I noticed Buckley and Ina sharing a hug. Ina, spying me for the first time lurking behind the trailer, gave me a thumbs up. Seemed like Buckley was finally forced into conceding. Ray looked at me with a Cheshire cat grin.

"Like I said, Ina Byers has amazing powers of persuasion."

Even though it looked like we had liftoff, there still appeared to be uncertainty on Buckley's part. She and Ina spoke for several more minutes in an urgent whisper. I strained to hear, but all I caught in the hushed tones was the word *marriage*. Very strange.

As she and Ina prepared to part company, Buckley caught sight of me, standing next to Ray. She smiled; I smiled back, rather insincerely, and gave her a foolish wave.

"That him?" she asked Ina. Ina nodded yes.

As Buckley climbed into the Ram's cab, she left Ina with this candid, cornfed assessment of me:

"He's adorable, actually. Fresh looking. Like a new foal who just slithered out of its momma's vagina trying to stand for the first time."

I wished she had kept that image to herself.

CHAPTER NINE

We were slowly walking the Lubbock County fairgrounds, drinking tequila coolers from a can, maneuvering our way through and around the hordes of fairgoers eating corn dogs and cotton candy. I spotted a child grasping the string of a large, helium-filled balloon for dear life, but apparently not tightly enough. It slipped from their tiny fingers, the child launched into a temper tantrum, and the accompanying wail shattered my eardrums. If that wasn't enough, the scent of livestock soured my sinuses. After twenty minutes, I had had enough and was ready to leave—but where? That was the problem. I had no real destination.

Buckley and I were a good twenty yards in front of Ina and Ray. We were not exactly having a grand old time, which was evident by the absence of sound between us. I could've broken the stillness but didn't because I had no idea how to break the ice. *How long have you been a cowgirl?* seemed mundane and showed my stupidity. Probably ever since she was big enough to climb aboard a pony and gallop to her heart's content, as any fool would know. I was relieved when she went first.

"Ina said you guys went to high school together."

Okay, this is probably going to make me seem like some pretentious asshole, but I was disappointed by her question. This was a yes/no inquiry. It lacked imagination. I was hoping for something related to poetry or history or my political affiliation. Something that went deeper. Philosophical. I played it another way—with honesty and frankness.

"Look, you mind if we skip the usual first date small talk and go into something a bit more definitive, like why you agreed to this county fair fix up? I gathered from your conversation with Ina—I guess you figured out I was kinda eavesdropping; sorry about that— you weren't exactly in favor of meeting me."

She took a beat before answering. Probably deciding whether to be honest or not. She went for honesty.

"At first, no. Then I changed my mind when I heard you were smart and your mother died when you were just five."

"So you felt sorry for me. This was strictly a pity connection."

"I never thought of it in that way. But now that you mention it, it is very sad. I'm sure you must've been traumatized."

"I remembered crying a lot and blaming God for taking away my mother too soon. From that day forward I put Him in the same category as Santa and the Easter Bunny—as charlatans and fakes."

"And you were only five when you made that decision?"

"I was very insightful for my age." I paused, then changed the subject, getting away from my attack on the Easter Bunny, who, for all I know, Buckley still believed existed.

"So tell me, Buckley, what's the real reason you agreed to this date?"

She didn't hesitate to give herself a moment to devise a good excuse. She went straight to the truth.

"Ina bribed me with a pair of very expensive ostrich boots and hard to come by concert tickets."

"So I heard. And that sealed the deal?"

"Pretty much."

"No offense, but I think you're lying. You're much too pretty to be needy for a date. I'm sure rodeo circuit cowboys are falling out of their stirrups just to get to you. Plus, I know you come from money and I can't imagine you're suffering from a lack of material things. You could probably buy yourself a damn boot factory if you wanted. Right?"

"Doesn't make me a bad person."

"More to the point, why would Ina go to such extremes just to get me a date?"

"I think she wanted me to keep you busy, so that you didn't wander off and head back to Bakersfield."

"And that was okay with you? Babysitting me?"

"The whole thing piqued my interest. I wondered what was so important that she needed you to stick around. As a normal person, I could understand—she wanted to keep tabs on your every move. But Ina isn't exactly normal. You can bet there's an ulterior motive. A hidden agenda. She's a game player."

"You think Ray was aware of the bribe?"

"Aware? He probably set in all in motion. He's more of a user than she is. Somewhere along the line there's probably a big payday. It's always about money with them."

It then suddenly occurred to me—Buckley's father was seriously wealthy. Could Ina and Ray be planning to somehow steal from him and needed me to get close to Buckley in order to pull off some sort of caper? A key to the front door. Combination to a wall safe. Password code for the high-tech security system. That was one crazy accusation, but not beyond the realm of possibility.

Meanwhile, Buckley and I overheard Ina and Ray in a heated discussion. Ina had had enough of Ray's bitching and criticizing the lowbrow bumpkins, whose idea of a good time was trying to tackle a greased pig. Ina took a defensive position.

"Hey, if it wasn't for those lowbrow, greased-up pig farmers, Emily Easterday would be out of a job and you'd be a security guard working the graveyard shift at some Detroit auto plant."

Then the worst possible incident happened. An unassuming techno-geek, carrying a couple smoothies, accidentally ran into Ray, spilling the smoothies, while knocking Ray's precious new sunglasses onto the ground. Ray went ballistic. I watched this exchange. It made me uneasy. Ray was now in this guy's face. His fists clenched. Ready to do battle.

"I'd say watch where the fuck you're going but it's way too late for that kind of advice, isn't it, pal?"

"Sorry," the geek said with a drop of sincerity and a whole lot of fear. "Sugar rush. Affects my equilibrium. I become a first-class klutz."

"Pick 'em up, asshole," Ray demanded.

"Excuse me?" the geek said tentatively.

I'm sure this guy, along with the small crowd of bystanders who were witnessing this tense exchange, couldn't comprehend the outrage Ray was gushing over a pair of stupid sunglasses. Glasses that he in fact stole from somebody else weeks ago.

"Don't make me repeat myself, dipshit. If the glasses are at all scratched, you owe me two hundred bucks."

The geek got logical. A mistake. Logic didn't compute in Ray's world.

"Normally, a conventional apology is enough to satisfy most people."

"I'm not most people. Here's your choice, fuck-stick. Pick up the glasses or pick up your balls at the milk bottle toss. A simple American threat."

Totally intimidated, the young geek decided it was best to pick up the glasses. He cleaned them off with his shirttail, then nervously handed them to Ray.

"Satisfied?"

"Not until you're out of my sight," Ray snapped.

The geek couldn't get away fast enough. Ina reacted with disgust and embarrassment, since the bystanders had been filming the altercation with their iPhones, and threatened to notify fair security and have Ray removed for his uncivilized manner. Their threats only pissed off Ray even more. He flipped his middle finger into their camera phones, yelling at them to go *fuck themselves*. Not cool. Two men stood up to his bullying tactics, getting in his face and suggesting he leave before someone got hurt. He didn't budge, said he'd gladly take on both of them—one at a time. He started to remove his shirt and precious glasses. It was like an after-school fight. Ina stepped in before there was a serious brawl with Ray coming out the loser. Although, since he was used to dealing with a much tougher element in prison, it's possible he could come out on top, pounding these guys into the dirt.

Ina, who normally would let Ray fight his own battles, apologized to the two brutes for his behavior, and pulled him away from a fight that could send somebody to the hospital and/or jail. The specter of serving jail time was a wake-up call for Ray, who realized being incarcerated would draw attention to his past arrest records. He wisely backed off and walked away with his fists still clenched for battle.

"Think there will ever come a time," Ina said, "where you won't be such a goddamn prick and have the urge to kick somebody's ass?"

"Some people play golf," he said, not attaching importance to this entire confrontation.

Thing was, I'd tried to avoid this kind of tyrannical personality my whole life. I was bullied in grammar school for being smart. For getting all A's. Labeling me a kiss-ass teacher's favorite. I once intentionally took a dive on a book report and got a B- just to prove I was a regular kid who put his jockey shorts on one leg at a time, just like them. A big mistake was not having a high opinion of myself. Yet here I was, years later, still wearing jockey shorts, lowering my values by associating with a fucking card-carrying psycho and his sidekick, an independent, uninhibited free spirit. I scratched my head, completely stumped as to what Ina saw in this loser. But why was I so mystified? Ina was not exactly a paragon of virtue herself. I turned to Buckley, hoping she might fill in the blanks.

"Maybe an unfair question, seeing that you and I could potentially strike up a strong connection . . ."

"Just say what you're thinking out loud."

"What's Ina's attraction to Ray?"

"Not hard to explain. Very obvious if you're really paying attention. Her flavor of man has always been the complex and the unconventional. She likes the bad boys. The roughnecks who were never taught manners. There's like a whole cluster of women out there who get the crap beat out of them, but always forgive and forget and come back for more. Leaving a relationship, no matter how abusive, was never easy."

Couldn't argue with that theory. I'd heard accounts of that happening all the time. Men who have even shot their girlfriends or wives and were forgiven. Often, violence is a familiar pattern for the woman, as well as for the man. It doesn't end until these women are dead. And even then, if they could come back from the grave and exonerate their partner, I suspect they would.

Having witnessed Ray's harsh temperament, Buckley had seen and heard enough for one day. Exasperated, she let Ina know it.

"Ina, I'm done. You can forget about the boots. I default on this date. It's been a rough outing. We'll talk tomorrow."

Buckley split without so much as a goodbye or a nod or a *nice meeting you.*

"Buckley, don't be so damn sensitive," Ina said. "We're gonna grab dinner, have a few laughs. Get thoroughly smashed. Smoke some weed. Give the boys blow jobs."

"I'll have to pass. I'm cutting down on laughs and blow jobs this month," Buckley fired back.

Ray grabbed Ina tightly by the arm. "C'mon, it's over," he growled. "Time to blow off this hayseed county fair." He then dragged Ina a few feet from where I was standing. But Ina wasn't having any of his manhandling.

"Stop fucking pulling on me, like I'm your pet."

"You just pulled me away from those thugs."

"That's different, I saved your ass and you know it."

A wave of fury rattled through me. Like Buckley, I had had enough of Ina and Ray. I threw my arms in the air, frustrated, and started to walk away from this exhausting melodrama. They tried to stop me.

I ignored their invitation to dinner. I was more focused on trying to catch up to Buckley. I rushed towards her, elbowing my way through the crowd.

"Hey, can we talk?" I shouted as I gained on her.

She spoke to me without looking back.

"It's nothing against you. It's Ray. He's a fucking animal. Don't get me wrong, I like Ina. She can be fun when she's away from him—but together they're poison."

"Look, I'm really sorry about all this unnecessary crap you had to endure on my account. It's my fault. If I hadn't come to Lubbock none of this would've happened."

She stopped and turned back to me.

"Why are you apologizing? You're not to blame for any of this."

"Apologizing feels like the right thing to do," I said.

"If you're feeling sorry for me, please don't. I can handle whatever is tossed my way. I've tumbled with the best of them. Thrown off my horse a hundred times, trampled by a pissed-off calf, kicked in the stomach by a three-year-old thoroughbred while I was grooming her. I can take a punch."

"Then why the tears?"

"Am I crying? I hadn't noticed."

Denying she was deeply bothered by something other than Ray's temper was an obvious deception to hide the truth of her tears. I attempted to de-escalate the tension.

"You feel like grabbing a drink or a coffee or a baked potato and wolfing it down with some jazz music?"

She took a beat.

"Too much to think about?"

"No, I like the choices, but I'd rather get a pizza and have it in your motel room."

As we walked to her truck, I couldn't help but wonder if my obsession with Ina Byers was dwindling, because for the moment I could think of nothing but sharing a slice with Buckley Griffin. For the first time since I arrived in Lubbock, I felt comfortable and my stomach wasn't churning and the desire to scream *help* disappeared.

The last thing I ever expected was to get it on with Buckley Griffin. Let me rephrase that. *The last thing I ever expected was to get it on with Buckley before the pizza arrived.* Our clothes strewn everywhere on the floor, my pants draped over a chair, her bra hanging from the lamp shape. It looked like a movie set for a cheap porno. The air conditioner blasted against our sweaty naked bodies. A bottle of Chivas sat on the nightstand along with a bucket of ice and two half-filled glasses.

Aside from her thick head of blonde hair, she was so utterly bare. Even the outer regions of her vagina sprouted only a light fine fuzz. It was dusk, so the remaining sun leaking through the gauze curtains darkened the room just enough where we could see every flaw on our bodies and every expression on our faces. She had an extraordinary figure. Smooth, tanned, supple skin. A thin scar that ran down her left calf was her only imperfection. And that was not a deterrent, but rather a victorious battle mark from when she had fallen off her horse and broken her leg during a calf-roping competition. I was deep inside her as she straddled me. I put my mouth on her nipples. She moaned, leaned forward, and stuck her tongue in my ear when she spoke.

"You're incredible," she said like she meant it.

"So are you," I repeated, but angry with myself for not saying it to her first.

"Fuck me hard, one more time," she said.

I did and after we both exploded, she dismounted, then lay beside me. Both staring up at the ceiling, panting like we just ran a 10K marathon around the room.

"Look, Jake, I really like you. This day turned out to be spectacular. And you are by far one helluva piece of ass."

What could I say? I was flattered. But I gave her most of the credit for the day's unexpected awesomeness.

"We have to do this again real soon," I said. "Like tomorrow morning when we wake up sticking to the sheets, smelling like sex and oozing bad breath."

She fought back those tears again. Tears leftover from earlier at the fairgrounds. I sensed I was about to find out the real reason for her somber mood.

"Sorry, but I can't see you anymore after tonight," she said. "At least not like this—naked and in bed, side by side, feeling complete."

"What do you mean? Why not?"

Then came the explanation. The last thing I ever expected. The one reason that would give any guy cause to flinch, quickly throw on his pants, and dash out the door, never looking back.

"I'm getting married tomorrow afternoon," she said with an air of nonchalance. I could've just said *congratulations,* but I didn't. I naturally reacted. Winced painfully before speaking.

"Wow. This is some news. Admittedly, I'm finding it very difficult to breathe right now."

I shifted and sat on the edge of the bed, waiting to hear the logic behind how these past few hours, from sunup to sundown, emerged into what it did—me connecting with a rodeo cowgirl and her fucking a total stranger on the eve of her wedding day. Perhaps that was an item on her bucket list.

She rattled off a litany of reasons why it was okay for her to cheat. Predictably, the double standard came into play. Bachelors go to Vegas and fuck hookers before tying the knot. Some men fuck their ex-girlfriends as a way of breaking ties with their past. People are disloyal now, so they'll be faithful in the future.

"Get what I'm saying?" Buckley asked, hoping it all made sense and that I would understand her rationale.

"I totally get what you're saying. But I also have to disagree."

"Why? Why can't the blushing bride have one last fling, fucking her brains out to celebrate the end of her independence?"

"She can. No one says you can't. There are no set rules. Just moral standards if you want to follow them. If not, that's fine too. But you can still be an independent woman while you're married."

"How bad do you think this was?"

"For you, maybe not bad. Shows you're a healthy woman with an interest in casual sex."

"This wasn't casual. I don't feel casual about this at all. Do you?"

"No. It's just that this would've been better without an ulterior motive. I'd like to feel that you slept with me because, well, you found me appealing and not just a fuck to service a last need before you become a wife and a homemaker."

Except for the buzz of the air conditioner, the room fell silent. She wanted to do it one last time. I was against it. Was this just her idea of one last hurrah? Or did she really want to have sex without the stipulation of it's what brides do before taking that giant leap into the valley of marital fidelity?

Of course, I softened. How could I not, seeing this beautiful woman spread-eagled on her back, asking to forgive her for being inconsiderate of my feelings? My thrusts became stronger, and as I was about to come, she initiated a pause in the action.

"What? Second thoughts? Feeling a sense of guilt? Your fiancé is on his way over here to cut off my dick?"

"Before I forget—you're invited," she said.

"Invited? Invited to what?"

"The wedding. I want you at my wedding."

After gasping and shaking my head in disbelief, I leaned over to the bedside table and downed one of the glasses of Chivas. You don't often get an invite to a wedding after sleeping with the bride the night before. Maybe this was a radical new approach to wedding etiquette these days.

"I can't," I said flatly. "This would be a definite conflict of interest. How could I look your husband, or any of your guests, in the face without feeling small?"

"People do it all the time. It's not an uncommon practice. I know a guy who fucked the maid of honor in a broom closet right before the ceremony."

"Sorry, but that's a horrible example. That makes the groom more of an asshole and the maid of honor a deceitful piece of shit cunt—excuse the language. Sorry, but I won't be there. Mainly because I might not be able to control my feelings and have this overwhelming desire to drag you to the broom closet before the *I do's*."

She was noticeably upset. Wounded, her voice cracked.

"Can I speak honestly here? I don't really know if I'm even doing the right thing by getting married," she said, while dramatically hanging her head in shame.

Now it became evident what she was seeking. She wanted my approval to bail.

"Why me? I don't know your fiancé. I know nothing about your relationship with this guy."

"I trust your judgment. You're smart. You have a solid grasp on what's right and wrong and what could be a huge mistake on my part. Maybe I'm too young, and it's too early for me to start a family."

I needed a question answered before I continued this debate.

"If Ina knew you were getting married, why did she pick you to babysit me? Of all the girls in Lubbock, she handpicked a bride to be. Makes no sense. Is there an underlying motive here?"

"She knew all along that I was on the fence. Should I call it off while I still had the chance? When Ina and I argued in the parking lot, I was ready to throw in the towel, but she finally convinced me that you could settle my doubts. That being with somebody, anybody, would help me decide which way to go. That I would see what a great catch my fiancé was. And you were readily available to be . . ." She hesitated, searching for the right word. I jumped in and completed her thought.

"To be what, a guinea pig? That I'd be the prototype of an ideal polar opposite of what you're about to marry?"

"I guess. I don't know. Maybe. I need a drink. This night has gone in the wrong direction," she whined as she grabbed the other glass of scotch and downed it in a single motion.

"Well, it's difficult to be objective knowing I was nothing but a litmus test. It's against my better judgment, but here's an honest opinion. I would say if you're in love and he doesn't smack you around, embarrass you in public, buys you all the basic amenities, washer/dryer, a fridge with French doors, and a double oven—go for it! Get married, live a full life, have a little red wagon full of kids and teach them to ride a horse and lasso a calf and skin their knees in a dirty corral."

She wavered for another few seconds before making up her mind. "Okay. I'll go through with it," she said like she was doing me a favor. "But I guarantee I'll be divorced in less than two years. And then I'm coming to hunt you down, Jake Reilly, and form a strong bond between us."

I wanted to say something positive.

"Seems like a damn good alternative," I said. Which might have been too encouraging. But I just didn't want to abandon her, and be the cause of her having a lousy day at the altar.

She grabbed her engagement ring from her purse and slipped it back on, kissed me hard, then whispered one last plea in my ear. Overcome by emotion, her voice cracked.

"Please show up," she said while leaning in and kissing me on the cheek. "It would mean a lot to me, Sharp Guy." By now she was fully dressed and walking out the door.

I stood there for a moment, perplexed—wondering how I should feel about her using the same endearment as Ina. Was she trying to use it as a tactic for me to change sides? Or maybe it was just her way of telling me Ina Byers was not the only fish in the pond who had issues. Didn't matter. What mattered was she touched a nerve. It got to me. I lay back on the bed and closed my eyes. It was a welcome silence. My head was spinning in several different directions. Too many to control. I fell asleep in my underwear on top of the bed and dreamt my life was simple. Until the sunlight blasted through the windows and woke me back to reality. And then I remembered who I was, and that my life was superficial, not simple. Chasing a real dream that was looking more and more like a *horrible mistake*.

CHAPTER TEN

Buckley's reception was going full tilt. There was an impressive ice sculpture of two rearing stallions resting on a massive buffet table in the center of a rolling backyard. A country band played in the background. Not a tux or suit in sight. Only the shitkicker chic look of rich *cow guests* in tight jeans, Stetsons, and their newly purchased Tony Lamas, fresh out of the box.

Ina, Ray, and I were just climbing out of the Mustang. It stood out amongst the limos, flashy luxury cars, some classic motorcycles, and even a few purebred horses tied up at a hitching post.

Ina was especially stunning wearing a low-cut black cocktail dress and sunglasses. Her four-inch heels had barely hit the pavement before she fired up a Sherman. She was out of her usual kick-ass black jeans garb, for good reason—to prove to the masses that she could be a lady when she wanted to. I must say, she looked remarkable amongst the leather skirts and pearl snap blouses. Ray looked like a dime-store version of Johnny Cash. As for me, I definitely fit in—dressed in a pair of jeans, denim shirt, sport coat, and a noticeable frown. I was desperately trying to control my nerves, anticipating the awkward moment when I would be introduced to the groom. That was a given. A certainty. I never should have come. Two drinks, then I ride off into the sunset. I was perspiring.

We crossed inside. Ina addressed Ray and I like we were six years old. "Play nice with the other kids," she said. Ray followed up with his own blanket statement.

"People who love this country-western hillbilly music crap can trim my hairy balls."

So eloquently put. I just knew, in due course, there'd be a brawl between Ray and some cowpoke that accidently bumped into him and spilled his drink all over Ray's formfitting T-shirt.

We headed for the buffet table, which took us past the slowly melting ice stallions. In my side glance, I saw Buckley coming towards us. Emily Easterday, the prominent evangelist, was escorting her. Buckley wore a nontraditional white wedding gown, short like a mini dress and low-cut. She was not afraid to show off her legs and serious cleavage. We finally linked up. Ina wasted no time starting up a friendly conversation. Both feeling a bit awkward, Buckley and I avoided eye contact.

"Check you out—aren't you the slutty bride, falling out her dress!"

Buckley took her remark as a compliment and posed like a model striding the fashion runway.

"Thanks for noticing," she said.

"I'm a noticer."

"You guys know Emily, right?" Buckley said proudly. Emily jumped right in without missing a beat.

"Sure they do. Her dad's my biggest contributor. God would spank me if I didn't show up." She looked around, impressed by the sprawling acreage and by the gala itself. "What a wonderful day of love and friendship and glory. Praise the lord for his influence." Ray responded with an *amen*. He'd probably get struck down by lightning if he said less. I couldn't imagine having sex with this woman. Her shrieking *Oh God* while climaxing I would see as a contradiction of faith, not me giving her pleasure.

Emily flattered Ray. "Hi, Ray, you look tired, pissed and adorable in your stolen shades. Ina, nice seeing you out of your grunge element."

"Is it?"

"Articulate as ever." She turned to me, placing her hand on my shoulder and squeezing, as if she was healing someone with an arthritic condition. "And you would be?" I started to introduce myself but Buckley beat me to it. Said I was Ina's friend from Bakersfield. Seeing the sights of Lubbock. You could sense the nervous quiver in her voice. So, I finished the introduction with a name:

"Jake. Jake Reilly."

"Emily Easterday," she said in her best lilting voice.

"I know who you are. I was at the gathering of your flock, the night the fat man had a gripe with God and took a header."

"Unfortunate. Deeply tragic. Obviously a very troubled man. I prayed for his soul that evening."

"But you couldn't reach up to the rafters and heal his anger, preventing him from committing suicide," I said, my own indignation coming through.

"You're a skeptic, aren't you, Jake?"

"I'm more than a skeptic. I'm a cynic. A prophet of doom. It disturbs me how you take advantage of people without a single shred of guilt."

"Freedom of speech, Jake. First Amendment stuff. Gives a person the right to say what they think. Free and public expression of opinions without censorship. So, the people I've saved from sickness and poverty might have an issue with you criticizing my work." She arched her eyebrows in a way that made her feel she had just got the upper hand in the conversation. But I didn't stop there:

"My father was a Vietnam vet. Had a severe case of PTSD. You think your power of healing could've prevented him from going insane? Don't even try to answer. I don't think so." My tone, a mix of petulance and arrogance even bothered me.

"Sorry for your loss," she said before she slipped her arm through Buckley's and guided her into the crowd to mingle with other prominent guests, who thought getting their picture taken with Emily and Buckley was a status symbol. It wasn't hard to see that Ray was pissed that I put his employer on the spot like that. I didn't apologize for my honesty. But he did get in my face.

"If we didn't need you, I'd break every fucking bone in your wise-ass face," he said. "I'm going to apologize for your fucking insolence." He then walked off, hoping to catch up with Emily before she got plastered. Drinking in excess was one of her guilty pleasures. The other was having sex with her star security guard after every sermon. I watched Ray as he waded through the crowd, bumping rudely into guests, causing some to spill their drinks on their expensive Western garb. A zillion things raced through my mind. But only one that piqued my interest—why did Ina and Ray need me so badly? And for what? I had hoped Ina could give me answers.

"Curious—why me? What talent do I possess that has Ray treating me with a slight degree of warmth? The truth. No bullshit," I insisted.

She grabbed my arm and pulled me closer to the bar. She asked the bartender for two scotch rocks. She lifted her glass and made a toast. "To you and me, Sharp Guy. Prosperous days ahead." We clinked and swallowed hard and fast. Then she told me how she and Ray had this exciting business venture and wanted to include me.

"Business venture? You mean like buying a Domino's Pizza franchise?" A waiter passed with a tray of champagne. Ina snatched a flute while dousing her Sherman in another. Unaware, the waiter didn't lose a step and moved on. She took a healthy sip, then launched into her sales pitch.

"It's a brilliant idea. We're planning to appropriate God's money. You up for it?"

"Am I up for what? Stealing from the church?"

"You know what's great about you, Sharp Guy? You get it right away. No need for additional, unnecessary explanation. Don't have to draw you a picture in the sand." She finished off the flute of champagne. "Not just any church. We're skimming a little off Emily Easterday's next big crusade collection."

I recoiled, then gave her a flat no. Never. It was a criminal act however you looked at it. I might be responsible for arson, which I could prove was a terrible error, but I was not a thief. I wasn't about to steal the hard-earned dollars that people, even naive, gullible people, donated to the church. She tried to twist the truth.

"It's nothing but a racket, Jake. A clever con. She's the thief. She deceives the believers into thinking Jesus was going to save them but needed to be paid for His trouble. The woman needs to be taught a lesson, and Ray and I plan to show her the error of her ways by hurting her in the collection plate. With or without you."

"You can count me out. Look for another partner. I'm sure there are plenty of inactive felons in Lubbock with the appropriate credentials, who would be glad to get out of the house and steal from Jesus."

Next she tried flattery, and it almost worked.

"Jake, I really want you to do this, and I'd feel a lot more secure with you on the job. You are brilliant. You are witty. You are the right man for this task. I never know which version of Ray is going to show up. The sensible, balanced Ray or the unpredictable maniac with a penchant to hurt someone." She then planted a gentle kiss on my lips. "Just consider the possibilities, Sharp Guy." She lifted her sunglasses and looked straight into my eyes. I tried to hold my stare, but couldn't. I politely excused myself, turned and walked away, not looking back. A very frustrated Ina wandered off to mingle, and I'm sure to instantly notify Ray that I was out. That she had no luck convincing me that the robbery would be risk free and financially rewarding.

Me, I just wanted one more drink before I left this whole Wild West show behind me. I crossed the expansive lawn and headed directly for a second bar located under a cypress tree. There were more bars at this wedding than you can count on two hands. Big drinkers, these Texans.

As I crossed the Great Divide, I wasn't paying attention to my route and accidently bumped into a guest. The impact landed him flat on his back. Amazingly, he didn't spill a single drop from the open bottle of Chivas he was holding.

I apologized, helped him up, and attempted to actually rub off the grass stains. Made up a ridiculous story about how I couldn't keep my eyes off an attractive girl crossing the lawn, when I should've been paying attention to where I was going.

"As long as it wasn't my wife," he said.

"Since I don't know who your wife is, I'll go out on a limb and say it wasn't her. But if it was her, she's very beautiful and caught my eye." I laughed. He didn't.

"If you were paying attention to the wedding ceremony, you'd know who she was," he slurred.

Holy crap. Since we never made it to the ceremony, I couldn't have known I just ran over the fucking groom. He took a healthy gulp of the scotch, then introduced himself, extending a hand. "Devon Moore. You must be a friend of Buckley's, since I've never laid eyes on you before."

"Yes. I know her from the rodeo circuit."

"You ride?

"I like to watch. Mostly a fan."

"Like a rodeo groupie?"

I admitted to it, and left it at that. Why degrade myself any more than I had to? We shook. His hand was sweaty. And here sprang forth my dilemma. Did I introduce myself using my real name or use a pseudonym? I chose to be anonymous for obvious reasons. Why I picked such a well-known actor I have no idea. It just rolled off my tongue as natural as can be.

"Powers Boothe. A pleasure to meet you, Devon."

"Walk with me in case I fall down," he said. I obeyed. Then, without warning, he began unloading his bag of troubles.

"A word of advice from someone who knows—don't get married unless you have to. Not because your parents saw this union as a business venture, between two wealthy Lubbock families. That would be a horrible mistake." There were those words again. He placed his arm around me like I was suddenly his best friend that he could confide in.

"The ink isn't even dry on the license, and my life is already spinning out of control." He took another full swig from his bottle. I listened to him vent.

"She doesn't want a honeymoon. Imagine that. She thinks a honeymoon is an insignificant waste of time and money, just to stay in the room to order room service and fuck. It's her opinion that we should give it to charity. Specifically, hand it over to the Emily Easterday Bullshit Fund. Have a taste."

He handed me the bottle and I drank with enthusiasm.

"This fucking proposal was the brainchild of Ina Byers," he added. "A friend of hers."

I took another nervous gulp, then handed back the bottle.

"Between you and me, I'm not a big fan of Ms. Byers. Trouble-maker. Has no respect for men. Not to be trusted."

I changed the subject for fear he might connect the dots and figure me out.

"Are you into horses too, Devon?"

"Not like my wife. My interest begins and ends at the OTB window. Just as a point of reference. Nothing else. I need an impartial opinion. What items does one pack for the honeymoon? I've got toiletries, change of underwear, KY jelly, Polaroid camera, and a vibrator. Would you agree? The perfect honeymoon getaway package."

I didn't answer because I didn't want to disagree and say that his choices seemed unromantic and sordid.

We reached the other bar and had managed to drain the bottle we were drinking from. He asked for another bottle. "If I can't take advantage of an open bar, who the fuck can?" He then raised the bottle in the air to make what turned out to be a very uncomfortable toast.

"Here's to you and me, Jake Reilly," he said, looking off at a beautiful girl crossing the lawn. *"But mostly to you. I just hope that I can satisfy Buckley as much as you did in your motel room last night. I understand I have a lot to live up to."*

Fuck me, I stood there while my heart made rumba thumps in my chest. My complexion changed to pale gray; I started to sweat and would have fainted if Devon hadn't shaken me out of this scary illusion. I told myself this was nothing but my guilty conscience playing tricks on me. Devon continued:

"Thanks for allowing me to cry on your shoulder, Mr. Boothe. It was a heavy load to get off my chest. Sad, but I'm guessing this marriage won't last two years. If that long. I could sense defeat during the vows, when my bribe just gave an unenthused nod and a shrug when asked if she planned to stay in the marriage *until death do us part*. The real pisser was, in a moment of sheer stupidity, I had her name tattooed on my arm."

"You can always draw a line through it."

"Yes, that bit of advice is not exactly helpful. Someone else suggested I just cut off that arm completely. Drastic but certainly a permanent solution."

After another generous swig, he reeled forward, and then zigzagged his way across the lawn to yet another bar located near the lake. Falling in could be inevitable. With no lifeguard in sight, I intently watched to make sure he didn't tumble in and drown. Fortunately, he made a detour and headed directly towards one of the bridesmaids, who was coming his way. Stopped in his tracks. Said nothing, just stuck out his tongue like a lap dog. She immediately slipped a hand into her bra and pulled a pill from its lining, popping it into her mouth then transferring it onto his tongue. I've seen this exchange before. An OxyContin was passed from tongue to tongue like a French-kissed communion wafer. I think it's some sort of game played in the druggy world, but I'm not sure. I made an impulsive statement to myself—what with the Oxy, plus all the booze he had consumed, Devon Moore's wedding night was on the brink of being a total disaster.

I'd had enough of this reception. I moved directly for the exit. I was fifteen feet from making a clean getaway when Ina intercepted me.

"Where you going, Sharp Guy? Not even going to stay for cake?"

"No cake for me."

"Not even a goodbye to the blushing bride?"

"We already said our goodbyes last night. No need to prolong the moment."

"So, there's nothing I can say to change your mind? Not even if I beg or grovel—which is something I detest? I'm willing to lower my standards just to get you onboard . . ."

"Please do not kowtow on my account. No words, money, or promises can persuade me to stick around. Up to this point it has been a real memorable experience. Give my regrets to Ray and the groom, who I suspect, when he sobers up, will discover he made a monumental blunder."

With that said, I charged out the massive wrought iron gate, feeling relieved that I was about to leave the melting ice sculpture and all the wealthy phony cow folks to their cake and traditional bouquet toss. Maybe in this hillbilly deluxe milieu the bride tossed a sprig of new-mown hay.

But in all honesty, I felt a tinge of failure. Came all this way to try and capture the heart of a boyhood crush and now I was leaving hurt and empty-handed. With nothing to show for it but a few glowing memories and a bruised ego.

However, my hastiness to leave was thwarted. I found myself stranded at the front entrance. I had no way back to my car. No transportation to the auto shop. I tried to hitch a ride with a limo driver. A Middle Eastern gent, maybe wearing a cheap dark suit and fake gold Rolex. I explained my dilemma. Underscored that the trip to town and back would only take maybe thirty minutes tops. He would not be missed, and I promised a generous tip for his time and gas. He was not eager to help, pointing out that he wasn't a fucking taxi service.

"You want to use my fucking service, make a fucking appointment." He handed me a card. I looked at it, then handed it back.

"You spelled *service* wrong. It's v-i-c-e, not v-i-s-e. Just sayin', as a fucking courtesy."

"If you don't fucking get out of my fucking face, it'll be a hearse driving you to town." I took his threat as somewhat harmless but got out of his face purely as a precaution.

Apart from stealing one of the horses or hitching a ride with an early departing guest ducking out to avoid the grueling cake cutting and the bouquet toss, I had no other choice but to trek fifteen miles back into town. It was hot as fuck. Maybe 101. The blacktop from the highway was sticking to my shoes. I felt like I was in the Mojave. I had gone no more than two miles when I started to visualize a mirage—those wavy splotches of reflective surface—like pools of water on the road ahead of me. Turning back would have been the smart move, but I kept going. Because going back meant facing Ray and Ina trying their best to persuade me to join their gang of swindlers. Why they needed me so badly was still puzzling. Trust? The power to control me? Who knows? I stopped to rest, leaned against an old broken fence. Wiped the sweat from my brow with the back of my sleeve. After a few long beats, I saw a car coming. I hoped this was my lifeline from baking in this oven and not a mirage. I positioned myself on the edge of the shoulder, and waved the car down. It slowed almost to a standstill. It was a Dodge Ram like Buckley's. Jesus, it *was* Buckley's truck. My pulse raced. I panicked, thinking it was the husband on a mission to take me down for fucking his bride. Ina and/or Ray must've betrayed me, because I refused to jump on their corrupt bandwagon. I sensed the tragic demise of the great thespian Powers Boothe was imminent.

The Dodge Ram finally reached me and came to a complete stop. Relief set in when I noticed Buckley was behind the wheel, crying, her mascara running down her cheeks while trying to stifle her sniffling. I hopped in; the leather seat was hot on my back from sitting in the sun so long. She drove off, flooring it. Without me having to ask, she rambled on incessantly: "I was looking for you. I needed you to talk me down off the ledge, hypothetically speaking. I made a mistake. My parents forced me. I was pressured to marry into money. I don't want to be attached to an investment banker. It's a boring, vanilla existence. By the way, what are you doing out here, walking in this heat? You'll suffer from dehydration, get creamed by a reckless driver and then story over—you're road kill."

An exaggerated perilous situation but nonetheless, I took her warning seriously.

It was at this point I noticed she had shed her wedding dress for jeans and pearl snap Western shirt, with her hair up in a ponytail. And there in the back seat was a small leather travel satchel. She continued to speak without a breath or a pause or a comma. "I have a full tank of gas, a Black AMEX card with a $200,000 spending limit. I say we head for Mexico, get me a quickie annulment, and then you and me, for starters, get a room in Cancun and begin again where we left off after our sensual pizza night."

She was talking crazy. It was over eighteen hundred miles to Mexico from Texas. It was apparent she was dealing with a severe case of buyer's remorse.

I tried to calm her down with a chunk of logic.

"Buckley, it's natural to be scared of being locked into one person after all the years of independence. Answering only to yourself. Not being obligated for someone else's happiness." Of course I had little experience in this area, but I was always good at talking myself down off the ledge during a panic attack. I then switched gears and was about to explain my reason for leaving Lubbock. But before I did, I made her swear she'd keep it under wraps.

Even though she promised, I was reluctant, because it suddenly occurred to me her father was a big supporter of Emily Easterday, and I wasn't sure how she'd handle this kind of news. I gave her the condensed version of Ray and Ina's plan to steal the donation money from Emily's revival. Her reaction was exactly what I expected—concern for Daddy's dough.

"How do they plan to pull it off?" she asked.

"I don't know."

"Rubber presidents' masks? Guns? Tear gas? A hostage situation?"

"I have no idea."

"Jesus, Jake, shouldn't we say something to somebody?

"There are consequences if you talk. You'd be suspected as being an accomplice. Accomplices serve jail time. Between eight and ten years. You want that?"

"Well, it'd be a lot better than being married to what's-his-face."

"No, it wouldn't be. Trust me, prison is more dangerous than marriage. Although some would argue there is no difference."

She sighed and then nervously fiddled with the wisp of hair that came unhooked from her ponytail.

"Buckley, go home and enjoy your wedding night. Party until the sun rises, then in the morning, under dry eyes, begin living your new life as Mrs. Devon Moore."

She took her time answering, and then in a soft whine, she begged me to have sex with her just one more time. A memory for her to ruminate on during those lonely nights when Devon worked late but was actually fucking his young secretary. There was obviously no trust in this fresh marriage. So, I guessed Devon already suspected her of being unfaithful. This actually eased my conscience.

Even so, I thought about lying and telling her that, while an unforgettable experience, what had happened between us would eventually fade away and become a distant memory.

But why would I say that? Why would I be so cruel? I wouldn't. So, I relented and broke my own vow not to have one last romp. She pulled her pants down just enough so that she wouldn't burn her backside on the hot bed of the truck. I never undressed, just unzipped and guided myself inside her. We took copulation to another level. It was vocal and it was vigorous. Fortunately the early departing guests driving by couldn't hear her cries of ecstasy or someone might have stopped to help a lady in distress.

An hour later, she dropped me off at the auto body shop. It was an emotional farewell. A lasting embrace. A series of quick kisses from her lips to my cheek sealed the goodbyes. I left her sitting in her truck and rushed to my Jeep in case she wanted a repeat performance. She started to drive off, braked, then got in the last word: "I'll see you in two years, Sharp Guy. Be sure and wait up."

I stood cautiously in front of Smitty, the hefty body shop owner. His guard dogs were blocking my car, preventing me from going anywhere until I paid the bill. Dangling the car keys in one hand and a sizeable wrench in the other, he demanded twelve hundred in cash before I got back my independence. Cash. Sure. An understandable ultimatum. No argument from me. But I was short fifty dollars and I knew this would result in a major hassle. I was hoping he'd let the fifty slide, once I explained that I spent every dime of my college fund to fix my car. Not a chance. He was a prick. Had no warmth for privileged college kids who thought they were better than him. I tried playing the sympathy card—made it known that I had no mother, no father. No living relatives. That I was now an orphan trying to eke out a life with nothing to show for it except the clothes on my back and the twenty-dollar bill I had crumpled in my shoe. That was the clincher. Hand over the twenty, he said, and he'd call it even. I conceded defeat. He gave me a disparaging smile, then tossed me the keys. As I sped away, I called him a *worthless, contemptible piece of shit*. He threw the wrench in my direction. It bounced off my rear fender. I slammed on the brakes and skidded to a stop. Got out of the car, picked up the wrench and heaved it back while exclaiming a thunderous *Fuck you, grease ball*. I got lucky—it actually hit him in the kneecap. I drove off, leaving him in pain, and spouting profanities while his dogs listened ambivalently with their heads cocked. That was my last memorable encounter in downtown Lubbock.

Twenty minutes later, I was on the Texas interstate heading back to California, as fast as my Jeep would allow. I felt relieved, except for a sharp, gnawing pang in the pit of my stomach. It bothered me how I just left Ina Byers without even a goodbye or a quote from the pen of Friedrich Nietzsche. Nothing. I just took off without looking back. I looked up at the Baked Potato matchbook that was wedged between the visor and the headliner. It was as if the damn potato was giving me a dirty look. Its eyes expressing a disgruntled stare. Overcome by my own insecurities, I tossed the matchbook out the window, thinking I had just rid myself of any future suffering.

Ten minutes ticked by, and in my rearview I saw Ina's Mustang. Was this just another one of those mirages, like the water on pavement? Was I feeling guilty about tossing out the matchbook? This was no mirage, I realized, as the Mustang gained on me and pulled up alongside. Ray was driving. Ina sat in the passenger seat, leaning out the open window. I looked at the road in front of me, then back at Ina. I blinked just to make sure this was a real sighting. We were now side by side, speeding down a flat stretch of Texas blacktop, when my cell phone rang. I answered it. Bad move on my part.

"What?" I muttered angrily.

"Jake, this is my last-ditch effort to get you on board. Over a half a million dollars for the taking. You get a third. Enough to rebuild the diner or open a sidewalk café in Paris if you wanted to."

We began having a heated conversation, traveling side by side, going seventy. It was a single lane. Needless to say, this was crazy dangerous. My palms start to sweat and I had to pee. I literally yelled into my phone:

"My answer is still no. I am not cut out to steal money from God, or Buckley's father, or the poor soul who drops his quarter into the collection basket to be cured from his aches and pains."

Ray steered the Mustang way too close for comfort, almost sideswiping me and shearing off the door handle.

"I thought you were a risk-taker," Ina said.

"Well, we both thought wrong. I've come to realize I'm more of a cautious kind of guy."

Up ahead were the turnoffs for Tyler, Texas, and California I-27. Staying in this lane, I would be forced to head for Tyler. I needed to swing over to another lane but couldn't because the Mustang was blocking my path. Ray jumped on the cell.

"Don't fight it, Jake. Do what feels right. Your choices are clear. Stay in the lane for Texas or take the Bakersfield turnoff to *Pussyville*."

Something inside me clicked, like a switch messing with my mind. I began to vacillate. I became indecisive. Up ahead I saw what appeared to be another mirage. Another optical illusion. A figment of my imagination. An official green highway sign that read:

PUSSYVILLE EXIT — 1/4 MILE

I looked over at Ina, who was staring directly back at me. Her smoky eyes locked with mine; they seemed filled with longing. I slapped my face several times with the palm of my hand to clear my head. I talked to myself to help me focus: *"Do not, under any circumstance, let the possibility of being with her cloud your sense of reason. You have a mind of your own, Sharp Guy—use it."*

We both approached the junction at the same time. One exit read: TYLER US-69 SOUTH. The other: CALIFORNIA I-27 NORTH.

The Mustang sped up, smoke spewing from its exhaust as it took the Tyler exit. Me, I slowed down, took I-27, weaving back and forth between lanes. But then at the last possible moment, I turned my steering wheel dramatically; the car swerved sharply to the right, almost flipping over as I decided to take the Tyler exit, skidding sideways over yellow warning bumps that rattled my teeth. Fortunately I came out of it safe. Without a scratch on the car or me. I just sat there on the shoulder of the highway, catching my breath from this absurd incident, wishing I were at a bar, slugging down bourbon like there was no tomorrow. A bar in some town other than Lubbock.

CHAPTER ELEVEN

I checked into the Moon Glow Motel somewhere off the main highway in Tyler. Again, not four-star accommodations, but reasonably priced, clean, but with an annoying ice machine that shook and reverberated like a hundred pairs of maracas trying to drown out the sounds of a mariachi band.

I pushed the stiff beige curtains to one side to stare out a grimy window into the parking lot filled with heavily travelled cars that had a sizeable amount of dead bugs stuck to their grills and windshields. I was unable to think clearly, yet coherent enough to form complete sentences while on my cell with my friend Parker, who was at work in his compact, undersized cubicle at the *Bakersfield Californian*.

"Look, I'm obviously a guy with a serious mental problem that needs attending too. Obsessed and possessed by a very complicated high school classmate—and the thing is, this fixation has haunted me, controlled me, and actually made me feel really good at times—until a little over an hour ago. I mean, never in my wildest dreams did I think I'd consider doing something illegal." I paused, tracing a sad smiley face on the grimy windowpane with my index finger. "Yes, I am talking a second-degree felony in Texas, which carries a penalty of two to twenty years in a state prison. Not something I could handle. Not an experience I want to share with others of the same sex, in a confined space." Parker gave me a handful of guidance.

"Okay. My advice is simple and makes all the sense in the world—run like a motherfucker back here and hide under the nearest bed covers you come too."

"Not exactly sage advice, my friend, especially if they're going to arrest me for torching my own place. I'd be better off taking my chances with Ina and committing this robbery."

"Robbery? You failed to mention it was a robbery. What, a bank?"

"Not a bank."

"Then what? A 7-Eleven? Armored car? Stagecoach?"

"Now you're being ridiculous. Let's turn this conversation around to something less unlawful. Read any good books lately?"

There was a long, strained pause.

"One hint won't give it away. I'm on the edge of my seat here!" Parker cried.

"Okay, a hint: it includes God."

"You're stealing God's wallet?"

"Yes. That's it. God's wallet, credit cards, and his identity. My question is, do you think I can get away with it? Will anybody notice if I walk around in an ancient tunic and sandals?"

"Now it's you being utterly ridiculous."

"Am I? Oh good, for a minute I was believing my own paradox."

Suddenly I became uneasy because there was rustling coming from inside the bathroom.

"Look, I gotta jump."

"What's the rush?"

"Ina just stepped out of the shower and I need to hand her a towel." That seemed very subservient after I said it.

I ended the call abruptly, leaving Parker hanging for an answer. On cue, Ina entered from the bathroom wearing nothing but a knee-length kimono and a grin. Tossing her a towel wasn't required.

"Hey, you look very . . ." I searched for the right word. *"Refreshed,"* was the best I could manage without using a blatantly sexist term like *edible.*

"I'm feeling cleansed. A Jack Daniels would be perfect right now." On the end table was a bottle of Jack and two glasses. I poured us both a drink. More for me. It settled my nerves, and if I drank enough it would also remove any fears, inhibitions, and misguided morals I'd brought with me from home. I suppose I'd suddenly become a bigger drinker than I cared to admit.

"Who were you talking to?" she asked.

"A friend from Bakersfield. Parker Rowe. Maybe you remember him from school. He was the editor of the school newspaper—*The Blue and White.*"

"The name doesn't ring a bell. But why would it? I made it a point to avoid reading that rag. I found most of the articles nothing but pulp sensationalizing bullshit school activities. What a fucking waste of ink."

She climbed on top of the bed, her knees pulled under her chin; she wasn't wearing panties. I'd be lying if I said it wasn't a complete turn-on. It was hard to divert my eyes, but I managed to adjust my focal point just as she grabbed a book from the bedside table and immediately began to thumb through it, ignoring me like I was just part of the plain, unattractive furniture and not even in the room. I zoomed in on the cover.

The Bullfighting Aficionado.

"Bullfighting. Never figured you for someone who'd be interested in that kind of cruelty."

She remained fixed on the book, not looking up to meet my gaze. "I love the artfulness of the kill. It's life and death drama. Bravery and blood. If you're a good boy, maybe I'll take you to Mascota with me someday. The bullfighting capital of Lower Mexico." Ina added this last detail with exuberance.

I think she had mentioned this place when we were distracting the Dobermans—showing off her bullfighting skills. She wanted her ashes spread there, amongst the bull droppings.

"If I'm being honest, this doesn't pique my interest. Seeing animals slaughtered for sport. I'll pass on the trip to Lower Mexico." I washed my dismissal down with the rest of my Jack.

"It'll take your breath away. It's very romantic. Very sensual."

"You obviously have an affinity for seeing helpless animals murdered in front of a bloodthirsty crowd. Sorry, not what I call an aphrodisiac."

"Jake, it's not a perfect world. People have differences of opinion, likes and dislikes. Take Ernest Hemingway, for instance—my hero. A brilliant author and an authority on bullfighting. Have you read *The Sun Also Rises?*"

"Yes. Hemingway. A talented bearded guy. I'm aware of his love of the Latin sport, as he called it. But just because fucking Hemingway liked to see bulls taken down to their knees, that doesn't mean I'm jumping at the chance at getting fifty-yard line seats at the Plaza de Toros bullfighting arena."

I then topped off our drinks, just to put a marker between my next set of questions.

"You're angry?"

"No. Maybe. Yes. Angry. Let's get back to the subject at hand—differences. Let's explore our differences. Yours and mine. That you're a thief. I'm not. That you're a criminal. I'm not. That you're not the same Ina Byers I knew eleven years ago. It bothers me."

"Hey, Sharp Guy, no argument from me. This is not the Ina Byers I knew eleven years ago either. It doesn't bother me. People evolve. I have a question for you: what did you ever see in me that was decent?"

"Nothing. That was the attraction."

She began to describe the harsh reality. That she and I ever getting together romantically was probably a long shot. But not unthinkable. Stranger things have happened.

"To be honest," she said, "being in a nonviolent relationship with someone who knows how to treat a lady with respect would be welcome."

I wasn't sure if she was playing me or not. Maybe she said what I wanted to hear just to stroke my ego. But I liked the feeling of being wanted by Ina Byers. Without warning, she slid out of her kimono, letting it drop to the floor. Excited, we both fell onto the bed. I stopped the action for a moment, knowing this was a dangerously bad idea. Even so, we began to make dramatic, pyrotechnic, vocal love, loud enough to upset the guests next door, who banged on the walls. We ignored the interruption and continued until Ina got a call from Ray announcing that he was on his way back from work. I was forced to cut this romantic evening short. I rushed my crescendo, and then quickly began to get dressed.

It wasn't difficult for Ina to sense my trepidation about pulling off this robbery without a hitch because, well, I said I was scared to death pulling off the robbery without being caught and sent to prison. She reassured me there was nothing to worry about. That I was in safe hands.

"Ray has it all covered. Putting together all the right pieces for this kind of heist. I'd be the last person to question Ray's abilities as a natural-born crook." She kissed me, then whispered in my ear: "There's a certain warped mentality at work here."

She didn't have to convince me of that. I just wanted to know what my role was in this caper. Was I the getaway driver? Or did I play a more integral part? Maybe I was in charge of distributing the ski masks? I never got a straight answer—more of a hollow promise that there'd be no fast getaway, and that a ski mask would not be a required accessory. I let it go. I didn't force the issue, but I wasn't stupid. She played it nonchalant, blasé in fact, because she knew I'd be unwilling to do whatever it was they had planned for me; I was prepared for the worst. I had this gut feeling—no, more of an ache than a feeling—that I should've backed out. But I didn't because, well—and I can't believe I would ever admit this out loud—they were counting on me. And as self-effacing as this sounds, I'm the type of guy who won't abandon ship when people are depending on me. Was I excessively nice or just fucking naive?

So I went back to my own room, stared at the ceiling for fifteen minutes, then fell asleep following the route of a thin crack from one end of the ceiling to the other. This time around it worked as a terrific sedative.

Later the following night, I found myself in the local sports arena soaking up the ideology of Emily Easterday as she spread the gospel. Emily had scrapped the tent show venue since the fat man took a header, and the area was cordoned off like a crime scene. Not to mention that a formal inquiry was being held, just to make sure his suicide wasn't an act of contrition.

The arena was packed to the rafters. I was told that tonight she planned to perform a resurrection, and that being among the congregation was considered a special distinction.

Emily, dressed all in white, was a vision of seductiveness. She stood center stage in front of an oversized neon blue cross that pulsated like a strobe light in a smoked-filled room crammed with hippies, flower children, and dropouts.

She was in mid-sermon:

"See, the Lord and I made this pretty sweet deal. He gives me the strength to cleanse and heal, and in return I give Him a healthy disciple."

Knowing beforehand that this was nothing but a dramatic exhibition of showmanship, mixed in with bogus healing, it was going to be interesting to see what she did and how she did it and to whom she did it too.

Ray, in his security position back stage, strolled the area like a Gestapo agent prowling the fences at a Nazi prisoner of war camp. He didn't carry a gun but was armed with mace and an expandable steel baton for self-defense. Ina and I were standing off to one side in the wings, getting a close-up view of the proceedings. Emily introduced a twelve-year-old boy whose clothes were worn and ill-fitting—I'm sure to help sell whatever dilemma he was living with, and which he hoped Emily could rectify with a single swoop of a hand and a *Praise the Lord* to go with it.

"Meet Kyle, everybody, who's come all the way from Fort Worth to be with us, to help rehabilitate a special friend!" she shouted. Everyone in the audience responded with a *Hello, Kyle.* The kid gave a listless wave. I was sure the audience expected Kyle's friend to be a schoolmate who'd been struck down with some incurable illness, and would be rolled out in a wheelchair or a hospital bed, or would hobble out on crutches. But they were wrong. The kid crossed over to center stage and joined Emily and an injured German shepherd named Max.

Max, wearing a camouflaged bulletproof vest, lay motionless on an elevated doggie bed bathed in soft light. Max perked up his ears while Emily told this touching story of how he was a military combat dog deployed overseas, trained to detect and locate unexploded bombs. The dog and his handler were hit by sniper fire while parachuting into enemy territory. The handler didn't make it. In the fall, Max broke two legs and had to have a third one amputated when he unfortunately parachuted into a land mine. According to army veterinarians, his hind legs were paralyzed, and he'd never stand upright again. When Kyle heard they were going to euthanize the dog and give him a military funeral, he adopted Max. I felt for the dog, and I respected the kid who adopted him, but if this Easterday woman could really turn lives around as advertised, why not choose a paraplegic war veteran to be the recipient of her so-called power to heal? Made no sense, and for me it was nothing short of reckless behavior.

But I watched the proceedings as Emily instructed Kyle to call the dog. Kyle cleared his throat, swallowed hard, then called him to come, using a military command: "Sergeant Max, front and center." The dog didn't budge. Its response was limited to a weak bark and a twitch of its ears. Kyle grabbed a leash. Emily pointed out that this was Max's directive that he was going into action. Kyle dangled the leash and ordered: "Max, heel." This time Max obeyed but only budged a few feet, dragging his hind legs like a combat soldier. Murmurs of *What a sad display* were heard throughout the crowd. Heartrending *ahhhs* originated from the darkness. Emily made the promise that Max would in fact march with his troop again. Kyle's tears puddled onto the stage floor.

I felt bad for this kid, being put through this kind of distressing drama. But that was the whole idea—getting the audience to feel a sense of stinging pain for both the kid and the dog. Noticing I was disturbed by it all, Ina tried to relieve my discomfort.

"Jake, it's all fiction. Evangelical competition today is fierce. Every once in a while Emily's forced to throw in a miracle or two to keep up with the forehead slappers. The dog isn't really a paraplegic. Sure, he's only got three legs, but he's an extraordinary pooch who has been rehearsed like a seasoned actor—and who, by the way, gets rewarded with a serving of lamb chops."

"Right. Just like the fat guy was a rehearsed seasoned actor who was fed too many lamb chops."

Ina couldn't deny that the fat guy was really a *disturbed* fat guy.

A hush fell over the crowd while Emily stood over Max, gently placing her hands on his hind legs and forehead. She looked to heaven. She spoke to God, or at least appeared to be doing so. In reality, her eyes were focused on a rigger eating a Philly cheese steak sandwich up on the catwalk. Max also looked to heaven, sniffing the air as the tantalizing aroma of the steak drifted down around his nostrils—a clever trick that caused everyone in the audience to praise this breathtaking image. Emily launched into her divine patter:

"Lord, we need a blessed miracle. Nothing short of spectacular will do. This dog has served our country and was trained to be a warrior. He deserves to be rewarded for his efforts on the field of battle. More than just a medal of honor—a revitalization of the strength that made him a hero in the eyes of this young man."

Emily pressed the palm of her hand down with force on Max's head, and dramatically reached her other hand toward the rafters. *"Max, the Lord gives you the strength to stand and walk."* Nothing. *"C'mon, soldier. Bring it on. Double time."* Still no movement.

"She's going about it the wrong way," I said to Ina. "The trick is to rub the scent of lamb chop on her upper torso. That certainly would excite the dog to stand at attention and excite a chorus of amens from the crowd." She ignored my haughty derision.

The kid, looking downcast, dropped his head on his chest and turned his back to the audience. As he did that, he purposefully folded his arms in front of him, dejected. This kid can emote with the best of them—Brando, Olivier, De Niro.

Suddenly, Max's ears perked up. This, I later found out, was his silent command to get to his three feet. He did so trembling, and the crowd reacted with amazement. Kyle casually scratched his ear. Another cue. Max tried to maneuver around the stage on his three good legs, but his gait was slow and he teetered like a drunken soldier on liberty in Tokyo. Another cue and another grand achievement. Emily continued to encourage the dog using her cleverest homilies. The dog started to walk at a normal pace. Another cue and the dog went into a full sprint, running down the stage steps, up the aisle, and exited through the back of the house. The audience leapt to its collective feet, clapping and cheering. Kyle hugged Emily dramatically and then started waving his arms in the air, finishing his bit by running down the stairs through the house shouting the fundamental pronouncement in the fake healing game: "It's a miracle!"

Miranda and the Heaven Seekers were now rocking the house with an uplifting song. The congregation was a virtual madhouse of spiritual turbulence. A concert atmosphere prevailed as the collection baskets begin to fill up like Jiffy Pop pans.

Ina then grabbed me by the arm and pulled me back stage for the next portion of the evening's hidden agenda. Keep in mind I had no idea what was coming next. Another miracle perhaps? Was she going to bring back John F. Kennedy from the dead? Jimmy Hoffa? There was no telling what was in store. I certainly had no idea that for me, this was the moment of truth. That tonight we'd be performing the robbery live without any rehearsal. I was sweating bullets, because I was never told what my role would entail. Ina positioned us in a pre-planned spot, near a large trash container. I demanded guidance.

"Okay, instructions. What do I do?"

First, she said, we would conceal our identities. She then reached into the trashcan and pulled out a shoddy looking blonde wig and slipped it on. Next she placed a Navy watch cap and mirrored aviator glasses on me. She then explained in detail what I believed to be a ridiculously flawed plan. Any second now, Ray and an armed guard, Hal, were going to show up carrying bank bags filled with a half million dollars that had been collected for over three months. Three months? I didn't ask why the money wasn't already safely deposited in some bank account because, well, I figured Ina had no idea. And she and Ray didn't care how Emily distributed the money. They were only interested in the fact that tonight was the night it was being transferred by armored car to God knows where. The bank? The attic in her house? Or maybe she just had a very large mattress in some unspecified hidden place and routinely stuffed all the money under it. Anyway, Ina continued to fill me in and explained my intricate role, which in my assessment wasn't exactly clever or foolproof . . .

Just as we spotted Ray and Hal coming around the corner, I was supposed to clutch my chest and fall to my knees like I was having a heart attack. That is correct, I was expected to fake a coronary. I was the diversion. The misdirection. While Ray, the other guard, and any other bystanders were paying attention to my acting performance, Ina would step away from the scene and cleverly switch bank bags with dummy bags filled with shredded newspaper. Ray stashed substitute bags in the trash container earlier that afternoon. A switch seemed simple enough. Problem was, I refused to play the heart attack victim, because my father died of congestive heart failure and recreating his death would devastate me emotionally. Not so sure I could be convincing enough, I suggested enlisting Kyle in the role of the distraught victim. He was a good actor and could surely pull off a kid having a spasm. I started to leave when Ina blocked my path.

"Jake, calm down. Forget being the victim. Fortunately we have an alternate plan."

"Good. Let's go with the alternate. I'll warm up the getaway ca—" Before I could complete my sentence, Ina pulled a hypodermic from her purse and plunged it into my neck. I became woozy and passed out, kissing the floor. Obviously a quick-acting sedative. Here's what I couldn't wrap my head around. Any schnook off the street could have played the diversion. It didn't take an Oscar winner to fake a heart attack. Not to mention, they wouldn't have had to share a big portion of the take by bringing in some stranger just looking for a quick payday. So, I asked myself for the second or third time—why the fuck use me? Why was I specifically chosen to be part of this faith healing rip-off? My winning personality? My attention to detail? The fact I seemed desperate to connect with Ina Byers, and that I could be swayed into doing what I was told and taken advantage of by her seductiveness and rough edges? I would say the latter was a pretty good guess. What did it matter now anyway? I was lying there face down on the floor, unable to move. But my brain and hearing were functioning just fine, so I was well aware they hadn't murdered me. And if killing me was in the cards, why not kill a stranger instead? Why me specifically? Any stooge could sell being dead. It didn't take a genius to die. I was rambling needlessly and it exhausted me.

Right on schedule, Ray and the second guard, Hal, appeared on the scene. Ray carried three large Lubbock National Bank money bags. Hal marched in front of Ray and was armed. When they approached Ina, she went into her pathetic distressed performance, frantically shouting for help using a strange bastardized form of Russian. The Russian threw Hal, and he became wary that this might be a setup. A deception. He drew his weapon and instructed the Russian woman in the bad blonde wig to raise her hands in the air and slowly back away from the victim. Neither Ina nor Ray expected Hal to freak out and pull his gun. Thinking fast on his feet, Ray assured Hal the situation appeared to be a legitimate emergency and suggested Hal holster his weapon. Hal remained unwilling and held onto it. Ray assured the Russian woman that they were there to help and would call 9-1-1.

Ina played it confused and started to babble.

"I don't think she understands a word you're saying," Hal said. "Doesn't matter we're not calling for help. If he dies, he dies."

He then pointed his gun directly at Ray's forehead and cocked the hammer back. Ray and Ina were naturally bewildered.

"What's going on, Hal?" Ray demanded. "This some sort of bad joke you and Emily dreamt up to test my loyalty?"

"It's my loyalty that should be in question. I'm handling all the cash from this point forward."

"Handling?"

"Let me use words even the phony Russian girl can understand—*this is a stickup*, to coin an old expression. I've been planning my own little robbery ever since I took this stinking job. Protecting the money of people who think God almighty is their guardian made me vomit. This whole scene you put together is the perfect cover-up that I needed to pull off my own little caper. I steal the money, leaving you and your pals to explain to Emily and the cops how Hal the guard—an alias, by the way—made you look like imbeciles. Never saw this coming, did you Ray?"

"I will fuck you up badly when I catch you," Ray said.

"Ray, your threats are laughable. You're nothing but a low-rent punk in a dark suit who thinks he's a tough guy." Then more vocal: "Now drop the fucking bags before I drop you, the blonde chick, and the dude on the floor trying to sell the idea he's suffering from a heart attack."

Hal nudged my head with his foot. I moaned just enough to make it seem as if I was still out of it, then took a beat before I grabbed Hal by the leg. Startled, he tried to yank free, but he couldn't move, because I had overpowered him with some sort of badly implemented wrestling hold. That was just enough time for Ray to try and disarm Hal. But easier said than done. They struggled, each attempting to seize the gun. A battle of brute strength against brute strength ensued. Pulling, tugging, pushing, shoving. For a split second Hal, still holding the gun, managed to free himself from Ray. Ray grabbed

Hal's hand just as he got off a shot that ricocheted off a ceiling pipe, traveled downward, and found its mark in Hal's temple. Hal dropped to his knees. Blood oozed from his ears and mouth. Ray smacked the gun out of his hand and watched as Hal fell flat on his face. So ended the battle, with Hal inadvertently taking his own life.

"Well, that was interesting," Ina, said with a profusion of sarcasm.

"Interesting, huh?" Ray snorted. "That bullet could've found its way to my head—then what?"

"Then you'd be dead, and I'd be forced to run off with Hal instead of you. Now that really would be interesting."

"Always gotta shove in a wiseass remark, eh, Ina?"

"What else do we have to say to one another that's meaningful, Ray? Except throwing wild insults back and forth."

Ina shook me—*hard*. I was now in a groggy, semi-conscious state but continued to play possum, in order to observe what was going down.

"You do realize Jake saved our asses, Ray?" she said.

"No time to give out medals," Ray snapped. "First things first. Wipe up the bloody mess. Then help me move the body, in case the gunshot might have alerted a late-night worshiper who was still praying for Emily to help them in their time of darkness."

With one eye open, I watched and listened to their plans. I could hear the panic in their voices. Before moving the body they quickly switched the money bags in the trash container, leaving the newspaper-filled bank bags lying on the floor next to me. Next, they dragged Hal's dead body a good hundred yards along the corridor and into the main area of the arena. It was cumbersome work. They left a trail of Hansel and Gretel-esque blood droplets along the way. They arranged the body with its legs and arms splayed out under the large neon cross. To make it look like some sort of divine suicide, Ray placed the gun in Hal's hand.

While they tackled this precarious undertaking, I had by now fully awakened from my drug-induced state and found the energy to swap the newspaper-filled bags on the floor with the real bags in the trash can, then rushed from the corridor with the real bags into an unlocked janitorial closet. The door accidentally slammed shut, causing a loud reverberation. The echo prompted Ray and Ina to come running back into the corridor where they had left me. But when they arrived, I'd vanished—as had the newspaper-filled bank bags. They were completely stumped, looking around in all directions. I could still see and hear them through the gap in the door.

Ina called out: "Jake, okay, you got the upper hand. Show yourself and let's work this out." There was a long pause as they impatiently waited for me to reappear. But no such luck. No sign of me anywhere. Of course, Ray was deeply pissed and did what he does best—threatened bodily harm.

"Once I get my hands on you, smart-ass, I'll snap your neck like a twig."

"Relax, Ray," Ina said. "He can't get far. He's drugged. Besides, he's got nothing but old newspaper."

Ray retrieved the bags from the trashcan. He didn't check them because he assumed the switch was still in play and the money was all accounted for.

"Okay, forget him, let's get out of here before we're caught," he said.

"I can't. I won't leave Jake behind."

"Ina, this is no time to suddenly develop a conscience. Now take a breath and move it."

Ray grabbed her by the arm and started to pull her down the corridor.

"No! How 'bout *you* take a breath. He's part of the plan. Always has been since he followed me from Bakersfield. We can't just abandon the guy because he ran scared. He's not like you and me. He's a decent kid with a set of morals. You wanna go, then go, but I'm staying until I find out where he is and what happened to him."

"Fine. Suit yourself. I'm taking the Mustang. You can catch a bus or walk for all I care. But I'm leaving before things heat up. And they will get sticky once Hal's body is found lying with a bullet hole in his brain. I'll meet you at the Moon Glow Motel in an hour."

Ray then rushed for the exit.

"You're a real compassionate guy, Ray!" Ina shouted after him. "But I knew that about you from the start, so it's no big surprise you only give a shit about yourself and your dick."

While I didn't witness the following scene between Ray Astemendi and Emily Easterday firsthand, of course—having been left behind in the janitorial closet—I have a good idea how it probably played out. I invoke my writerly right to employ artistic license liberally.

⚜

Ray hustled into the parking lot holding tightly onto the three bank bags. He didn't seem to be concerned about the chances of being seen. He casually opened the trunk and tossed in the money bags. Just as he was about to slam the trunk shut, Emily Easterday appeared, driving up alongside of the Mustang and rolling down the window.

"Hop in, Ray. I'm in the mood," she said with pure sexual proclivity.

Ray knew he was always on call to feed her sexual appetite. But this was not the time for him to give in.

"Listen," he finally said after a gaping pause, "I can't tonight. I sort of promised Ina a night out."

"You're rejecting me over that twisted girl?"

"It's not a matter of rejection, Em."

"Then what is it? Why the sudden indifference, Ray? I don't turn you on anymore? You've suddenly become immune to sex? What?"

"It's strictly a matter of keeping her happy. Making her think we're one of those dangerous couples you read about in those steamy fiction novels."

"I never knew you ever picked up a book, Ray. I'm impressed. Thing is, I don't understand why she deserves a night out." Her tone suddenly changed when she turned her attention to the bank bags in the trunk. "Wait. Stop. Never mind about the sex tonight, or you and Ina's steamy fiction tryst. Just tell me why my bank bags are in your trunk and not in the back of the armored car and on their way to my vault?"

"Look, it's not what you think."

She slid out of her car to examine the bags up close.

"What do I think, Ray? Please tell me."

"That I'm ripping you off."

"Are you, Ray? You taking advantage of our relationship? Thinking that just because you're fucking me you can squeeze in when my back is turned and steal from me?"

"No. I wouldn't do that. Sure, I can be a prick sometimes, but I know better than to steal from your flock, Em."

"What about your compadre, Hal? Perhaps the two of you conspired against me? After all, the money is there, just yearning to be taken. An irresistible temptation by the Devil himself."

"You got this all wrong, Em."

"Do I? I'm thinking you saw an opportunity to get rich quick."

"That's total crap."

"Prove your loyalty, Ray. Open the bags and show me it's just your dirty laundry," she insisted.

He took a much-needed pause, exhaled, and experienced a sickening chill. This was not going according to plan. What was the alternative? Confess and take the heat? Be arrested and jailed for attempted robbery? Or knock her unconscious, drag her body next to Hal's, and make it all look like a crime of passion? But who was going to believe that a young beautiful healer like Emily Easterday had a thing for someone like Hal, an ordinary schmuck completely out of her league?

Neither of those options were necessary, because the contents of the bank bags were nothing but shredded newspaper. The paper Ray originally swapped with the cash bags. Emily demanded a credible explanation. Ray, trying to piece this all together, managed to think of a reasonable lie.

"Okay, Em, here's the truth. I'm embarrassed to admit that Ina and I were splitting town in the morning. I was planning on leaving a note. I've had it with this life of witnessing afflicted people with multiple disorders crawl up on stage to be cured by your so-called miracles."

He claimed the newspaper was for wrapping up the breakable household bric-a-brac. Emily was unconvinced.

"Since when do you and Ina have anything resembling bric-a-brac? Where's the money, Ray? Where's my goddamn money!" she screamed.

"You have to ask Hal. He's always been in charge of the cash transfer. Maybe this time he decided to keep it and skip. Maybe you're right. The temptation was too great."

She smirked, took a deep breath, and then got back in her car.

"I'd have to be pretty stupid not to sense that something has gone really sideways. I have that special intuitive gift, you know. A gift from God that gives me the power to grasp human behavior." A beat. "I'll give you a fifteen-minute head start before I call the cops. *And may God have mercy on your soul*, when they catch up to you and that whore of a girlfriend."

A very unhinged Ray slammed the trunk shut, but it didn't catch. Fuck it. He left it open, jumped in the Mustang, and peeled out.

❦

Meanwhile, I was still hidden inside the janitorial closet, while Ina, who had discovered my whereabouts, stood outside pounding on the door, speaking in a loud whisper. The pounding, along with her voice echoing, was deafening.

"Jake, I know you're in there. I can hear you breathing. Ray split with the cash. We're meeting him later. Hal shot himself, in case you missed it. For the time being, all is clear, but that can and probably will change at any moment. Come out and we'll discuss how to escape from Emily Easterday and her devoted flock when they come after us, throwing fucking stones."

I slowly cracked open the door and peered out to make sure Ray wasn't waiting for me with a knife to cut off my balls. It seemed safe so I exited the janitorial closet. Ina instantly went into a defensive mode.

"Before you yell and call me disgusting names for getting you into this, I make no apologies. Sometimes a plan goes all to hell."

I swallow a quick blast of anger: "You drugged me, for God's sake!"

"It's all part of pulling off a long con. You have to improvise once in a while."

"At my expense. What if I was allergic to the drug, and died?"

"But you didn't. It was just a splash of veterinary tranquilizer called ketamine. Harmless. Nonaddictive."

"You're wrong. That shit is dangerous. I happen to know that enough of that stuff can bring an elephant its knees."

"Okay. Sorry. I screwed up. But I only did it to help the cause. To sell the con."

"You said Ray has the cash," I asked, only because I overheard their whole switch scheme and wanted to hear her side of it.

"He does. Yes. All five hundred thousand."

"Then what is it that I have here?" I held up the bank bags.

"Shredded newspaper. Ray hid identical bags yesterday and made the switch when you went down and became the diversion."

"You're positive Ray has the money? That he took the right bags—that his clever changeover worked?"

"What are you driving at, Sharp Guy?"

"That you and Ray aren't as clever as you pretend to be. That Ray has absconded with the shredded paper, and I have the cash, and that you and I should leave Ray behind and head for Bolivia."

"That's crazy talk."

"What part is crazy?"

"That you have the money."

I opened just one of the bank bags for exhibit. She was surprised—*floored* would be more accurate.

"If you feel your heart racing and need calming down," I said, "this would be a good time to inject yourself with a splash of your veterinary tranquilizer." This produced a slight smirk.

"C'mon, we need to get out of here," she said.

We headed for the parking lot, even though Ina knew her car wouldn't be there. On the way she grabbed a fire extinguisher off the wall. There were a few random cars still in the lot. She headed straight for a silver Ford Taurus.

"We're taking this one. Get in," she said.

"Get in? Where's your car?"

She ignored the question, then smashed the driver's side window with the extinguisher. The car alarm went off. I quickly jumped in while she hot-wired the ignition switch. In a matter of minutes we were speeding towards the edge of town.

"Nice move," I said. "You can bet this car will be reported stolen within a half hour,"

"Highly unlikely. This is Hal's car. He's in no condition to report anything, or even drive for that matter."

"Where we going?"

"It's not Bolivia."

CHAPTER TWELVE

We wiped our prints from Hal's Taurus with Kleenex tissues, and then ditched it in a nearby ravine. Walked five miles and met up with Ray at the Moon Glow Motel. The Mustang, as well as my Jeep, were parked in front of room 15. The Mustang's hood was still warm from Ray's speedy escape from the arena.

As we arrived, Ray was pacing outside like an expectant father on uppers. He was noticeably anxious about one, losing sight of the money, and two, Emily's veiled threat to call the police and have Hal and him arrested for fraud for ripping her off of the five hundred grand.

"She said that?" I asked.

"In so many words, while she was firing me. As of now I'm an unemployed felon."

"Her being a cunt shouldn't be a surprise," Ina said.

"I'm being accused and I don't even have her damn money. It somehow got up and walked away out of the trash can on its own. It's one of those fucking miracles she performed."

He turned and stormed inside the motel room. We followed.

Why I decided to be the nice guy and make him feel better about himself, I have no clue. I mean, he left me behind to face the authorities, take the blame, and be sent to jail. But in the back of my mind I was thinking about protecting myself from any criminal charges. Giving up the money and letting Ray and Ina do what they seemed to do best—run.

I told Ray how I switched the bags, because I was pissed about how they both had treated me. With no regard for my safety. I threw the bags onto the bed.

"Here's the damn money, Ray. But keep in mind there's a slight defect in the whole caper—I forgot to take the mirrored glasses. I left the pair I was given as a disguise inside the janitorial closet. They'll eventually find my prints all over them, put two and two together, and figure out that I was your partner in crime. Seems like you're fucked if I decide to blab under hot lights. Unless, of course, you kill me, like you did Hal, then make a run for it."

There was a natural long pause while Ina stared down Ray, waiting for his response. He became unusually good-natured.

"Hal's death was an accident. We fought and he got the short end of the stick. End of story."

"Problem is," I said, "you won't be around to plead your case, because knowing you, you'll run. You'll run because deep down you're a coward, Ray."

"You're wrong."

"I'm not wrong and you know it. Sure, you exude this tough guy exterior, but inside you're like a jelly donut."

With that observation, Ray moved towards me, fists clenched, preparing to punch me in the face. I would not expect less. Ina stepped in.

"Okay, both of you, stop this bullshit now. Can't you see what he's doing, Ray? He's angry because you left him behind. And even so, he got the only thing you cared about. Not me, not Emily, not Hal. The fucking money. So he's testing your loyalty."

I allowed Ray to stare me down for five seconds.

"She's spot-on, Ray. Up to this point, after all I've just done for you, you're still not appreciative. You can't bring yourself to say *thanks*. You think that word makes you weak. Labels you a pussy. Try it, Ray. Say it. See if you melt. See if anyone here laughs in your face for being a nice guy. Know what? I'm taking drastic measures. I'm confiscating the stolen money I had the wisdom to grab and leave you to your sulky mood, believing that all people are against you."

I literally started to walk out with the bags of money. I had no idea how Ray was going to react. Throw a lamp at my head. Wrestle me to the floor and pummel me senseless. So naturally I was surprised when he gave way to civility.

"Okay. You're fucking appreciated. Thanks for doing what you did." Ray then sat on the bed and put his head in his hands, frustrated. "What else? Do you want a blow job to prove I'm a team player?"

"Jeezus, guys, this is getting a bit perverted," said Ina. "Do I have to turn the lights down low and switch on some romantic music?"

Feeling awkward, I had to change the subject so I jumped in and took control of the conversation, like I was suddenly appointed the kingpin of this ragtag gang. I proposed a plan. Surprisingly, they paid close attention and seemed to go along with the idea of staying out of sight until early morning, then, under the cover of an overcast sky, sneaking out and getting as far away from Texas as possible. It wasn't a real clever plan but it made sense to just get the hell away from the crime scene before the cops were on our tail. It was agreed without any further mention of blow jobs.

I turned on the TV just to take my mind off all the unpleasantness. A really bad idea. The robbery was the lead story on the ten o'clock news. I started to turn it off but Ina and Ray wanted to know what was being reported. If they'd be mentioned. A journalist is on the scene reporting that a Hal McGrath, a second security guard connected with Emily Easterday, the evangelical crusader, was found dead, sprawled under the glow of a twenty-five-foot neon cross. Early reports indicated it was a suicide. Probably another unhappy man who lost his faith in the Lord was the reporter's commentary.

"Once they catch up with Emily, you do realize we're all fucked, right?" I nicely pointed out.

There was a long, miserable silence as the mood in the room turned pale, especially when Ray and Ina's picture flashed on the screen as persons of interest, with a chyron generated caption warning: *Do not to approach as they're considered to be armed and dangerous.*

"Congratulations on your recent status making the most wanted list. Very impressive," I said, knowing the sarcasm would only piss them off—which was my objective for treating me like a second-class citizen.

With their faces now plastered all over the local and network news, Ina, noticeably worried, asked me for a favor. Since I was probably in the clear and safe from being recognized in public, she wanted me to make a drugstore run and get some platinum hair coloring, a pair of barber scissors, and a baseball cap for Ray. With all the bad publicity, she and Ray needed to change their identities to something less recognizable.

"What's preventing me from just taking off?" I asked.

"Nothing," Ray said. "This would be your chance to go back to Bakersfield flat broke and guilt-ridden that you left us to hang."

"In the same way you left me, right?" I responded.

"Look, I realize I'm not exactly someone you can trust. In the eyes of most people I'm a bad guy, with bad intentions. Always have been. You tend to hate the fucking world when you were dumped into the foster care system most of your life. Beaten by foster parents who could give a crap how you turn out as long as they get a monthly check for giving you a roof over your head. For some people it's a racket. Actually, it's pretty common. I took a page out of my foster parents' cheat book, got caught up in the an illegal lifestyle, and used the shrewd lessons learned to my benefit."

"A lot of kids have come out of foster care just fine," I said. "You're just a bad seed. You enjoy being a roughneck. A bully. It gives you some sort of social status."

"Christ, now you're here giving me a psychological evaluation."

Ray, angry again, turned off the TV and flung the remote across the room.

"Then don't do it for me, do it for Ina. It's no secret you have this *thing* for her. This schoolboy crush. I would go so far as to say you've fallen head over heels in love. You have it bad, like a pill-popper has an addiction. Right?"

There was an awkward moment while I turned to Ina to see her reaction. She just shrugged. I wasn't about to deny his assessment, and for good reason—it was true. Nevertheless, was I willing to put myself at risk, go out into public view and buy a bottle of fucking hair dye for the cause?

"You ever love anybody, Ray?" I asked. "I mean, except for yourself."

"Should I be lying down, Sigmund Freud?"

"Please, I'd like you to answer the question as best you can. I promise I won't think less of you if you've never loved anyone in your life."

"I'm sure there must've been someone along the way. But for the most part, I try not to get too attached to people."

"So you have no feelings for Ina, is that it?"

"Never said that. Ina's different than most. Unique. You of all people should know that."

"Look, Jake, it's no use discussing anything emotional with Ray," Ina broke in. "He's not wired for starry-eyed romance. He's strictly unsentimental. To be honest, I'm not sure why you have this sudden interest in his feelings."

"It's strictly a matter of wanting to be more acquainted with the person I'll be sharing a prison cell with."

"Look, if you're afraid of getting nabbed, don't make the pharmacy run on my account. It's not worth the risk," Ina said with a small measure of sincerity.

Ray grabbed a handful of cash from inside one of the bank bags and stuffed it in my pocket. Not sure if it was a hundred dollars or a thousand. But it was a substantial amount.

"And a bottle of Jack Daniels," Ray demanded.

"Excuse me, but I never agreed to go on this pharmacy run."

"Then use the money for gas on your way back to your life of monotony."

Not a horrible suggestion. But was I ready to get away from these two? I had to make a quick decision. My stomach was doing flip-flops. My brain was pounding in unison with my stomach. And suddenly I spoke . . . not what I expected to say, but it came out plain and to the point. I turned to Ina, reading the passivity in my eyes. "Any particular brand of hair dye?"

❧

Moments later, I was moving slowly down the street in my Jeep. Although the traffic was light, I had no idea where I was going. I jerked my head back and forth like a Wimbledon fan, seeking out an all-night drugstore. The music blaring on the radio was interrupted by a news flash, warning people to be on the lookout for Ina Byers and Ray Astemendi, who were wanted for questioning regarding *the Holy Trinity robbery*—that's what the press had designated it.

My heart sank to the floorboard and I started to breathe heavily. I pulled over to catch my breath and reassess my options. After a quick count, I estimated I had at least a thousand dollars stuffed in my pocket. I thought to myself, was this enough to just take off and get away, as Ray so succinctly suggested? But maybe not. Perhaps roadblocks, spike strips, and a car chase were in my future . . .

One of those spectacular Jason Bourne chases, speeding down narrow Italian streets at seventy miles an hour. Four or five small Fiat police cars are on our tail as we weave in and out of traffic. This entire pursuit takes place as resounding brittle strumming violins and cellos play under the action. The Polizia are gaining, so we take a circuitous route up on the sidewalk, whizzing past tourists having coffee at sidewalk cafes, nearly mowing them down as they scatter in all directions. We continue to try and lose the cops but it looks futile as we reach a dead end. We hang a quick left and barrel down a set of steep concrete steps that rattles our teeth. The steps lead us to another street. Another left turn, only this time we're going against traffic and end up crashing into a vegetable truck speeding our way. Produce is strewn everywhere, bringing the chase to a halt as police cars skid and crash into one another, allowing us to get away.

I shook my head to clear the nightmarish vision. Once I got the courage to drive on, I finally spotted a CVS pharmacy and pulled into the parking lot, turned off the engine, and heaved a long sigh, as if the chase had really taken place. For those few minutes I was transferred into an artificial reality that made me forget I was on an empty Texas thoroughfare looking for a lousy drugstore. Isn't imagination grand?

The whole night seemed like a weird acid trip. Not that I'd ever experienced LSD. It's just a known fact that the drug can produce the most maddening psychedelic images, and I was definitely experiencing something similar. Neon signs made a kaleidoscope effect. My directional signal dazzled like a strobe light. Not sure, but I may have witnessed the Beatles striding through the crosswalk on Abbey Road. I supposed this was all just the residual adverse effects of the damn animal tranquilizer that still lingered in my system.

After getting their cover-up supplies, I headed back to the motel, avoiding the Italian Polizia.

⌇

It was midnight when I arrived back. The Mustang was gone. Probably kept out of sight for obvious reasons—potentially being spotted by an inquisitive cop circulating the neighborhood, for one. I finally went inside and, like the Mustang, Ina, Ray, and the pile of money were nowhere to be found. My backpack sat forlornly on the bed—the only vestige of our brief, unholy alliance. I leaned against the doorjamb, feeling all the emotional food groups: hurt, anger, exploitation. I took a deep breath and went into the bathroom to splash water on my face. Maybe this was all just a bad joke orchestrated by Ray. It wasn't. On the mirror was one word printed in red lipstick that pretty much filled in the blanks—*Adios*. My gag reflux started churning. I tried to puke but I was dry. I had been conned big time. Sending me to the store was an obvious ploy. My heart was beating too hard, and I felt panicky sick. I talked myself down from reading too much into the *Adios*. I spoke out loud into the mirror to help the words sink in: *Don't be fooled by this, Jake. "Adios" is not a clue. It has no deep implication whatsoever except to say "so long, sucker" in a romantic language—not "tag you're it, I'm headed for Mexico."*

One bright side. I discovered three thousand dollars in my backpack. I supposed this was Ina being generous and that she kept it from Ray, who would've rejected the idea of a charitable contribution with a flat *fuck him*.

⌇

An hour later, I was sitting in my Jeep washing down a tasteless cup of coffee from the motel lobby. Rethinking the horror of it all and deciding what I do next. Was there any doubt that I should turn myself around, head for home, and make a slight deviation by checking into the nearest mental ward? That would be too sound. Too predictable. Instead, I made a foolish, impetuous decision. I put the car in gear and headed south. Extremely south. South of the border, actually. Do I have to spell it out? No. This was the unavoidable move; I knew it the instant I was left the cash and the word *adios* was smeared on the bathroom mirror. Like the Baked Potato matchbook cover, for me, it was another sign. Evidence of why I was so damn obsessed and why I must continue the search for Ina Byers. A very foolhardy move, but I was convinced that Ina Byers could be turned around. Go from bad to good. Just enough to make her think twice about what she was doing associating with the likes of Ray Astemendi, and where it would probably lead her—either behind bars or dead. I had nothing else to lose except more of my dignity.

Admittedly, I was in the grip of an obsession that I was powerless to resist.

I was contemplating getting some advice from Parker or at least him telling me that I was psychologically impotent and needed professional help. Getting in touch with Parker would be pointless. What I really needed to do was stop beating myself up for having feelings. That much was clear.

CHAPTER THIRTEEN

As I drove along Mexican Federal Highway 1, at a good clip, the radio played the familiar sounds of traditional Mexican folk music. Every so often I'd catch a recognizable phrase like *el amor* or *la muerte*. Love and death. The journey was tedious. Nothing to break the monotony except the occasional tumbleweed and flurries of dust. Miles of flat, dreary landscape broken only by a thin strip of highway. I passed a stranded motorist in an overheated Ford truck that had seen better days. Rolling past endless desert, I found myself stuck behind a dilapidated tractor inching along, struggling to make it to its journey's end.

The trip was not without incident when, further down the highway, I got a flat tire and was nearly run over by some preoccupied motorist, who just missed taking off my ass as he whizzed by. Pissed, I felt justified in flipping him off and calling him a *cocksucker*

I stopped at a gas station where a mangy mutt sat out front, welcoming customers with its gravelly bark. I asked the Mexican attendant if by chance a weathered red Mustang stopped for gas recently. He hardly spoke a word of English and displayed only three teeth in his head when he smiled. I tried another tact. Using my index finger, I drew a crude picture of the Mustang emblem in the dust on my hood.

"Ford Mustang," I said loudly, like he'd understand English if I screamed it. He shook his head, and I got a *"No entiendo, señor,"* out of him. On the way back to my car, the mutt attempted to bite my ankle. That was all I needed, to be struck down with rabies in this remote Mexican village.

From this point, I checked into another dreary motel with an unpleasant odor to it, and spent a sleepless night staring at the cracks in the adobe ceiling. Over the past few weeks I'd noticed that every ceiling has a path of cracks to follow and stare at. It's what makes all the lousy motels indistinguishable, and what makes the sleepless nights sleepless. It's like a traveler's lifeline that usually led back to the same dismal motel room with the same uncomfortable mattress, crowded with bedbugs that rode on your back until you took a shower and drowned the little fuckers.

I was too distressed to think about anything except catching up with Ina and shaking the damn truth out of her. Tracking her was all based on my hunch she was headed for *Mascota*. The bullfighting capital of Lower Mexico. My instincts were a significant long shot, but I went with them just the same. I had really nothing else to go on except instinct.

The following day, with my Jeep caked with mud and a menagerie of dead bugs riding for free on my windshield, I drove past a road sign in Spanish:

Entering Mascato—Population 3006

Main Street was empty. Not remotely as exotic or romantic as Ina described. More of a dust bowl. I drove slowly down a rugged thoroughfare. No cars, no people. Another barking dog chased my Jeep for a few feet, then took off after a stray *gato*. I stopped in front of Mercados Público—a small Mexican market, where an ancient Coca-Cola machine stood out front like a monument to American capitalism. It was definitely no Safeway Supermarket.

I approached a Mexican man who was slumped in a worn-out car seat, with his feet propped up on a crate that had *manzana rojas* stenciled on its side. He was asleep under a sweat-stained New York Mets baseball cap.

"Excuse me, señor. Sorry to interrupt your siesta," I said loud enough to wake the dead, but he didn't budge. I held up my iPhone, displaying a candid photo of Ina I had taken, while she was lounging in her kimono.

"By chance, have you seen this woman? Ina Byers. Dark hair, dark eyes, pale skin, slender build, rough around the edges. A small scar on her knee from where she tripped and fell on a rusty beer can as a child. Ring any bells?"

The man lifted the bill of his cap, looked right through me, then pulled the bill back down over his eyes, shutting out a world he obviously wanted no part of.

"I'll catch you later when you're more focused," I said as if he understood every word I offered. I drove a few blocks over to a small gas station that only had two pumps: *Regular* and *Ethyl*. It was as if I had suddenly time-traveled back to the fifties. However, the price was a different story altogether. This old guy was charging almost four dollars a gallon, in contrast with twenty-seven cents back in the day.

To appear good-natured, I filled my car with three gallons of gas. I showed the attendant, who was wide-awake under his own baseball cap, Ina's photo. He stared at it blankly, then shook his head. I didn't want to be insulting but I felt I had to comment on the town's lack of character.

"No offense, but I expected Mascato, the bullfighting capital of lower Mexico, to have a lot more charm and less—how do you say it in Español?—dirt." He steered me in the right direction, and gave me a rambling lecture in the process.

"You are talking about the town of *Mascota*. This is *not* Mascota, señor—this is *Mascato*. With the O, not the A. You want the A, not the O. We are the O. The A will be much more to your liking—the weather is much better and won't stick to your shirt."

More info than I needed.

The man introduced himself as Alejandro. We shook hands. I kept my name to myself. He then unfolded a map on the hood of the Jeep, and pointed to where we were and where I needed to be. Told me Mascato with the O was a mountain city and far too treacherous to go by car. The train was the best way to travel, not by car, he emphasized. But there was a problem. The train didn't run these days because of an unfortunate landslide onto the tracks, destroying the locomotive and killing the engineer—who was his cousin, Rodrigo. His wish was to be buried alongside the tracks, so he could feel the reverberation of passing trains as they rolled over him. That the townsfolk planned to do, as soon as they locate what's left of his body from under the mass of earth that smothered him.

Anyway, it seemed the safest and only way to travel was to take the local airline, that was coincidentally owned and operated by Alejandro and his second cousin. I could only hope that this family's history of dying on public transportation wasn't a curse. I left my Jeep with Alejandro who charged a nominal fee of fifteen dollars a day for parking. This time I was smart enough not to leave my dad's gun behind. And in my favor, the airline itself was small enough that I didn't have to pass through a metal detector before boarding. Single engine, held maybe ten passengers. I was told by a fellow passenger who kept crossing herself, that if the landing was successful, to tip the pilot a few pesos. This was not an airline tradition I needed to know before takeoff.

An hour and fifteen minutes later, I disembarked. Out front of the Mascota airport, I looked for a taxi or some form of municipal transportation to take me to the nearest motel. All I saw were classic American cars lined up in front. These timeless beauties belonged in a car show, not on the rugged, dusty streets of a Mexican town, being used as taxis. As I headed for a metallic blue four-door '57 Chevy, a Mexican kid, maybe thirteen, wearing jeans and a Doors concert T-shirt, cut me off, shoved a flyer in my face, and began to recite a sales pitch.

"A special price for you today, señor." I grabbed the flyer and without looking at it, folded it, stuck it in my back pocket, then automatically told the kid I wasn't interested in whatever he was selling. Probably a free drink at a strip joint in beautiful downtown Mascota. I climbed into the waiting Chevy. The nervy kid followed me into the back seat. He was relentless, shoving yet another flyer in my face.

"My uncle has the finest, and only, bullfighting school in all of lower Mexico," he bragged. "Many gringos come. The ones who live have great stories to tell."

"Not exactly an illustrious sales pitch, kid," I said, hoping he'd give up and go leap on some other out-of-towner. I turned to the taxi driver and instructed him to take me to a clean, inexpensive motel. The kid didn't take the hint to get out. I gave him a warning. "Kid, scram or I call the policía." The kid, clearly realizing his effort to sell me on the bullfighting school had failed, said something malicious in Spanish, then for emphasis slammed the car door in my face. I didn't want to know what the kid said. Why ruin my first three minutes in Mascota with words of slander and character assassination? I'm pretty sure I heard the word *pendejo* mentioned. Which, according to my driver, meant *asshole*. I'd been called worse. Just not in a romantic language.

I was finally driven to a nearby motel. On the way, my driver offered his name, Hiram Salazar, and his many services—as a tour guide, escort service, bodyguard—that came with a small fee. He also offered me a one-time discounted price on the pair of size ten handmade leather Western boots he was wearing. Only sixty American dollars. Usually you paid two hundred in Miami, he said. He then raised his leg to display the boot. "Fits like the glove. The finest of all the cowhides," he said in his best broken English.

"No need for used Western boots or an escort, but why would I need a bodyguard?" I asked. He was straightforward and did not sugarcoat the very real dangers awaiting tourists walking the streets of Mascota at night. So, to ensure my safety, I decided not to walk the streets at night, and passed on the bodyguard offer.

Ten minutes later, we arrived at the Motel Marbella. Right off the main drag. It had a pool and cable TV. Perfect. I would use neither of those amenities. The room was clean and displayed framed posters of prominent bullfighters: Manolete, Juan Belmonte, and Rafael Gomez Ortega. All of whom were probably highlighted in Hemingway's nonfiction book about the traditions of Spanish bullfighting, *Death in the Afternoon.*

I had just gotten undressed to take a much-needed shower when the kid's flyer fell onto the floor. I picked it up with the intent of trashing it, but something caught my eye. There was this colorful picture of a matador with a flowing cape, darting out of the way of a charging bull. It certainly didn't read like a free drink coupon at the local cantina. It was edgy, on the fringe of being brutal. In bold red lettering it said: *The Cervantes School of Bullfighting. Experience the Artfulness of the Kill.*

I instantly flashed back on Ina promising the same daring adventure. There was a definite theme going on in this quaint town, and I bet Ina Byers was hiding smack in the middle of some Mascota neighborhood.

Six p.m. I was having an early dinner at a local *restaurante* when a young girl, maybe in her mid-twenties, approached and sat down across from me uninvited. She was Latina. Attractive and assertive. She wanted to know if I was interested in a date tonight. *Date* I was sure was code for *party in my room for a nominal fee.* Just like the kid who was offering a special deal for bullfighting lessons, this young lady had a special rate as well. A hundred and twenty-five US dollars for forty-five minutes of companionship. I quickly discovered, she worked for an escort service. So as not to offend her, I responded gracefully, without being insulting.

"Your price seems reasonable, miss . . ."

"Carmen. Call Me Carmen."

"Your price seems very reasonable, Carmen, but I'll have to pass, because . . . well, I'm on a strict budget. Companionship was not a planned activity on my itinerary."

"Too bad. You seem like a person who knows how to treat a young lady like she's a grown woman."

Okay. I'm not stupid. I can detect a come-on when it's thrown in my face. "Look, I'm here on personal business—looking for a friend. Nothing more than looking. No time for extracurricular romps. So you might as well swing over to another table and find someone else who'll take the bait and jump at your offer."

She leaned in and suddenly switched gears.

"Maybe I can help find this friend. A woman, yes? I am most popular in this town. You pay me twenty American dollars an hour. I promise results."

"So you are a working girl as well as a detective. A rather diverse combination." She gave me a blank stare. "Diverse—a mixed bag of careers," I explained. She winked, so I guess she understood my query.

"Si. Yes. I do many things, except sell drugs. I am in bed with many mens, but not ever with the Mexican drug cartel. I give you a 20 percent discount in case you change your mind." She grabbed the palm of my hand and with an ink pen wrote *20% de descuento* on it. No signature. No expiration date. No hint of what it was good for. Sex, detective work, or a car wash? Nothing. "Buenas noches," she said before she hopped over to the next table, confronted another American male with his wife no less, and launched into her pitch all over again.

Needless to say, I found this whole exchange uncomfortable, as well as upsetting that this girl was prostituting herself at such a young age. I finished dinner and headed back to the motel. As I left, my eyes were glued to Carmen as she worked on the American couple, and I accidentally bumped into a busboy who was clearing dishes. I apologized profusely. "No problemo, señor," he said graciously.

He knew where my eyes were looking—at the beautiful Carmen. I did not dispute his keen awareness and moved on to my motel, conveniently located across the street. I stopped to buy a copy of *The News*, a Mexican-English language newspaper, from a vending machine, in case I got bored.

At my door I found Carmen patiently waiting. She must have slipped out the back way and beat me across the street. She was leaning against the jamb, blocking the keyhole. The couple at the other table obviously passed on her offer as well, and she'd come to give me an even more reduced rate.

"You don't give up," I said.

"I come to give back your *billetera*." My what? She held up a wallet. It certainly looked like my wallet. Impossible. I checked my back pocket—a natural reaction—making sure it is in fact gone. It was.

"Where'd you find it?"

"In the hands of the busboy," she claimed.

"He found it? How lucky of him."

"Yes. In your back pocket."

This was baffling. But it seemed this girl had been witness to the lift and confronted the busboy to give it up, or she'd make sure he never worked another job in Mascota. Guess she had that kind of influence in this town.

I was grateful and offered her a small reward. She turned it down. I insisted. She didn't want any money. Said she felt badly that a thief stole from me.

"You are a guest here in my town, on my street," she said, as if she were a spokesperson of the chamber of commerce. "Stealing from our visitors is committing the sin." She crossed herself, taking the incident to another level—as if this was a religious offense.

Anyway, I felt obligated to give her something. At least take her to lunch to show my gratitude. Then it occurred to me how to satisfy the both of us: I took advantage of the 20 percent discount scribbled on my palm and slept with her. A quick beat. Now before you judge me as a crude, despicable person and criticize my morals, take into consideration that I was contributing to the tourist trade of this town; not to mention I'm a red-blooded American guy who sometimes yearns for intimacy. It's not unnatural. It's healthy in fact. Freud, I guarantee, would sit up, take notice, and give me a high five.

The next morning I planned a surprise visit to the Cervantes School to ask a myriad of questions. I called for a cab. Coincidentally or intentionally, the same cab driver, Hiram Salazar, was idling out front in his '57 Chevy, waiting for me. He was in mid-conversation with Carmen. She was leaning in towards the open driver's side window, covertly slipping him a wad of cash. When she saw me coming she gave me a sly wink, then took off in the other direction.

I slid into the cab and wasted no time asking questions that were none of my business, but curiosity got the best of me.

"That girl, Carmen, the one you were just talking with, she approached me . . . " I never finished my sentence.

"She works for me. She is one of my best girls. I may not have mentioned that I am also the manager for some very fine quality señoritas."

I took a pause before accusing him of being a pimp.

"A pimp? That is an old, tired name from the movies. For me, I like being called a manager. I help the girls make a good living. We all need to make a good living. Even the prostitutes, who have kids to feed and rents and medical bills to pay."

"And as the manager you, too, make a profit, correct?"

Choosing not to answer, he kept quiet for a few beats.

"You still want to hire my taxi, señor, or do you prefer to ride in another cab with a, how you might describe . . . less moral driver?"

"I'm good where I sit. Sorry if I insulted you."

"So, you do not want your money back for her service?"

I just shook my head. Why get into a discussion about whether I was satisfied or not? I didn't admit it, but I did like his money back guarantee concept. It put a whole new spin on modern-day prostitution.

Hiram put the car in gear and drove off. "For your information, señor," he said a mile or two down the road, "the girl is working to go to the law school in Mexico City. Wants to be an abogado—an attorney—and defend prostitutes who are treated unfairly. She has a moral purpose for being a prostituta herself." He said this as if he was defending his own daughter.

I understood her goal and respected her motivation—sleeping with numerous men to save illicit incarcerated women. However, when you said it out loud it didn't seem to have the moral uprightness it was meant to have.

⚬

Fifteen miles and twenty-six minutes later we arrived at what appeared to be a ranch. Its acreage was massive, with three large bullrings located right outside my car window. There was a bull in the center of one of the arenas. It had rubber tips on the ends of its horns. He was old and pissed off. His snort was weak. His stomp, decrepit. The snot from his nose, disgusting.

Inside the ring with him was a nervous young Japanese student being tutored by a Mexican instructor. I couldn't help but notice that the instructor was also old and decrepit. But in contrast to the bull, he had no visible signs of a snort or snot dripping from his nose.

The student stood mid-ring, his cape positioned off his hip, to one side of his body. I watched intently as the bull charged with all the speed it could muster in its shaky, arthritic legs. The ground beneath his feet rumbled. The student attempted to make a pass but misjudged his position. Consequently, the bull plunged its rubber horns into the student's chest, sending him flying into the air; he landed on his ass and settled in the wet spot where the old bull had taken a desperately needed leak. I'm no expert, but it was obvious somewhere during the study course, this kid didn't pay attention. The veteran instructor stepped in and distracted the bull. The student rose to his feet, brushed himself off and limped out of the ring, embarrassed. He passed by me, and I couldn't help but give him some reassurance: "Better luck next time." The kid didn't care for my comforting words and told me *to go fuck myself* using his best English.

Then from behind me, I heard a deep voice with a thick accent, combining Spanish with his own shape of English.

"There are no lucks in fighting the bulls. Only the skill and *la tecnica correcta*. The boy, he makes the wrong moves. He will be very sore, yes, but worth the pain to accomplish *el arte perfecto*." Translation: the perfect artistry.

I turned and found a fifty-something man. Overweight. His belly hung over his belt. Unshaven. Unpolished. Chewing an unlit cigar. He offered me his hand, saying, "I am Rafael Cervantes. This is my school, which I built with my two only hands." We shook. His hand was rough. Probably had never touched a skin moisturizer in his fifty-plus years.

"Yeah. Your school. I get it. Impressive. Jake Reilly."

"Come, I show you around and find you a nice cape in your size."

"It's okay. I'm just browsing," I said firmly. He put his arm around me, opened the gate to the bullring, and started to lead me inside. I told him that I was here looking for a woman, nothing else. Mentioning a woman seemed to arouse his juices.

"Ahhh, yes. Plenty of womens in Mexico, señor. I know many of them." I showed him the iPhone photo of Ina, hoping he recognized her. He studied it, squinting, rubbing his unshaven chin, to help summon his memory.

"Her name is Ina Byers. Very *bonita*. She may have taken a few lessons. She loves the kill."

Our conversation was interrupted by the thunder of approaching hooves. We both turned to see the decrepit old bull charging. He eluded the old instructor and was barreling directly towards the open gate where we were positioned. Rafael was calm but also sensed danger. He instructed me not to move any muscles.

"Do not show the bull that you fear him. He knows the smell of fear. He knows if you are a weak-minded coward."

I could only think how insightful he was for a bull. At the last possible moment, Rafael removed his leather jacket, stepped in front of me, and used it as a cape, passing the bull with a flourish. I thought, how very coincidental—this was the same prudent move Ina made with her blouse, challenging the Dobermans. Who knows, maybe this Rafael could give me answers. Once the old bull was safely returned to its enclosure, I showed Rafael Ina's photo again. This time he adopted a more lecherous point of view.

"Si. Very beautiful. Very much a woman. Fiery."

"Very fiery. Then you know her?"

"Not as much as I'd like. I must confess, I would very much like to have the dirty sex with her."

This made me extremely uncomfortable. But he didn't stop making tactless, lewd remarks.

"And you, señor. I am sure you have these urges, same as me. It's like a poison in our guts. To mount the fiery womens from behind till they squeal like pigs. Yes?"

"Yes. Maybe. No."

The perverted route this conversation took flustered me. And then out of the same warped mouth came an appreciation of my dilemma.

"Hotel El Paradiso. She is there."

"Are you sure?" I asked, almost choking on the words.

"Si, señor. Señorita Byers. You will find her having lunch in the courtyard at *mediolia*." Translation: in the noontime.

I asked how he knew this. He said it is his job to know what went on in Mascota. "I am also the mayor, señor," he confided.

So, my instincts were right. She fled to the safety of Mexico. Grateful, I gave Rafael a manly hug, which he perceived as a gesture that we were now the best of friends, and that he could open up and share his personal life with me.

"Maybe later, after you attend to your business with Señorita Byers, we get drunk on tequila—me and you—and toast the womens who have tasted our pleasure," he said with a sly grin.

I just gave him a friendly nod and smiled rather than make a commitment to pay tribute to my sexual conquests—which were few, and would not in any way be enough to lead to a drunken stupor.

204

At exactly noon I found myself in the passenger seat of Hiram's '57 Chevy. We're headed for the Hotel El Paradiso. Traffic was light. But my stomach was heavy. I was both tense anxious to confront Ina, who I anticipated would be defensive, nervy, and not at all blown away that I had caught up with her. I didn't forget about Ray. Unless they split the money and went their separate ways, which I doubted, Ray was still a key factor to contend with. My instincts told me that he was close by, making sure the half-million dollars was not far from his grasp.

I shifted in my seat. Hiram noticed my uneasiness and suggested I needed to relax.

"By showing that you are the coward will only hurt your chances of having the upper hands," he said through his rugged accent.

"Was it F. Scott Fitzgerald who said: *Revenge is a dish best served cold*?"

Hiram, not having a clue who I was referencing, let out a boisterous laugh as if the quote was humorous.

"She has no idea whose head she's messing with," I said. She'll never get the chance to underestimate me again. I've got a lot of pent-up anger and I intend to use it."

This time Hiram conveyed a less complicated opinion.

"I think maybe this woman, she has you by the cojones." He grabbed his crotch, making it clear he was referring to his balls. I couldn't argue with his evaluation. I wanted to, but his perception was probably spot-on. I needed a drink. Something stronger than a beer. As luck would have it, Hiram had a bottle of tequila stashed in the glove box. In this country, tequila was the antidote for whatever ailed you. Fever, snakebite, women troubles. I couldn't help but notice that hidden behind the bottle was a *pistola*. I reacted with wide-eyed surprise. He sensed my trepidation.

"For the passengers who ask for *los guardaespaldas proteccion* and desire to walk in the night," he said. "You have a gun, señor? For the protection? In Mexico, a gun is like having the benefit of a larger cock."

I wasn't about to go through the whole back story about how I have one—a gun, not a large cock—and all the details of why I brought it with me, and how I left it hidden inside an air conditioning vent in my motel room. I instead chose my words carefully to illustrate my position on owning a weapon . . .

"A gun? No. I have no gun. I'm not a fan of guns. Besides, I come from a fairly small town. Not that a small town doesn't have its own set of problems. Just don't need a gun to solve them."

Hiram, I could tell, didn't buy my small-town logic. Didn't matter; this conversation was over, and it was time I started drinking to build my confidence, and to calm the anger just enough so that I don't seem like an out of control lunatic.

I took two (or was it three?) healthy gulps of the tequila before we rolled up in front of the hotel. I have to say, the Spanish architecture was four-star. Pretty sure it was in the Spanish Colonial Revival Style. I slugged down a fourth sip, just in case the first three weren't effective. Pretty sure I was prepared to do battle. Hiram decided to hang back and make sure I didn't suddenly become *el cobarde*—the coward.

I hopped out of the car, nearly falling over from the effects of the tequila. Dizzy and hot, I slowly entered the lobby of the Hotel El Paradiso. It had quaint, traditional Spanish decor. Mediterranean wall sconces. Traditional rustic furniture with tooled leather backs. Wall to wall, terracotta Spanish tile flooring. I looked around, but I had no place to direct my anger because the lobby was empty. A ghost town of a foyer.

My focus was suddenly drawn to the courtyard.

It was laced with blooming bougainvillea. A bubbling fountain. Shafts of soft afternoon light fell on a wedding in progress. A priest, dressed in his usual garb, stood before a man wearing sunglasses and a woman in a white peasant dress. Their backs were to me. I supposed the hotel staff, consisting of the manager, the bellboy, and the cook, made up the wedding party. Wait . . . I suddenly noticed a familiar face among them—Carmen. Was I surprised? Not really. This girl got around. She was standing next to the bride. I speculated that this was one of those rare occasions when a steady John had fallen in love with a hooker and taken her to the altar. Carmen served as the maid of honor, sending off one of her *prostituta* peers to live a legit life in suburbia. Hey, my unconventional imagination is simply working overtime.

The tequila was finally doing its job. I nearly tripped as I inched closer to get a better view, but making sure I didn't disturb the proceedings. And then, without warning, I got lightheaded. Thought I was going to pass out, so I leaned against a four-foot vase for support. It rocked back and forth and nearly toppled. The noise interrupted the solemn event and all heads turned collectively in my direction. I managed to elude the stares by hiding behind a pillar. And then, as if I was watching a home movie, I saw the players' faces with the utmost clarity. I rubbed my eyes and blinked several times just to make sure this wasn't another one of those illusions I had been experiencing on the blacktop. It wasn't. It was definitely Ina and Ray reciting their wedding vows. A fucking nightmare of a scene. It felt as if my heart was about to pound right through my chest.

I finally got up the nerve to take a better look and peeked out from behind the stone pillar like some jealous lover. A very bad idea. The sight of Ina and Ray looking blissfully happy devastated me. This was the one thing that every man didn't want to be faced with—the ultimate rejection by a woman. This was what Dave meant when he said he was afraid to ask out my mother for fear she'd turn him down and marry someone else. I felt an overwhelming wave of abandonment and I hated it.

Ina's feminine intuition must've kicked in because she suddenly turned in my direction and saw me staring from behind the pillar. I tried to look into her eyes and meet her gaze but I had neither the strength nor the courage to do it. So, I distanced myself and slowly backed away. But not before I vomited a river of tequila in that huge vase. A class act I wasn't.

An hour later, I was in the middle of packing and getting ready to checkout of the Motel Marbella. Couldn't wait to put this town in my rearview. It had brought me nothing but more tense moments and a habitual hatred for travel. I grabbed my dad's gun from inside the A/C vent and quietly headed down to the front desk. The clerk greeted me and said there was no charge for my stay. My jaw dropped. I couldn't understand why I was given such preferential treatment. His explanation was vague.

"*Los saludos de el director.*" Translation: compliments of the manager. Then, using his best English vernacular: "You earn the free stay. *Felicidades.*" For emphasis, he ripped up the bill in front of me like confetti and let it float on top of the desk.

I paused before commenting: "While I appreciate the gesture, señor, my stay here was not by any means free. It was a costly mistake on my part, showing my face here in Mascota. Besides the usual travel expenses, I paid the price big time. I learned an expensive lesson about finally calling it quits and throwing in the towel. I'm not a quitter. I've always carried out any risky undertakings to the fullest extent, but in this case . . ." I lifted my arms in the air. "I surrender unconditionally."

The clerk, noticeably glassy-eyed, just nodded and smiled as if he understood what I was trying to convey. I bid him an *adios*, then went outside into the warm sun. It felt good that I was leaving this journey behind me. The trip served no purpose, but what did I expect? An open arms welcome from two people who manipulated me and profited from my keen mind and my ability to grapple with complex problems? Was I that naive? I would say not. By getting married they had, in effect, joined forces and shown their contempt for me, branding me utterly worthless. That was probably the last straw. No, it *was* the last straw. *Motherfucking cocksuckers!* I screamed that last phrase loud enough that heads turned from all directions, and a few dogs barked as if they actually understood the insult.

⌘

Twenty minutes later, I was slumped in the back seat of Hiram Salazar's 1957 Chevy, speeding along Main Street and heading for the airport. My obsession for Ina Byers was no mystery to Hiram. Emotionally, I was hiding nothing. Funny thing was, he didn't feel bad for me. For him, losing a woman was part of life. It wasn't the end of the world. Women come and go. Some relationships are grand, some are ordinary, while most others are morally wrong.

"You have to accept defeat or you suffer and die," he said. "It's that simple. If you choose to continue to breathe, then you find yourself another woman to take her place and fill the closets that your last woman left empty."

That was his philosophy. Empty closets refilled with women's clothing. If only it were that simple; it would make all relationships a lot less painful when they're over.

209

Before dropping me off, Hiram, in a soft, almost embarrassed tone, announced that he had paid for my motel room. Why he decided it was important for me to know this, I'm uncertain. Recognition, maybe? Or was this just a preamble before mentioning that he actually owned the Motel Marbella? Yes, I was surprised, especially if it were true. But why would he lie? With his right hand to God, he swore he inherited it from his mother, Marbella. I asked myself the obvious question: why would a guy who runs his own motel drive a taxi and pimp for whores? I suppose the best answer is: *why not?*

It was windy at the airport, an indication the flight would be dangerous and bumpy. Just as I exited the taxi, the young kid who shoved a flyer in my face before once again accosted me. This time it advertised a 20 percent discount on salsa lessons.

"My sister, she is *la instructora*. You will be *el experto* in two hours, for only six dollars American," he claimed.

"I'm leaving town, kid. I have no use for dance lessons where I'm going. Back to the place where I feel the most comfortable—Back to *Pussyville*."

CHAPTER FOURTEEN

It was 5:30 a.m. when I crossed the Bakersfield city limits. It felt cathartic. So as not to attract any attention, I drove way under the speed limit, crawling through the city, and headed for the diner's final resting place. It was eerie as well as calming, being back here with so many fond memories banging around in my head. The not so fond memories, although few, seemed to be less disturbing compared to what I'd been through in the past few weeks. At least my Jeep was in the same condition as I'd left it when I'd picked it up at the Mexican market in Mascato with the O. Alejandro, the attendant, asked me how my trip was. I paid him the ransom for getting my vehicle back without comment.

I stood motionless, staring at the charred remains. Someone had spray-painted the words *burned just like their burgers* on one of the surviving planks of wood. I found it to be a clever proclamation. Within a few minutes, I heard the wail of a siren in the distance, getting louder as it came closer.

My tiptoeing into town made no difference. Somebody who was up early walking their dog, or jogging, probably noticed me and called the cops. I thought about running. But why? I had come back for the sole purpose of taking whatever punishment was handed to me for committing the crime. Leaning against my fender, slathered with gray primer, I waited patiently for the law to arrive, arrest me, and read me my Miranda rights. The sirens were almost on top of me. Odd, but I wasn't that fearful. If anything, I just felt a sense of failure. In a matter of a few hours, I'd have a police record. My face would be plastered across police websites as a convicted felon. I felt sure they were going to interrogate me, until I cracked and revealed the whereabouts of Ray Astemendi and Ina Byers, and my involvement in the Holy Trinity Robbery. Come what may, I wasn't about to give up Ina, no matter what strong-arm tactics they planned to use on me. Ray, however, was a whole different story. I just might tell them what they wanted to know and help send him to prison. But I'm getting ahead of myself.

The police cruiser finally reached me. I swallowed hard, and wiped the beads of sweat leaking from my brow and upper lip. However, that whole feeling of hopelessness quickly changed to confusion when the cruiser zoomed past me. Its flashing lights and blaring siren faded in the opposite direction. Was I no longer a threat? Were there no 9-1-1 calls or meddlesome locals walking the neighborhood, anxious to turn me in?

It actually bothered me that I wasn't apprehended. I specifically came back to ease my guilt. I phoned Parker, to tell him I was back and how I planned to turn myself in at the sheriff's office before they sent a posse out after me. After five rings, he answered with a bright "Hey, I was just thinking about you"—apparently having read the caller ID.

"Yeah, it's me. I'm back in town. Went by the burnt-out diner and now I'm going to the cops to surrender. Arms skyward. Waving a white flag in the air."

"Why? What stupid stunt did you pull now?"

"Same stunt—arson. Time to come in from the cold."

Parker then relieved my guilt. Told me I was exonerated. That Richard Salvetti, the homeless guy, revealed that it was nothing but a terrible accident due to the flip of a lit match. Told the detective and the arson squad assigned to the case how I left the diner in his charge while I traveled for a few months. Even showed the cops the diner keys as proof. Said if they needed his written statement he was living the good life in Tent City.

I found it incredible that they even believed his story. He could've just found the diner keys in the rubble, and made up the rest. Don't get me wrong; I wasn't complaining that I was found innocent and that all charges were dropped. I breathed normally for the first time in weeks. It just took me by surprise, and I was trying to control the exhilaration, so I didn't act as though I was pleased that I wasn't caught.

I could tell that Parker suddenly shielded his phone with his hand before speaking in a whisper. "Look, I'd ask you to stay with me, but I'm in a relatively new relationship and I haven't unpacked all my stuff just yet. We're still in the trial period, so a long-term situation is not exactly set in motion."

Parker didn't do relationships. He did one-week stints, then ran, or was told to take a hike. That's a nicer version of how most women asked him to exit the bedroom and their lives. So I was surprised to learn he had moved in with this girl that he met at the car wash: Denise Hicks, a former classmate who now made her living as a court reporter. I understood his apprehension. The last thing he needed was me making what sounded like an already stressful situation intolerable. Denise interrupted the conversation, spitting orders with a drill sergeant's gruffness.

"If he's really desperate, he can stay with us this one night. On the couch. No pets. Last thing I need is urine stains on the carpet."

I passed. Said I'd be more comfortable staying in my car or getting a motel room until I landed on my feet again. Wasn't sure if her urine stain comment was directed towards the possibility of a pet or me.

"I'm here if you need anything, buddy," Parker said before clicking off. I gave this relationship a flimsy two weeks before it collapsed. Her demeanor, especially the *no pets* proviso, made her seem a tad domineering. Parker didn't do well with overbearing women. The intimidation factor usually plugged in right after the first unfulfilled early morning sexual performance, when, after only two minutes, he'd begin to wilt inside her before going entirely slack. Not his fault that he was in a hurry to please himself.

Now that I was off the hook for causing the fire, I had a decision to make. The diner itself was history, but I was still a property owner. I could borrow and rebuild. But why? I hated the restaurant business. Didn't need that kind of pressure anymore.

For now, I opted to clean up the rubble, then with the money I had left over, rent a small camper, roll it onto the patch of diner dirt, and call it home until I could relocate to a much safer, quieter climate. I wasn't out of the woods yet with the Lubbock police, and probably now the Feds, who surely had launched a vigorous investigation into the death of Hal, the security guard.

In the back of my scrambled mind, I anticipated it was only a matter of time before they connected me with the whole Emily Easterday con. Looking over my shoulder would become a persistent twitch.

Two months later I was flat broke. I had used up all my cash and maxed out my credit cards, using them for food, electricity, and property taxes. To avoid arousing any suspicion, I had to maintain the outward appearance that I was still an upstanding citizen. The smart move would be to sell the land and get the fuck out. Or at least sell it back to the bank, take a loss, and use the small profit to buy a thatched hut on a cheap Caribbean island and write my novel. God knows I had a lot of story to spin these days.

Meanwhile, I just needed to get out and stretch my legs, and find work. Nothing complicated or strenuous. Something that would entail the least possible amount of responsibility in my life.

The following morning, I walked into Milt's Coffee Shop—a one-time fierce competitor who had always tried to undercut our prices, even if meant he'd lose money. Anything to piss my father off. The feud lasted until Milt had a nervous breakdown, which drove him to therapy and a life of meditation to curb the anxiety and soothe his bleeding ulcer.

I spent my last five dollars on a cup of coffee and a slice of an apple butter Danish ring. I was convinced that there was no food more overrated than Danish—a pastry that seemed stale even when served fresh.

There I sat, alone in a booth, racking my brain to find employment. Scanning the want ads was a depressing task. Every fucking job opening was related to the damn computer industry or nursing. They all demanded you had experience. I had crap. I was an unpublished author, a former diner denizen, and a thief. No employer clamored for those special skills. Frustrated, I started to circle an ad that was looking for an exterminator trainee. Depressing. This was what my life had become—applying for a job learning how to murder vermin. This didn't agree with my stomach, which began to tighten up in knots. Realizing there was no relief in sight, I took my frustration out on the apple Danish and smashed it with my fist hard. Very loud. Very scary for some. My rage caused a lot of people to flinch, and brought forth an employee carrying a large stainless spatula. Apparently I was about to be eighty-sixed from Milt's Coffee Shop. As the figure got closer I realized it was not the bouncer but Helen, my former waitress, dressed in a white double-breasted chef jacket. She was noticeably distressed, but even though we hadn't seen each other in a good three months, she was as motherly—and brutally frank—as ever.

"I don't think I've ever seen you this mad before, Jakey," she said, sitting down with a grunt. "Life must be treating you cruelly."

"Yes. Cruelly. What are you doing here?"

"Life has also treated me poorly. Or should I just say, it's put me in the poor house. I needed the money and Milt needed a chef. Bills had stacked up. Plus, you can't send a daughter to college without cash. Living the American dream with debt hanging over your head is a rough road to travel. Don't tell me you came in here because you had the overwhelming desire to kill a perfectly good Danish? I never thought you'd show your face in this town again."

I told her the whole sordid story. Didn't leave out a word or a syllable. Everything that was true, everything that was criminal and heinous. How I witnessed a fat man fall to his death during an uplifting sermon by a beautiful but fake lady evangelist. How I had been the drugged patsy in a heist that went horribly wrong. How I had chased Ina Byers, my enduring crush/professional bad girl, clear down to Mascota with the A (not to be confused with Mascato with the O), and watched in revulsion and disbelief as she tied the knot with Ray Astemendi, my nemesis/professional shit stain.

She softened. "Well, you gave it your best shot. The girl turned out to be a misfit. Not your fault she's a con artist and a murderess. Now what? No job. You're broke. You're living in a trailer the size of a deck of cards, and your clothes need to be washed, or even better, burned. But in your case, you should stay away from matches. Pardon my candor, but you're not in any condition to take on a job, let alone look for one. You look like a bum and smell like a sewer rat."

"Thank you. I needed that kind of motivational speech to pull myself up by my bootstraps and rebuild my character."

I mentioned my long-term plan to sell the land and use the money to leave the country and rediscover my priorities—and myself.

"Sure, but in the meantime you need to survive."

She made me a decent breakfast and loaned me enough money to buy pants and a shirt. In addition, she phoned a friend and three days later I got a clerk job at the local Food Barn Supermarket. Not exactly a career-building position, but a cut above being an exterminator trainee. Also, working at a supermarket was perfect for my needs. I had access to food and toilet paper. All the necessities to stay alive. Uncomplicated. No worries about making sure my dad wasn't in his pajamas, yelling *incoming* every so often when he imagined we were being attacked by Vietcong rebels.

That morning I made a promise to Helen: when I sold the property, I'd make sure she was compensated for all that she had done for my dad and me.

"Not necessary. Just clean up your act and get the fuck away from here, before the authorities catch up to you," she said, almost in tears.

Always watching my back. Always thinking of my well- being. What would have become of me without Helen Mayfield's constant devotion to my pitiful cause?

On my first day, wearing a new pair of stiff pants and a crisp white JCPenney button-down shirt that itched, I squirmed under the scrutiny of a supervisor who was evaluating me. Andrea Miller. Middle forties. A makeup junky that also bathed in cheap perfume. In all honesty, it was depressing returning to Bakersfield. Especially under these circumstances. Running into customers who once ate at the diner and wanted to know what happened to my life. Why hadn't I written the Great American Novel as I always proclaimed I would? Needless to say, I was disappointed in myself, as well. What happened to that ambition? Seemed like it just suddenly vanished. I lost the will to be creative. Maybe it would return. Probably not.

So, in a head-scratching moment, I raised the question—why would anyone stay in Bakersfield? I'd run across many of the same faces since I'd been back. People I grew up with, who never had the energy to leave. It was a town that bred complacency through cable TV and those damn membership warehouse stores that offered a tub of ketchup the size of an oil drum.

An elderly lady, eighty or so, stepped up to buy her daily groceries. I ran them over the scanner. Bread, cheese, vodka, Greek yogurt, oatmeal, orange juice. She had the ingredients for a screwdriver and was fooling nobody by hiding the booze between the cheese and the yogurt.

"You enjoy your work, young man?" she slurred in a sweet voice. I just shrugged because the truth was, I hated this job but it served a purpose. She continued: "It's important that you like your work. Life is too short to be saddled in a job that makes you hate the world and the people in it, like the damn fascists, don't you think?"

I looked up at her. Her eyes were strained and bloodshot. Her face was troweled with pancake makeup to hide the wrinkles and crevasses she'd acquired over the years.

"You have an easier question, ma'am?" I said. "Like, what's my political affiliation, or how much do I weigh? I ask only because I'm in no mood to get into an in-depth conversation about whether I enjoy being a supermarket cashier making a minimum hourly wage. But I'll answer you just the same, because part of this menial job is to have a back and forth exchange, no matter how trivial, with the customer."

I leaned in and whispered: "I hate this job with a fucking passion. But it's serving a purpose. Keeps me connected with reality, and also works as a reminder that we shouldn't take our lives for granted. Because as soon as you walk out that door, you could be hit by a bus and die a tragic death and never get to drink your vodka and eat your cheese ever again. Have a wonderful day, and thanks for shopping at the Food Barn."

"You are one wretched fuck," she maliciously responded.

"I appreciate the review on my very first day," I said. "Concise and honest." She slowly and methodically shuffled towards the automatic doors that, if she were not careful, could damage this old woman critically. I entertained a fleeting vision of the carnage, and smiled wickedly.

The job was already turning on me, and I was sick of this banter. I was ready to call it quits and throw in the apron when the conveyor belt slowly sent two bottles of tequila my way, breaking the tension. Checking out one more customer would not kill me. As I begin to scan the liquor, I heard a familiar voice cry out: "And a pack of Sherman Naturals."

I slowly looked up and my suspicions were correct; it was familiar all right—too familiar. Ina Byers was grinning back at me. She looked in bad need of sleep, but still managed to look appealing. Her presence rattled me a bit, and in my distraction I found it hard to function, until Andrea, the training supervisor, elbowed me in the ribs, saying, "Don't forget to ask how the customer is doing."

I became angry, loud, and tried my best to hide the fact I was clenching my jaw, my fists, and the cheeks of my ass.

"Oh, I don't have to ask. I know exactly how she's doing. She's doing just fine since she came into over a half million dollars of stolen money. Am I right, Miss Byers? Or should I say, Mrs. Astemendi?" My sudden outburst caught the attention of every shopper within a hundred feet. Heads turned. Mouths dropped open like trap doors. They were all anticipating her cussing me out—calling me an impertinent fucking sonofabitch. Instead, she put on a brave face and said: "Ray took off with all the money." She looked as if I should feel bad for her and forgive her for cheating me and treating me like her car—*a piece of shit.*

"No cash? Then will you be paying with a credit card? A card that isn't maxed out would be preferred," I said flatly. There was a pause. Shoppers were again anxiously awaiting her reply. Even Andrea, that paragon of efficiency and propriety, was agog.

"Look, I thought maybe I could apologize and explain things."

My turn to react. My throat was dry. The corners of my mouth had that sticky white stuff (like Elmer's Glue) that gathers when you're parched and can hardly speak. So, to slake my thirst, I opened one of the bottles of tequila that were still positioned on the conveyor belt, took a long swig, then addressed the crowd.

"I have to be brutally honest about my feelings—the contempt I have for this woman is excessive. In a word, she's a fucking bitch. I don't apologize for my unrefined outburst. Believe me, it's a well-founded designation."

"For the record, I wasn't treated exactly fairly either," Ina said, grabbing the bottle and taking her own healthy gulp. It had become a supermarket drinking game. By now most activity in the place had stopped, as all eyes were riveted on us, watching the drama unfold.

"Oh, please spare me the sanctimonious, exploited girlfriend slash wife, hearts and flowers speech," I said.

Ina suddenly moved closer to me, and whispered, trying to keep the conversation somewhat private. She rattled on with energy. I just listened, skeptical of her story.

"The guy is mental, okay? It was always his idea to rip you off. I knew if I didn't go to Mexico with him, I'd end up in a shallow grave in some border town. I married him to make him think he could trust me." She went on to tell me that as a cover, Ray found work as a security guard in a newly opened Indian casino just outside of Mascota.

"Knowing Ray, he was planning a way to rip off the casino," Ina continued. "A dangerously insane goal that I wanted no part of. So, after a few weeks, I got up the nerve to split. Without the money. Took that joyride of a plane back to safer ground. Got my car at the airport and days later, here I stand, a victim just like you."

Andrea, found an opening and jumped in. "Do I need to call the manager?"

"No need, this will all be over soon," I said. "I first need to call her a liar and a cheat just one more time before my thirst for revenge is satisfied."

I take another swallow of tequila. Then another. My behavior did not go over well with the store manager, who slunked over and threatened to fire me on sight.

I appreciated his warning, pointing out that I wasn't just drinking for the sake of drinking. I was drinking to get drunk and rid myself of the bullshit that this *woman* was throwing at me. He fired me on the spot, a move met with storewide applause. But it didn't stop the rancor.

Ina tried to convince me that her pointed reference to Mascota—the bullfighting capital of lower Mexico, and the town where she wanted her ashes scattered—was intentional. A clue for me to follow. "Why would I mention that if I planned on ditching you?"

"Okay, yeah. My mistake. You're one of the good guys, taking my side," I said with tremendous sarcasm. "And your clue was perfect. I found you, and where did it get me? Capriciously rejected, and now ringing up toilet paper and Cocoa Puffs in the center of *Pussyville*." Calling Bakersfield *Pussyville* did not go over well with the locals. The applause became a resounding outpouring of *boos* and *fuck yous*.

I turned to the protesting audience and directed my contempt at them.

"Here's what I know for certain, people—that Ina Byers and all her drama is finally out of my system. And I can say without an iota of regret—fuck her. Fuck her duplicitous boyfriend, Ray. And fuck the bogus evangelical preacher Emily Easterday and her synthetic tabernacle."

With that said, Ina gave me a parting smack of bitterness.

"Boy, did I have you pegged wrong. You're not as smart as I thought, Sharp Guy." She then tossed a handful of cash onto the counter, gulped what was left of the open bottle of tequila, grabbed the second bottle, stuffed her precious Shermans in her leather bag, then sprinted towards the front door, flipping me off as she exited. All that without a pause or taking a single breath. It was a sight to behold.

"Well, that was a fun stroll down memory lane. And may I point out that the only thing good that came out of our so-called relationship was the sex. She was a standout fuck, in case anyone is curious." Did I regret making that comment? Not really.

Having been fired, and now half shit-faced, I turned to the manager and supervisor to bid them a fond fucking farewell, and tell them that paying me for half a day's work was not necessary. It was at this point that the room started to spin and I threw up in a grocery bag filled with perishables. The customer—and all who witnessed this display of cascading vomit—retched in unison. When I came up for air, I noticed Ina's Mustang pulling out of the parking lot. I rushed out through the automatic doors and chased after the aged pony car as it pulled into traffic onto Chester Avenue.

CHAPTER FIFTEEN

A desperate pursuit ensued. Me on foot. Still juiced; feeling the effects of the tequila was not in my favor. The task at hand: negotiating a series of unanticipated obstacles. The first being a four-foot hedge of rose bushes I vaulted over, nearly falling head first into the prickly patch. Then I found myself maneuvering around an abandoned couch that some asshole had inexplicably dumped in the middle of the street. It was a treacherous obstacle course of inanimate objects.

Continuing at a rapid pace, the Mustang made a sharp turn on 24th street. I detoured through the park, raced past an empty public pool, reappearing on the street an instant after the Mustang whizzed by, going at least forty. Now gasping for breath and getting that feeling I might puke again, I found myself smack in the middle of the intersection. Horns honked; brakes squealed; a street sweeper barely missed me. Undeterred, I cut down another street—14th, I think—and ran past an abandoned movie theater. I had to stop to catch my breath or I'd faint dead away. A moment in time—I recalled going to this theater and making out with Melinda Miles in the back row. It was 1989. I was thirteen. *Goodfellas* was on the bill. She thought it was too violent and had feverish nightmares about Joe Pesci. She never went out with me again.

Suddenly, in my peripheral, I spotted the Mustang heading towards Union Cemetery on Potomac Avenue. I geared up and resumed the chase. I surmised, but I could have it wrong, that she was going to visit her grandmother's grave. I kept the car in my sights as best I could. After no more than a hundred yards, my calf started to cramp up. I massaged it as I ran. This did nothing but aggravate it even more. But somehow I managed to maintain a lively pace.

Up ahead, big trouble loomed—a railroad crossing. And as luck would have it, a freight train was barreling in the direction I needed to cross. I was now limping like a wounded animal, hoping to jump the tracks before the train crossed the intersection and killed me, which would regrettably end my pursuit. The engineer noticed the potentially dangerous situation and went into emergency mode. He hit the whistle several times, the screech echoing like an opera singer trying to reach high C. I rejected the warning and continued to try and beat a freight train travelling at a good clip, about 50 miles an hour. Sure, I could've stopped and waited for the train to pass like a sensible person, but no, I was determined because the length of the train easily reached a mile, and I would have lost sight of the Mustang if I stopped and waited. You see this kind of thrill-seeking performed in movies, but in real life you're not on the edge of your seat, but on the cusp of serious disaster. Flattened like a crêpe suzette. The train was just about on top of me when I jumped in front of it. It was fucking dangerously close as I felt the air stream of the cars whoosh by, and me clearing the train and the tracks by just a few feet. I tripped and fell on the other side of the tracks, skinning my knees on the loose roadside gravel. My new pants were torn, and my kneecaps were bleeding. But that stupid stunt didn't discourage me. I slowly rose and limped onto the cemetery grounds, able to spring in front of and block Ina's Mustang as it pulled into the parking lot. She slammed on the brakes. Both my hands rested flat on her hood. It was hot, and my hands were nearly blistered by the heat of the engine. I took a much-needed pause, not really to rest, but to contemplate how I had made it to this point. I was gasping for air, my knees were bloodied, and now I had a hot, sharp pain on my left side. I was a mess. The only upshot—I had sobered up.

I looked at Ina, who was staring back at me, shaking her head in disbelief. A beat, and then she casually rolled down her window.

"You some sort of lunatic?"

I violently pounded on the roof of her car, the same way I destroyed the Danish. This helped release a lot of frustration, but not enough. I lost it . . .

"It goes way, way beyond lunacy. It's more like demented, masochistic, indescribably self-destructive, might-as-well-slit-something behavior." I took a breath. "I was minding my own business, leading a bland life, until you had to come back. And, okay, yes, I'm crazy about you. No one in his right mind would go to this much trouble to win over someone as bitter and twisted as you. Would somebody in this cemetery, who's not dead, like to tell me why?"

Ina started to answer, but I stopped her. "No. No talking. You don't get to offer a reason. You've said and done enough." Another deep breath. And as I was about to rant even more, Ina leaned out the open window, grabbed me by my crisp white shirt collar, pulled me towards her, and had the audacity to kiss me long and hard, which threw me totally off-balance, interrupting my seething train of thought, and rendered a calm stillness within me.

❧

In less than a half an hour, we found ourselves partially naked at the deep end of the empty public swimming pool. How we got there was a mystery. Finishing off the second bottle of tequila had muddled our minds. So trying to make sense of this was impossible. But neither of us cared. The important thing was that we were fully naked and enjoying the moment.

Ina was leaning against the pool wall, her bare legs wrapped around my waist. We were vocal, moaning and screaming out sexual instructions to each other. It was a three-ring circus of intense copulation. I wished the shoppers at the Food Barn were here to witness that I was right about Ina Byers being a person of exceptional sexual ability.

An hour later, or maybe it was only ten minutes that seemed like an hour, we fell asleep in each other's arms, in the shallow end. We were rudely awakened not only by the sunrise blasting in our eyes like a laser beam, but also the annoying grind of a bulldozer chewing up chunks of cement, then spitting them out into a waiting dump truck. This particular morning marked the beginning of a huge city demolition project. In the abandoned pool's place they were building a multi-million dollar shopping center. We were the last to ever use the public pool, albeit not for its original purpose.

While Ina chauffeured me back to the Food Barn and my car, I reflected on two things. One, why didn't I chase her in my car; and two, why did I chase her at all? What was I expecting to get out of this once I caught up to her? My share of the money? The truth? An apology? Sex? Yes on all those impulses.

A sudden slam on the brakes hurled me forward and shook my body pretty hard. The seat belt nearly decapitated me.

"What the fuck was that all about?"

"A dark blue sedan just ran the red light."

"Not a big shock. Most of the people in this town are unaware there are rules of the road. Their minds are usually in another galaxy, contemplating the never-ending dilemma—how to break off their marriage or relationship in a civil, non-violent manner."

The Mustang sat in the middle of the intersection, idling. Cars were honking for it to move. She didn't react. I turned to her. Her complexion was pale. White as paper.

"You okay?"

"No. I'm sick to my stomach."

"Pull over, I'll drive."

"That blue car. The driver—it was Ray."

"What are you talking about?"

I found this to be impossible. It was a mistake. A look-alike. A doppelgänger.

"Not a mistake. It was definitely him. I'd know that profile in the dark." Her confidence was unshakable.

I suddenly got cold and clammy. If she was right, her safety was in jeopardy. Perhaps even mine, if he found us together, and his jealousy kicked in. I couldn't live this way in constant fear of this psycho. Something had to be done. What? Who knows? But something impactful. Something final.

By now, there was a symphony of horns honking incessantly. On top of that, motorists were yelling obscenities as they maneuvered around us like an island in the pavement.

"You better pull over," I suggested in a calm voice. She drove to the curb, turned off the engine, then lowered her head into her chest.

"The glove box. My Shermans. Light me one, please." Please? She never said please. The tension must be at a historically high magnitude. I lit her a cigarette and handed it over. She took a drag and exhaled, only this time there was no perfect smoke ring, just a thick cloud that hung over us like a pall. I began questioning her at a rapid pace. I couldn't get the words out fast enough.

"What the hell is he doing here? Let me rephrase that—if he took all the money, what the hell is he doing here?"

Ina slowly lifted her head. The look on her face registered fear mixed with guilt. Something I've never seen from Ina Byers.

"I'm listening," I murmured.

"Jake, it all comes down to trust, okay? As long as I can remember, I've always had this deep-seated hang-up about trusting people. Men specifically. You can't deny most of them will do anything to get what they want, right? Anything. Lie, cheat, even in some cases commit murder."

"Sure. I don't know. Maybe most. Where are you going with this bitterness towards men?"

She rolled down the window, stuck her head out and took a deep breath, just to put space between her next sentences, which didn't exactly give me peace of mind.

"Ray never took the money. He never ran out on me with the money. I took the money that he had hidden in the floorboards of our motel room, and then I ran. He's come here to seek revenge against me, but he mostly wants the loot, I'm pretty sure."

It was difficult to accept her confession as truth. By now I had lost faith in anything she said. Was this just another excuse to somehow involve me in another underhanded scheme? Probably.

"Excuse me if I'm not as gullible as you want me to be," I said, "but I don't buy your story."

"Think about it. Why am I here? Why else would I come back to this godforsaken whistle stop? To place a flower on my dead grandmother's grave? No. To share half the money with you, Sharp Guy. To divvy up the take."

"And when were you planning to tell me about this share and share alike idea?"

"When it felt right. But now none of it matters. He's here, he's angry, and getting back at me seems to be his objective."

"Since it's between the two of you, drop me off at my car, and I'll slip out of the way of the skirmish."

Suddenly, her cell phone rang. We both jumped. Exchanged worried looks.

"Who knows this number?" I stammered nervously.

"No one, except maybe Ray."

"I thought you said you ditched Ray's cell?"

"I did. Tossed it in the Rio Grande. But I guess that didn't stop him from buying a burner phone."

"To soothe the butterflies flitting around in my stomach, answer it. Just to make sure it's just some kids who found the phone and are making a prank call."

She answered it, putting it on speaker mode. An angry voice issued an ultimatum.

"I want my fucking money. I'll call you tomorrow to set up an exchange. So sit by your phone. I know how to reach you. And no underhanded bullshit, like bringing in the cops to trace the call, or you and your clever friend will suffer the consequences." *Click.* End of the one-sided conversation.

And just like that, while working the checkout stand at a neighborhood supermarket, trying to remove myself from the workforce, I was back in the fray—wedged between a lunatic and yet another life-threatening situation.

As we drove, both shaking our heads in disbelief, both feeling the probable danger that lay ahead, I couldn't help but notice the barely masked fear on her face. I felt bad and only wished I could give her solace, but I felt vulnerable myself, so promising her protection would have been a ridiculous reassurance.

We both agreed the smartest move would be to give Ray back the money. That way we eliminated running the risk of any sort of bloodshed. But this was no guarantee. I saw him smile when the fat man took his Humpty Dumpty fall. I believe he got off on seeing people trying to escape from life-and-death situations, and failing. It was his sick hobby. He enjoyed threatening people until they cracked under pressure.

That night, our strategy was to stay at my camper and play it safe until we could come up with a plan. But after careful thought, it occurred to us Ray would definitely stake out the old diner location, just waiting for us to show up, then move in and take us by surprise. As a precaution, we stopped off and picked up a few items, including my dad's pistol. Bringing the gun was Ina's idea. Totally justified. We still needed a place to lay low until we figured out how to contact Ray and hand over the five hundred thousand. I was assuming that figure still held up, and that Ray and Ina hadn't gone on a shopping spree in downtown Mascota.

"By the way, where is the money?" I asked.

All I got was: "In a safe place. Once we set up a meet with Ray, I'll go dig it up."

"So it's buried."

"Yes."

"How about a helpful hint as to where?"

"Not far from here."

I gave up trying to get a straight answer. Left it all up to her to make the exchange. We decided to spend the night at the least obvious hiding place—the Silver Angels Retirement & Assisted Living Facility, where Ina's grandmother took her last breath. Now a desolate building, it was waiting to be demolished because it had failed dozens of inspections and didn't meet city codes. The building was boarded up and locked tight. We couldn't find an accessible entrance, so I managed to rip off a piece of plywood that was haphazardly nailed over a window. The noise awakened a stray cat that let rip a characteristic high-pitched shrill, like it was climaxing.

Inside it was dark, dank, and smelled like disinfectant and urine. We rummaged around, stepping over broken glass, discarded mattresses, a broken-down wheelchair, puddles of stagnant water, and even a few rats scampering in all directions, hoping to elude the clutches of the cat. After a few minutes, we found an area that suited our needs—the rec room, where the retirement crowd probably spent endless hours playing pinochle, while discussing their aches and pains and displaying their surgical battle scars. We set up camp in a dry corner. We had stopped off at a neighborhood Mom-and-Pop store and got provisions: a few candles, a bottle of tequila, and some pre-made cellophane-wrapped sandwiches. We fired up a couple candles. They highlighted the walls that were covered in graffiti. *I got laid here in 2004 stood* out in red spray paint. Kids from the high school must've adopted this place their personal fuck zone.

"Or maybe it was one of the old farts bragging about slipping it to one of the broads, before he kicked the bucket," Ina said, always going for shock rather than decorum.

Finally feeling some sense of security, we poured ourselves a drink, tried to ignore the stench of urine in our sinuses, and speculated about Ray's demands and what he would probably have us do. Ina pretty much had him pegged and knew the drill. He'd set up a drop. We'd be given a time and place and instructed to toss the money bags probably in a dumpster located in a dark alley behind some random Chinese restaurant. Only because he had a thing for Chinese food. Very predictable, but according to Ina, Ray was old school when it came to unscrupulous activity. For one, he wouldn't trust Ina for a minute, so he'd send a paid flunky to make the pickup. His suspicion and mistrust of people in general only intensified his belief that the police would be hiding in the shadows, ready to pounce and make an arrest. Although this last bit of conjecture was highly unlikely, since the money was stolen, Ray would not rule out Ina bringing in her own muscle and taking him down in broad daylight if need be. The mutual distrust made it hard to understand why they were a couple and what they saw in each other.

It was all very classic film noir for my taste, but hey, who was I to judge the effect Peter Lorre and John Garfield had on the small-minded Ray Astemendi?

After two hours I got impatient and said my piece. "Just call the guy and have him meet you in a safe place with lots of witnesses and bright lights. A restaurant. A supermarket. A lighting fixture store. Tell him that's the only way he gets the money: by doing it your way.

You got the upper hand. You have the money. If he wants it, he has to play by your rules."

"Okay. Sure. On paper this is sound advice, but Ray is not above using violence, no matter what the circumstances. He will use any means necessary—gun, kitchen knife, baseball bat, run me over several times in his car. I'd really like to deal with this on a risk-free level. Making sure that I come out of this alive."

I tried changing her mind but without success. She was determined. Nothing for us to do but eat and drink until we heard from Ray. The sandwiches were inedible. We were starved. Hadn't eaten all day. The smart alternative was to order takeout rather than risk picking something up ourselves. Ina arranged to have a pizza delivered on the corner of Pine and 30th. Said someone would meet the driver with the cash in thirty minutes. If he was there on time, there was a ten-dollar tip in it for him.

In twenty-five minutes we were both on the corner waiting for the delivery guy to show. We walked, leaving the Mustang hidden behind a dumpster in the rear of the retirement home. The pizza was delivered six minutes late, but we gave the kid the ten-spot anyway. For him to even show up at a random corner and not a residence took balls.

As we headed back to the rec room with our now cold pizza, a shaky, angry voice from behind threatened us.

"Hand over the pizza or I break your legs, and you'll never dance at your sister's wedding."

"I don't have a sister," I said. "Therefore your threat, while colorfully worded, has a fatal flaw, pal."

Ina, on the other hand, was not impressed by his flashy phraseology. Prepared, she swiveled around to face our aspiring pizza mugger, while pointing my dad's .45 in his face. I had no idea she had brought it and was also surprised it was loaded this time.

"I think it's the other way around on the pizza slash dancing warning, fuck-stick."

The guy was wearing a handkerchief over his nose and mouth like a train robber. He instantly dropped the fireplace poker he was using as a weapon and raised his arms in the air, surrendering himself.

"Oh God, please don't shoot," he pleaded. "Show a little compassion. I'm craving a little sustenance. Except for a dry dinner roll I found peeking out of a trash bin, I haven't had a decent meal in days."

Ina demanded he remove the mask and show his gutless face. He did. I gave a little gasp of astonishment, because I recognized our assailant despite his disheveled appearance and horrible stench—not that that wasn't his usual state. It was Richard Salvetti, my homeless friend from school. We exchanged hellos like we were best friends, and then I introduced Ina. She didn't remember him. I took the opportunity to thank Richard for documenting my innocence in the diner fire.

"No problem," he said. "You can repay me with a slice of that pizza and we'll call it even."

Suddenly, out of the darkness, a car turned the corner, going at least fifty, and headed directly towards us. Ina and I flinched, anticipating that it was Ray. He had found us. Ina pointed the .45 directly at the car windshield, ready to take out the driver. I envisioned a shoot-out, gangland style, in the middle of the street. I would have ducked for cover but there was nothing for me to duck behind except Richard. Both Richard and I lay flat on the sidewalk—a bad idea if the car decided to jump the curb and run us over. Fortunately our instincts were wrong and Ina didn't have to shoot the driver. My guess was it was one of those chicken-shit husbands, skipping town and abandoning his family.

We breathed a collective sigh of relief and hustled back to the safety of the retirement home along with Richard, who was still expecting a ration of pizza.

I suggested to Ina we enlist Richard's help. My idea went something like this: Richard parks the Mustang a block from the drop site. He leaves a note on the windshield to meet Ina at a nearby restaurant filled with witnesses who, if they had to, would come forward and identify Ray if there was a skirmish.

"Why can't *I* just park my own car?" Ina asked.

"Let's not forget," I replied, "Ray is a sharpshooter. Who's to say he won't have you in his sights once he spots the Mustang traveling on the street? Bam, he snuffs you out like a rusty shooting gallery duck."

"We talked about this, Jake. We do it my way."

"Which is what? You failed to mention how this is going to go down."

"Haven't figured that out just yet. But I'm working on it."

"I hope you're not considering using that animal sedative again. It'll be useless against a gun. Especially in the hands of Ray Astemendi, crack shot."

Richard flinched. He shifted nervously, nearly choking on his slice of pizza.

"Did you say Ray Astemendi?" he asked.

I nodded. "Yes. Why? You know him?"

Then his obvious uneasiness became blatant nonchalance.

"Me? Not really. I knew a Ray from AA. And for a minute I thought . . . but he had an Armenian last name. Bedrossian, I think. Ray Bedrossian."

"You sure? Because when you heard his name you kind of flinched."

"I think flinching is a thing inherent in most addicts. Besides, it's more of a shudder than a flinch. An unexpected craving for . . . are you cold? I'm cold. I need to go outside in the sun."

"There is no sun. It's ten o'clock," Ina pointed out. "What's really going on, Salvetti, you going through withdrawals?"

"No, I'm good. Well, I could use a taste, but what I really need is a few dollars to tide me over. Fifty would be nice. A hundred would be nicer. Someday I'll pay you back. But don't count on it."

"Sorry, but I don't have that kind of money," I said.

"She does. The girl does. She seems to have a great deal of cash. Fifty, just fifty."

"Not going to happen," Ina said flatly. "Take the rest of the pizza and call this your lucky day, considering that you got the sustenance you were craving, after you first threatened us with the fireplace poker."

He turned to me with disappointment mixed with anger on his face. "This is the thanks I get for saving your ass from going to jail and being tagged an arsonist?"

"I have no say in this, Ricky. It's her money. Not mine. I'm just along for the ride. If it were up to me, I'd give you a few dollars to keep you afloat for a month or two."

"I just need enough to score a couple Oxys, so I don't crash."

I slipped him a twenty. He grabbed it, then disappeared back into his world.

"I saw that you slip him some cash," said Ina. "Nice gesture. Maybe I was a little rough on the poor guy. I'm dealing with a lot of pent-up anger issues right now. And my charity and goodwill levels are at an all-time low." She paused, looking at me with a serious expression. She fiddled with her hair before speaking in a hushed, consoling voice.

"Not to worry, Sharp Guy. I'll find a way to get to Ray, and resolve this problem. I will not let anything happen to us—to you. You have my word."

She then kissed me on my cheek. Why? Probably to establish her sincerity. Okay, sure, her sincerity about keeping me safe was somewhat commendable. However, I took her word with a grain of salt. I'd learned to be extra cautious when it came to trusting Ina Byers. Reading between the lines was a must or you'd find yourself being injected with animal tranquilizer or falling into a snake pit covered over by twigs.

In any event, I had another, much more plausible way to go. I suggested that we anonymously notify the Lubbock police of Ray Astemendi's whereabouts.

"They arrest him for the murder of the security guard," I said, and we rest easy, without any sort of confrontation. We walk away with all the money and head for Bolivia."

Except for the Bolivia part, Ina claimed she had already thought of that, but her fear was that Ray would snitch and implicate her, in exchange for a lighter sentence. Maybe even plead temporary insanity and try to get placed in a psychiatric hospital. Her only safety net was to give Ray the money and let the cops track him down later. By then she'd be long gone. As for me, I needed to have my own escape plan, because you can bet the first place Ray would look would be in my backyard. There was no safe place for me to hide. I was a dead man, unless I sold my acre of land and hightailed it to safer ground. I was starting to sound like a Western folk hero.

CHAPTER SIXTEEN

The following day, around noon. Ina had lost her patience because Ray had failed to get in touch with her as promised. What else was knew? He was a slacker. She decided to put her own plan into motion and was on her way to the Padre Hotel, an historical landmark with a tragic past, located deep in the heart of the Arts District. There was a terrible fire on the seventh floor in the 1950s that resulted in many deaths, including Ray's parents. Going on a hunch and nothing else, Ina was thinking Ray would seek revenge for their death. Maybe even be crazy enough to start another seventh floor fire as a testimonial. Ina's instincts were right. Sitting out front was the same dark blue sedan that ran the red light and almost collided into us. Plus, it displayed Mexico plates.

Ina parked behind the sedan, got out, and checked inside for any clues. Two empty Modelo Especial beer bottles sat alone on the front seat. Ray's preferred brand. It confirmed her suspicions that he was in the hotel. She went inside to the front desk. I accompanied her for moral support—not that she needed any. The clerk reeked of Aqua Velva and was sending off *Do Not Disturb Me* signals. Ina stood and waited. He pretended to be intently reading a magazine. She cleared her throat. Finally, without looking up from his magazine, the clerk muttered: "Under what name is your reservation?"

"I have no reservation. I just need to ask a question, then I'll leave."

"What kind of a question?"

"The kind that requires a simple yes or no answer. Is there a Ray Astemendi registered?"

The clerk slowly looked up. His eyes were bloodshot. His nose a purple hue. A sign of an acute alcoholic issue.

"Sorry, miss, house privacy rules. Afraid I can't say."

"It's actually Mrs. I'm his wife."

"You have proof? Can't be too careful. I'm not saying you're lying, it's just we don't want any trouble."

"What kind of trouble?"

"The usual trouble when a wife or girlfriend goes into a jealous rage, bursts into a man's room unannounced, and finds him with another woman. Then shoots both of their entangled naked bodies while in the midst of copulation. You can never get the blood stains out of the sheets, and the management will charge me and take the cost of new sheets out of my paycheck for not being more vigilant about who I let upstairs without proof of who they are."

"He paid you, didn't he? To play the idiot clerk. To turn anyone anyway looking for him."

"Again, I'm not at liberty to say."

"Tell you what. Blink once for yes, twice for no. That way you won't have to speak or break your precious rules. Is Ray Astemendi in this fucking hotel?"

"I think we're done here, miss," he said without a blink.

Ina leaned in closer to this weasel.

"Let me give you some ugly specifics on who you're sheltering here. His parents died in the fire of 1950. He blames the hotel for its faulty wiring. He's primarily here to preserve the memory of their death. Seeking revenge. Probably staying on the seventh floor near the ice machine, where his mother and father perished. You needn't blink because I know I'm right. You can choose to keep your mouth shut and protect him from whomever—but I'd give him this note before all hell breaks loose." She stuffed a piece of folded paper in his jacket handkerchief pocket. "You'll want to get this to him on the double. The sooner the better, because all your guests who are staying here at the Padre are in serious jeopardy. By morning this place could be draped in yellow crime tape, with chalk outlines of where the dead bodies were found. You've been warned. Have a pleasant evening."

The following scene—in which I have once again employed considerable dramatic license (a budding writer's prerogative) was cobbled together from my later conversation with Ina about her fateful meeting with Ray Astemendi.

⌖

A few hours later, the Mustang was parked outside St. Paul's Church on 17th Street. Inside, Ina sat on the priest's side of the confessional booth, nervously fiddling with a couple of Mexican bracelets dangling on her wrist. She lit a cigarette and a parishioner who was just exiting the church immediately got her attention. "Excuse me, but this is a no smoking house of worship."

"Sorry, my error," she replied. "I'm a bundle of fucking nerves. My very first confession. I'm one of your card-carrying heretics."

After a few beats someone entered the other side of the confessional. A penitent? No, but the voice was familiar.

"I got your note, and was a little surprised you picked a church for our little parley."

"You never called, as planned so I took the liberty of getting this show on the road. Figured a church was the safest place to cover my ass from flying shrapnel, considering your temper."

"The sanctity of the church won't protect you."

"Nor you either, Ray." With that came the distinct sound of a pistol's hammer being cocked.

"Wow, you came armed. Classy."

"Never can be too careful with religious fanatics these days, Ray. You of all people should know about fanatics."

"Why'd you run out on me, Ina? We had a good thing going, I thought," Ray said, knowing it was a damn lie.

"You thought wrong. You treated me like crap. You were fucking that evangelical whore behind my back, not to mention a cluster of other young women you helped find Jesus with your own personal hands-on technique. You weren't exactly the epitome of trust and coziness. So I took the money, thinking it was only a matter of time before you put a pillow over my face and ended the good thing we had going."

"So, let's cut the small talk and get down to business. Where's the fucking money?"

"In an attaché case under your seat. It has a combination lock. As a safety precaution, I'll e-mail you the combination once I'm safely out of sight of your crosshairs. Understand?"

"Very thorough. You thought of everything."

"Not everything, Ray. Never figured you for a backstabbing, treacherous piece of shit. I must be slipping. Usually I can spot a cocksucker from a mile away."

"Always the one with the sugary mouth, huh, Ina?"

It was nearly sundown. The Mustang was rolling down Truxton Avenue at a moderate speed. Ina was behind the wheel, I was riding shotgun, and hearing for the first time how Ina compromised the mission.

"What do you mean, you gave him most of the money?" I asked, stupefied.

"Most meaning a third. Call it payback for my years of devoted acceptance of his late-night Bible studies with Auntie Em."

"So when he discovers the shortage, we—rather, *you*—can assume what, that he'll come after you guns a' blazin'?"

"I'm not worried. He knows I'm carrying. And he knows I'll use it if I have to."

"You'd kill him in cold blood? You'd commit murder without a second thought?"

"Yes. Maybe. I dunno. Christ, I'm starting to sound a lot like you—indecisive."

"Are you listening to yourself? Apparently not. If it were me, and I knew the sick, lethal capabilities of Ray Astemendi, I'd be on the first stagecoach out of town—to quote another dated Western cliché."

"You're right. I should run."

"But you're not. You're sticking around. Why?"

"Guess I don't want to give him the satisfaction of thinking he intimidates me and can control my life."

'"Answer me this: what will you accomplish if you're dead?"

"I'll know that I pissed him off. Infuriated him. And even dead, I will get pleasure out of knowing he'll still only have a third of the money. I win. He loses. Let's get drunk."

The Mustang pulled into the parking lot of a neighborhood liquor store. Its neon sign sputtered as if it was about to die an electrical death at any moment. While Ina hung out by the car, I went inside to buy a bottle of tequila and a pack of Shermans. The clerk behind the counter was a little elf of a man, standing on a crate; he was maybe five feet tall—that's including the crate. Before I even placed my order, he made it clear that he didn't take crap from anybody.

"If you're here to rob me, I'd think twice," he warned. "My right hand is under the counter, gripping a sawed-off shotgun that's aimed directly at your fucking balls."

"Been robbed a lot have you, sir?" I gulped.

"Too many times to count. They come in wearing ski masks and point handguns at my head." His voice quivered just recalling the nerve-racking events.

I assured the little man that I was only there for a bottle of tequila and a pack of smokes. I casually mentioned I was a staunch supporter of the NRA and the Second Amendment. However, he didn't see this as a sign of me being an ally and didn't take his hand off the shotgun during the entire transaction.

A few minutes later, we were back on the road again. It was 6:45 p.m. The sky has an orange tint to it. "Where we going?" I asked.

"A special place. Into our past."

"Just curious, where's the rest of the money? Or is that also hidden in the past?"

"What does that mean?"

"It means, where's the money? It means, where have you stashed the money. It means, why are you being so vague about the money?"

"Jake, calm down. I have everything under control. The money is nearby and in a safe place, just waiting for us to grab it and split up the take."

Extremely ambivalent, I shifted and wrung my hands nervously.

"Honestly, after ruminating on this until my brain cramped up, I'm not sure I want my share. It's dirty money that so far has generated bad karma."

"Jake, don't be stupid. You've earned it. Without you the whole scheme never would've worked, and we would've walked away empty-handed."

"You're giving me too much credit. Any talentless chump could've taken my place. You don't need to be a brainiac to fall down and play a heart attack victim. What I'm trying to say is that I could never live with myself, knowing I've used that money to enjoy a cushy lifestyle. I've repeatedly said this, and you don't seem to take me seriously."

"Fine, feel guilty. Then give your share to charity. A worthy cause. Or burn it, like the diner—if that'll help you sleep nights."

Five silent minutes ticked by. My stomach flip-flopped without my permission. Then reality set in. I had no job. Nowhere to go. No future plans, except to try and sell the dirt my diner once perched on. I was like a person without a country. Treading water, waiting to sink and drown. It's funny how your principles of right and wrong alter when you're desperate, knowing poverty can strike at any time. I surrendered, which somewhere down the line, in my questionable future, I would probably regret.

"Okay. Fine. Put a tight lid on the guilt. I'll take 10 percent of my third, which is somewhere in the neighborhood of sixteen thousand, six hundred dollars. No more, no less. The rest is yours."

"Okay, then, Jakey, you have a deal."

We actually shook hands to solidify this transaction. In my mind I had just committed a mortal sin. I'd agreed to accept God's stolen money. I would surely burn in hell. If there is a hell, which I am inclined not to believe. I'm convinced there is no separate location for good and evil. Bad people go to the same place good people end up. They all fade into this stream of nothingness.

Another half mile, and I hear the tires crunch over gravel. Then a few more feet, and we pulled up to a chain link fence with a sign that read: Private Property No Trespassing. Although the area looked familiar, I still didn't have a clue where she had actually taken us. Ina jumped out and opened the gate. Beyond the gate it was dark, but I could see a silhouette of what I thought was a roller coaster. As we drove further inside, she turned on the high beams and I realized we had come in the back way of Collins Fun Zone.

"Holy crap, it's still standing!" I shouted like an excited kid scarcely able to contain himself as he waited to ride the Ferris wheel.

"Our youth," Ina sighed, waxing philosophical. "When life was filled with bitter disagreements over fundamental issues. Teenage conflict."

She parked the car near an embankment. This was where she and her unruly friends took target practice at Coke bottles and beer cans set on the ledge of this broken-down railway depot that was once a short stopover for commuters heading north. *Kill the Can!* was the battle cry as they riddled the targets with hundreds of rounds of .22 shells. The depot barely stood erect, weathered and riddled with bullet holes. Its walls were inscribed with the names of those who roamed this hallowed ground, and dates spanning decades.

A half hour later, we were perched on the hood of the Mustang, overlooking a ghost town of an amusement park. Most of the tequila had been consumed, and we were very buzzed. The only light came from the full moon bathing us in a silvery glow. As Ina lit a Sherman, she posed a question: "Ever stop to wonder how you're gonna die?"

"No. Never. Maybe once, when my mother died of cancer. Seemed like a natural thought, worrying if it was hereditary or not. But for the most part, it never entered my mind."

"I mean, if you knew beforehand," Ina persisted, "would it make it easier?"

I hesitated, and took a sip of tequila.

"I gotta say, you have a way of taking the edge off a good time."

I leaned in to kiss her, lifting her sunglasses so I could see her full face in the moonlight. I winced, noticing one eye was bruised and swollen.

"Whoa. Care to explain the shiner?"

"Bumped my face in the confessional booth. They're a lot more cramped than I remembered."

I didn't believe her. This was Ray's handiwork.

"I know I'm repeating myself, only because I really never got a sensible answer, but I can't for the life of me understand why you ever stayed with Ray. It's not that his mean streak is unpredictable."

"You live, you learn, you get smacked in the face enough times, and you finally end it before he kills you. That's how it worked for me. I stuck around, hoping it'd get better. I was a fucking naive dreamer."

She then finished off the bottle of tequila, tossing the empty onto the ground in front of us. While it spun like a top, she slipped the .45

pistol out from inside her jacket and fired one shot—shattering the bottle into small shards, while at the same time piercing the worm right through the heart. The sound echoed in the night air.

"Nice shootin'. You certainly know your way around a gun. Where'd you learn to shoot like that?"

"Girl Scout camp," she said with a straight face.

"And here I thought the Girl Scouts were only known for their Thin Mints."

She ignored my attempt at humor and gave me a true account of how she became such a crack shot.

"Had this first date with a guy who took me to an indoor shooting range, bought me a cheeseburger, then fucked me goodnight. That guy was the all-intimidating Ray Astemendi. It was an unforgettable night, which was the very first entry I scribbled in my diary."

Ina Byers I guarantee never had a diary.

"Okay, Sharp Guy, your turn to let loose." She offered me the gun.

I backed off, but she turned me around by rationalizing how my father wouldn't have kept the gun if it weren't a reminder of his heroism. And how he used it to protect our country from its enemies. I saw the logic of her argument, and agreed to play *Kill the Can* in my dad's memory. A little sappy, but sappy inspired me enough to fire the damn gun.

She moved the car so that the headlights peered through the weeds and undergrowth, spotlighting the dilapidated depot in an eerie fashion. I'm sure it was a mixture of the booze, the headlights, and the moon that put me in a surreal frame of mind.

We trekked through the tall grass, then over the old railroad ties, and positioned ourselves in front of what was left of the depot. Ina handed me the gun. It felt different than when I held it against the kid's head in Needles. Must've been because it was loaded this time. It now became a real weapon of destruction. She then stood behind me, positioning my arm at the right level. She walked me through it.

"Finger on the trigger. Cock the hammer back. You're gonna squeeze with your index finger like you're gently massaging my clit."

This image alone had me longing to squeeze the trigger. The wind howled around us. Ina leaned in, pressing her body against my leg.

"You gonna leave your knee there?"

"Only if it helps your aim," she whispered seductively.

"Now shoot directly in the center of the door. Don't worry about hitting anything but the door. Empty the clip like you mean it. As if you're some sort of, I don't know . . . a crime-fighter, taking out the bad guy who's holding an innocent child hostage in an abandoned Iowa farmhouse."

"What? Is that image really necessary? Is that what you conjure up every time you pulled the trigger playing *Kill the Can* in high school—a child in danger?

"No. I'm just trying to make this moment fun for you."

"By painting me a grim picture of a child being held captive. That to you illustrates fun?"

"Forget there's a child. Put aside the hero worship crap. Just shoot the damn gun, Jake."

Now I was pissed. Maybe that was her intention all along. To rile me enough so that I'd blast away without a second thought. I pulled on the trigger and unloaded six rapid shots. The raucous gunfire set off a chorus of barking dogs in the distance. I looked at the barrel and noted with satisfaction it was actually smoking, just like in the movies. More holes were drilled into the old wood, and it now had all the hallmarks of, well, a railway station that'd been murdered to death several times over and was begging for mercy.

"How'd it feel? Pretty fucking extraordinary, I bet."

"Yeah. There was a certain charge in it. A certain rush that gives you a sense of power. A sense of persuasiveness. Know what I'm saying?"

"I do. Yes. Exactly. A gun wields enormous domination," she said, then kissed me as if it were some sort of reward for firing a gun for the first time.

"Okay, this next time we'll aim at a smaller target. Gimme a second to set up a couple targets."

"I'm out of bullets."

"I've got an extra clip in my pocket. Hold tight."

To be honest, I wasn't anxious to shoot the gun again, but I didn't want to get into another debate about my moral principles towards firearms. She hustled down the steep grassy embankment like she was pushing through a dense forest. I watched as she placed empty bottles on the ledge. For no more than ten seconds, I shifted my focus on the gun muzzle and was amazed by the heat that still generated from it. When I looked up, she was nowhere to be seen. Vanished. I called out over the prevailing wind.

"Hey, where'd you go? Pee break?" Nothing. No response. Worried, I headed down the embankment to make sure she was okay. I called out again. Still nothing. I carefully approached the structure, just in case some unwelcome varmint leapt out and wanted to gnaw on my leg. I spoke loud and succinctly. I could see my breath in the coldness of the night air.

"See, a lot of guys would have a real problem with this kind of disappearing act," I said aloud, to calm my anxiety. "It would probably deflate their ego. Belittle them. Not me. I'm not easily unnerved by a girl walking out on me, after I unload six bullets like I'm John Dillinger."

The door to the depot was ajar. The Mustang's headlights still illuminated the area, and I noticed boot heel drag marks on the ground, leading inside. Thinking nothing of it, I reached for the door handle, which was nothing but a piece of rope that had been nailed to a weathered plank. As I started to pull on it, the headlights flicked off and the area became pitch-black. I could barely see, so I used the flashlight app on my iPhone. At the same time, I heard tires frantically spin on the gravel. I swiftly turned around and saw the Mustang speed away. I was bewildered, stunned, and angry, all at the same time. I didn't get the joke, if in fact this was a joke. My smartphone flashlight caught something inside. Opening the door wider, I saw a body lying motionless. Even dead maybe. Needless to say, this alarmed me. My heart started beating rapidly, and I hyperventilated. I felt dizzy but not bad enough to actually faint. Taking a closer look, I made a harrowing discovery: it was Ray Astemendi wearing his Ray Bans. He was on his back. I shined the light on him to get a better look. At first I remained calm until I leaned down and removed the sunglasses. Blank eyes stared back at me. I checked his carotid for a pulse. Nothing. No doubt he was dead. A million things raced through my mind. I went for logic. He wasn't happy with only a third of the money. He followed us here. When the time was right, he was intending to kill us in cold blood. But I got to him first. One of my six bullets must have found its mark. I was too flustered to check the body for an entry and/or exit hole. In fact, the thought didn't even occur to me.

I fell into a state of panic bordering on delirium. Even though this appeared to be a horrible accident, it would still be considered murder. In my hysterical state, I was forgetting that Ina took off, leaving me behind. In a lucid moment, I developed a hypothesis. When she noticed Ray dead on the ground, she became unhinged and took off, leaving me holding the bag, and saddled with having to explain to the cops why and how I found a dead man inside the old Santa Fe depot on private property that was clearly marked No Trespassing. From where I stood, I was plainly guilty of involuntary manslaughter. It didn't look good for me, especially if I was counting on Ina to come forward and reveal how Ray's death really went down.

A feeling of hopelessness washed over me. Suddenly feeling totally paranoid, I started running through the underbrush, catching a branch now and then that seemed to thrash at my face like I was being flogged. Where was I running to? I had no idea. I just figured the safest thing to do was to run from the scene, convincing myself that if I ran far enough away, it would all disappear. I blamed all this on the damn cartoon potato, with its mirrored sunglasses and groovy demeanor. The image and its misleading advice came back to haunt me. Was I really blaming my actions on that damn matchbook again? Yes, I was. Because, well, I couldn't place any sort of responsibility on myself.

In the moonlight, I worked my way towards The Stonemark apartments on Q Street, where Parker was now living with his girlfriend, Denise Hicks. I hoofed it past the entrance of Union Cemetery. It was desolate, like the city streets. No sign of life anywhere. I must've run twenty blocks, if not more, before I realized I still had a chokehold on the gun grip. It was unsettling. I hatched a random irrational thought: should I toss it in the bushes or a dumpster? I wasn't thinking straight. No way would I get rid of this reminder of my dad's heroism. I'd run at least five miles without tiring. Amazing how I seemed to possess all this energy.

Guess killing someone, even if it was a freak accident, really gets your adrenaline pumping.

It's two o'clock in the morning when I finally made it to Parker's place. Dizzy, I leaned forward, touching my head to my knees, trying to balance my equilibrium. Finally, I stood erect and knocked hard and fast. I waited impatiently for the door to swing open. There was no answer. I knocked again, only this time even much harder, using my fist like a battering ram. No response.

"Parker, open up, I killed someone tonight!" I screamed at the door.

In that same instant, I realized that was not a smart announcement. A neighbor, or a light sleeper, might have heard my confession and called the cops. Finally the door opened a crack, the chain lock stopping it from going further. It wasn't Parker. It was the girlfriend. She was rubbing her eyes awake. And although I was in a state of shock, I couldn't help but notice that she was very attractive, and that I could see her nipples protruding through her flimsy T-shirt. A very nice distraction.

"What the fuck is your problem?" she said in a fierce whisper. "The words *kill someone* woke me from a sound sleep. You have any idea what time it is?"

"Sorry, I need to speak with Parker. Bring Parker to the door and I'll explain everything in detail."

"You're, Jake, right?"

Words failed me, as if I'd suddenly forgotten my name. I'm only able to manage a nod.

"Jake, you're shit out of luck. Parker moved. We broke up. It didn't work out. He's too needy for my taste."

I asked where he moved to. Back home? Another place? She was not a vast storehouse of information.

"Maybe he shacked up with another girl who doesn't have a problem mothering him," she said.

"A name? An address? A wild guess will do, as long as it's where I can find him."

"I'm slamming the door on you, Jake. And it's going to hurt if you keep your fingers there."

In desperation, I told her the whole, unvarnished story of Ray Astemendi's accidental (I refused to say untimely) death, and my conviction that Ina Byers had set me up. I hoped she'd feel bad for me, or at least could give me some advice, since she was a court reporter and had a handle on the law. Her suggestion came too fast, without a stick of sympathy.

"Turn yourself in, tell the cops the whole story, and hope they believe you enough to follow up on what seems to be an implausible truth."

I pleaded. Raised my hand to God and swore it was all true, and I just needed one lousy favor—a ride to my car. There's a long pause as she deliberated.

It was 2:45 in the morning when Denise finally felt a twinge of compassion and gave me a lift.

We were in her Honda Civic headed for my Jeep, which was parked alongside the rental camper.

"This is against everything I believe in," she said. "I need solid evidence. Yet here I am, an accessory to murder."

"Denise, you're just dropping me off at home. It's not as if you're driving me across the border into Canada."

"So what's your plan, Jake? You have a plan? I've sat in on enough court proceedings to know that the accused always had a plan. A plan that usually backfired, but a detailed strategy just the same."

"You're not exactly helping my confidence here," I said.

"You're going to need more than a handful of confidence, you're going to need a good trial lawyer," she said confidently.

"Lawyer. Yes. If you have the name of a lawyer, can you write it down when it's more convenient?"

I assumed I was being chauffeured to my car, and was naturally taken aback when Denise pulled up to the Bakersfield Police Station and stopped at the unloading zone. A quizzical stare from me was not enough . . .

"What are you doing?"

"A favor. I'm doing you a favor."

"The hell you are. You're throwing me to the wolves. I thought we had an understanding."

She paused. I hated pauses, because usually what came next was a mouthful of absolute nonsense. And I was right.

"Turning yourself in is the smart move here, Jake. Eventually they'll discover the body. They'll get your prints off the sunglasses you stupidly touched. Not to mention, when they dig the bullet out from Ray, you can bet, if you think this Ina person set you up, the shell will be a perfect match for the round shot from your gun."

And that's when it hit me like a ton of bricks. The bullet. I saw no bullet hole anywhere. I had this theory, purely speculative but something concrete that could clear me. I needed to go back and check out Ray again. Denise was skeptical about returning to the scene of the crime. She was nervous that, by now, the police would have an entire investigative team on site. Since the crime only happened an hour ago, I found her reason to stay clear unconvincing.

I pleaded. Said I had to examine the body again. If my instincts prove to be accurate, they could substantiate my innocence. After a few minutes of nudging and pushing and prodding and threatening to hijack her car, she gave into my pleas.

We headed back to railway depot. I was almost sure my intuition was correct. When we arrived, there was no sign of the cops or that the area had been disturbed. Ray's body was still in the same position. Flat on his back. His sunglasses still resting on the bridge of his nose. And my instincts were well founded. The evidence we discovered was overwhelmingly in my favor. We turned Ray on his side and saw evidence that he was shot in the back. Denise had been in enough courtroom dramas, and seen enough crime scene photos, to recognize entry and exit wounds when she saw them. Which made it impossible for me to have killed Ray even by accident. I suppose he could have had his back to the door, but that seemed unlikely. With this newfound detail, Denise proposed we clean up the area of anything that could tie me to the crime. Smart thinking. I wiped my fingerprints from the sunglasses with my T-shirt, swept away our footprints with a tree branch, and picked up the .45 caliber shell casings from where I unloaded the six shots into the door of the railway station. Unless we missed something, I was greatly relieved that I couldn't be charged, or that I was even at the scene. Unless Ina came forward and said otherwise. But why would she? She'd be incriminating herself.

Even being this meticulous, Denise thought I should inform the police. Make an anonymous call from a pay phone and tell them where they could find the body.

"A pay phone? And where would I find a pay phone these days? That was a mystery in and of itself."

"You're right. Stop and buy a burner phone."

I totally nixed the idea of a phone call to the cops. Wouldn't make me feel any more secure. For me to feel that I was out of danger, I needed Ina to corroborate my innocence. I needed to track her down and somehow force her to admit her guilt, putting me in the clear. This was highly unlikely. Forcing Ina Byers to do anything was a hopeless undertaking. To put my situation into plain language *I was royally fucked.*

Denise decided to help me locate Ina's whereabouts. Denise had a GPS tracking app that could track down another phone location. Said she used it for a part-time job, freelancing for this law firm, serving delinquent asshole fathers who had missed their child support payments.

According to the tracking device, Ina was just leaving Union Cemetery. My instinct told me she was visiting her grandmother Pauline one last time before leaving town. Denise stepped on it like she had pursued and hunted down people before. She took corners and shifted gears like a Formula One driver. I liked this girl's take control attitude and found myself admiring her own intuitive nature. I didn't disguise my checking her out. Probably shouldn't have been so blatant. She noticed.

"You're staring at my tits. What's up with that?"

"Sorry, it's just that they're staring back at me, and the thing is, you're not the kind of girl Parker usually hits on."

"What is that supposed to mean?"

"You're, well, more attractive and seem to have more on the ball—in contrast with being rural and domestic, which he usually went for."

"Is that a compliment or a come-on?" She slammed on the brakes and turned to face me. "Let's get one thing straight, Jake, before we go any further. I am not ready for another relationship that isn't going to work out. You might be good-looking and my type—if I had a type. But there's no way I'm sleeping with you. Understand?"

"Sure. Completely. We will not stop this chase to have sex."

She laughed, realizing her anxiety was utterly ridiculous.

Just as we arrived outside the cemetery, the Mustang sped by in the opposite direction, headed for the freeway on-ramp. I instructed Denise to *follow that car!* as if I was the hero in a 1930s gangster movie, and had just jumped into a taxi to chase down Edward G. Robinson.

She did a one-eighty in the middle of the street and floored it.

"Wow," I said, "that was some move!" It gave me a rush of exhilaration.

"My dad was a stunt driver before he died in an unfortunate crash that went sideways. Car unintentionally flipped on wet pavement, skidded into a turn, and plowed under a tanker truck filled with gasoline. The explosion rocked the neighborhood. He was killed instantly. I sued the production company and the stunt coordinator for not complying with safety regulations. It's still in the courts. If I win the case, I'm leaving this slag heap for a better life."

It wasn't the first time I heard someone call this dusty Kern County city a slag heap—and probably not the last.

"Sorry for your loss. Losing a father can be demoralizing. Lost my dad to PTSD and heart failure."

"Well, we certainly know how to turn this car chase into a warm, uplifting look back into the deaths of our patriarchs, don't we?"

I remained quiet until the Honda was tailgating the Mustang.

"Prepare yourself," Denise warned. "I'm pulling up alongside, so this would be the perfect time for you to say something smart and persuasive."

As the Honda inched closer to the driver's side of Ina's car, I lowered my window and screamed with no regard for anything, except making Ina Byers understand the gravity of the situation:

"I know you killed him. I have proof. Pull over and face the fucking music!"

"Okay, not to seem critical," Denise said, "but *Face the fucking music* is a little outdated. If you have anything more current that doesn't put you in the same category as a hundred-year-old gangster, I'd go with that."

Denise tried to maneuver the car so it wouldn't sideswipe the Mustang. Now side by side, we looked over at Ina. She drove with one hand on the wheel, while the other was flicking the ash off her Sherman. She gave me a friendly smirk, then flipped me off.

"This would be the perfect time to use that present-day allegation you've been saving to really get her attention."

I calibrated; at the depot, I had shot off six rounds, leaving me one last round in the magazine. Knowing this, I pulled the gun from my hip, stuck it out the window, and shot at the Mustang's rear left tire. I wasn't even close. The bullet bounced off the asphalt, causing sparks, lighting up the night. Denise braked. She was noticeably shaken.

"What the fuck? Have you completely lost it? You just can't randomly fire a gun on the 101 Freeway. People could get hurt or die from a ricocheted bullet."

"Sorry, I lost control of my senses. I figured action speaks louder than words. No more guns. I believe I'm out of bullets anyway."

Meanwhile, I noticed the Mustang speeding away and leaving Denise's Civic in the dust.

"Don't slow down. I swear, no more flare-ups of insanity coming from me. We can't give up the chase. I still need to obtain some sort of closure on Ina Byers. You know, I think the word *closure* is over-used, because there'll never be closure. The dilemma or unresolved conflict or whatever issue the person faced will still haunt them even after closure is achieved."

"Jake, I'm starting to feel really concerned for how you're handling this. A high school crush deceived you into murdering her boyfriend. And to what end? Money, greed, a thirst for power? Or is it just a sick game with this chick?"

"A game? What do you mean?"

"From what little you've told me about Ina Byers, I get the sense she thrives on taking advantage of people. That this is her drug of choice—being a bully. Using people to satisfy her addiction."

Denise floored the gas pedal and again we were in hot pursuit of the Mustang. What she said might be true. I wasn't sure what to think at this point, but what I did know was that if I made it through this predicament unscathed, I'd never become infatuated with a weird, spacey female again. I'd stick to the strictly innocent type who refused to make love in daylight hours and blushed when regarding their vagina as a pussy.

CHAPTER SEVENTEEN

We had seemingly driven an infinite amount of miles. The sun had just started to rise over the Sierra Nevada Mountains. The Mustang whizzed down a lonely stretch on Highway 190, past a road sign: Death Valley National Park.

I couldn't believe that Denise had stuck with the pursuit and taken me this far. I asked why.

"I wanted to turn back at Barstow, but a voice inside me said, *Don't be a dick, help this guy come to terms with his dreadful mistake.* To be honest, your personality reminds me a lot of my father. He was a weak man too. Pussy-whipped, if I'm being honest. My mother had him wrapped around her finger. He never had the balls to stand up to her. You're doing that. Taking control of your spineless personality trait. Guess I'm living his pathetic life through a person who is willing to finally say *Go fuck yourself* to the woman he adores. The woman who has driven him to the brink of psychological destruction."

"I think there's a compliment in there somewhere. Is there? Or am I just searching for honeyed words?"

The Honda had gained on the Mustang. It was only several car lengths behind. A beat, then came . . .

"She had a kid. Died at birth."

"Please don't get maudlin on me, Jake. Recalling the death of our fathers is all I can handle on this outing. I'm fresh out of tears, and the emotional lump in my throat has gone soft."

"No tears. No need to respond, just listen."

I proceeded to tell her what had been haunting me ever since I saw the name Dean tattooed on Ina's calf. How I thought the kid might have been mine, because the name Dean was a character from Kerouac's classic novel, *On the Road*. Dean Moriarty. The same book I considered the greatest novel of its time. The same book she was reading on graduation day back in 1995.

"That's a lot of speculation without firm evidence, Jake. It could all just be coincidence. A fluke. Also, it could be something you wished was true, allowing yourself to romanticize the sketchy physical relationship you had with her."

"Sure. Makes sense. Smart analysis. I hate the fact that you may be right. So, where do you think she's going?" I asked to change the subject.

"Wherever it is, she's gonna need petrol real soon. That Mustang is a gas guzzler. Built in 1979. V8. Gets no more than eleven miles per gallon."

Fifteen more miles, and it looked like my luck had changed. Steam was pouring from the hood of the Mustang, like a smoke signal calling for reinforcements. The car crossed the highway and slowly pulled into a turnout. Ina got out and raised the hood, then reacted appropriately. "Damn this *piece of shit* car!" she screamed, scaring the crap out of a few birds perched on a tree growing out of the side of the ravine. They flitted away, squawking.

Denise hung back, and stopped the Honda on the shoulder a safe distance away. "You're on, Jake," she said. "Go do what you must do to make your life whole again. Just no physical shit, like punching her in the face, even though you have the urge. What you decide to do about the money, well, I can't advise you. A third might be rightfully yours, but I'm guessing she's not going to give it up so easily. Maybe you can convince her to give you enough to help pay for gas back to Bakersfield and the price of a good lawyer."

I got out and cautiously moved towards Ina with the stealth of a hungry cat preparing to pounce. Slow and calculating.

I made first contact. "Don't grab that radiator cap. You'll burn the hell out of your hand."

"Always helpful, even in a pressured situation. What do you want, Jake? Your share of the money, an explanation—or are you here to smack me for fucking up your life?"

It was hard to think straight. I nervously ran my fingers through my hair, just to stall the unavoidable question . . .

"Why me? Why the fuck did you pick me?"

"Jake, I think that's obvious. You were hooked. Obsessed. I had to do nothing but smile and make empty promises and you fell into place. I needed a fall guy. Both you and Ray fit the bill."

She slammed the hood shut with force and the trunk popped open.

"Well, I've gotta call Triple A. They've catered to my many car troubles over the years. I'm sure I'm on their speed dial." She moved past me and crossed to the trunk.

"I took the bait," I remarked. "The planted matchbook cover was an obvious dangling carrot."

"Not really, that was just an accident that went in my favor."

"And Ray?"

"Ray? Jesus, poor naive Ray. The whole scam was my idea. The security job. The heist. Even the idea of him wearing dark glasses to look more menacing. He was as much of a patsy as you were, Jake."

"Why'd you have to kill him? Sure, he was an evil cocksucker, but killing him was a bit harsh."

"I didn't kill him, Jake. You did. With your dad's gun. Of all your wild shots, one found its mark."

"You know that's bullshit."

"That'll never hold up in court," Denise pointed out, walking up beside us.

"Who the fuck is she?" Ina snapped.

"My ride," I said. "My witness."

"You sleeping with her, Jake? Nice. Good for you. She's attractive, and I bet she has a high IQ and doesn't mind having sex in daylight hours."

"Stick to the subject matter. How'd you pull it off?" I demanded.

"Strictly off the record," Denise chimed in.

"What is she, a cop?"

"Court reporter, with a lot of knowledge when it comes to the law," Denise answered. "What's right, what's wrong, what's just your common everyday killer instinct homicide, with no regard for human life."

"Before you start sending me to the gas chamber, it was actually an accident," Ina said. "When I met Ray at the church, and he forced his fist through the center divider in the confessional trying to grab my throat, I stabbed him with the hypodermic needle that was filled with the last drop of the animal tranquilizer. It had no immediate effect. Wasn't enough to cause any damage. We struggled. He grabbed my wrist. I couldn't pry it loose. His grip was too strong. I used the butt of the gun to knock his hand away. During the scuffle, the gun somehow went off in my favor. It wasn't premeditated. I drove to the old railway depot, removed Ray from the trunk, and was able to drag him inside. The rest you can figure out on your own."

"I admit you even had me convinced that I killed Ray. It's not unconceivable that one of my stray bullets could've found its mark. But that would've been an impossible shot, since he was shot in the back."

Ina turned her back on me, ignoring my allegation.

"When I found him he was lying face up," I further explained, "and a shot to the back would've caused his body to fall forward, with his face down in the dirt. His sunglasses would've fallen off, maybe even broken."

"You figure that out all by yourself, Sharp Guy?"

"He had help," Denise said. "I've been in court enough times to hear a district attorney make their case and put an alleged killer away for a lot of years."

Ina swung around and faced us again.

"Even if it were fact, when the cops investigate and the ballistics report matches the bullet to your dad's gun, you're as good as guilty, as if you shot Ray yourself. You can call it a horrible accident and maybe you'll get a lesser sentence."

Denise jumped back in and added: "For the sake of argument, let's concede you probably had Jake's gun with you as protection when you met Ray at the church. You needed some sort of reinforcement.

But I'm guessing something went wrong. We discovered the needle mark in Ray's neck; when the drug didn't have an effect, like you said, he came at you, like a madman, fists flying. You had no choice but to shoot him or you'd be history. But there's a twist here, isn't there? You survived because you didn't do the shooting. There was an accomplice. Another fall guy. Someone who desperately needed cash. Or someone who was infatuated by your charms and was willing to risk it for a heavy sexual payday. You promised to sleep with him or her for a favor, because you knew taking out Ray alone was going to be impossible."

Ina ignored the accusation and fired up her ubiquitous Sherman.

"You're grasping at straws, girlie. But I can tell, you're good at guessing games."

"Maybe she's not grasping at all; in fact, she makes a strong argument. There's a short list of guys I know—besides me—who are enamored by you: Archie, the fat bartender, the infatuated cemetery worker with the piercings. Was it one of them?"

"This conversation is becoming a yawn," Ina said. She stomped out her cigarette and nervously lit another one.

"Try this on for size," said Denise. "Maybe you employed a junkie who needed a quick fix and was stone cold broke and would do anything for a couple bucks. I'm guessing he was only supposed to scare Ray with a warning shot over his head, but he was so cranked up his aim was off. It all went sideways and he shot Ray in the back, killing him. Game over. Anything in that area close to being an accurate yawn?"

There is a long pause while Ina digested Denise's theory.

"You should be a mystery writer," Ina snorted. "Or at least scribble children's books. You have a knack for fairytales."

I conjured up the names of more guys that might be desperate for a quick payday. Then I slapped my forehead when it became obvious, and the plot thickened.

"Holy crap, it was Richard Salvetti, wasn't it? Our homeless dinner guest. A known druggie. You paid him to shoot Ray, didn't you? You took advantage of his frailty. He would've done anything for a slice of pizza and an ounce of cocaine. That's it, isn't it? Case closed. End of story."

"You're on a fishing expedition, Jake."

"She may not have pulled the trigger," Denise said, "but she's just as guilty of murder as your friend, if in fact that's a true account of what went down."

"You guys are good together. A latter-day Nick and Nora Charles. She suggests *dope addict* you come back with *homeless pizza guy*." Ina stomped out the freshly lit cigarette, then leaned on the fender of the car, folding her arms in front her as if she was about to tell a good story. Which she was . . .

"So here's how Ray was really taken out. Pay close attention, it gets a little muddled in places. You're right; our school friend Richard Salvetti was somewhat involved. He came to me and asked to be part of the money exchange. I said no fucking way, until he explained how he knew Ray a good two years before I even met him. Way before Ray and I hooked up, he was a bottom-feeding drug dealer. Mostly sold to lower pay scale addicts. A little diazepam, some OxyContin, a couple of Vicodin, a handful of Quaaludes. A variety of pharmaceuticals, like in a box of chocolates. Seems two of his steady customers were Richard's parents. Ray sucked them dry of every penny they had, including Richard's college tuition. It was rumored they died of a lethal overdose of some highly toxic heroin.

Richard was certain it had to be stuff that Ray had slipped them at a discount. When Richard had heard, during our pizza exchange at the retirement home, that I was dealing with Ray Astemendi, he nearly shit his pants and saw an opportunity to seek revenge for his parents' deaths. Keeping that in mind—he did not shoot Ray in the back through the rear of the confessional with your gun as planned. I gave Salvetti your gun to do the deed. That left me defenseless. So, to prevent Ray from attacking me through the confessional, I made it seem as if I had a weapon to protect myself. But I had nothing. Only the distinctive sound of a gun being cocked on my cell. Just like I did with the *cat meows* at the body shop. It worked. Ray took the bait. Thought I was definitely carrying and he backed off."

"Clever," I said. "So did Salvetti kill him or not?"

"He was prepared to do it but never got the chance. I left the confessional and went outside for a smoke. I assumed Salvetti was waiting outside for Ray to show his face and put a bullet in his brain. I heard a gunshot and figured it was done. But no more than one minute had passed when Salvetti came looking for me, all flustered. Hyperventilating. Not because he was overwrought about shooting Ray in cold blood, but because he found Ray slumped over in the confessional, already dead."

"What!"

"You heard right, Sharp Guy. Ray had died by the hands of an unknown assailant. We never knew who it was. It remains a mystery."

"You expect me to believe that crock?"

"I expect you to believe you're in the clear. That Ray died, but not by your gun. All Richard did was help me put his body in the trunk of my car. Ray was a bastard. An abuser of women, physically and mentally. I think we should view his death as a cold-blooded murder carried out by a phantom hit man. And give this guy a standing ovation."

"So, let me get this straight. One, Richard Salvetti didn't kill Ray. Two, you're trying to sell me on the idea that you have no clue who shot him, yet knowing all this beforehand, you still decided to pin it on me? Man, that is cold. Why? You hated me that much?"

"It's got nothing to do with like or dislike. It's a matter of preservation. Saving my own skin. You were—are—the most unlikely person to commit murder. You don't have as much as a parking ticket. While the real murderer is still at large, you're safe. You've been handed a *get out of jail card.*"

"But that goes out the window if the bullet that killed Ray was a .45 caliber. A .45 caliber that somehow turns out to match my gun. Then what?"

"Then to make sure there's no chance of any comparison, you should get rid of the gun. Toss it in the drink, before they come knocking your door down with a search warrant and a pair of handcuffs."

"I no longer have a fucking door. Thing is, I have no proof that it wasn't me who killed Ray Astemendi. I'm fucked."

Denise turned her attention to Ina. "What Jake needs is a really airtight alibi clearing him of any wrongdoing. Like your testimony. But I have a hunch that's not going to happen. Also, by you admitting the truth, you've now implicated both Jake and me in this murder. Nice job."

"It's not my job to look after you two. If you think you're in jeopardy—split. Run. Leave the country. Change your names, dye your hair, and get a facelift. But if the police do their job well, they'll find a dead body and never trace it back to Jake Reilly."

The words *phantom killer* rattled around in my head like a tilted pinball machine. I'd have to be really naive to accept that as fact.

"I need to call a fucking tow truck," Ina announced.

In defiance she slammed the trunk shut. It didn't catch, springing back open. She crossed to the passenger side door.

"Denise," I said, "please tell me why I'm still here and not running away from this madness?"

"Because you threw right and wrong out the window long before you knew this girl was a villain. She can do no wrong in your book. You idolize her so much you overlook her faults."

"Oh good, for a minute I thought I was dealing with a serious emotional problem."

Denise took my hand in hers. She had heard and seen enough.

"C'mon, let's go. We have enough on Ina Byers to fry her. We both witnessed her confession. I even recorded it on my cell."

Denise tugged on my arm, but I didn't budge. I pulled my hand away, then spoke in a whisper: "I'm not done. I need to verify one important thing. I need to know the truth about the kid."

Then I swallowed hard and turned to Ina. My voice cracked, while my heart skipped several beats.

"Is Dean my kid, or not? The truth would be decent."

Ina said nothing, just glared at me and inhaled deeply.

"Does it matter? Would it really make a difference if I said he was? Would it make you feel better knowing that you lost a child at birth, and that you'll have to live with that awful tragedy for the rest of your life?"

"That's not an answer. That's a painful excuse," I said, frustrated. "I'd like a yes or no. Even a maybe would do."

"You're not going to get it today, Sharp Guy," she said. She yanked on the door handle. Nothing. Stuck. It finally opened after several more hard pulls. She grabbed her mobile off the seat, slid inside, and punched in a number. She instructed an operator: "Yeah, I could use a tow. I'm stuck on Highway 190, right off Zabriske Point. It's a red piece of shit Mustang that's ready for the boneyard."

As she continued to give more details and her auto club number, I walked to the rear of the car and saw a sports bag lying inside the trunk. It was covered in fresh, moist dirt but unzipped enough to see the stolen cash staring back at me.

"So, I'm curious: where was the money hidden?"

"Like I said, in a safe place. Buried next to my grandma Pauline's grave. Brilliant, huh? Bribed another high school classmate with a fistful of dollars—the delusional cemetery worker, who shaved his head and pierced his nose just to impress me. Here's an added feature that I'm sure you'll appreciate—or not. Most of the five hundred thousand is in the bag. I never gave Ray his third. The attaché case was stuffed with paper. Just like the switched bank bags were at the Easterday swap. You work with what's already been proven. God, don't you just love it when the B side of a record turns out to be the smash hit?"

Denise slid up behind me and whispered in my ear. Her breath was warm and minty fresh; I hung on her every word.

"Jake, she's nothing but a fucking manipulating bitch. My next move would be, grab a handful of cash, jump in the car, and drive away while you still have your sanity and your self-respect."

I nodded as if I was about to take her advice. But instead, I lost it. Struggled to keep my temper. My first inclination was to grab the bag of money and toss it over the cliff, making sure no one pocketed even a dollar from the robbery. Instead I went for temper tantrum and began slamming the Mustang's trunk repeatedly. This caused the passenger door to close on its own while Ina was still in the car on her cell with Triple A. With every slam came the painful realization that this kid Dean was definitely mine. Denise backed off, realizing it was pointless to try and curb my rage.

I kept slamming. Ina reacted to the reverberation that was now a full-blown annoyance. "Hey, easy. Take your damn frustration out somewhere else, but not here. Not during my time of exasperation."

With each vibrating slam, I was not aware the car was inching forward slightly. Or that there was a disaster in the making. I slammed one last time, and the car started rolling towards the edge of the cliff. Somehow she must've unconsciously left the car in neutral. Ina tried to open the passenger side door from the inside. The handle came off in her hand. She was locked inside.

Her *piece of shit* cry echoed in the gully below. The car seemed to finally be deteriorating and gasping for its last breath right before our eyes. Both Denise and I ran alongside, and tried to open the door from the outside. Nothing doing. Our attempts where futile. Denise yelled for Ina to step on the brake. Ina extended her leg over the center console. Nothing. The pedal sank to the floorboard. Now real panic set it. As Ina scooted across to the driver side door, the front wheels of the car rolled several inches over the side of the cliff.

"I could use some serious help here, Sharp Guy."

Even though Denise probably had misgivings about helping Ina, she obviously felt a tinge of empathy. "Hand brake!" she yelled. "Try the hand brake!"

Still straddling the center console, Ina leaned over and groped for the hand brake under the left side of the dash. She could barely reach it. With her palm now slippery from sweat, she was able to pull the brake handle, but it didn't catch. She tried again. This time it caught but the yanking motion jostled the front end, which caused the car to tiptoe even closer towards the edge. The car teetered precariously. And to make matters even more dramatic, the engine began to overheat on its own. Smoke poured out from under the hood like an overworked steam locomotive trying to crawl its way up a steep incline. I felt totally helpless at this point. Ina looked directly at me and for the first time, I saw real fear in her eyes. A different Ina. A vulnerable Ina. Her face expressionless drained of color.

"Put the car in gear!" I repeatedly yelled.

But my advice was too late . . . the Mustang careened over the edge like a kid's toy car. Denise screamed, expecting the worst. I had a knee-jerk reaction and tried to grab the rear bumper, as if I suddenly had the superpowers and could pull the car away from the edge.

I watched hopelessly, as the Mustang was now airborne. All I could think about was what Ina asked me a few weeks ago . . .

"Ever stop to wonder how you're gonna die?"

Then, as if someone were listening, the Mustang slammed into a tree that was growing twenty feet down, off the side of the mountain, and came to a shaky rest. More smoke billowed from the engine, and the right front tire separated from the axle and flew into the air like a Goodyear Frisbee. Both Denise and I were standing at the edge of the incline. Staring. Riveted. Watching the car teeter. We exchanged looks. Denise read my mind.

"Don't try it, Jake, it's too dangerous. Besides, you have no obligation to rescue her." I heard the words *dangerous* and *obligation*, but I ignored the warning and climbed down the treacherous incline towards the car that hung on the tree like a giant Christmas ornament.

Denise was beside herself. "I'm calling for help! Wait! Where the fuck are we? What highway? I need directions!"

A car passed by; she tried to wave it down. No such luck. The car zoomed past, uninterested. The driver probably didn't want to get involved with this crazy person flapping her arms; for all they knew, she was trying to fly off the cliff.

Meanwhile, I was inching my way down the side of the cliff, moving as fast as I could, trying to reach the tree. I'm not a climber. Even as a kid I never climbed a tree. Never saw the value in it. A cat got stuck—tough; it was on its own. I reached a branch. Hoping it was sturdy enough to hold me, I swung myself around to the car window. Inside, Ina was unconscious. Her bloodied head rested against the cracked windshield. I pounded on the window, and screamed with hopeless emotion:

"You had no right treating me like one of your losers. I was sincere, played by your rules. Up front about my feelings. And now that I seem to be your only lifeline, you expect me to just forget your fucking impertinence and manipulation and toss you a safety net?"

I pounded the glass as hard as I could. My fist made a splintering noise. I thought I might have fractured my hand. It began to throb. Now my hand, my neck muscles, and my heart were beating in frantic harmony. Without thinking, I pulled the gun from my waistband and began to fire wildly at the windshield. Click, click, and click. Nothing. It was empty. And then, by some twist of who knows what, Ina's eyes blinked awake. She was suddenly conscious and responsive. She spoke in a hushed, peaceful tone.

"Don't try and rescue me, Jake. Let me crash and burn. This'll make it easier for both of us. I won't go to jail, and with me gone, your obsession, since the ninth grade, will finally come to an end." She lost consciousness again.

I continued anyway. "I'm in no mood to have this conversation. I'm saving you, whether you like it or not. I'm that kind of guy. Death is not my idea of obtaining closure."

It then occurred to me that possibly things would have turned out different if I had jumped in and saved her, metaphorically speaking, in the ninth grade. That she would have turned out to be a much more understanding and thoughtful person with some advice from me. Maybe not. Maybe there was nothing I could have done or said to change Ina Byers from being who she was—a hard-nosed rebel.

As I clung feebly to a branch with my injured hand, I reached for the door handle with my good hand. It was mere inches from my grip. I finally grabbed it, yanked it for all I was worth, but the car lurched forward, freeing itself from the tree.

I may have said a prayer, or some strained version of *Oh my God,* as my world shifted into slow motion, watching the car sail downward like a bird learning to fly for the first time, eventually slamming nose first into a bolder and flipping over on its back. It then crashed into another bolder and flipped again, only this time the trunk lid separated from the rear end and the stolen money drifted into the air, like confetti raining down on a tragic parade.

The car plummeted to the bottom and exploded like a scene out of an old war movie. Surreal. Then came silence. Denise, who had witnessed this horrendous spectacle, had covered her mouth to muffle her screams.

Pretty sure I was screaming too, but I was too busy vomiting to notice. In my shaky condition, still gripping the tree branch, I thought about how my father must've reacted when he witnessed an Army buddy taking a hit and dying in front of him. There was nothing he could've done to save him. Screamed for a medic that came too late, then ducked into a foxhole, hoping he wasn't the next casualty.

When I finally stopped hyperventilating, and wiped the tears from my eyes, I cautiously and painfully, with my injured hand, climbed back up the cliff face to solid ground. I found Denise sitting on a rock with her head in her hands. Devastation was writ large on her face.

"It wasn't real. It was like watching my father, performing a dangerous stunt," she cried.

I sat down next to Denise and cradled her head in the crook of my arm. The silence was uncanny. Even our breathing was reduced to a quiet, placid rate. I wanted to admit, but didn't, that at that particular moment I was genuinely attracted to Denise. I thought this was just an impulse someone had after experiencing a nightmarish death. You yearned for intimacy, wanting to share the moment in a more emotional, impassioned way. Maybe not. Maybe it was just me seeking, I don't know—closure.

We waited for a good forty minutes before a parade of rescue vehicles showed up—tow truck, police cruisers, and a coroner's van. The battered and burned Mustang was lifted out of the gully, dangling on a crane. The scene resembled one of those arcade games where you lower a claw, trying to latch onto a cheap prize. Regrettably, this was not a game, and the Mustang was not a prize I'd want to take home as a souvenir.

CHAPTER EIGHTEEN

Three days later, Denise and I were called into the Kern County Courthouse to give a detailed statement. By now they had found Ray Astemendi's dead body, still faceup inside the old Santa Fe depot. The forensics team was in the process of doing ballistic and DNA tests. They even took shoe print photos at both Saint Paul's Church and the railway station. Why the church? Nothing that I know of gave any indication that the church was related to Ina's crash. They obviously had some evidence that we didn't know about. Like a blood sample or an eyewitness that heard the gunshot and saw Ina and Richard Salvetti discreetly slip Ray into her trunk and speed away.

Needless to say, I was edge-of-my-seat-nervous as we were thoroughly questioned by homicide detectives. Denise and I only gave them our side of the car wreck, and how it came to be that all that money was scattered at the scene. So as not to appear suspect, I speculated and told them that rumor had it—and they could verify this from the news agency that covered the story—that Ray and Ina were responsible for ripping off Emily Easterday. Made sense that the stolen cash was probably stored in the trunk of the car. When the car hit the bottom of the ravine and exploded like a reenactment of Hiroshima, the cash must've shaken loose and rained down like residual radioactive particles. They didn't appreciate my illustrative comparison. Duly noted. I also mentioned that it seemed like I was doing their job for them—figuring out what their crime scene investigators were being paid to do. They didn't appreciate my snide remark either. Again, duly noted.

Fortunately, they didn't connect the dots and never linked me with the murder or my part in the Holy Trinity robbery. I left out a lot of pertinent info, for good reason. Why incriminate myself? Told them just enough to satisfy their investigation, and put names to faces and faces to crimes committed in Lubbock. I purposely left out Richard Salvetti being a vagrant and possibly the hit man who took out Ray Astemendi in Saint Paul's Church, because it might've been retribution for his parents' overdose. I primarily left it out because, well, if Ina was right about this *phantom killer*, then I'd be wrong. And being wrong would just confuse things, and they'd question my legitimacy as a reliable witness. And maybe even dig deeper and discover I lied about not being at the railway depot on that fateful night. The forensics team and pathologists took my fingerprints and swabbed my cheek for DNA. *Just to eliminate me from suspicion* was their reasoning. After a good two hours of intensive questioning, Denise and I were released and couldn't get to the nearest bar fast enough, where we slugged down a few drinks while discussing our future together. We agreed there was an attraction but plainly knew there wasn't going to be an *us*. Too much traumatic baggage to rehash all over again. We decided to spend at least one more unforgettable week together before going our separate ways.

⌘

The next morning, Denise and I were up bright and early. I was brewing a pot of French roast coffee while she was on the phone with an ADA friend, who worked at the Bakersfield district attorney's office. Her friend had some inside scoop on the Ina/Ray case, and was willing to share it. This was all of no significance, but it seemed both Ina Byers and Ray Astemendi were found guilty of killing Hal the guard, and robbing Emily Easterday's New Rebellion Crusade. Ray's death still remained a mystery. According to the ADA, Salvetti got away clean and was never charged for any crime. However, the skeptics thought he might have gotten away with murder. Unfortunately, Richard's body was found weeks later in his hotel room in Paris. The Four Seasons Hotel George V, to be exact. A thousand dollar a night accommodation. The death certificate indicated the cause was an overdose of amphetamines. I gathered he got paid well by Ina to afford a stay at the George V. The room service tab was over four hundred, including tips. Try wrapping your head around all that.

My dad's pistol, conceivably the murder weapon, might have been an important piece of evidence, but it was never found—either at the crash site or in my possession. Yes, they had a warrant to search my camper. I had nothing to hide because I had buried the gun next to his grave at the Veterans National Cemetery. I wasn't a true suspect, but more of a person of interest, based on Emily Easterday's testimony that I was a close personal friend of Ina and Ray. And that I was an atheist who probably got his rocks off stealing from the hand of God.

Lubbock detectives even questioned Buckley Griffin. She played it smart; said nothing to incriminate herself or me. She tried calling me several times but I didn't pick up for fear the cops were monitoring the call. Plus, reconnecting with Buckley didn't seem like a good idea. I read in the gossip columns that her marriage was in trouble. She caught her husband having an affair with one of her bridesmaids, who was also supplying him with drugs. Ain't love grand?

A few days dragged by. Maybe four days and three nights and a sleepy afternoon. I felt like I'd been driving in the slow lane of the freeway in a golf cart. Sluggish. Lacking energy. I finally sold the empty lot to a developer who planned to open a quickie lube and oil change business that promised fifteen-minute service. Just what this town needed, another enterprise that I predicted will fail because most Bakersfieldians weren't in a rush to make their lives better or more convenient.

The whole ordeal of signing over the land deed was a lot more uncomfortable than I expected. Letting go of the last crumb of my childhood memories had a profound psychological effect on me. I withdrew back to those days for a split second and caught up with myself at age seven, playing in the same dirt I had just sold. Making mud pies in a freshly dug trench filled with rainwater, then hurling the hardened dirt clods at passing cars to get their attention, hoping they'd stop and eat at my parents' diner. It was my fruitless attempt at promoting the $2.98 steak and eggs breakfast. It was a wasted effort, but I remembered getting praise from my dad for enduring the profanities that were hurled back at me by angry motorists. The day I heard the words *fuck you, kid* stuck in my mind as being truly historic. I took a big loss on the land sale. After broker fees, paying off the mortgage and the portion that I promised Helen, I was left with $65,000. Just enough to live on for maybe a year or two if I was thrifty and cut out meals for the rest of my life.

I planned to stay at least one more week but in truth, I was ready to move on and kick this small town lifestyle to the curb. Denise understood my restlessness and didn't try and talk me out of moving on. First order of business was to return the camper to the rental people. It had served its purpose—a refuge to shelter me from the elements, and a place to cry and talk to myself in the mirror when things got tough, and I needed someone who understood me to listen.

My next move was strictly an impulse decision that freed me of all material objects and greater responsibility—I sold the Jeep to a used car lot. I was deeply saddened to let it go. It, too, had served me well, transporting my emotions from infatuation, compulsion, and obsession back again to the real world and the harsh realities of my life. It would be sorely missed.

So, there I stood, twenty minutes later after closing on the land deal, leaning against a wooden pillar, on the boarding platform at the Amtrak station, drinking a lukewarm coffee from a paper cup, stripped of all my worldly possessions. All I had left was the clothes on my back and a check for $65,000 stuffed in my front pocket like it was a crumpled grocery list. I had just got my cue to board the train when two plainclothes detectives, wearing rumpled suits and neckties tied in bad Windsor knots, slid up to me and whipped out their identification. Admittedly I was a bit unmoored. They informed me that they were still looking into the murder of Ray Astemendi, and Ina Byers' unfortunate mishaps, and needed to ask me a few more questions—down at police headquarters. Mishaps? Did they now recognize this murder as a mishap? And Ina's tragic death as just an unlucky accident? I naturally went into defensive mode.

"Am I a suspect? Do I need a lawyer?" I asked, annoyed that I was about to be detained. I was not told by these two Columbo lookalikes if I was now being declared a person of interest. They just smiled, shrugged, then put me in the back seat of their undercover Dodge Dart and drove away. For all I knew they could be taking me to an abandoned warehouse, to be interrogated under bright lights. And when I didn't give them the answers they wanted, they would beat the crap out of me, then drop me at the city dump to be buried in a fucking landfill. Then again, they could be legit and I was just dramatizing for no good reason except fear, anxiety, and guilt—because I was about to be caught red-handed as an accomplice in the Emily Easterday robbery and the dead guard *mishaps*. One of my dad's Valiums would have been a welcome mood-calming enhancer at this particular time.

At police headquarters, I was put in an interview room. Cold, cramped, with gray walls and bright incandescent ceiling lighting that buzzed and gave me a headache. I was offered a beverage. I passed. After fifteen minutes alone in the room, I was nervously drumming on the metal table with my fingers when a woman finally entered. She was not at all attractive; homely, actually. Ugly, if I wanted to be really cruel. She wore a man's suit that was way too large for her small frame. She was all business. She introduced herself as Detective Jo Lewis as she slid into the chair across from me. There was no sign of a smile or anything resembling a charming personality. She turned on a tape recorder and established the time, date, her name, then segued into my vital statistics—only child, both parents deceased, never been married, no chronic conditions or substance abuse charges to speak of. Having had breezed through that without a scratch, she proceeded to give me the third degree. My words, not hers. Before her first question, I asked why I was picked up. The adept Sergeant Lewis failed to give me a straight answer. So, I was tight-lipped, making sure they couldn't push me into saying anything incriminating. All business, she finally opened up a file folder and produced a series of shoe print photos. One series taken at St. Paul's Church, the other sequence taken on site at the railway depot. None of them seemed to match in a way indicating they could have been worn by the same person, who was at both places at different times.

"So what does all this have to do with me?" I asked defensively. "I am not a shoe expert or a cobbler."

"Look, you wanna be a smart-ass, do it on someone else's time, not mine. We're just following up on some new leads that keep tripping us up."

"Sorry, I'm just anxious. I try to avoid rooms without windows. I'm claustrophobic. Stems from a childhood phobia. Postage stamp-sized bathroom with no windows." This was my first lie to the police, and it wouldn't be my last.

Detective Lewis didn't care about my fear of windowless small spaces and continued with the interview, shoving the series of shoe prints from the church across the metal table closer to me. She licked her top lip with her tongue, and that's when I noticed she had the beginnings of a mustache. She obviously didn't believe in using a depilatory cream. Just so you understand, since this was my first taste of being interrogated I was naturally a bit on edge, which is unusual for me. Normally I'm pretty calm. What I'm saying is, the whole mustache reference was purely me being defensive before she put me in some sort of uncomfortable position. It was strictly a shield to separate me from unpleasant events—like this. But I never mentioned her mustache or her rosacea skin condition.

"We believe one of these shoe prints belonged to the person who killed Ray Astemendi," she explained. "They were found in the church around the confessional booth. Pointy-toed, usually made by a cowboy boot or a European oxford. There's also this." She then produced from the same folder a clear, sealed evidence baggie. Inside was a scrap of a paper corner, obviously torn from a larger piece of paper. It showed the tip of a bull's horn with the words *Lower Mexico* printed in red. I knew exactly what I was looking at—the remnants of a Rafael Cervantes bullfight school flyer. This stirred up plenty of bile. I shook my head and denied knowing what it meant or what it was.

"Curious, where'd this come from?" I asked.

"Saint Paul's Church. You been to Saint Paul's Church recently?"

"I try to stay away from any houses of worship. Any form of religious sanctuary, actually—I was brought up in a nondenominational household. Sure, we celebrated Christmas but for all the wrong reasons—exchanging gifts, drinking eggnog, the mistletoe thing. That's how my family celebrated Jesus Christ's birthday. Nothing in the spiritual vein at all."

"Moving on. You been to Mexico lately?"

Again I lied, because there was no way of them checking that out. I drove, crossing the border with thousands of other tourists, then flew on a nondescript airline.

"Mexico—not lately. In high school, a bunch of us piled in my car and—"

"Never mind." Again, she had no interest in my personal habits as a kid and moved on.

"Forensics found no prints on the scrap of paper, which was discovered inside the front entrance. Only a series of numbers hand-written in pencil on the back in Spanish. One, two, one five, two one six, six. The numbers mean anything to you?" she asked.

I was quick to answer.

"Nope. Means nothing. But if you're looking for a lay opinion, I'd say that it could be someone's lucky lottery numbers."

"And the scrap of paper? Anything jog your memory?"

"Could be the corner of an advertisement flyer. The kind you find stuck to your windshield wiper. Most people, including myself, would be irritated by it, rip it from the wiper, and toss it on the ground. How it made its way into the church, your guess is as good as mine."

"I'm thinking it was stuck to the bottom of someone's shoe, and came loose," she said.

"Yeah. Could've been. Smart analysis. This is why you're the detective and I'm a former hash slinger trying to leave town to seek a better lifestyle. Curious—what led you to the church in the first place? A witness, perhaps? I only ask because I'm an aspiring novelist, and I'm thinking of possibly using that kind of clever storyline where the main character is killed in a church."

"Who said anyone was killed in the church?"

"So, no one was killed in Saint Paul's Church? The mention of the church was just a guess. This is you trying to piece together little tidbits, hoping they'll connect, isn't it? Interesting how you guys work. Listen, why have I really been summoned back here? Am I now considered a suspect?"

"It's all a matter of routine. You mind if we swab the inside of your cheek so we can rule out that all of the DNA in the church isn't yours?"

Either this woman was drunk or had a serious memory problem.

"Not to seem, you know, impertinent, but I was already swabbed for DNA, fingerprinted, and frisked during my first visit to this constabulary. But if you want a repeat performance, be my guest. Swab away. I have plenty of DNA to spare."

"Not necessary. My mistake. I've got a lot on my plate these days—I'm in the middle of a nasty breakup with my partner."

Sorry to hear that. *"There is always some madness in love. And always some reason in madness—Friedrich Nietzsche."* My recitation of Nietzsche did not sit well with Detective Lewis.

"Yes, well, I don't think this Nietzsche character was ever in a lesbian relationship and caught his partner fucking another woman after the pride parade last September. Anyway, back on track—I would like to take a quick sweep of your hands for gunshot residue. Again, just to eliminate you."

As she was performing the sweep of my hands with a special GSR instrument, I was now worried I could be in serious trouble. Didn't they rule me out already? Were they having second thoughts about me being innocent? I squirmed just a little.

"Curious, just to be accurate for my book about the guy killed in the church. How long does gunshot residue remain on the skin? On the hands? On the body itself?"

"I would say four to six hours. But washing your hands, or even sliding them in and out of your pocket, can erase any residue. Even suicide victims can test negative."

"That's good to know—in case I might want to shoot myself, I'd be cleared of any wrongdoing."

She released an aggravated sigh, and I just knew she wanted to smack me. But she didn't. Instead, she smacked off the tape recorder, stood, and then gave me a dismissive look.

"Sarcasm fits you very well, Mr. Reilly. You're good at it. Okay, sharp guy, you're free to go, but don't leave town just yet. Stick around for twenty-four hours in case I have any other clever questions to throw at you."

Since I was forced to stay for another day I requested they drop me off at the nearest park, where I planned to sit on a bench, watch pigeons eat bread crumbs, and brood until I was released and granted the freedom to resume my life with the common folk.

In the park, I sat on a damp bench and racked my brain, trying to come up with my own set of conclusions. I put together an arbitrary suspect list, based on the information given to me by the detective and my own personal facts. I started with the pushy Mexican kid who shoved the flyer in my face at Mascota Airport. But I couldn't imagine he'd come all the way to California to kill Ray Astemendi. What would be his motive? And did he have the balls to actually shoot a man in the back? Stranger things have happened. For now I put his name at the bottom of the list with a question mark. But I didn't rule him out.

Next came Rafael Cervantes. The mayor. An overweight, oversexed predator who reeked of cigars and tequila and boasted of fucking every woman that came his way. He seemed like the type of man who would have dealings with Ray in some unethical/shady arrangement that maybe went sour. Drug trafficking and money laundering siphoned through his bullfighting school came to mind. I placed him in the middle of the list with an asterisk. Needed some evidence of him dealing with the Mexican cartel.

And finally there was Hiram Salazar. Cab driver. Motel owner. Part-time pimp. All-around good guy. Possibly, Ray tried to take over his turf. Had visions of being top dog in Mascato. Stepped on people's toes. Made the great mistake of challenging Hiram, who carried a .45 caliber pistol and had no misgivings about using it. Maybe the gun was the same bore that was used to kill Ray. For now, he was my prime suspect.

Although Ina made it clear that she didn't know who killed Ray, she may have held back a vital piece of information, covering for the real killer. But I'd never know this, would I? I'd become exhausted trying to solve this murder. And since the police were treading water looking for any clue, I feared I was their only link to solving it, and they would hound me until I told them what they wanted to hear—which was really nothing, since I was just as much in the dark as everyone else.

I pictured Detective Jo Lewis and her team of old school detectives gathered around a smoke-filled room swapping theories and ideas, trying to put together a case based on their flimsy clues—a shell casing, size 10 pointy-toed shoe prints, and a scrap of paper with eight numbers written on the back in Spanish. *Uno-dos-uno-cinco-dos-dos-uno-seis.* I wasn't there, but I imagined the consensus in the room was that the numbers were either a code of some kind, an international phone number, or access to a numbered Swiss bank account.

I fell asleep sprawled out on the bench and was awakened by a cop ordering me to go home or get a room. I chose neither and decided to get a meal at the local surf and turf restaurant. That idea hinged on if they could cash a check for $65,000. A last supper commemorating my final departure from the land of lost souls, perhaps. I read, by way of the obits, that they planned to bury Ina's remains next to her grandmother. I hadn't forgotten her wish to be laid to rest in downtown Mascota, but there was no way I was about to carry out her wish, and get on that rocky flight back to the bullfighting capital of lower Mexico. Besides, no matter how much she had infatuated me, at this point in time there was too much bad blood between us. The regard I once had for her had vanished. Well, maybe not completely. There would always be some emotional attachment. I mean, you just can't wipe clean your feelings after a pretty remarkable girl says you're by far the sharpest knife in the drawer. She did say that, you just weren't there to hear it.

I was in the middle of my entrée when I looked up and in walked Emily Easterday. She looked great, wearing a sleeveless blouse, miniskirt, and a sexy smile. She walked in the room ahead of an attractive young man no more than twenty-four. I tried to hide my gaze because, well, I knew there'd be a lot of questions thrown at me that I'd refuse to answer or couldn't answer, and I wasn't in the mood to be snubbed by her fucking superior attitude. But I wasn't so fortunate; she saw me and crossed the room like she was onstage performing one of her fake healing miracles. Her companion was not far behind. She stopped at my table. People around the room watched her every move. They knew who she was, but I cleared it up for those who might not know why they were staring. I spoke loud enough for the cooks in the kitchen to hear . . .

"Emily Easterday, evangelical superstar, as I live and breathe!"

"Living and breathing. That's more than we can say for Ina, Ray, and Hal the degenerate guard—right, Jake?"

"What is it you want, Ms. Easterday? Besides stating the obvious about dead people who find it hard to breathe."

"For starters, I want the half million dollars that was stolen from me, but that's not going to happen, is it, Jake? It's all a pile of ashes in the bottom of a ravine."

I intentionally dropped my napkin, hoping after I picked it up, she'd be gone. No such luck.

"So, why're you in Bakersfield—big evangelical convention in town? A wild time led by an illustrious potentate in a red fez?"

"We're setting up our cross at the outdoor amphitheater at The Park at River Walk. Bringing my worship service to the good folks who are in need of cleansing and spiritual healing in the California sun."

"Sorry, I'll have to miss that performance. It's on the same night I wash my hair."

I nodded at the guy, who now stood close to her, posing with his hands stuffed in his slacks pockets like a department store mannequin.

"Who's this, the new boyfriend? Ray's replacement? Does he know you're a charlatan? Does he know the meaning of charlatan?"

The guy clenched his fists inside his pockets, then moved towards me like he was going to defend her reputation through some sort of aggressive action. He spoke in a thick British accent. Proper it wasn't.

"Should I handle this bloody wanker, miss?"

"Bloody wanker? Are you an East Ender, mate? I detect a slight working-class cockney enunciation. Does he know the meaning of enunciation?"

"Ignore him, Simon. I'm used to biting comments thrown at me by clueless people who don't understand the gift of healing that I possess. Did they ever find out who murdered poor Ray?"

"Not yet," I said, "but they have a bundle of bloody suspects. Not literally, figuratively. I'm sure they already called you in for questioning. I'm also sure you, in your infinite, dynamic way, used your flirtatious sex appeal, and your personal relationship with God, to sway any allegations that you might have been in on the robbery to boost your own pocketbook. I have to say, I love how this conversation is flowing. Accusatory, yet not too vicious—where you command your watchdog to attack and bite me on the leg."

That pretty much ended it.

"Nice chatting with you, Jake."

I expressed a slight smile, and nothing more, just to be neighborly.

She moved off to sit at table in the back. Away from the sinners. I couldn't help but notice that Simon was wearing a pair of pointy-toed Italian oxfords. Thought nothing of it until I realized his shoes could match the shoe prints found at the church. If they happened to be an exact match, that certainly cast a whole new light on the phantom killer. It would eliminate Hiram Salazar as a prime suspect and put Emily Easterday center stage for having a good reason to have Ray killed. You steal a half million dollars from Emily Easterday, you had to expect some form of retaliation. A slap across the face, being hollered at, a bullet to the back of the head. Something malicious. Something final.

If this Simon character killed Ray, where did Ina fit in? For a minute she claimed Salvetti killed him, and then took it back, saying it was a phantom menace. None of this jibed. *Dubious* was becoming the word of the day. Also, why did Ina try and pin the murder on me? What was behind that? Trying to throw off and misdirect the law and cover for the real killer that she was in collusion with? I added Simon the East Ender to my list of suspects but hadn't completely written off the idea that Ina played a prominent role.

I needed serious help because my list of suspects was growing. Someone to bounce ideas and theories off of and to supply me with a couple Tylenol for my raging headache. I headed straight for Denise's place. As a court reporter, she had a knack for piecing together dicey situations. Plus, I wanted to see her one more time before I left town. Which was now twenty-hours and counting.

CHAPTER NINETEEN

It was 8 p.m. Denise had just washed her hair and was dripping when she answered the door. Without a word, she instantly pulled me into the bathroom, where I sat on the toilet (lid was down, thank you very much). I got to the point and ran down the relevant information. We began to deconstruct the murder of Ray Astemendi, while her hairdryer operated at full throttle. It made it difficult to catch every word, prompting her to intermittently switch the dryer on and off between thoughts. Fifteen minutes later her hair was dry, and we were sitting at the kitchen table, drinking wine while trying to devise a plan of attack based on what we now knew.

Ray Astemendi was murdered inside the confessional booth at St. Paul's Church, with a slug to the back of his head—that was a given. Our first suspect, based on what Ina told me, was Richard Salvetti, who pulled the trigger. Supposedly unintentionally. Up until now there was really nothing to substantiate her claim. It was Ina's word against mine. However, new leads had cropped up. The scrap of paper from lower Mexico and the shoe prints raised the question: who trampled through the crime scene from Mexico? We both changed our minds and agreed on a new primary suspect—Hiram Salazar. Mainly because he owned a .45, wore rough out, pointy-toed cowboy boots, and was familiar with the bullfighting school flyers that he found on his windshield daily. So for the moment that eliminated Salvetti. Again, we went back to the lingering question—why would Hiram want Ray dead? Motive, motive, motive. And if Hiram did do it, where did Ina fit in? Did she and Hiram plot the crime as a team? So far we had nothing solid to go on, only speculation.

Now we came to Emily Easterday with the British boyfriend wearing pointy-toed Italian-made Oxfords. If it was him, that meant Emily had to somehow be involved. And we knew she definitely held a grudge and had good reason to eliminate Ray. Then there was my own harebrained scenario—that maybe they were all guilty. Made a pact. Like the characters in Agatha Christie's *Murder on the Orient Express*. They all had personal reasons to murder the boorish businessman, Ratchett aka Cassetti.

We focused on seven players—Ina Byers, Hiram Salazar, Rafael Cervantes, Rafael's pushy thirteen-year-old nephew, Jorge, Carmen De La Vega, Simon the Brit, and, of course, Emily Easterday.

We took a break and had sex for an hour to clear our heads before we started over, and tried to figure out how to get a look at the soles of Simon's shoes. Even if we accomplished that, then what? We had no way of matching his soles with the soles the cops had on file. I would have to go directly to the police to see if there was a match. My guess was, they wouldn't release that information during an ongoing investigation. It was all too risky and would put me in a very vulnerable position. I'd have to admit that in some way, I had information regarding the robbery, Ray's murder, and Hal's alleged suicide.

The smart thing for me to do would be to drop the whole thing and let the professionals figure it all out. It wasn't my job to solve this murder. But I did have a responsibility to make sure the right person was brought to justice and charged for killing Ray. With Ina dead, I was the only one who knew that Ray killed Hal with Hal's own gun. This was also a lingering unsolved mystery. But if I came forward, my testimony could help put the missing pieces together.

There was obviously a missing link that was driving both Denise and me nuts. A large, gaping hole. She suggested we should clear our heads again and have sex before we tackled our next move. My God, what had we become, entry-level sleuths?

An hour later we came up with a clever plan to catch a glimpse of the sole of Simon's shoe. Clever is not exactly the right adjective. More like ill-advised but doable. It involved Denise and some feminine charm—of which she had plenty to spare.

⁜

We showered—together—had another run at sex in the shower, then dressed in our most inconspicuous evangelical street clothes (whatever that was) and with a burst of adrenaline, made an appearance at Emily Easterday's New Rebellion Crusade. This was the same venue where I happened to see the Doobie Brothers perform years ago—the outdoor amphitheater at The Park at River Walk. The house was packed with the usual followers and fans of her spiritual renaissance. Our only mission was to track down Simon, and put Denise's plan to work.

An hour later, Emily had just performed her closing miracle—restoring the hearing of a young girl who suffered a hearing loss in one ear, when at the age of ten, shoved a marble down her ear canal, piercing the eardrum.

With one hand cupped over the girls' bad ear and using the other ear as a conduit to God, she screamed, at the top of her lungs, her own concocted sanctified bullshit into the good ear.

Just like in the movie *It's a Wonderful Life*, in which George Bailey lost his hearing while saving his brother Harry from drowning, she, too, had experienced a similar tragedy trying to save her baby sister from perishing at the bottom of a swimming pool. Her bravery was rewarded—she saved her sister.

As far as I was concerned, this was not exactly an extraordinary feat. I mean, the thing was, yes, the girl couldn't hear in one ear, and yes, she was heroic and saved her baby sister, but like George Bailey, she had perfect hearing in the other ear and had led a remarkable life. Not exactly a showstopper using screaming as a healing device. I think Emily Easterday had stolen the George Bailey story because, well, she had run the gamut of complete human emotion and was desperate for anything that would appeal to her fan base. And it must've paid off because a surplus of *amens* rattled the arena, praising Emily's power to carry out such a spiritual achievement. Arms were raised up to heaven praising God for his divine supremacy. The chorus sang an up-tempo song, which signaled the ushers and attendants to march up and down the aisles like robotic devices, pass the collection plates, and rake in the cash. While Frank Capra, I'm sure, rolled over in his grave. Plus, I pose the question—who's to say the girl was really deaf? I didn't rule out, that the girl was an actress, recruited from the local scam artist talent agency.

From our seats in the tenth row, Denise spotted Simon. He was standing to one side of the stage and was wearing an earpiece

(FBI style) just like Ray once did. We knew that Simon, like Ray, performed as Emily's security captain. He held a black bank bag and collected the donations as the ushers poured the proceeds into it like a cascading waterfall of dollars and cents.

It was time for Denise to make her solitary move and approach the suspect. She was not without anxiety and trepidation, because if in fact he was the killer, that meant he had homicidal tendencies, and the last thing she wanted was to say or do anything to set off his temper. Undetected, she tiptoed her way backstage, hidden from view by any crewmembers who might question her presence. All I could do was watch and hope I didn't have to come to her rescue. I had snuck over and situated myself at the edge of the stage and could see and hear their interaction. It was almost impossible to see Simon's shoes from where I stood, but the tops of his white socks were visible. Who wears white socks with brown Oxfords and black slacks? A man with no style who dressed himself in the dark.

At the last possible moment Denise decided to scrub her original plan of attack: pretending she knew him from a pub in England. She instead rushed up to him and played it like a crazed groupie on speed. Talking incessantly.

"I love your shoes. Very stylish. Italian, yes?"

"What? You can't be here. Now move it," he demanded.

"I need to get a pair for my boyfriend. He's Italian. Born in Naples. Mind if I take a quick snapshot? Thanks. You're a dream."

"Yes, I mind. Leave. Now."

He became physical and pushed her away. Denise didn't let up. She whipped out her smartphone and started to take several pictures of his shoes.

"I said sod off, you cow."

She then took him by surprise, and with all the strength she could manage, lifted his leg by the ankle to display the oxford's sole. He lost his balance, nearly toppling over and losing his grip on the bank bag. She was able to snap a picture, but not before he nearly took off her head, executing an axe kick like some martial arts fighter. Denise got the subtle hint that she was in serious danger and rushed off the stage, out of the arena, and into the parking lot.

We met up at her car, jumped inside, and made a hasty getaway like we had just done something criminal. Denise was still a little shaken.

"That cocksucker nearly took my head off," she said shuddering.

"I saw. You were very brave."

"Brave? I literally peed my pants. Before we do anything else, I need to change my underwear. I refuse to drop this evidence shot off at the police station smelling like the toilet floor of a gas station."

There was actually no rush because of a slight hiccup in our next planned move. I couldn't deliver the sole print in person. I couldn't risk them accusing me of being one of the people behind the Ray Astemendi murder. The iPhone photo would have to be sent by email or text, anonymously. We decided to hold off for now until we had a safer, more plausible way to go about it. We were in unfamiliar territory.

It started to rain when we drove away from the arena. Interestingly enough, we noticed Simon and Emily getting into a car. Her car. They appeared awfully cozy. He got behind the wheel. From our vantage point we saw them in a clench, kissing one another long and hard. No doubt this was more than just a late-night Bible study with Auntie Em. We had a choice of either following them or going straight to the police. Question was, what did it profit us to follow them? What could they possibly lead us to? We needed confirmation on the shoe print before we dove into anything that might get us hurt or made us look like an unreliable source of information.

Fifteen minutes later we were back at Denise's apartment. She changed her underwear, her pants, her blouse, and her outlook reinforcing the idea that some British men were definitely proper wankers. I was loosening up in the kitchen, watering a hanging plant that was dying while I downed my second glass of wine. These days death seemed to be following me. The diner, my dad, Ina, Ray, and now a philodendron begging for its life.

I think my twenty-four hour proviso had lapsed. Didn't matter, I wasn't going anywhere. Leaving Denise hanging was not an option. Yet she had other ideas . . .

"If I were you, I would not hesitate to leave town. Ride like the wind. Let me deliver the shoe print to that detective, while you hop on the first stage leaving Dodge." A beat. "Did you hear me?" she yelled louder.

"Yes, I heard!" I hollered back. "Found the Wild West reference to be very unique. But I'm not budging. I'm too caught up in this mess that's plagued me since I rolled into Texas, allowing a pathetic cartoon potato to usher me into a fulfilling life of crime. I need to make sure I'm cleared of any charges. Understand what I'm saying?"

"Yes. Plagued. Texas. Potato. I get all the highlights. But I think you're overreacting. Being paranoid for no good reason. They have nothing on you except, I dunno, bad judgment on who you had breakfast with in a Texas diner, where an old man with dementia rear-ended your car, which triggered a sequence of bad luck events and threw you into a tailspin. So what? People have experienced worse."

"What people? Name names, please, so I can follow up and see if they've ended up either in prison or killed for holding back vital information."

"Killed? You think maybe someone wants to kill you because you know too much? Too much about what—literature?"

"About how Hal the guard really died. The possibility his family members are out to seek revenge and are tracking me down."

"And how would they know you witnessed his death?"

"You look hard enough, you find things out."

"So then, while they snoop around, they'll discover it was an accident."

"You're right. I'm just being paranoid."

"I'd change my name just to be safe, however."

"What?"

"Just kidding."

The back and forth rhythm of the conversation made me dizzy. I departed the kitchen and slumped down on the couch in the living room. I propped my feet up on the coffee table and relaxed. I was nursing a third glass of wine to help gather my thoughts but got distracted and turned my attention towards the framed autographed one sheet of the movie *Bullitt* with Steve McQueen that hung on the wall. I wondered what Steve McQueen would do in this kind of dilemma. I'm sure it would've entailed jumping over a barbed wire fence on a motorcycle. Which didn't help me whatsoever.

Denise finally reentered the room fully dressed in dry clothes. She plopped down next to me. Close. Her body heat radiated up and down my legs. It warmed my soul.

I poured her a glass of wine and we fell silent for the longest time, taking small sips and racking our brains trying to come up with how to proceed with our own private little unauthorized investigation. We were warned by the cops to stay clear. Don't get involved. Let them do their job. Don't disturb the crime scenes, stop looking for clues, and suspend approaching any potential suspects with English fucking accents.

We finished off the bottle of wine and had nothing to show for it except a stain on my shirt, where I had carelessly dribbled. I headed back to the kitchen to try and remove the stain with club soda. She had no club soda so I tried using 7UP. As I blotted, I launched a cloying question that travelled from room to room, hovering over an exhausted Denise, who had her eyes closed, taking a catnap.

"Have I ever told you how much I really adore everything about you?"

I waited for a response, which I had hoped would've come sooner, or at least that she'd come running in and pounce on me with great affection. Nothing. Instead I got this in-depth reaction:

"Adore? I don't think I've ever been adored. This is definitely a first, being adored. I know there was a time when this one guy put me on a pedestal. Never adored me though."

I had to laugh out loud to myself.

I reentered with the stain still visible on my shirt. The 7UP made it worse. I now had a round red spot that looked like I had been in a paint ball gunfight. I continued to try to impress . . .

"I'm especially fond of your hazel eyes, turned up nose, and sandy hair, not to mention your well-developed brain."

Her eyes slowly blinked open. "Yes. This is without a doubt a first. No one has ever adored my well-developed brain. I am flattered. Truly I am. Not to seem ungrateful by your generous compliment, but I need to know: will you still *adore* me the same way once you take a closer look and discover that my eyes are blue, my nose straight, and my hair a reddish brown?"

Now it was her turn to laugh.

"What's so funny?" I asked.

"I find it rather hilarious that when we first met you were more interested in my tits than my eyes."

"What can I say? I'm a repulsive, despicable person." Then I noticed. "My God, you're right, your eyes are very blue."

We shared a laugh, and just as we were about to extend our audible foreplay into something more physical, my cell phone rang, breaking up what could've been a killer of a romantic moment.

It was police detective Jo Lewis. I flinched, because I may have spoken too soon about me being untouchable. They must've found something that connected me with—well, everything. She sounded insistent and wanted us—me specifically—to meet her at the station in an hour. She had a walk-in witness who was there to spill some details germane to Astemendi's death.

We couldn't wait the full hour. The anticipation of who this witness was had us ramped up with curiosity. We were there in fifteen minutes, arriving breathless, as if we had leapt off the sofa and ran all the way.

When we arrived, I was briefed. Denise listened with rapt attention like she was watching a box-office smash. The summarization went exactly like this: seemed a man, rugged looking, dark complexion, dressed in jeans and a well-worn leather jacket, came in, identified himself only as a person from Mascota, Mexico, confessed that he also wanted to kill Señor Astemendi dead, but got there too late. That's as far as it got until he specifically asked to speak to Señor Jake before he would say another word. No last name, but it was very clear who he wanted to talk to. But why would this man go out of his way to confess to a crime he didn't commit but wanted to commit—and would've committed if he had gotten there first? This puzzled Detective Lewis and the other members of her squad. I was brought in hopefully to fill in the blanks.

I was not as perplexed as they were. Figured it had to be one of three people: Hiram Salazar, Rafael Cervantes, or Carmen De La Vega. But I couldn't imagine why any of them would want Ray dead. Or how they might be involved. Motive baffled me. But I didn't admit to any personal ties for fear they'd see it as a conflict of interest. Showing favoritism would not be in my favor.

The detective told me they were looking into this further before formally detaining the man on the basis of his being an accomplice. And of course giving out more information that might lead to the gunman's whereabouts.

The first line of questioning was standard. Find out where this man was on the day of the murder and match the pointy-toed cowboy boots he was wearing with the forensic shoe prints.

This seemed like the most opportune time to hand over the Simon shoe photo Denise took. However, we held off until we got a clearer picture of what we had walked into.

Both Denise and I were ushered into an interview room to make an identification. Denise had no idea who this man was. Never seen him before in her life, she said while shaking her head. Me, on the other hand, a whole different reaction. Shaking my head wouldn't sell the shock on my face. But why was I so surprised to see Hiram Salazar sitting uncomfortably on a metal chair and not behind the wheel of his '57 Chevy? I shouldn't have been—after all, he was at the top of my suspect list.

I got a warm welcome.

"Nice to see you again, Señor Jake. Carmen sends her best regards. You are looking *un poco pálido* [a little pale]. You sick? Maybe shocked to see it is me?"

"Actually, I'm not that shocked. You were at the top of my—never mind, I think we all could use an explanation. Why are you here, for one? Two, why are you confessing to wanting Ray Astemendi dead? And for what reason? Was he blackmailing you? Did he maybe discover you were dealing drugs with the Mexican cartel and threatened to turn you in unless you paid him handsomely?" Paid him handsomely? That last sentence seemed to crop up like I'd stolen it from some B movie.

"What? No. You got it all wrong. I do not deal drugs."

"Then what? Tell the detective, or she'll find a reason to arrest you for conspiracy to commit murder."

The detective turned to Hiram. "I know, everything he just said is a lot to digest. For me too. Let's start with this piece of evidence. Did you accidently drop this scrap of paper from a flyer at the scene?" She produced the evidence, which was sealed in a baggie.

"Si. If you look on the back, the numbers 1215-2216 are written in Spanish. For my eyes only, from Senorita Ina Byers. A coded message giving me instructions. It was the time to be at the church and the address. It must've been stuck to the bottom of my boot and fallen off when I ran away scared."

"So then, if we take this to court, along with the other evidence we have accumulated against you, you'd be willing to say under oath that you committed this crime? And Ina Byers was an accomplice?"

"I don't know the meanings of accomplice," Hiram said, looking at me for an interpretation.

"*Co-conspirador.*" I just happened to know that translation from my third year Spanish class.

"*Conspirador?* No. You put the words in my mouths. You maybe not understand what I say. I came in with my hands in the air, giving up because I, Hiram Salazar, figured it was only a matter of times before you peoples had the proof of me being at the crime place. At the church." He crossed himself in a spontaneous gesture of piety. "But I admit now in front of you and God that I did not kill Señor Ray but had good reason to want him dead very much."

"Did you know Richard Salvetti, a known vagrant and drug addict," the detective said, "or have you ever had dealings with him?"

"Dealings? No dealings. Salvetti was already at the church when I arrived and found Señor Ray dead *en el confesionaro* box. I never met Salvetti before that day. We both had our reasons to want him dead, this is true. Ray sold Salvetti's mother and father the bad drugs that killed them, and my problemo was also *muy malo.* For you to know—that *pendejo* of a man got my daughter, Anna, pregnant. Pregnant!" He slammed his fist on the table violently. "She was only fifteen. Quince! Under the age. A child. A virgin."

There was a natural silence in the room. I needed to lean against the wall to keep from falling over because I was now dizzy from his confession. I had no idea he had a young daughter. But why would I?

Hiram filled us in, which helped us to understand how this all happened.

"My daughter, she met Señor Ray at the evangelista's revival in Texas, when she went to the religious night with her aunt Lourdes, who had very bad *artritis reumatoide* in her hands and wanted to ease the pain. Señor Ray saw her in the crowd and liked my daughter very much. She was very beautiful and looked much older. He took her to many nice restaurants and showed her a good time around the town. One thing led to another thing and now she is having his baby."

"Jesus. Did he rape her, Hiram? If this is a case of statutory rape, he should be castrated." I swallowed a quick gust of anger and kicked a chair across the interview room. This, of course, raised the eyebrows of the group. Lewis had to calm me down. Act civil or I'd have to leave was what she ordered. I complied. It just pissed me off that that motherfucker took advantage of this young girl. I bit my lower lip, stood in the corner, and listened.

Lewis went on: "So, señor, do you think your daughter was raped?"

"I am not sure. Maybe, yes. She was a virgin. Maybe she fell in love with him. At fifteen she was maybe, how do you say, *enamorado* by his machismo."

"Enamored," I translated unnecessarily.

Everyone understood what he was saying. She was infatuated and got sucked in by his macho bullshit.

"She wanted to keep the baby but is too young to be a mother. Her Aunt Lourdes and me, we have tried to talk her out of doing this, but she believed maybe this was God's will. She is very religious, my daughter. When Senorita Ina found out about what Señor Ray did, she called me in Mexico and the three of us—her, Salvetti, and me—agree to make sure Señor Ray never take the advantage of young girls again. We decided to chop off his cock in his sleep with a *machete*."

Okay. A little too graphic for my taste, but we all understood his pain and were touched by his comments. Understanding a father's overprotectiveness for his daughter is not a difficult concept to grasp.

"Think about it," I spoke up, "three people, all of whom were affected by Ray's unscrupulous, nasty conduct, combine forces to have him terminated. I mean, fifteen or not, you just don't kill someone because they got your daughter pregnant. Do you? Murder is murder. Even I know that you can't just turn your back on the law and do what your heart tells you to do. In this case, taking out the motherfucker who violated your young daughter."

Detective Lewis chimed in. "Jake is right, murder is murder no matter what the motive. I can't overlook that Señor Salazar may have committed a crime, no matter how heartbreaking his story is."

"I swear on my daughter's life, I did not kill Ray Astemendi in the church with a bullet to his head," he said with an emotional crackle in his voice.

It wasn't my place to change the subject but I did anyway.

"What about the money stolen from Emily Easterday?" I asked.

"I know nothing about any stolen monies."

"Forget about the money for now," the detective interrupted brusquely. "Most of it is gone anyway. Burned. But what I need to know is how the Englishman, Simon, fits it?"

"I know nothing about any Englishman. But I'm thinking he was here to also send Señor Ray to the early grave. A paid *el asesino* maybe."

"Paid? Do you know who hired this man?" Lewis asked.

"No. But if it was him, I'd shake his hand and throw him a fiesta."

The detective turned to me as if I were now part of the team and suddenly had all the answers. This was the moment Denise showed the photo of the pointy-toed Italian oxford. And I revealed how I thought that this British bloke was working for Emily Easterday in more ways than one. Head of security for her Counterculture Foundation and part-time hit man when she had the urge to eliminate people who were disloyal to the inner circle and bad-mouthed her idealistic philosophy. That last bit of knowledge was nothing but pure speculation on my part, but not an unrealistic statement of fact.

They took a fifteen-minute coffee break. I passed. It gave me time to pace, organize my thoughts, and theorize about the situation. Again, strictly a wild stab but not unrealistic: Ina hated Ray for cheating on her, but mostly because he used her crusade as a dating service to meet desperate, distraught women seeking a quick fix to mend the grief in their private lives. The man was scum. The ultimate slap in the face, however, was that he didn't accept responsibility for knocking up Hiram's daughter. According to Hiram, Anna came to Emily in her dressing room after one of her spiritual gatherings, and asked for help. She wanted advice about how she should handle Ray's denial that her child was his. Emily did not take this news lightly and made a promise she'd handle it.

Coffee break was over. Everyone gathered again in the interview room. Detective Lewis looked tired. The bags under her eyes were even more pronounced and fleshy. I let everyone get settled before I presented the burning question:

"Where do the shoe prints fit it? Are they Hiram's? No. He is not an Italian oxford kind of guy. Can we agree he's strictly a Western boot guy? Yes. So, I'd say that eliminates him from the suspect list."

Denise finally handed over the iPhone shot, which we quickly discovered were not a match with Simon's shoes either. That in itself now seemed like a waste of energy, getting his shoe prints and putting Denise in a bit of danger. Although he seemed to be off the hook, no one counted him out. After all, once a crook, always a crook. Detective Lewis was at her wits' end. Seemed like the cops had reached an impasse. Or had they?

Upon Detective Lewis's orders, the police went back and surveyed the crime scene at the church, based on Hiram's statement that he thought Ray was shot in the confessional by a third party. Then his body was moved to the depot by Ina and Salvetti. A bigger question was introduced: if the three of them were innocent, what purpose did moving the body serve? This stumped the room, but not me. I knew why: because Ina wanted to pin this murder on me as a safety precaution to cover her own ass, and also to cover the asses of Hiram and Salvetti. But I wasn't about to slip that piece of the puzzle on the table, because it would put me at the crime scene where Ray was found. As far as the police were concerned, I was nothing but a private citizen trying to help them piece together this crime. And it was only because of my past connection with Ina Byers and Ray Astemendi that they were hoping I could come up with viable clues that would help them track down the real killer. I had no idea who they thought I was—one of those crazy psychics who claim to have the ability to find a missing child by feeling a piece of clothing, maybe?

As I already mentioned, the police went back to the church for a quick once-over in the event forensics had missed something. Which they had. A .45 caliber shell casing was discovered lodged under the baptismal font. Ballistics matched the bullet taken from Ray Astemendi.

Based on Hiram's testimony that Emily told his daughter, Anna, she'd handle Ray, they went out on a limb and had the forensics team thoroughly reexamine Easterday's dressing room at the outdoor amphitheater at The Park at River Walk, and the surrounding area.

As luck would have it, they discovered a .45 caliber pistol hidden in the giant neon blue cross hanging from the rafters. Another ballistics test proved that it was in fact the murder weapon. Although there was no evidential proof, Emily was taken into custody as a prime suspect for the murder of Ray Astemendi.

Denise and I were not allowed to be present during Emily's interview. But we did watch on a monitor inside an adjacent room.

Detective Lewis sat across from Emily Easterday and her lawyer, a big shot attorney from a high-end Beverly Hills law firm. He looked like he just stepped out of a Tennessee Williams play, complete with long white hair and a southern accent. "My client only agreed to this sit-down because she wanted to abide by the rules," he said with a syrupy drawl. "Bring the true assailant to trial. For the record, she is making it emphatically clear she is not guilty."

Emily stood up as if she was about to perform one of her legendary miracles on Detective Lewis. A real theatrical move if ever there was one. She looked to heaven. The bright fluorescent lighting rebounding off the ceiling caused her to wince and shade her eyes.

"I'm sure I look frightful in this lighting," she said before speaking in her most persuasive manner. And always, she used dramatic hand gestures to sell her deathless oratory. "I'm willing to take a polygraph test to prove my innocence. I am a lot of things to a lot of people, but a murderer? I am far from being that kind of individual. I pride myself in helping the less fortunate. When I said to that dear, distressed child, Anna, that I would handle Ray, what I meant was exactly that—I would handle Ray. Take him to task. Make him see the error of his ways using the power God has given me. Words and prayer. I had that kind of influence over Ray—but I obviously never got the chance to render my thoughts and use my divine power.

Someone, not me, took the law into their own hands and handled it in the way they saw fit—with the gun you found in my cross."

I applauded her performance. Although she couldn't hear or see me, she knew her soliloquy proclaiming her innocence was award-winning.

There was a pause while Lewis pondered if Emily suddenly had the upper hand or not. With no real proof, Lewis was at a disadvantage, and the lawyer used his legal leverage.

"If you're going to hold my client, you need more than just a gun found in a large acrylic cross. Is the gun hers? Are her fingerprints on the gun? Have you considered that some religious hate group that is out to destroy Ms. Easterday's reputation might have planted the gun? If your answer to all those questions is a flat *no,* then we're leaving. Interview over."

Emily and her attorney headed for the door.

"Wait! Not so fast," said Lewis. "Everybody just stay put. This is far from being over. You leave when I say you can leave. That's how it works here. I'm in charge until someone of a higher power says different." Lewis gazed obsequiously at the drab gray ceiling.

"By that you must mean our Lord and Savior, Jesus Christ," Emily said in a sublime manner.

"In your world that may be true, but on mine it's the chief of detectives on the floor above us."

The questioning dragged on for another grueling forty minutes. It went nowhere. Lewis tried every trick in the book to cause Emily to slip up and give false evidence, but she came out of it without a scratch that could damage her reputation.

Denise and I met with Detective Lewis an hour later in the police station canteen over a cup of something charitably called coffee and an alien-looking cheeseburger that I'd be too embarrassed to serve. She was nice enough to keep us in the loop. Why? Who knows? I think she was just frustrated and was getting pressured by her superiors to solve this case and needed an objective point of view.

She had no choice but to release Emily Easterday, because she had an ironclad alibi. Seemed she and Simon were in a hotel room at the time of the murder. Room service corroborated they never left all night. Auntie Em was putting her evangelical powers to good use with a butt slap and a tickle, I imagined. To support their alibi, the pathologist estimated that the murder took place at the church between 12:30 p.m. and 2:00 p.m. and was moved to the depot, where they found his body, sometime after that. Ina, Salvetti, and Hiram Salazar agreed to snuff Ray at 1:30 p.m. However, Richard and Hiram didn't show up until 1:45 p.m.—fifteen minutes later. And Ina, who left the confessional to go outside and smoke a cigarette, had no knowledge that Salvetti and Hiram Salazar were late, and showed up after Ray was killed by a third party—an unknown man or woman, who by then had taken flight and was presumably hiding somewhere in the city.

Thing was, I wasn't that quick to eliminate our elusive Englishman. Lewis wasn't willing to disregard his culpability, but she had nothing on him that would stick. I was still convinced that Emily Easterday recruited him through some devious UK connection. I theorized he slipped out of the hotel room undetected, went to the church, killed Ray at 12:30 p.m. and was back in time to pop Emily one more time before the two o'clock checkout time. How he knew Ray would be at the church was still a mystery. But if this guy was a professional, he had ways of knowing. I think he got wind of where Ray was staying and followed him just as he was leaving the Padre Hotel to meet with Ina at the church.

When the forensics team discovered the shell casing under the baptismal font, they also concluded that most of the shoe prints were actually made by the priest, Father Anthony, and not Simon. After further inquiry, it was learned the priest's Italian oxfords were a gift given to him by a bishop friend staffed at the Vatican. Of course, it was no coincidence he was at the church at the time of the murder. It was he who actually called 9-1-1 after hearing shots fired. He was alone in the rectory preparing for his Sunday service. So his whereabouts at the time of the murder were not confirmed by anyone but him. He said there was no living person who could vouch for him, However, he added, a statuette of Mary, the mother of Jesus, perched on a shelf inside his rectory office, was always looking over him. Well, that wasn't good enough for Lewis and her band of rumpled detectives. The next day, Father Anthony was brought in for questioning.

CHAPTER TWENTY

Gathered inside the police station interview room, Father Anthony sat across the table from Detective Lewis and a young detective, Patric Siddens, who was acting as a witness to the quizzing. Since we were so deeply rooted in this investigation, the police agreed to overlook protocol and let Denise and I watch and listen to the discussion through the two-way, semi-transparent mirror.

Let me set the scene: Detective Siddens turned on the tape recorder. Lewis spoke and enunciated slowly, so there was no confusion about what was taking place.

"The time is 16:30. Present are Detective Jo Lewis, Detective Sergeant Patric Siddens, and Father Anthony, who they are questioning at this time in connection with the Ray Astemendi murder that occurred on Wednesday, the twenty-five of May, 2014 at Saint Paul's Church in downtown Bakersfield. Let it be known that at this time Father Anthony is not a suspect, but rather a person of interest to help ascertain a few details related to the case."

Denise and I are watching the action from the cheap seats, behind a two-way mirror. It was clearly noticeable that Father Anthony appeared fidgety, wringing his hands nervously. He was offered the usual choice of beverage—coffee, tea, water. If it were me doing the offering, I'd have served a cup of sacramental wine just to keep things friendly. They apologized for bringing him in and said it was just a formality since the murder took place at his church, and that they were making every possible effort to get to the bottom of this horrible crime that occurred in his parish. The church had been sealed off with crime tape and declared off limits until further notice. Parishioners would have to go pray somewhere else, or let their sins build up until the confessional booths were reopened for business.

Father Anthony tried to be accommodating. Even before Detective Lewis got started, the priest reiterated that he was the one who called 9-1-1, but by the time the first responders showed up there was no body or anything resembling a shooting. The confessional was bare. Which of course left the cops scratching their heads.

"If there's anything I can do to help bring this tragedy to the forefront, you can count on me to be cooperative," he said with as much sincerity as necessary to maybe fool us into believing he was genuinely concerned, and of course to be found not guilty of any crime himself.

Maybe he should have been concerned. I for one was skeptical. Why? His posture. Slumped over, with his arms tightly cradled around his waist as if he were carrying a heavy load. Hiding a secret. That was the vibe I got from Father Anthony. More than just the shameful secrets he heard at confessions, about how Uncle Ernie pinched his niece's cheek, then her ass, when she was thirteen. And how it affected her trust in men. Something a lot juicier. I'd served and conversed with enough people in the diner to know when a person was riddled with guilt. It was how they looked around the room, veiling their plate, making sure no one was judging them by the way they ate their bacon and eggs.

Denise didn't want to believe the priest was an unsavory character.

Lewis first asked if he minded if they took his prints and swabbed his mouth for DNA, just to eliminate him from the list of possible suspects. He automatically became defensive, which to me sent a message that he was hiding something. I got the highest grade in my psychology course and it was about to pay off.

"Am I a suspect?" the priest questioned. "I get the feeling that I'm being looked at as the bad guy here."

Boom, there you go, a sure sign he was about to stumble and try to wriggle out of the truth.

"Everyone within spitting distance of the church is a suspect, Padre," Lewis said. "It's how we work. Point a guilty finger until the killer trips up, and when he or she does, that's when we throw the net over 'em. But I'm sure you have nothing to hide. Right, Padre? According to the 9-1-1 emergency operator you called in at around 12:45."

"Yes, that seems right."

"And how many minutes before that did you hear the gunshot?"

"It would only be a guess, but not more than five minutes."

"So you waited five minutes before calling it in?"

"Yes. I guess I was trying to reassess what I heard. Why?"

"Because if you heard the gunshot at say, 11:45—"

"Which I didn't."

"And you didn't call until 12:45, that would be a problem. There'd be an hour unaccounted for. The reason I question the time is because, according to the forensic team, the murder took place sometime between 12:45 and 1:45."

"How can forensics determine time of death without a body?"

"I'm the one asking the questions, Padre. So, in your statement you said you heard a shot at 11:45, which is what, an hour and fifteen minutes earlier than our team guesstimated. So something doesn't add up. Where did that extra time go?"

"I could be off maybe a couple of minutes but no way a full hour and fifteen," Father Anthony insisted. "Look, I know what I heard and when I heard it. I can't prove what I heard, nor can I pinpoint the time of the murder. Maybe what I heard was a car backfiring and thought it was a gunshot."

"Okay. Interesting. So it's possible you heard a car backfiring at 11:45 and not a gunshot."

"It's possible, yes. I'm not an expert on the sound a gunshot makes. Even you have to admit a car backfiring makes an almost identical sound."

"Once you heard the noise of either the car or the gunshot, did you go where the sound came from and check to find out what was going on?"

"I did not, because if it were a gunshot I certainly didn't want to put myself in harm's way if a shooter was on the premises."

"But you still called 9-1-1 not knowing if it was just a car backfiring, yet you told the operator you heard shots in the church. Correct?"

"Yes. I guess I did. I'm sure if I had called in about hearing a car backfiring the operator would have hung up, thinking I was a lunatic. Am I going to be detained much longer? I have a meeting with the bishop at six o'clock."

"I'm going as fast as I can. We're here to give you the benefit of any doubt."

The priest suddenly grabbed his stomach, I think because it was sending a message to his brain to be careful of how he presented his now shaky story to the police. Although he agreed to have his DNA and prints taken after the interview, even the detectives sensed nervousness in his speech.

Denise and I paid close attention as Lewis resumed the interview at optimum energy. Her next question was straightforward; at the same time it caught me off guard to the point I nearly choked on my own spit. I couldn't even imagine how the padre felt. His heart must've been pulsating like a New Orleans jazz band leading a funeral. She leaned in, then asked the pivotal question:

"So, Padre, answer me this: how did your prints manage to find their way onto the murder weapon?"

Naturally he was a bit rattled. Shifted in his seat. Tugged at his priest's collar that seemed to be cutting off his air supply.

"My prints? Are you sure? Why would my prints be on a weapon of destruction? I am a pacifist. A disciple of Jesus Christ. I abide by the Sixth Commandment: *Thou shalt not kill.*"

"My thought exactly. I get it. You're a pacifist. A peace lover. That's what baffled us. What we're trying to determine is how a disciple of God managed to get his prints on the gun. A freak twist of fate?" Lewis asked this in a calm, windless tone.

Father Anthony looked to heaven, I supposed for guidance. Then he lowered his head, let out a sigh, and became defensive again. Said there had to be a mistake. The forensics people messed up. Either that or someone must've set him up, planted his prints on the .45 pistol. There was a beat while Detective Siddens leaned over and whispered something into Lewis's ear. Lewis nodded, then turned back to the priest, flashing a smug grin.

"My sergeant makes a valid point. No one said it was a .45 pistol, Padre."

They were good. Chalk one up for Siddens. Father Anthony tried desperately to backpedal.

"I must've read somewhere that the murder weapon was a .45 caliber gun. It was all over the news. Or maybe one of my parishioners mentioned it in passing."

"Sure. But the gun caliber was never publicized, sir. That fact has been intentionally kept under wraps while we continued to investigate."

"Perhaps I became aware when the investigating team discovered the shell casing under this baptismal font. Yes, I'm sure that's it."

Lewis leaned in, trying to throw him off his game and catch him in another lie.

"Not only were your fingerprints found on the gun hidden inside Emily Easterday's neon cross, but your Italian shoe prints were also found in and around the Rebellion Crusade platform area. Is it just coincidence that you and the killer shopped at the same shoe store?"

The father shrugged rather than say anything else because his testimony so far had gotten him deeper into trouble.

"Where were we? Right. You were about to tell me why your shoe prints were all over the crime scene."

"Not unusual. My shoe prints are probably all over the church grounds. I'm there every day. Roaming the parish. I perambulate for exercise. As for my shoe prints around the crusade platform, I believe I was invited to meet Ms. Easterday on stage after her homily."

"Can she vouch for you?"

"Probably not. Because in truth, she never showed up. I waited for fifteen minutes, pacing around the cross area. I was anxious and very disappointed. I was looking forward to exchanging points of view, sharing our different ideologies."

"In my line of work," said Detective Lewis, "there is only one ideology: find out the truth. And if it's a lie, well, then you have no alternative but to call them on it, even if you happen to be wrong and embarrass yourself. But in this case I'm pretty sure I'm not wrong."

"I'm not sure I'm following your line of questioning. Are you insinuating I'm lying?"

"Well, yes, I guess I am. I don't buy your story about meeting Emily Easterday and exchanging religious tidbits. . . I happen to know, through a reliable source, that on that particular night, she had no intention of meeting anyone except her bodyguard slash boyfriend, Simon, at a hotel."

"All that proves is that she must've forgotten about our meeting. Nothing else. Her not showing up certainty doesn't explain why my prints happened to be found on the murder weapon."

"True. This is true. But let me explain what I think went down. And Sergeant Siddens here is going to be so impressed by my police work, he'll buy me a drink later." Siddens chortled under his breath. He didn't look old enough to even be allowed in a bar, let alone buy a drink. "I'm not sure of your motive, but I think you killed Ray Astemendi in cold blood while he was just about to exit the confessional booth. You shot him in the back of the head, then waited an hour before calling 9-1-1. He never saw it coming. This gave you time to dispose of the gun in the cross, then dump the body at the old railway depot to cover your tracks."

"Dump? I dumped nothing. After calling 9-1-1, I finally got up the courage to take a look at the confessional booth, where I heard the shot, and there was nothing there. No dead body. Nothing. No blood. No sign of a shooter. No sign of a struggle. Nothing. I swear."

The priest began to shake, either out of fear or out of guilt.

"Isn't swearing a blasphemous act against God?" Lewis pressed.

"Yes. But not in this case, and you know it. Excuse me, but am I being charged for something? If not, I'd like to leave, or at least call a lawyer who can get me out of this room."

"Do you think you need a lawyer, padre?"

"I don't know what to think. All I know so far is that I'm shaking like a leaf. You've made me very uncomfortable with your subtle accusations."

"I'm losing my touch. I tried not to be subtle."

"He's weakening. He's definitely hiding something under that dog collar," I said as I turned to Denise, who I could tell was about to disagree with me.

"I don't see him weakening. I see a man scared that the police might charge him with murder, because he made a call to 9-1-1 and when they showed up, there was no sign of foul play."

"Let's not forget his prints were found on the murder weapon," I said.

Denise appeared flustered. "For the sake of argument," she said, "let's say they were planted, as the priest suggested. Who would do that and what would be their motivation?"

I took a beat before answering, because I had no clever answer to give her.

"I think we need to have sex right now to clear our heads and reconsider the clues, the suspects, and the motive."

"Wow, that sounds like a terrific idea. Did you bring a mattress and a bottle of wine?" she quipped.

"Seriously, I think we need to be patient before showing Father Anthony the door and declaring him innocent. I realize it's not our call but look, I would love him to be not guilty. The last thing I'd want to see is a priest go to the gallows. But if he is the killer, I have full confidence that Lewis will get him to own up. And when he does, I bet his reasoning is going to be a hum-fucking-dinger."

"I love it when you use the King's English so properly. Honestly, I don't know what to think. Everything you've said makes sense. But why? What prompts a priest to take a life? If it's a fact that he murdered Ray, then stalled for an extra hour before calling it in, that's an outright mind-blower."

"Hey, who knows what devious thoughts are nestled inside the mind of a killer?"

We stopped the guessing game and returned our attention to watching Detective Lewis press on with her interrogation. She didn't hold back. There was no *good cop, bad cop* in play here. Only a determined cop using whatever method it took to get this priest to raise his hands and surrender.

"It's time for you to confess your transgressions, Father Anthony. Get it off your chest. Living with this kind of immorality hanging over your head has to be damning to everything you believe in. Righteous indignation, I think you'd call it. You'll go straight to hell, and never have a place in the kingdom of heaven. I plan to stay here until you hand us a guilty plea. Even if it takes all night. We have plenty of coffee to keep us awake. Lousy, not fit to be drunk coffee, but it does the trick."

"What about my one phone call?"

"That's only a myth, Father. Something played out in the movies. It's nothing but a convenient plot device. In any event, we're coming around third heading for home, so the one call you're asking about could be a consideration once we get what we're looking for—your admission of guilt and/or a why you did it, and who actually pulled the trigger."

There was a long pause. Why the hesitation? Who knows? Something was churning inside this man's head. Maybe he was forming his best defense as to why he committed murder. Possibly going for an insanity plea to lessen the charge. Coming up with a name to place blame. A scapegoat. A parishioner who pissed him off once.

The priest then hung his head for a brief moment, as if in prayer or shame, or maybe he was gonna lose his breakfast. When he lifted his head, there emerged the despairing and fearful look of a broken man who knew he had deceived his faith. He admitted his guilt.

"I'm ready to confess my sins," he said, crossing himself.

"Take your time and don't leave out a word," Lewis said.

His face flushed crimson. He took a drink of water, I'm sure to wash down the fear in his throat. It was his turn to experience a different side of the confessional. He gently slid into his confession, admitted he had hidden the gun in Emily Easterday's neon cross, trying to incriminate her. He slipped up and forgot to wipe his prints. An amateurish mistake made by a desperate man, in a hurry to flee the scene. At this point the priest in Father Anthony had disappeared. His reverence had given way to dark corruption.

"When I returned, the body was gone. I swear. I have no idea who took the body. Unless Ray was not dead and crawled away on his own. Which I doubt, because I shot him square in the back of his brain."

Now the question was put on the table: why did this priest want Ray Astemendi dead? And why try to pin it on Emily? What could possibly be his motive? A deep breath, and then the truth began rolling off his tongue like a well-rehearsed Sunday sermon. He acknowledged he had a problem with Easterday passing herself off as a disciple of God, when she was really nothing but a fraud taking advantage of Christian values just to feed her own ego, and taking the Lord's name down into the gutter where she lived. But vengeance was the primary motivating force. And here came the grand scheme. The crowning point.

Another sip of water seemed to help unearth more words. It was almost as if he'd been practicing the speech.

"My hatred for Emily all began in Texas on the tenth of May when a *pathetically overweight man* stood up on the rafters, balancing himself on delicate guy-wires that creaked with his every move. While the crowd below feared for his life, he gave them what they wanted to see—a grunt, then a flying leap to his death. A poor man who suffered from an eating disorder. A man who came to Emily's crusade to ask God, through her so-called power, to reduce his waistline. She chose to make a spectacle of his plea. That was my motive. To help a man who had no control over his gluttonous eating habits. A horrible incident that her personal security guard, Ray Astemendi, found amusing. He remarked, as he was showing me the door by the scruff of my collar, that it was no loss, just one less *fat guy*—his uncouth term—to devour all the Twinkies. Yes, it was I who administered the last rites. I was there in the audience and rushed the stage to help this poor fellow in his time of need."

I turned to Denise, hit hard by this priest's confession. "I knew I recognized this guy. I was there. Saw him rush to the stage as he just admitted. At first I thought what a kind gesture, but trust me, there's more to this than just an unselfish act."

Father Anthony continued to open up the floodgates.

"I tried to talk him out of coming to Texas to see Emily but his mind was made up. He had tried every diet on the planet and this was his last-ditch effort to try and remedy his bulimia. He believed Emily Easterday's preordained palm on his obese stomach would make him thin. Ridiculous? Yes. But he needed some form of saving grace and he felt I couldn't give that to him. He meant no harm to anyone."

Father Anthony took a much-needed breath. He was on some kind of roll, like he had just opened a vein and displayed all the tendons.

"Thing is, with much love in my heart and a great deal of repentance, I openly confess without shame that he was family—he was my kid brother—and I avenged his death with another death. I killed Ray Astemendi, because I blamed him for pushing my brother off those guy-wires. God will not absolve me. If anything, He will strike me down with a firm blow, then send me to hell to gather with all the other infidels and maggots."

My stomach clenched. I felt bad that I was right about the priest. It was over. Murder solved. The older brother had avenged the younger brother's death leap.

"Poor guy," said Denise. "Takes the law into his own hands. Disregards his faith and kills to avenge another man's weakness. Not exactly the conduct of your ideal vicar."

It was time for us to leave. We got what we came for— answers to Ray Astemendi's death. We were drained from the emotional admission and needed a stiff drink. Possibly two or three. We were at the door when Father Anthony continued to give even more testimony. I could tell he was in this maximum guilt mode and had to get everything off his chest. He was noticeably exhausted. He hung his head for a second. Then in one angry, singular motion, he ripped off his clerical collar, tossing it on the floor. I assumed this was his way of renouncing his faith. What came next pushed a button that prompted Denise and me to stick around.

"For the record, the gun I used to eliminate Ray was my father's revolver that he used to extinguish—and I use the vernacular of the era—rat finks and stoolies in the early forties."

As anyone can imagine, Denise, the detectives, and I were trying to take that last detail seriously. Seemed to be a little hard to swallow and out of character for this priest. C'mon, rat finks? Lewis picked it up exactly where I would have, if I were in her shoes. A man who used such archaic language needed to be analyzed.

"Interesting choice of words, Padre. Want to shed some light and tell us who your father was? And please don't think we are naive enough to believe he was Al Capone."

"Gary Anthony Rizzo. Known by his rather surly colleagues as Gary the Gent. The mob guys were given nicknames to mask their real identities from the police and outsiders. In the case of my father, he always tipped his fedora before killing someone. For that reason he got the moniker Gary the Gent."

"Yeah. Very clever. And very gallant of him, tipping his hat like that. Sorry, but I never heard of your old man. But why would I? He's slime from another era. An era when gangsters took over city blocks of gangland territories to gain supremacy and killed anybody that got in their way. Nice goin'. If he were alive today, I'm sure he'd be proud of your accomplishment." Lewis took a beat as if to savor her next action. "Padre, I'm arresting you for the murder of Ray Astemendi. There was a pause, while Sergeant Siddens read the good Father his

Miranda rights. Just as Siddens completed the legalities, another cop entered the room, handcuffed Father Anthony and started to escort him out the door and into a nice comfy jail cell, where he'd remain until his arraignment. I never let them reach the door.

"Wait, stop!" I said aloud to myself. The idea that his dad was a *wise guy* piqued my interest. I wanted in the room to ask a question that, if I didn't get an answer to, I'd be counting cracks in the ceiling for the rest of my sleepless nights. I broke the rules and barged into the interview room. All heads turned. Detective Lewis jumped out of her seat and shielded the priest because I flew in like some madman. I assured her everything was cool. My curiosity was running full tilt, and I just needed to ask the lingering question that was surely also on the lips of everyone hearing this priest's confession. She let me continue without restriction but put me on a five-minute time limit. I looked straight into the eyes of Father Anthony. I tried not to blink so he would understand that I was serious.

"What's your question, son?" he said in a friendly, timbre.

"Okay. I need to know: what provokes a mobster's kid to become a priest? The truth, not some bullshit sob story you'd tell on a radio talk show."

I could tell that both Lewis and her sergeant found my question perceptive. We waited while Father Anthony turned to Lewis with an incredulous stare.

"Who is this guy anyway? A reporter doing a story on bent priests?"

"Nobody important. Not a reporter," Lewis said. "You don't want to answer, don't. The kid is an aspiring writer. There's a curiosity that comes with that kind of sensibility." She added, "He and Ray Astemendi were mutual acquaintances."

"What difference does it make, knowing why I did what I did? I killed a living, breathing human being. Isn't that enough? My reason was simple: to stop him from living."

"It's more than that. It's a matter of good versus evil," I said.

He was standing and took a seat before answering. Why? Was his answer so devastating that he might fall down revealing it? He swallowed. Why do people need to swallow before telling the truth? Is there some biological process that helps bring up the truth that's been lying in the pit of their stomach for years?

"I had a vision," he said.

I stopped him right there. "Okay, that is horseshit. You had no vision. You saw your father killing people, and rather than follow in his footsteps you took the easy way out and hid behind the Bible. Because—"

"Because I needed to atone for his sins. Because as a kid, growing up in his shadow, people treated me with respect only because of who my father was. They didn't like me for who I was. While at the same time these same people were afraid to approach me. They didn't want anything to do with me. My close friends were delinquents. They had police records by the time they were twelve years old. Mug shots instead of class photos. This is not the kind of unconditional love that a kid desires from his father. I needed a real father figure, not some guy who carried a gun to parent night. So I turned to the one person who could make me feel whole and safe and understood my needs as a kid growing up in the backstreets of Chicago—God. My safe house was the church."

The room fell silent. Except for me, everyone present was visibly touched. I hated that story because it wasn't the total truth. He knew it. I'm sure his dad beat the crap out of him to toughen him up and mold him into the kind of person he was. A bully. Just like Ray Astemendi. He didn't kill Ray because he called his brother a fatso. He killed him because he reminded him of the father that tormented innocent people. Persecution is the thing that drove this kid to rush to the nearest seminary. And after all these years, he took a page out of his father's wise guy handbook and became the one thing his father always wanted him to be—a thug in a collar. Amazingly enough, the padre didn't deny my theory—probably because I hit a home run. He stood up, swallowed again, and then was escorted out of the room.

I had to admit, it was a thrill to be part of this investigation. Me, Jake Reilly, a private citizen, given the authority to question a suspect. It had to be the most satisfying experience I'd ever had. Even better than fucking Ina Byers for the first time in the diner. I mean, Detective Jo Lewis broke the rules for me. She could get busted down to a desk job, or worse, directing traffic. You just don't hand over the reins to a guy who's scared pissless of horses. But she obviously had confidence in me. Filled with a sudden, heavy gratefulness, I kissed her on the cheek.

"What's that for?"

"Just thanks." I felt my eyes tear up. I looked away for a second to blink them off, and Denise said, "Nice goin', sharp guy." Detective Lewis paid me the ultimate compliment. Thought I should consider police work. Thought I'd make a terrific detective someday. Thought I had what it took to understand the human psyche and what makes people tick. That's half the job. The other half was disciplining yourself from being conned by a criminal's sob story and letting it influence your decision to find them innocent or guilty. I said I'd think about it, but truth, there was no way I'd wanna be a cop. Long hours, bad coffee, and in some cases putting your life on the line and dying at the hands of a lunatic who hated the world around him and wanted to end your career with a bullet because you were overweight. No thanks. An afterthought—I got lucky helping to extract the truth out of this priest only because it was close to home. Also, experiencing the bullying tactics of Ray Astemendi firsthand helped.

Father Anthony was stripped of his priesthood and found guilty of murder in the first degree for killing Ray Astemendi in the confessional booth of his own church. His lawyer was already preparing the appeal, claiming temporary insanity—specifically, that Jesus Christ influenced his decision to commit the crime. This defense was enthusiastically chronicled by a group on its website, *freefatheranthony.org*.

Although the plan never came to fruition, Emily Easterday was convicted of being an accomplice and constructing a plan to assassinate Ray Astemendi. She was sentenced to two years in a low security federal correctional institution. Two weeks before her trial, a surprise walk-in witness came forward saying they had overheard Ray encouraging the *fat man* to take a dive in order to propel his disbelief in God onto the front pages of newspapers and religious journals. And since Ray was Emily's employee, the courts felt she was responsible for his actions and attached another six months to her sentence. After her release, the bad press forced Emily to disband her crusade and quietly slip away from the evangelical circuit into obscurity. There were rumors, however, she worked under an alias as a cocktail waitress at a Lubbock bar and grill called the Baked Potato. As anyone can imagine, this made me grin from ear to ear until the corners of my mouth hurt.

Simon Flynn, aka Aiden Byrne, a former member of the IRA, was eventually caught trying to flee the country on a plane headed for London's Heathrow Airport. A European Arrest Warrant had been issued for Aiden's capture in connection with a London Docks murder that had taken place a year ago. Before being extradited,

Aiden was questioned by the FBI about his attempt to murder Emily Easterday and his connection in the Ray Astemendi killing. With nothing to lose and a life sentence already looking him in the face, he opened up and confessed that he had never actually met Father Anthony. It was strictly a cash deal made over the internet. His assignment, orchestrated by the priest, was to get up close and personal with Emily Easterday, and then, on a specific afternoon, finish her off. He would receive his full payment of fifty thousand dollars once Father Anthony had been texted a photo of a lifeless Emily Easterday. He never got a nickel because it was a homicide that went sideways, as a result of a maid that interrupted him just as he was about to thrust a pillow over Emily's face. Both the maid and Emily fought him off just enough to send him over the balcony, where he fell four floors into the pool and was apprehended two days later trying to board a plane at LAX.

Hiram Salazar was released on his own recognizance and went back to Mascota to live with his young daughter and to help raise his grandchild. He gave up his position as the manager of the escort service, and promoted Carmen as his successor. He actually fulfilled Ina's wish and had her body cremated and her ashes spread just outside the courtyard of the Hotel El Paradiso. Although they failed in their attempt to eliminate Ray, Hiram was grateful Ina included him in taking this *bastardiedora mujeriete* (womanizing bastard) permanently out of commission. To show his enduring appreciation, Hiram often sends thank-you cards to Father Anthony, who is serving a lifetime prison sentence with no possibility of parole.

Richard Salvetti did unfortunately die of a drug overdose, in Paris, as previously reported by the left-wing newspaper *Le Monde*. After helping Ina transport the body to the railway depot, Ina felt a surge of humanity and gave Richard a substantial portion of the stolen money. She had suggested he get as far away as possible from the tragic lifestyle he had endured while living in Bakersfield—a community that persecuted him as a loser, an eccentric weirdo for wearing a trash bag overcoat, and for begging for change in front of supermarkets and on street corners. He was a misunderstood soul who obviously could not keep it together, and whose only friend was a bottle of booze, a cigarette butt, and a line of coke. Before her death, Ina tried her best to have Richard buried in the same cemetery as Jim Morrison, Edith Piaf, and Oscar Wilde—Père Lachaise Cemetery. A ridiculous attempt. Such is life. Or death, as the case may be.

⌘

Denise and I said our final goodbyes at the train station. It was a teary-eyed and emotional scene, ending with a promise that someday I'd return and we'd pick up where we'd left off: on her sofa drinking red wine in moderation and considering giving romance a shot. Our like-mindedness was reflected in the fact we were both true agnostics; we also had a genuine dislike for mean-spirited, egotistical people—and broccoli. It was apparent we had a lot of the same interests too. Sentimental movies that made you weep in your popcorn, Thai food, proper British mysteries where it's hard to understand a word they're saying without using subtitles, rock music, Rachmaninoff's *Piano Concerto No. 2*—to name but a few.

⌘

Nightfall. Spring 2014. There was a chill in the air, but it was comfortable inside the moving train that was headed north. I was located in an empty club car, sitting alone next to the window, looking out at the dark shadows of the landscape that whizzed by in a blur. Felt like I had been here before, on this exact train, travelling alone with nothing but my thoughts, my fears, my ambitions. It was sort of unsettling, not knowing your destiny. But isn't that the idea of living a full life all about? Being surprised at every turn. If you knew what was coming, like how and when you were going to die, how abnormal of a journey would that make? That being said, who, at this point of my life, was responsible for my welfare? What I mean by that is, who would take care of the little stuff in the event I got deathly ill and suddenly dropped dead? Who would bury me? Who would sit at my bedside until I breathed my last breath? I had no family to speak of. It all boiled down to a handful of acquaintances—Helen, Denise, Hiram, or if I was really desperate, Andrea the supervisor at the Food Barn. I wondered—could a person hire someone to grieve for you? Was there an agency, like an escort service, that provided a warm body to sit at your bedside, hold your hand, and lament? I made a mental note to look into that. Maybe I had just stumbled upon my next career, as a hired mourner. Twenty-five an hour plus travel expenses. I took a breath and distanced myself from this insane notion because the truth was, when I died, my thoughts would also be dead, and whoever the people were that wept for me or threw dirt on my grave shouldn't be an object of concern. Or should they? Again, that was assuming I was buried and not cremated. I made another mental note to write down instructions for somebody to follow. But who? This was a dilemma.

On the horizon, I could make out the silhouettes of the broken-down Fun Zone Ferris wheel, the National Cemetery, the empty swimming pool where Ina and I had sex with no end in sight, and the diner in all its glory—while burnt hamburger fumes lingered in my sinuses—before it perished. All just in my head but an accurate reminder of my life as I lived it. I did the best I could, considering the unhealthy obsession I had with Ina Byers. Although she would never know it, she gave me something of great value. The thing I always wanted—liberation, breathing room, a chance to experience life in the *no looking back* lane. She encouraged me to expand my horizons and push for new frontiers.

In the reflection of the window, the perfect smoke ring hung in the air until it dissipated as fast as it appeared. The scent of Sherman Naturals engulfed my nostrils. This was nothing but another illusion that I feared might emerge whenever I wanted to be reminded of how I fell in love with such a complex, independent, willful bad girl.

The real shame: I never actually told Ina Byers that I loved her. Although it was clearly evident to everyone who knew about my all-consuming infatuation, I never came out and said the words. This would have made a real difference. Probably wouldn't have changed how she felt about me, but rather how it made me feel about myself. Sure, I would have risked the worst possible outcome—rejection, or *getting the brush-off,* to coin an outdated cliché. But it's all about taking risks and accepting the good with the bad, and the bad with the *horrible.* There's that word again. It had been constantly following me through my journey.

I banged my forehead lightly against the cool window glass. Not enough to do damage but just forceful enough to exhibit my frustration for letting such a significant opportunity slip away.

I closed my eyes for a quiet moment. I could feel the moonlight cast its glow on my face. It calmed me, until I was interrupted by the sudden loud vibration of the rails clattering over the trestle.

I redirected my attention out the window, just as the train sped past a sign that comforted me. A life-changing epiphany.

YOU ARE NOW LEAVING PUSSYVILLE

ACKNOWLEDGMENTS

I've got to start with Chuck Barris, whose brilliant decision to hire me as the head writer for the unequivocally outrageous, GONG SHOW that ran from 1976 to 1978 then in syndication from 1988 to 1989, will always be the most memorable and significant career experience in my life. A mentor, a friend who selflessly gave me my big break and the chance to spread my artistic wings as a crazed, unhinged, uncensored writer. RIP Chuckie Baby.

Many thanks go to Charles Shyer. My friend for over fifty years. His talent as a writer, producer and director, not to mention his input in the original Ina Byers screenplay, certainly helped make this book come to life.

My editor and proofer Kevin Cook, who almost went stark raving mad correcting my many mistakes. He deserves a medal of valor and a truckload of Tums.

A very special thank you to Pamela (Crane) Cangioli and her company Proofed to Perfection. A class act. Thanks for sharing your valuable marketing skills.

Ghislain Viau, of (Creative Publishing Book Design) a talented designer. His innovation is highly visible as seen on the front cover.

Lary Borkin and Ed Tait—always there to push my books to the lovely folks in Edinburgh.

Kate and Riley Spencer—there's never getting around mentioning the love and support your kids give you.

Laurie Spencer—her love and affection is what kept me afloat.

And lastly—Archie—always by my side—a writers' best friend. Never a thumbs down. Never a harsh word. Good dog.

ABOUT THE AUTHOR

LARRY SPENCER has written and published three very power-fully written novels. *The Tipping Point Of Oliver Bass, Material Things* and his most recent, *In Search of Ina Byers*. He has proudly been a Writer's Guild of America member since the late 70s, having written and produced a swarm of highly successful TV shows, which culminated into writing several feature films. He lives in Valley Village, California with his talented wife, Laurie and their equally talented dog Archie.

www.ingramcontent.com/pod-product-compliance
Lightning Source LLC
Chambersburg PA
CBHW020919110726
47900CB00001B/221